RAVE REVIEWS FOR DEBORAH MacGILLIVRAY'S *THE INVASION OF FALGANNON ISLE*!

"What makes MacGillivray's romance so special are the eccentric characters, right down to the cat, and Desmond and B.A.'s growing relationship."

—*Booklist*

"This is an entertaining, humorous and heartwarming tale of love, friendship and a bit of magic. The hero's struggle to make peace with his past and the heroine's determination to help him are nicely depicted. The secondary characters are great fun, especially The Cat Dudley, and the peek into the lives of the main character's siblings whets the appetite for their stories."

—*RT BOOKreviews*

"In a word, 'Perfection!'"

—Huntress Reviews

"*The Invasion of Falgannon Isle* is a masterful tale woven by an incredibly talented author. The juxtaposition of the modern day intrusions with the timelessness of Falgannon Isle creates a world readers will want to visit, over and over again."

—CK's Kwips & Kritiques

"Ms. MacGillivray creates characters that seemed so alive that I almost believed Falgannon Isle really exists. If it did, I would really love to move there! *The Invasion of Falgannon Isle* is one of my best reads for 2006—it ha
laugh-out-loud moments,
the paranormal, and a gre

THE COMING STORM

The soft breeze ruffled his wavy black hair and caused his silk shirt to ripple. He'd unbuttoned it half-way down his chest and had no T-shirt underneath. One long leg was stretched out before him; the other was cocked against the low creek-stone wall for bal-ance. Jago Fitzgerald was waiting—waiting with that stillness inherent to all of nature's nocturnal hunters. Men like this were quite treacherous to females. They sensed small changes in a woman's body, reaction to the lethal peril they posed. The pounding of her heart, the rapid short breaths. And—damn it—the tightening of her breasts.

Fortunately, Asha's black sweater hid that reaction from this arrogant man in the darkness. It was her little secret. A woman needed every advantage in dealing with a male like Jago Fitzgerald, for she had the un-shakable sense Netta was right.

He was waiting for *her*.

Other *Love Spell* books by Deborah MacGillivray:

THE INVASION OF FALGANNON ISLE

Riding The Thunder

DEBORAH MacGILLIVRAY

LOVE SPELL

NEW YORK CITY

LOVE SPELL®

October 2007

Published by

Dorchester Publishing Co., Inc.
200 Madison Avenue
New York, NY 10016

ISBN-10: 0-505-52692-1
ISBN-13: 978-0-505-52692-2

Printed in the United States of America.

For Monika Wolmarans, Leanne Burroughs,
Dawn Thompson, Diane White, Carol Ann Applegate
Sandi
and
Bobby "Boris" Pickett

Riding The Thunder

Prologue

June 1964, Kentucky

"I *don't* believe you want to marry me!" Laura cried.

Not crocodile tears either, Tommy Grant knew. Laura Valmont felt things more deeply than most people, one of the special traits that first attracted him to her.

She had just moved to the small Southern town of Leesburg, Kentucky, when he first laid eyes on Laura. Not there one day, she'd taken on three bullies cruelly tormenting a stray cat. Fifteen, womanhood blooming on her body, she failed to recognize the peril she'd stepped into on that hot summer afternoon. With singular determination, and wearing the aura of a warrior princess, she had placed herself between the mangy cat and the older thugs—Monty, Reed and Ewen.

They were dangerous, *not typical bullies*, but out-of-control, budding psychos—especially Monty. There was something seriously *wrong* with Montague Faulkner. Raging hormones saw the situation as combustible as tossing a lit match into gasoline. Tommy doubted Laura noticed all three had serious hard-ons as they watched her, almost licking their lips. It wouldn't have slowed her down. Her sole focus was on rescuing that piteous cat.

At nineteen, Tommy was a shade taller than the younger Reed and Ewen, but not Monty. Monty had three inches and a few pounds on him. Nevertheless, the punk stepped back when Tommy moved before Laura, shielding her. Monty was a bully, and like all bullies a coward at his core. Once you crossed him, there would be trouble down the road. Tommy would have to watch his back. There'd be hell to pay—one didn't clash with Montague Faulkner and not expect to find his tires slashed or his windshield shot out. *Or worse.*

Tommy had asked drolly, "Is there a problem here?" The steel of his words had instantly diffused the volatile situation.

It never occurred to Tommy until much later that with her act of rescuing the cat, and his rescuing her, their lives had changed in a single heartbeat. He might've as well gone down on his knee and proposed then and there. *The die was cast*, as the old-timers loved to say.

During the following two years, she'd made his life hell. In the small town of Leesburg there was no escaping Laura. Anytime she caught him on a date, she'd stared until he had this strange fear his balls would shrivel and drop off. She'd buzzed around his home, brought flowers for his widowed mother, and aided in planning tea parties and summer barbecues. His mother wore a knowing female smile saying, *bide your time, son, you're already hers.*

At first, he'd fought the inevitability. What red-blooded, twenty-year-old male wanted a wide-eyed teenager mooning around him, even if that sweet seventeen-year-old had a pair of world-class breasts and an ass that made him swallow his tongue? Heaven to look at, she was a severe pain in the groin and numerous cold showers to get over. Seventeen still had that sign: *Look but don't touch.* Sane males ran for their lives. He ran. Only, Laura had made up her mind. He never stood a chance.

Last summer when she turned eighteen, she'd come at him, no-holds-barred. In short order, everyone in the jerkwater town knew they were a couple and would marry soon. It was only a matter of setting a date.

Precisely what now had Laura in a tizzy. She had graduated Leesburg High back in the spring. With no intention of going to college, she wanted to get married, and next week wouldn't be soon enough. A year seemed a lifetime away to her.

"Damn it, Laura, I want to get married, too. I have one more year of law school—which you know well. What? You want to marry and move in with my mother and uncle? That'd be fun. I can't swing it, honey. Let me graduate. My uncle will take me into his practice then." He explained the facts—as he had weekly since her graduation. "My part-time clerking isn't enough for us to live on."

"Maybe your uncle would help us if we got married—"

Tommy gritted his teeth. This broken record of explanations was getting him nowhere. Sighing, he repeated it all once more, hoping he would *finally* get through to her. "My uncle barely has enough to keep his law practice going. Leesburg isn't the richest place for an attorney. Poor man has spent his life taking care of my mother and me after dad died. He just doesn't have the money, Laura. I *can't* ask him."

"But he gave you this new car for your birthday, Tommy."

She referred to his fire-engine red Ford Mustang. One of the first made, Ford was so high on the car that they jumped the gun and released it weeks ago instead of waiting for the mid-September rollout of new '65 year cars, calling it the '64½ model.

"My Chevy was falling apart. He was ticked he had to cancel appointments three times to come pick me up because of it breaking down." Tommy pleaded quietly, "Please, be reasonable. You know we'll marry this time next year. You can be a June bride. A *beautiful* June bride." He squeezed her hand and glanced over at her, love filling his heart.

"Oh, Tommy, my dad is being transferred out of state.

They're moving next month. Mom broke the news to me last night," she choked out.

"What?" Tommy took his eyes off the road, unable to believe she was serious. He had to swerve the steering wheel back when the car accidentally crossed the centerline. Traffic on Leesburg Pike was dangerous. They promised the newly opened I-64 would someday help the situation; however, since construction remained mostly in unconnected pieces, heavy trucking traffic still came flying down the pike at a breakneck speed. An oncoming trucker gave Tommy a blast of his horn and then held up his middle finger.

"They said if we don't get married . . . I have to go with them." Laura sat stiff and pale in her seat. "To Texas."

Rattled, Tommy failed to notice the black pickup bearing down on them—until it banged the rear bumper. Damn! His Mustang was only weeks old and already a dent in the rear end. Tommy could see his insurance rates going sky-high. What he didn't need—another expense. He was saving for an engagement ring—Laura's Christmas present.

"What the hell?" Tommy looked in the rearview mirror, trying to see who was driving. The harsh glare from the evening sun bounced off the windshield, nearly rendering it a mirror. Another slam to the rear said the first hadn't been an accident. Someone was clearly ramming the heavy truck into them.

"Tommy, are they nuts?" Her head whipped around trying to see.

The DJ on the car radio announced, "This is Coyote Calhoun on *WAKY* dedicating this Golden Oldie to all the Lauras out there, Ray Peterson's mournful ballad about star-crossed lovers, 'Tell Laura I Love Her'."

Ordinarily, Laura would turn the song up. *Their song.* Four years ago, the tune had made it to number one on the *Hit Parade* and it was still in the jukebox at The Windmill Restaurant where everyone hung out. Slot H-13. Since the lovers in the song were named Laura and Tommy, the song had become theirs.

The truck sped up and slammed against the rear of the Mustang again. Both Laura and he jerked from the impact, which nearly pushed the car into the back of the cement truck ahead of them.

"Tommy, I'm scared. What are they doing? That driver is stark-raving mad!"

Tommy glanced in the rearview mirror again. In slow motion, Tommy saw it all happen, too damn fast to prevent it. The driver revved the truck's engine and smashed into the car once more. Hard. The cement truck started to slow to make a left turn onto Richmond Pike.

The cliffs were coming up. Tommy dared not let this madness drag on as there was a likelihood they could be forced off one of the sharp S-turns. He hit the gas, hoping to swing around the truck before it halted to turn. As he did, the Ford truck slammed into the car, jarring them forward. Too late, Tommy saw the *Peterbilt*, which had been blocked from view by the cement truck, barreling down on them from the other direction. The driver never had a chance to hit the brakes.

Tommy swerved back into the right lane, but the truck crashed into the Mustang again, pushing them forward. Tommy cut the wheel hard at the last instant, trying to go into the small creek running parallel to the road's far side. He couldn't do it fast enough. Crying tires, busting glass, grinding metal . . . a painful scream Tommy heard as the semi plowed into the side of the Mustang.

Laura.

They say life passes in front of your eyes just before you die. *They lied.* It wasn't the past that flashed through Tommy's mind as he lay there trying to move, trying to breathe. *It was all the things in life that would never be.* The wedding he'd hoped to share with Laura in a year's time, her so beautiful in a white gown. Images of him coming home to her, a small black-headed baby boy in her arms. Christmases, New Year's Eves, birthdays. Making love in the rain. Everything that Laura and he would never have.

Tommy sensed he was bleeding from his mouth and nose. Blood was in his eyes and streaming down his chest. He hurt. Bad. Yet, all he could think of was Laura. Beautiful Laura with her auburn hair and laughing brown eyes. The woman he loved more than life.

He reached for her hand. "Laura!" he choked through tears and blood. The instant he touched her he knew she was dead. He laced his fingers with hers and held on, knowing there was no life without her. "Laura!" He screamed in madness.

His body felt on fire. He couldn't breathe. Obscenely, Ray Peterson crooned, " 'Tell Laura not to cry, my love for her will never die.' "

"Tommy, wake up! Tommy!"

Tommy jerked up, then looked around, wondering if the collision had been merely a bad dream. The world was in sepia, a strange, gold shimmering twilight. Laura glistened with faery dust. She laughed and tugged on his hand, and for an instant he glanced back at the wreck. Cars were stopping along the road, and people ran to the smashed Mustang.

Not a dream. A nightmare.

"Tommy, this way." Laura smiled, pulling his hand.

"Laura, wait. I love you." He yanked her into his arms, squeezing her so tightly she'd have a hard time breathing. Tears filled his eyes and streamed down his cheeks. "Oh, Laura . . ."

She kissed him. "Shhhh! We must hurry before someone gets our booth at The Windmill. I want a Cherry Coke and then to slow dance to our song."

"But Laura . . ." He hesitated, looking back at the wreck, confused.

She reached up and gently pulled his face around toward hers. "It doesn't matter, Tommy. Nothing matters but that we're together. We'll always be together. Just like the song, Tommy, our love will never die."

Chapter One

Present Day Kentucky

Lifting the icy-cold bottle of Coors to his mouth, Jago Mershan froze in midmotion, then groaned as if he'd received a stiff blow to his solar plexus. His whole body tensed as everything about him receded to gray. Nothing could've prepared him for the impact of Asha Montgomerie on his senses.

Jago's eyes tracked the woman who'd slid out of the black Jaguar and strode across the parking lot, the image of warm honey suddenly foremost in his mind. Only, his sweet tooth wasn't throbbing. His pain centered lower—much lower. The jukebox switched to Bob Seger's pulsing "Come to Papa," causing the right side of his mouth to twitch into a hungry predator's smile. Low laughter rumbled in his chest as his eyes never left Asha.

He whispered, "Yeah, come to papa."

She was tall, around five-seven, the height increased a shade by the heels of her brown leather Wellies. Her black jeans fit snugger than his English racing gloves and lovingly displayed the long, sleek limbs that could wrap around him—ah, a man—and never let go. Being a lowly male, he thoroughly appreciated how those firm breasts filled a 34D to perfection, no Miracle Bra needed, no Pamela Lee implants. Bodies like hers were a throwback to the heyday of Marilyn Monroe and Jane Russell. Placing her hand on the porch rail, Asha followed the spiral up the creek-stone stairs, her body undulating in a quiet, feline grace. Those superb breasts swayed perceptibly with each step, the black scoop-necked sweater revealing tempting cleavage.

As she moved alongside the row of plate glass windows, Jago was treated to her profile, the derrière promising a male could enjoy watching her walk away nearly as much as seeing her coming toward him. Well, almost. Observing those mobile curves approach, a man would tingle with the anticipation of getting his hands on that firm flesh.

Sunlight caught and was refracted through the full glass door as Asha opened it, blinding him for an instant. Then she rematerialized, born from the brilliant shafts. The setting sun's aura followed her with an arcane sentience, greedily clinging to her to form a red-gold halo about her, a breath-stealing shard of time that burned deep into his soul. When he was old and gray, he'd recall this instant as if yesterday and remember its power, how it moved him.

Not a classic beauty, Asha's face was arresting, feline. Her jawline hinted at the Montgomerie stubbornness, though the faint cleft in her chin softened the effect. Jago's body bucked as he imagined running the side of his thumb over that shadowy dip, seeing those cat eyes watching him, spellbound by his action. A flicker of arrogance flashed in those amber eyes, but the haughtiness was understated, carried off with a regal self-assurance few women ever truly achieved.

Asha glanced about the room in a disinterested fashion, her hair rippling like silk down her finely arched spine. Golden brown: Jago deemed that label pathetically inadequate. Asha's locks shimmered with a thousand golds, fiery to pale auburns and vibrant browns. That mane provoked an appetite to see it spread across a pillow as he drove himself into her slick, welcoming body, to feel it draped and cool over his burning skin. A hunger that would force a throwback like him to howl.

A wicked smile tugged at the corner of his mouth when the jukebox changed tunes and the singer began *ah-ooing* about "The Werewolf of London." Given a British passport was in the glove box of his leased Jeep Cherokee, and the fact Asha provoked him to consider howling, he chalked one up for odd quirks of fate and timing.

It was fascinating to observe the emotional shifts on male faces as they watched Asha pass. Clearly, they wanted her. Oh, did they want her! Nonetheless, Jago doubted any would approach her. She stared men in the eye, dismissing them with a bat of her long lashes with a poise that would send all but the most voracious meat eaters running. They would look her up and down and lick their chops, but the power, the regnancy radiating from her would humble all. Most would feel guilty for even daring to look, to wish, knowing they were unworthy. Only sheer morons with nothing to lose would take the risk.

Or a man as assured of himself as Jago.

Asha's aloof scan of the dining room finally reached him. Her tawny-brown eyes widened as their stares collided. The witchy force of those cat eyes rocked him, stole his breath. Lightning sizzled along his nerves as the odd moment in time lengthened. All else faded. Never had he felt so connected to anyone.

Then, with a sweep of her lashes, she pretended not to notice him.

"Nice try, Asha," he said under his breath, then took a long draw of his beer to kill his parched throat. *Jago Luxovius Fitzgerald Mershan, you're one lucky sonofabitch—or cursed*, he mused.

Asha spoke to the hostess, her words lost to restaurant chatter. Evidently, she requested the blinds be dropped, for the woman did just that, plunging the diner into shadow. Asha went ahead and seated herself in a booth about halfway back, on the side opposite of the long row of windows.

Jago's position on the stool at the counter was dead center on the aisle, affording him a splendid show. Oh yeah, this Scottish miss had one sweet ass! The way she moved sent his blood into a low, rocking thrum, similar to a Harley-Davidson jump-starting in his chest. Yep, that's what Asha reminded him of—his classic '67 Harley Electra Glide in black—all sleek curves and lines, created so a man craved to climb on for the ride of his life. He contemplated if Asha made love Harley-style: zero to a hundred mph in the blink of an eye.

It would be riding thunder.

He nearly laughed aloud, realizing if he told her that—in all sincerity meaning it as the ultimate compliment—she'd probably deck him. Only a man would think comparing a woman to a Harley—not just any bike, mind you, but a Harley—was the highest praise. He recalled that old Robert Palmer song "Bang a Gong," and the stanza about a woman being built like a truck. Females just didn't get what Palmer wailed about. Men did. It was one of those *Men are From Mars* kind of stalemates. Few things born of man could bring Jago to his knees faster than a vintage Harley or the perfect woman.

And Asha Montgomerie, without a doubt, was the perfect woman. A man's hottest fantasy come to life. His fantasy for far too long. Over the years he had studied dozens of photos of her. Then back in May at her grandfather's funeral in England, he'd seen her from a distance. Brief glimpses that little prepared him for the up close effect this woman had on his system. It took all his control not to get to his feet, go to her, put a hand behind her neck and devour that small, pouty mouth.

Jago wanted her as he'd never wanted a woman before. Without hesitation he'd take her, possess her, brand her and never look back. Damning all consequences. Because like her, he too was a throwback. Too bad he was here to tear her safe, secure world apart. Before the dust settled, she'd likely hate his guts, despise him just as powerfully as he craved her.

Jago prayed he didn't destroy them both before it was done.

Chapter Two

Asha stared at the menu—not that she needed to read it. The Windmill served Cajun gumbo on Thursday, fresh halibut on Friday, Saturday and Sunday, a grilled New York strip that would melt in your mouth every day of the week, along with BLTs, club sandwiches and burgers and fries. She was aware Kentucky catfish was no longer a specialty on the menu, thanks to the sprawling suburban population of Lexington polluting the Kentucky River with their sewage. She knew the prices. Wouldn't have to ask for availability. Small wonder since she ordered the food supplies each week.

She usually ate after the supper crowd thinned for the evening. Only, she had spent the day on the horse farm and was now ravenous, even though it was barely five. She'd eat early and be ready to handle the cash register, leaving Rhonda free to concentrate on seating customers as they shuffled in.

The long fingernails of her left hand tapped out a restless rhythm on the Formica tabletop while she feigned attention with the plastic covered menu. Asha tried to block out the man sitting at the counter, drinking a beer. Her eyes had spotted him the instant she came in, though she affected pretense that she hadn't. Inside, her heart bounced against her ribs with a bruising force. Men like him were *hard* to miss. A female *sensed* their presence as much as *saw* them, some basic animalistic instinct that set off alarms.

"What'll you have, Boss Lady?" Netta asked, setting a glass of ice water on a paper coaster. With a grin, she pulled a Bic pen from behind her ear, popped her gum, and waited.

"You ever wonder why we put paper coasters under our drinks when it's a Formica top?" Asha asked blandly. She knew Netta was waiting for more than her order. The waitress wanted to gossip about Mr. Tall, Dark and Potently Sexy sitting on the stool.

Netta shrugged. "The Windmill has always put paper coasters under glasses." She snapped her gum again and lifted her eyebrows. "You know what happens if you try to change anything around here. More than the natives get restless."

Ignoring the comment, Asha folded the menu and handed it to the blonde. "New York strip, medium-rare, and a salad with French dressing. I'm famished."

Netta spun exaggeratedly on her New Balance sneakers, her eyes sweeping over the man at the counter. "Hmm . . . I'm famished, too." Giving Asha a wink, she took the order to the small window to the kitchen. She attached the ticket to the wheel, spun it around for Sam, then dinged the bell to get his attention.

The stranger on the stool again drew Asha's gaze, compelled her to look at him. *Dared* her to look at him. She tried to mask her glance, nonchalant, as though bored and seeking diversion, letting it sweep the whole room until it finally reached him. She failed. Their eyes locked and Asha nearly flinched as she felt the focus of his mind. A throb of radiant sexuality sent a shiver of physical awareness through her body, slamming into her womb with a force she'd never experienced.

This man *unnerved* her. Rarely did men do that to her. Actually, *no* man had. With her intense catlike eyes, she could look down her nose and set even the strongest ones to feeling like slugs. The ability was second nature to her, she turned on the frost and glared as if he were something she'd stepped in.

As a rule, that sent them running. Not this one. As though he not only knew the rules to the game, but also had a cheat sheet, the stranger leaned back against the counter with a wolfish grin and looked his fill. Not even pretending to do anything else, he just stared at her. It was damn unsettling. She couldn't even pretend to gaze out the windows at the pastoral scenery of the horse farm across the road; she'd asked Rhonda to close the blinds against the harsh afternoon glare.

"Here you go." Netta set an iced Pepsi, a salad and a basket of rolls before her. She stepped so that her body blocked Asha from the stranger's view. "You *know* that man at the counter?"

Thankful Netta had given her the perfect excuse for taking her eyes from the invader, Asha broke a roll and buttered it. "What man?"

Netta gave a mocking laugh and popped her gum a couple times. "Nice try, sugarplum. Men like that are impossible not to notice."

"Never saw him before in my life." Asha sipped the cola. Oh, she would remember this man had they met.

A master gossip, Netta excelled at knowing when to tell all, when to hint. With her smart mouth and flashing baby-blue eyes, she'd charm a person's life history from them in a wink. The Windmill likely had higher profits this past year and a long line of regulars due to Netta's down-home charm. What she knew about the stranger would be forthcoming.

The only way to play the game, Asha mused, was to answer a question with a question. "Why would you think I know him?"

"Sexy Lips has a foreign accent. British I think, like yours. Gives a gal shivers." Netta hugged herself and then chewed her gum. "Also, I get this sense he was waiting for something . . . *maybe you*. My granny *knew* things. She passed that on to me."

"Steak's up, Netta," Sam, their cook, called through the open space, setting a plate up on the warmer.

"Back in two shakes." Netta went to pick up the inch-thick steak and returned to place it before Asha. "Eat up, sugarplum." She glanced sideways at the black-haired visitor and raised her eyebrows. "Looks like you're gonna need all your strength."

"I sure enjoyed that dinner. You tell Sam that, eh, Asha?" Melvin Jackson said, picking up a peppermint from the bowl at the side of the register. He unwrapped the cellophane and then popped the candy into his mouth, waiting for her to ring up his ticket.

Sam poked his head up in the small window. "Sam heard your big mouth flappin'. So, you liked the gumbo?"

Melvin patted his round stomach. "Damn fine meal—though just a pinch too much sassafras and not enough filé powder."

"Bah. It was perfect." Sam frowned and waved in dismissal. "My granny, born down on the Bayou Teche, was teaching me how to make gumbo while you were barely an itch in your daddy's britches, you old coot."

"Who's an old coot?" Jackson snapped, though it was with a twinkle in his eye.

Asha counted out Melvin's change, only half listening to the routine these two went through every Thursday night. Each week, Melvin came in for the gumbo dinner; each time he and Sam fussed over the filé powder and sassafras. A running game between the two. Tonight, however, she could barely keep her attention on them. She felt the stranger watching her. Perturbed, she tried to tune him out, ignore him as if she remained unaware of his presence. It was impossible. Her skin tingled, knowing his eyes followed her every move.

"'Night, Netta, Sam, Asha!" Melvin waved as he opened the door and stepped out into the warm October night.

Asha had just stuck the receipt in the basket by the register and closed the till when Sexy Lips leaned across the counter and asked, "May I have another Coors?"

A shiver slithered over her body, a cross between female fear instinct and instant turn-on. Wow! An image of that deep voice whispering sweet nothings to her in the middle of the night was enough to give her a hot flash.

As yet, Asha couldn't determine what color the man's eyes were, due to the recessed lighting, but their power rocked her to her toes. Forcing herself to turn to the glass-doored cooler behind her, she removed a Coors. She used the Pepsi-Cola wall-mount opener to snap off the top.

"Twist-off my arse," she grumbled, then handed it to him.

As his fingers closed around its neck, hers flexed in a spasm about the brown bottle. *Did beer have salt*? Her grandmother had taught her and all her sisters never to pass a warlock salt. Asha now wondered if that included salt as an ingredient. Maeve had been Scottish, born on Falgannon Isle in the Hebrides, where the past wasn't so distant and superstitions were the norm. Maeve believed if you passed a warlock salt, you'd open yourself to obeying his suggestions. When Asha had pressed why, Maeve said it was an old warlock's trick, a test if you'd bend to his will. Asha guessed she should've clarified if that was salt in *all* forms.

The stranger's black brows lifted, questioning her hold on the bottle. Perplexed amusement twinkled in those penetrating eyes, eyes the shade of green garnets, nearly so dark one might take them to be deep brown or black. They held a power, a force that rattled her.

Again, Falgannon Isle came to mind, where her sister BarbaraAnne lived. The island was under an ancient curse, which could only be broken if her sister—the Lady of the

Isle—married a green-eyed man with black hair. She couldn't help but think of B.A.'s curse as she stared this man in the face. Maybe she should pass B.A.'s address to him. He had black hair, green eyes and his voice held a sexy hint of Ireland—all three requirements to fulfill the dictates of B.A.'s curse.

A burning flare of jealousy exploded in the pit of her stomach. Strangely, she didn't want her sexy blond goddess of a sister anywhere near this man.

Dismissing the weird thoughts, she released the beer.

"Thank you." A hint of laughter touched his words. "For a moment I thought you were going to arm-wrestle me for it . . . though I can't say I'd be averse to the idea of a *tussle*."

She opened the till again, and set about arranging the bills so that the faces all pointed in the same direction. Any excuse to avoid those probing eyes. "Not for a beer. I don't drink beer."

"Beer, or alcohol in general?" he asked.

"Beer." Asha closed the register, trying to think of some other chore she needed to do. An escape. There wasn't anything, so she drew a cola from the fountain and held up the glass. "I'm a Pepsi addict."

"That still doesn't answer my question. Drink anything besides Pepsi?"

"The occasional whisky—without the E." Asha forced herself to appear cool, calm and collected. Then why did her heart pound so erratically? No male had ever caused this reaction within her, on par with sticking her finger into an electrical socket.

"What's wrong with beer?" the stranger pressed.

"I don't care for the taste." She shrugged one shoulder. "Sue me."

His dark eyes danced with mischief. "Have you ever drunk a Coors?"

"No, I once drank a Dark Isle and a Wee Heavy."

"Dark Isle? Wee Heavy?" he inquired.

"Scottish ales."

"Ah, room temperature ale. You should try Coors. Big difference between American beer and European ale." He pushed the bottle toward her. "Try it."

She stared at the container, once again worrying if beer contained salt. This was too much like the Wicked Witch offering Snow White the poisoned apple, but instead of a witch she faced a warlock. Damn! She regretted now that she hadn't paid more attention to her grandmother's warnings.

He remarked, "First, you almost won't let me have the beer, now you stare at it as if I'm offering you a cobra."

"I'm working." Asha grasped at the convenient reason.

He laughed softly. The low sexy rumble wormed its way under her skin, spreading goosebumps across her body. "Chicken." His brows lifted in a dare.

Damn, she really wished she knew if they used salt in brewing beer. "I don't drink with strangers."

He leaned forward and stuck out his right hand. "Jago Fitzgerald."

Asha stared at it. A beautiful hand. You could tell a lot about a man from his hands. The fingernails were clean and manicured, not a nail biter, saying he wasn't the nervous sort. No calluses, yet they weren't soft. She judged he had some sort of indoor job, but used those strong hands on weekends to exercise. The fingers were long, elegant. Hands of a magician. Hands of a lover—hands of a bloody warlock trying to trick her into doing his bidding!

"Jago?" She tested the resonance of his name. Though his accent was British, he pronounced it with a long *a* Irish sound. Instead of *Jag-o*, it was *Jay-go*.

"It's Old English for—"

"James, I know. I just never met one walking around before." He waited for her to accept his hand. When she didn't, his left brow arched. *Well, damn him, no man called her chicken twice!* She took his hand. It was warm, dry. "Asha Montgomerie." A shiver went up her arm, lodged in her shoulder, then her neck. *Yeppers, he was a ruddy warlock.*

His handshake was firm. His thumb traced a small circle on her palm three times before releasing it. *What? Was that some sort of old warlock school handshake?* Asha wondered.

For an instant something hot flickered in his dark eyes. Asha had the odd inkling he thought about using that hand to pull her to him and kiss her. Then it was gone. She chalked it up to a trick of the recessed lights.

He let go. She thought she'd passed the test rather well, outside the electrical shock and imagining he'd wanted to kiss her. Then his left hand waggled the Coors by its long neck. Caught up in thinking Netta was right—he *did* have sexy lips—Asha blinked, recalling he had goaded her to take a drink of his beer.

She slowly accepted the Coors, saw a smug smile almost escape before he reformed his face to seriousness. Taking the brown bottle, she turned it around and stared at the label.

"What? It's a *Coors*." He laughed.

Oh, she liked that laugh. "I was looking for a list of ingredients. Every bloody thing has ingredients and daily nutritional requirements these days—even bottled water. But not beer. *T.M.*"

"T.M.?" he queried.

"Typically Male. Don't mess with male bastions like beer."

"What's to know? Barley, hops, water and yeast?"

She hesitated and then admitted, "I wondered if there was salt in it."

"On a low sodium diet?"

She smiled, suddenly enjoying the banter. "Something akin to that." Feeling silly, she took a sip, then passed him the bottle back. "Thanks, but no thanks. I'll stick to Pepsi, Cherry Coke and 7-Up."

"Cherry Coke? If you're a Pepsi addict, why not Cherry Pepsi?"

"Cherry Coke is an old favorite around here," Asha replied

evasively, then chided, "You want a burger and fries with those beers?"

"I'm waiting 'til the supper crowd thins a bit more. Then I'd like one of those strip steaks with onion rings. And don't nag. I've only had three beers in the last two hours. I'm not driving; I only have to stagger a few feet up the knoll." He winked. Winks like that should be outlawed as unsafe for female consumption.

"Up the knoll? As in one of the bungalows?" *Oh great, he's right next to me.* Talk about temptation under her nose!

Jago nodded with a roguish twitch at the corner of his mouth. His eyes shifted to Netta as she came through the swinging door, carrying a tray with slices of strawberry pie, each topped with a swirl of whipped cream.

"Hey, darling," he said, "on your next pass into the kitchen how about tossing one of those steaks on the grill for me? And a side of onion rings?"

The blonde batted her lashes at him, then glanced to Asha and winked. She tossed over her shoulder, "Sure thing, Sexy Lips."

"Sexy Lips?" he repeated. His black brows lifted at the nickname. "I can live with that."

Damn Netta! Go ahead, feed the man's ego, Asha thought. Sexy Lips? Hell, *every inch* of the man, head to toe, was drop-dead sexy.

If he was sticking around, that spelled trouble for her.

Suddenly, the jukebox came on. Asha closed her eyes and groaned as the song started playing.

"*Laura and Tommy were lovers. He wanted to give her everything . . .*"

Asha sighed in resignation. It was a great song, one that seemed to last through the ages. "It certainly lasts around this place," she muttered, glowering at the Wurlitzer 2700.

The jukebox had been new in 1963, and now was worth a small chunk of change, a collector's item from the silver era. This one would go for ten times the market price of others, since each booth still had its original wallette table changer. But the bloody thing had a mind of its own. Oh, did it have a mind of its own!

Netta came back with her tray empty, catching Asha's questioning glare. She shrugged.

"I thought Colin took that song off the jukebox," Asha said.

Netta laughed. "*You* try taking it off."

Asha scowled at the shiny chrome Wurlitzer that looked brand new instead of decades old, as Ray Peterson soulfully crooned on, "*Tell Laura not to cry. My love for her will never die . . .*"

Chapter Three

Jago's request took Asha by surprise. "Supper rush seems over, and business has slowed. Why don't you keep me company while I eat, Asha Montgomerie?" Netta had just informed him it would only be a couple minutes until his steak was ready. "I hate dining alone."

Asha looked up from scribbling notes for next week's food order. Instinct was to brush Jago Fitzgerald off the way she did all males who tried to push past her 'no trespass sign', but as she stared into those dark green eyes everything faded to a blur. She could only focus on him.

The crazed jukebox with a mind all its own had stopped its tizzy fit, spinning "Tell Laura I Love Her" endlessly, and now behaved, playing "Against The Wind." As Asha stared at Jago, she felt close to him in some fey way, as if there were some connection between them, a bond.

Maybe it was Bob Seger's ballad evoking emotions, but she believed he hated eating alone, and he was right; business had slowed. A couple shared a banana split in the back booth, and one of the motel customers was finishing up his meal with a slice of pecan pie. Derek bussed the tables that needed cleaning, and Netta was already changing the menus to show tomorrow's specials. Just another typically slow Thursday night.

Giving in to temptation, Asha put down the pencil and closed the order book. "All right, I'll take a break and eat a piece of pie."

Pleasure lit Jago's eyes. "Where shall I sit? Anyplace special?"

"Anywhere is fine. It's always slow Thursday evenings."

Jago started to slide into the first booth on the left. A big one, almost C-shaped, it was large enough to seat eight people. Asha panicked, her command coming out in a yelp.

"Not there!"

"Anywhere,—just not *here?*" He waited for an explanation.

Asha grasped for a reason to offer. How did one elucidate that there were unspoken rules about The Windmill—and not just The Windmill Restaurant, but also the drive-in and the swim club? There existed certain boundaries everyone around the three places quickly learned not to cross or else. Like the last time Colin removed "Tell Laura I Love Her" from the jukebox, the following morning they had found every plate in the restaurant shattered and in a big heap on the middle of the dining room floor. If you parked in slot H-13 at the drive-in or sat in that particular booth, you were courting trouble. People refused to discuss these 'peculiarities' with Asha since she'd returned to take over the businesses; ask them a direct question about the odd occurrences and they practically ran. Still, Asha was Scot and thus respected things outside the norm. She embraced these quirks as part of the ambience of The Windmill. She was unsure how an outsider would react to her suspicions, however.

She eyed the booth he'd started to sit in. All manner of catastrophes befell any unsuspecting diner who dared occupy that booth after dark. During the day, it was all right to use it, but after the sun set you could bet something weird would happen. Trays might be dropped into the unfortunate person's lap, or the bus-cart might careen into the table, sending a load of dirty dishes everywhere. Once, a flying plate had hit a man in the back of the head. No one had witnessed the 'Frisbee toss,' but everyone muttered suspicions.

"Less cleanup racket if we sit a few booths away." *Nice save.* She patted herself on her back. "Now, let me fetch a piece of pie."

As she passed the jukebox, it changed to "I Will Follow Him" by Little Peggy March. Asha stuck out her tongue at the temperamental thing.

Pushing through the swinging door to the kitchen, she went to the food locker, took out a pie and cut two slices. Jago hadn't ordered dessert, but she figured he couldn't watch her eat these plump berries with the strawberry glaze and not want a slice himself.

She returned and set both saucers down on the table, causing Jago to raise his sexy black brows. "Compliments of the house," she said.

"Thank you—for both the pie and the company."

"You're welcome. I've been on the go all day. I can use a breather."

And boy, could she! There was an odd, almost feral stillness about Jago Fitzgerald, a trait inherent to nature's most successful predators. He unsettled Asha, on par with a white tiger wandering in and making himself at home in the middle of her restaurant. She cautiously studied him while he ate, every move deft, elegant, understated. Oh, this man intrigued her. Maybe too much.

"You manage all this?"

"*This* being the motel, swim club, the restaurant, laundromat and drive-in? Actually, I own them. The horse farm on the other side of the road is owned by my father and brother, but everything on this side belongs to me. When Mother died, she left me a quarter interest in the horse farm and half ownership of these businesses. I cut a deal with my father last year. Traded him my shares in the farm, and he made me total owner of The Windmill and the house on the river."

"Odd place for businesses—out in the middle of bloody nowhere."

"The horse farm was once part of a land grant from George the Third. During the War Between the States, it was a horse plantation. This building was the overseer's house. As you can tell, this diner is grafted onto its side. When the landowner died in the late '40s, there was a protracted and dirty fight amongst the numerous heirs. They were forced to break the property into five separate tracts and sell them at auction. Mac—my father—bought this one."

"Valinor Revisited? Isn't that an odd name for a horse farm?" Jago smirked in a teasing fashion, then took a sip of coffee.

Asha shrugged. "Mac is a big Tolkien fan. My grandfather knew him. I guess we're lucky he didn't name the place Bag End."

"Okay, the farm I understand, "Jago sounded intrigued. "This is, after all, the heart of the Blue Grass State. Only, I'm puzzled by these other businesses in the middle of undeveloped farmland."

Asha warmed to the subject, proud of the area. "The first business on this spot was an icehouse. People used blocks of ice for iceboxes back then. They needed a place centrally located, not too far away. Seeing an opportunity, the owner started selling beer and soft drinks by the case to boaters heading to the river for the day. Back then, this highway was the main artery for commercial travel from Michigan to Florida. We're the halfway mark on the Blue Highway. Truckers required somewhere to get gas, to eat. Travelers needed a motel, a stop on their way to Florida. Mum renovated the overseer's house into the restaurant, and then they built a small motel extension. The swimming pool was added for the motel guests' pleasure. Later, traffic slowed when I-64 opened back in the early '60s, so Mum changed it to a private swim club. The laundromat was necessary for the workers. I'm not sure where she got the idea for the drive-in." She shrugged. "She was a rabid movie buff. I thought ours was the last one in Kentucky, but Netta informed me there are a dozen left. They're having a rebirth, people discovering the fun again. We do a strong business on weekends. With houses for the workers on the other side of the drive-in, The Windmill has grown into a special quirky microcosm."

It struck Asha how her tiny community was somewhat similar to B.A.'s island in Scotland. Her oldest sister owned the small island in the Hebrides, which had a population of less than three hundred. The Windmill was similarly isolated, and people who worked and lived here were just as eccentric, wanting a place in the world where things were slower. That was why she fought her father's recent pressure for her to sell.

Asha wasn't getting rich. She'd returned to take over running the businesses three years ago, just after her mother's death. She needed a purpose in life. She'd envied B.A.'s Falgannon, and sensed The Windmill could provide her with the same satisfaction. As long as everyone was paid and she was able to maintain the complex in the same style, Asha was happy here.

Jago's comment interrupted her reverie. "It's also a little odd to find a Scot running the place."

Asha pushed her empty pie plate aside. "Though my mum was a Scot, she was raised in Kentucky from the time she was nine-years-old. I grew up on both sides of the pond. One of the bones of contention in my parents' marriage and then divorce was that she never felt comfortable in Britain. She'd always want to come back here. The Windmill holds many wonderful recollections for me . . . it's a storehouse of memories for many people, which is why I'd like to see it continue. In some ways, we're in a time capsule. When I-64 took away the traffic, everything stood still. We've remained in a time warp, stuck in the 1960s around here with a passion."

"You dumplings need anything?" Netta had come to remove their empty dishes.

Jago shook his head. "The meal was delicious. I look forward to being well-fed while I'm staying here."

Netta stood patiently waiting for more information. When Asha rolled her eyes, Miss Gossip of the Year finally caved in. "Fudge, you ruin all the fun, Asha. I'll just have to needle it out of you later."

Jago watched Netta vanish into the kitchen, then remarked, "She's a character."

"All at The Windmill are." Asha shifted in the booth, leaned her back against the wall and stretched out her legs along the seat. "So, what are *you* doing in my little nowhere burgh? With that accent you're on the wrong side of the pond."

"Speaking of accents—*burgh*?" he teased, "You can take the lass out of Scotland, but you can't take the Scot out of the lass."

She stuck out the tip of her tongue at him. "Och, roots run deep. Why the thistle is our national flower; they often go down thirty feet. So, what drew you to my *burgh?*" she asked again.

"I'm a developer. I'm in the area to scout around." He watched her intently, obviously waiting to see her reaction to that pronouncement.

Asha just stared, unblinking. *Oh, bugger.* Sexy lips or no, she'd just got the kicker of a feeling Jago Fitzgerald was the front man for Trident Ventures, the big money people trying to buy the horse farm and The Windmill. There'd already been two offers and counter-offers; however, Trident was pressuring her father to include The Windmill as part of the package. Mac didn't like her living in Kentucky, wanted her closer, so he used the offer as a lever to get Asha to return to England to live. She'd flatly refused. The businesses were hers, and there wasn't anything Mac could do to force her to sell. Evidently, Trident had decided to send their rep to negotiate face-to-face.

"Never trust a pretty man," she muttered under her breath.

Jago leaned forward and placed his elbows on the table. "Beg pardon?"

She blinked innocently as though she hadn't spoken. "Scout? For what?"

"As you said, this wide spot in the road is centrally located."

"Oh, great. What the world needs—another Wally World." She drank her 7-Up, trying to calm her rising irritation. She failed.

Jago shifted in the booth, stretched out his long legs and observed, "I see you rank developers slightly above used car salesmen and lawyers."

"They take beautiful countryside and turn it into Plasticland. If I want to shop, I can drive into Lexington and have my choice of half a dozen malls. I don't want any on my doorstep. The thought never occurs to developers that anyone might *like* how things are."

"No one holds a gun to people's heads. They don't have to sell."

"Good. Thank you. I'm *not* selling, no matter what anyone says. Go back to Trident, tell them I don't care how they pressure Mac or if he sells the horse farm. The Windmill stays." She slid from the booth before saying something she'd regret, then paused, having one more tidbit for Mr. Sexy Lips Developer. "I don't like Trident sending their hired gun to muscle me. I don't take harassment well. I tend to get mean. Very mean."

Instead of looking affronted, he just smiled. "Sassy thing, aren't you? Guess it goes with the red hair."

"My hair isn't red," she snapped. Picking up a strand draped over her shoulder, she pretended to study it. "It's . . . well . . . crabby tabby."

"Crabby tabby?" He chuckled.

"Oh aye, and that describes *me* rather well, too. Push me, I hiss and the claws come out," she warned.

He sipped his coffee and watched her with a predator's

stillness, which set prickles tingling along her spine and neck. "Ever get up on the soapbox and find you mistook the situation?"

"You aren't from Trident?" she challenged.

He evaded, asking, "Now that I've eaten, may I have another beer?"

He slid from the booth and followed her to the front of the restaurant to perch on a stool at the counter. Asha went to the cooler, took out a Coors, opened it and set it on a paper coaster before him. She commented, "I noticed you didn't answer my question."

"Yes, Asha, I represent Trident. But not as a hired gun, as you so colorfully put it. We felt there was a need to study the area. Sheath the claws, Crabby Tabby. You don't have to try and boot me out of the motel—yet."

Netta came from the kitchen and plopped down on the stool beside Jago. "My feet hurt," she grumbled. "They promised these high-priced New Balance shoes would stop that. Guess I have to break them in first, you think? Asha, hon, give me a cream soda with lots of ice. I'm dying of thirst."

Asha took a glass off the shelf, filled it with ice and Big Red. She set it on a coaster in front of Netta, along with an Almond Joy—Netta's nightly end-of-shift indulgence.

"So, have you finished giving handsome here the third degree?" Netta asked impishly.

Asha's eyes met Jago's, and she was barely able to focus on Netta due to the mesmerizing power the man exuded. "He's a bloody developer," she said, using her sour words as a shield.

Netta let out a howl. "Could be worse. He could be a used car salesman."

Jago lifted his beer in a small salute, glancing pointedly to Asha. Netta leaned toward him and bumped shoulders.

"But then, Sexy Lips," she cooed, "I'd let you park your socks under my Serta Sleeper no matter if you were a telemarketer, forever calling me at 8:00 a.m. and waking me from my beauty rest."

"Down, Netta, you'll give him a big head." Asha chuckled. It was hard to remain straight-faced around the saucy, thirty-something woman with bleached-blond hair and china-blue eyes.

"Shucks, hon, I'd like to make *something* big on him." Netta winked at Asha.

Asha shook her head with a smile. "Stop propositioning the customers, Netta." The rebuke was a running joke. Part of her earthy charm, Netta propositioned the customers with great regularity; they'd be disappointed if she didn't. In some ways Asha wished she could take life with the same seek-your-fun-where-you-may attitude. Having faced hitting the big 3-0 just three weeks past, she felt the pinch of her moral standards and the limited opportunities. She loved The Windmill, but being in the middle of nowhere didn't present one with the widest range of dating prospects. Worse, her *high raisings*—as some around here put it, referring to her being a Brit—made the local lads seem a tad mundane. Demolition derbies and tractor-pulls just weren't her cup of tea.

The maniac jukebox began playing "It Hurts To Be In Love" by Gene Pitney. "*How long can I exist wanting lips I've never kissed*?"

Netta looked at Asha, and they both broke out laughing.

After she flipped off the overhead lights inside the diner, Asha locked the restaurant's door, then glanced around the parking lot. It was empty, typical for an area that would roll up the sidewalks at 9:00 p.m.—if they had any. The incandescent light spread the greenish cast to the area, creating long shadows, its quiet hum the only noise in the still October night. Asha followed the walkway around to the facade of the building, turned left, keeping on the flagstones until she reached the motel entrance, the vestibule of the old overseer's house.

Delbert Seacrest leaned on the counter of the front desk, half dozing when Asha came in. The old man reminded her of a pudgy Alec Guinness. She chuckled softly and said to herself, "One of the perks of owning The Windmill. Not everyone has Obi-Wan Kenobi for a night manager."

"You talking to yourself or me, Asha? If it's me, speak up. I don't hear so well these days." The elderly man yawned, aware Asha wouldn't say anything to him about catnapping on the job.

It was so slow during the week that often having a night manager seemed silly. However, eighty-seven year old Delbert enjoyed the job, said it kept him from being alone all the time. Having no family, he lived in the large rooms at the back of the old house, and tended to set his own hours. Asha smiled. The Windmill was his family now.

"Something big city developers wouldn't understand," she muttered lowly, and then passed him the bank bag containing that night's cash from the restaurant. He shuffled off to place it in the safe until Asha could deposit it, a chore she usually did on Monday mornings.

"How was business?"

"Brisk for a Thursday. Keeneland's opening helped. We're catching their travelers taking the scenic route." She went behind the desk, spun the registry book around and glanced down at the page half-filled with names, dates and the guests' origins.

Jago Fitzgerald had checked in late Monday night. She'd been at the river house Tuesday and Wednesday, and then had gone straight to the horse farm bright and early this morning. That's why they had missed each other until tonight. Delbert had initially put him in room five, then moved him to the bungalow this afternoon when it became available. That made him her neighbor.

Directly behind the restaurant was a small courtyard with five self-catering cottages, arranged in a horseshoe pattern. Each had sliding patio doors so one could enjoy the lovely garden and fountain, and came equipped with a small kitchenette, living room, and bedroom. Asha maintained one for her part-time residence, a second for her brother, Liam, when he took the mind to stay. The other three they let to travelers, wishing to remain in the area for a longer visit.

So, Jago Fitzgerald was her neighbor. Knowing that unnerved Asha in ways she didn't care to think about. Not sure what she was looking for, she studied the precise script. Most men's handwriting was little better than chicken scratches; his was neat, elegant. He gave his address as London, England. What did she expect to suss from a name she already knew and a vague English address? Restlessly, she tapped her fingernails on the book.

She looked up when the elderly manager ambled back from the office. "Delbert, did Mr. Fitzgerald pay with a credit card?"

"I intended to mention him to you, Asha. He originally requested a bungalow, but they were full up—that honeymoon party for the Gibsons. I put him in five until they checked out. I really hated to lodge such a fancy gent in number five, but that was the only room available."

Asha frowned and winkled her nose. "The one with the cracked ceiling tiles?"

Delbert nodded, sticking his hands in the pockets of his oversized sweater. "I sort of felt bad, him being quality and all."

"Yeah . . ." She sighed. "It's on my to-do list, Delbert, which gets longer every day. Not many around here are able to redo ceilings. Colin cannot handle it due to his vertigo, so I'll need to hire someone from Lexington or Leesburg. It'll cost me an arm and a leg. Still, with all this windfall business because of Keeneland, I should be left with some extra cash to toss around for repairs."

"You know, Asha, my offer stands. I could help out a bit. I have some money saved and it just sits in the bank not doing much."

"You're a dear heart, but I'm determined to do all this on

my own—prove something to myself, you might say." She patted his arm and gave it a small squeeze. "How did Fitzgerald pay for the room?"

"The first two nights, cash. I moved him to the bungalow this morning when it became available. He paid for two weeks in advance."

"Cash again?"

Delbert nodded. "Nice crisp hundred dollar bills. He stays around here for a few weeks, you can fix your ceiling tiles."

Asha glanced back at the office safe, glowering. "Maybe I should check them. He might be a counterfeiter."

"Girl, you always had a runaway imagination. Your mother figured you'd be a writer."

She shrugged. "So far, I can't muster enough discipline or time."

"Well, don't go writing about counterfeiters when you do. One look at Fitzgerald rules that out. He's money. Wears a Rolex. Tips well, too. He's quality . . . like you. That intimidates *some people* around here, gets their inferiority complexes perking. Besides, I always check big bills. They had that funny little strip thingy in them. They're legit. So is he." The old man paused as a distant look came into his eyes. "He reminds me of someone . . . a long time ago . . ."

"Don't say 'in a galaxy far, far away,' " Asha teased, picking up her purse where she'd set it by the register. "He works for Trident Ventures, the bunch trying to buy Valinor. They sent in their gunslinger to put pressure on me. Me is *not* a happy camper."

Delbert laughed. "Ah, well, they can't buy what you aren't selling, eh? Get a good night's rest. My rheumatism's acting up. I'm going back to my room to prop up my feet and watch Leno, maybe catnap a bit."

" 'Night, Obi-Wan," Asha said, but he'd already turned and didn't hear her jest. She pushed out the door and continued around the side of the building to the bungalows.

She was halfway down the driveway leading to the small

courtyard when she noticed Jago. Wary, she pulled up. Oh, not that she feared he might harm her. This threat came from a different direction, and was more dangerous.

He sat on the rock wall, the white of his shirt shimmering in the autumn night. His hand lifted to his mouth, and from the small flare of red, she saw that he was smoking.

"Strike two," she growled so he couldn't hear. "A developer *and* a smoker."

Asha didn't care for smoking, detested how the scent clung to clothes, hands and hair. While she hadn't been that close to him in the restaurant, she failed to notice telltale signs of a long-term smoker. No nicotine-stained fingers, no 'cloud' around him. Also, he hadn't indulged while in the diner, so he wasn't a chain-smoker. Still. Continuing on, her slow steps carried her nearer. Jago took another draw and she saw it wasn't a cigarette, but a long, thin cigar—cigarillo, she believed it was called.

"Worse than cigarettes." Her mouth pursed in censure. Cigars often left a foul smell on men who puffed them. Oddly, the cigarillo looked natural to Jago. As the warm breeze swirled around them, she detected a sweet cherry scent.

"Hello, neighbor." His low voice rumbled with a sorcerer's cant.

Hello, neighbor, my foot! Warning gongs were going off in her brain. If she was smart, she'd slug him with her purse and make a run for her cottage. Lock herself in. *Then* she might be safe from this virile warlock and his potent magic.

The soft breeze ruffled his wavy black hair and caused his silken shirt to ripple. He'd unbuttoned it halfway down his chest and had no T-shirt underneath. One long leg was stretched out before him; the other was cocked against the low, creek-stone wall for balance.

Jago Fitzgerald was waiting—waiting with that stillness inherent to all of nature's nocturnal hunters. Men of his caliber were few and far between, and quite treacherous to females. They sensed small changes in a woman's body, reaction to the lethal peril they posed. The pounding of her heart, the rapid, short breaths, and—damn her body—the tightening of her breasts.

Fortunately, her black sweater hid that reaction from this arrogant man in the darkness. Her little secret. A woman needed every advantage in dealing with a male like Jago Fitzgerald, for she had the unshakable sense Netta was right.

He was waiting for her.

Chapter Four

Wanting was a dangerous thing. Asha knew this. Everyone wants something: a Lamborghini Murcielago, more money, a closet full of Prada shoes. With many women it's to pig out on chocolate. That didn't mean getting what you wanted was *good* for you.

Asha suddenly wanted Jago Fitzgerald with a soul-deep craving that was alarming. Terrifying. Wanted him enough to reach out and take whatever he offered, asking for nothing but tonight. She could see the whole scene play out in her mind. His mouth taking hers, savagely. Her clinging to him with a passion the like of which she'd never known.

She wondered if he would make love with that same controlled force now emanating from him, or would he snap and let loose demons because he too wanted? Both scenarios rattled Asha. Both images were frighteningly vivid, crackling with the power of clairvoyance. Worse, she figured he was likely aware of her hesitation. Aware of why.

As badly as she desired him, she reminded herself this man was passing through. Oh, he'd enjoy a hot fling to wile away his stay in Hicksville, Kentucky. If so, he should target

Netta, not her. Asha didn't play with customers—*Rule Number One*. She wasn't part of the package at The Windmill.

"How long are we to be neighbors, Mr. Fitzgerald?" she asked softly.

He smiled. Not a fool, Asha didn't trust that smile. It was the same smile the Wolf wore when Little Red Riding Hood exclaimed, *My, what big teeth you have*! Women were born knowing *not* to trust a sexy smile like that.

"I want to gain a feel for the area. Ramble a bit. I plan to use The Windmill as my base—if that's all right. Why I wanted the bungalow instead of a room—I like to spread out . . . have room to work." He lifted the cigarillo to his lips, took a draw and then exhaled a narrow stream of smoke into the air. The cherry-scented smoke swirled around her with a wizard's magic.

"I should be fool enough to help the enemy by providing a roof over your head?" Tired after being on her feet most of the day, Asha considered joining him on the rock wall, but deemed that would be *too* close.

"I'm not your enemy, Asha." His white teeth flashed in the night. "And I *am* a paying customer."

"True, you are a customer. Whether you prove to be the enemy or not, I shall reserve judgment." The autumn night seemed to enfold around them, to cocoon them in an intimacy that left her breathless. It was the sheer force of this man. His radiant heat reached out and nearly overwhelmed her fragile sense of self-preservation. She needed to get away from him, *fast,* before it was too late. "Goodnight, Mr. Fitzgerald."

" 'Night, Asha Montgomerie. *Pleasant dreams*," he wished in a low sexy voice that promised they'd be about him.

Asha started to walk away, but those soft words made her turn around. Jago still sat, smoking. The sensual hint of cherry trailed after her, taunting her for being a coward. Yes, she was a coward. She ran when she wanted to step between those strong thighs, press her body against his chest, and see if that cherry smoke tasted as tantalizing as it smelled.

Never in her whole life had she ever considered taking a stranger to her bed. While a modern woman, there was still a wee dram of old-fashioned morals within her. The only way a man would make it past all her carefully erected guards and to her bed would be through love.

She had a feeling Jago Fitzgerald could be the exception.

Yes, she craved to take those few steps to him, maybe shock him with her surrender. However, as she thought of doing that—was just a breath away from doing it—images of a balefire seared her mind's eye, of two lovers coming together with a passion that would burn out all reason.

Swallowing back her yearning for him, she turned on her heels. And fled.

Yes, wanting was a dangerous thing.

Jago watched Asha rush to her bungalow and unlock it. She reached inside, flipped on a light, and then with a glance over her shoulder, entered. Sliding the patio door shut, she turned and relocked it. Hesitating, she stared with haunting eyes out into the night. At him. The instant spun out, making it hard for him to breathe.

It wouldn't take much to push the hand of fate and knock down those barriers she was carefully constructing between them. She wanted him. Oh, how she wanted him. It probably terrified Miss Prim and Proper just how much she did. An intelligent woman, she recognized she was his for the taking, that had he reached out and kissed her, he'd be in her bed this night. No words, no promises, just her sweet surrender. The needy look from those tawny eyes set his brain on a slow burn. Made him nearly forget his best intentions.

With a sharp yank, she pulled the cord on the heavy drapes, and shut him out of her contained little world. He didn't like being shut out. Still, despite his annoyance, he smiled, seeing that her bungalow was next to his. He figured she likely had a personal code about never dating customers. Picky women often made such rules.

"And Asha is very particular, aren't you, love?" He said the words as a challenge.

Taking another drag on the Swisher Sweet, he relished the hint of cherry in the tobacco. Damn cheap-arse cigar, but one fine smoke. His brother Desmond always sniggered at his choice of cigars. Of course, Desmond did everything first class. Were he to smoke, only Havana's best would be good enough for him. Jago didn't indulge often, but at times a smoke was relaxing. It allowed him to savor the moment. Like now.

He wanted nothing more than to go knock on that glass door with the drapes pulled against the night. *Against him*. See if Asha would let him in. He wanted to push past the line she'd drawn in the sand, see if she'd make an exception for him, test if she'd break those rules. There was a restlessness inside him. A queer, itchy feeling that had been creeping up on him for the past ten months.

The restiveness had first started back in winter, though he couldn't now precisely pinpoint the date. He recalled going to the refrigerator looking for something, though he wasn't hungry. He wondered if the compulsive action was caused by lingering childhood memories when food had been scarce. That seemed logical. He'd noticed when watching television, he'd constantly flip channels; nothing held his attention. And women . . . they'd become like his incessant trips to the refrigerator—plenty of choices, but nothing for which he truly hungered.

Jago couldn't recall the last time he wanted a woman the way he ached at this moment for Asha Montgomerie—craved her until reason faded and age-old instincts to mate possessed his mind. What he felt for her was primitive, raw. It was dangerous. In more bloody ways than one.

So odd, Trevelyn and he were twins, yet their approach to women was wholly different, dissimilar even from their elder brother Desmond. Desmond liked women; he just didn't like them to cling—especially after the novelty of the relationship wore thin. Trevelyn loved sex. He ran through women like one might a box of tissues when you had a cold. Strange to think of sharing a face and body with another being, yet inside that wrapper was a person poles apart. Trev was a tiger on the prowl. And himself? Jago sighed . . . not sure what he was anymore.

The disquiet within him had grown worse after Sean Montgomerie's funeral last May. Desmond, Trev and he had attended the service in England, sitting at the back of the ancient Norman kirk so that no one would notice them.

His brothers and he had been obsessed with bringing down Montgomerie's empire, vengeance pure and simple for their father's death. It had taken years, but Desmond had finally orchestrated the man's financial downfall, starting with claiming Falgannon Isle, Valinor Revisited and the estate in England, Colford Hall. Asha's grandfather Sean had once put up those properties as collateral for a loan, then defaulted on payment. The deliberate act had left Michael Mershan with a loss of his personal fortune, and facing jail time for misappropriation of bank funds in granting the questionable loan. As a result of the scandal, he had committed suicide when Jago and his brothers were children.

To say Desmond felt cheated by Montgomerie's death was putting it mildly. His brother had wanted to look the old man in the eyes when he handed him the papers showing the multi-billion dollar empire Sean had built was crumbling and why.

Well, the financial plans were still in place, and Desmond and Trev were pig-headedly determined to go through with them. True, there was a fortune at stake. Only of late, Jago questioned the whole idea. Montgomerie was dead. What did any of it really matter now?

All he had to do was close his eyes, and that memory of Desmond at thirteen was in his mind. Just like yesterday, he saw his brother, feverish, so sick he belonged in bed, yet dressing at three in the morning, getting ready to deliver papers. It didn't matter that Des was sick, didn't matter that he'd eaten nothing the night before, or that he'd sat and rocked their mother most of the night while she was in the grips of one of her black depressions. Des always did his paper route, knowing the extra money he brought in often meant the difference between them eating and not.

That memory haunting his soul, Jago knew without hesitation he would walk barefoot through Hell for Des. If finally settling this business with the Montgomeries would give his brother the sense of peace he desperately needed, then Jago knew he'd walk on the hot coals of his conscience to do it.

Taking another pull on the Swisher Sweet, he cast his mind back to Sean's funeral. Asha and her sisters—Montgomerie's granddaughters—had sat in the second row. Seven breathtakingly beautiful women, the kind of women men fantasized about. The front row held their six brothers, father and two uncles. Jago vaguely recalled them, as handsome as the granddaughters were beautiful.

Clan Montgomerie's motto was *Look Well.* Though he assumed that meant *Be Vigilant*, in this instance it also applied to the appearance of the striking males and females of Sean's line. If the scientist who'd cloned Dolly the Sheep ever got around to cloning human beings, he needed to look up the Montgomeries.

Jago recalled how Desmond had stared at BarbaraAnne the whole time. Once she had turned and looked directly at Des. To Jago, it seemed the whole world had held its breath as the two stared at each other. Needless to say, he hadn't been surprised when Desmond announced he'd be the one to go to Falgannon Isle to handle that end of the business for Mershan International and Trident Ventures. Jago had never said anything to Desmond, but he was aware his brother had carried a picture of BarbaraAnne in his wallet for nearly fifteen years, cut from some magazine.

Desmond likely thought of it as a goal, as a reminder of what drove him. Jago figured his brother failed to recognize that he went to Falgannon for more than his role in taking down Montgomerie Enterprises. He wondered how long before Des recognized that fact.

"'Oh, what a tangled web we weave,'" Jago muttered, then flicked the ashes off his cigarillo.

At the funeral, much to his irritation, Asha had never turned around, so he'd spent the whole of the service staring at the back of her head. It was hard from that distance to tell her from her twin sister, Raven, or for that matter from her elder sisters, Katlynne and LynneAnne. The four women were dead ringers, variations on a theme, with only small differences in their height and hair. Asha had the lightest auburn locks, with pale almost blonde streaks.

Jago had been outside in the parking lot before he finally got a good look at her face. Quite vividly, he recalled standing by the car, watching Raven and Asha coming down the steps of the ancient kirk. They were twins, and yet, Asha had seemed unique somehow. Maybe being a twin himself had endowed him with a perception attuned to recognizing finite differences others missed.

As he hadn't been surprised when Desmond booked a flight to Scotland, Jago had fathomed in that breathless instant that he would be the one to come here to Kentucky.

"Destiny, the bitch, sure plays cruel tricks with people's lives." He laughed softly, mockingly.

Jago took one last draw on the Swisher Sweet, the taste going flat. He dropped it and ground the butt beneath his boot. Instantly, the disquietude was back.

The light in the living room of Asha's bungalow winked out, increasing the penned animal mood within him. Like a big cat in a zoo, Jago wanted to break free of this invisible cage that caused his edginess. No, that light going off didn't help the situation one bit. Was Asha in bed? Did she sleep nude? Were the sheets soft flannel, crisp linen or sleek silk? What material rubbed against those full breasts? Images filled his mind of them locked together in full-tilt, ride-'em-cowboy sort of sex. How would she taste? Would she want—as the Pointer Sisters crooned—"a lover with a slow hand," or would she give measure-for-measure, as sudden and wild as a spring thunderstorm?

A fresh vision flashed in his mind: him holding her body spooned against his, lazily listening to the rain on the roof as they drowsed. It was a vivid picture devoid of his gnawing restlessness, and for a moment, an intangible sense flowed through him, spreading in gentle waves of tantalizing warmth. The sensation shifted through his veins, then lodged in his chest, both unnerving and welcome in the same breath.

Then the old hunger returned, tenfold, nearly overwhelming him. That damn wanting and yet not knowing what his soul cried for.

Giving up, Jago stalked disgustedly toward his bungalow. He wondered how many times this night he would get up, go to the refrigerator, stare for a few minutes and then slam the door—coming away with nothing.

"For a change there's a good excuse for that bit of nonsense—I don't have any food in it yet." His mood brightened. "I'll just have to get Asha to show me where to shop tomorrow."

Chapter Five

Asha came out of the motel office and pulled up short. The black Jeep Cherokee sat, engine running, at the end of the walkway. "Bloody warlock read my mind?"

Jago leaned over the passenger seat and opened the door from the inside. "Hop in, Asha, you're getting wet." He flashed that killer, mega-watt smile. Asha wanted to slap the smug expression off his handsome face.

Exhaling, she unslung her purse from her shoulder, slid into the Jeep and closed the door. There was no scent of cherry smoke, just clean male and the light hint of citrus, bergamot and wood found in Armani's *Pour Homme*. Last year, while searching for the perfect Christmas presents for her brothers, Asha had fallen for the scent, even bought it for cousin Edward. She adored it, and had almost purchased a bottle for herself, just to keep and smell. She'd eventually nixed that idea, thinking the fragrance required the body heat of a man to make it complete. Having no male around, it would only serve to torment her. That Jago wore that cologne—or one similar—flustered her.

"Good morning, Asha. Have you breakfasted yet?" He

shifted the Jeep into gear, pulled down the motel drive and turned onto the narrow outbound road, wipers swooshing in a soothing rhythm.

"Actually, I'm not much of a morning person, so I don't usually have breakfast." As she fastened the seat belt, her eyes took in the details of the sexy man.

Jago wore a black turtleneck sweater, black jeans and a camel-colored, suede bomber jacket. His right hand rested lightly on the gearshift between them. The small gold ring on his pinkie matched his Rolex. Elegant. Understated. His effect on her system was anything but.

"Ever notice you have a habit of evading direct replies?" Jago coasted the sedan to the end of the short lane and waited to pull onto the highway. "Which way? Or are you going to ply me with another evasive answer?"

She fought a smile. "Left. To Leesburg."

"Can we shop for groceries in Leesburg? While I look forward to meals at The Windmill, I'd like to have basic staples for my off hours. Sandwich stuff. Some utterly fattening Krispy Kreme donuts. Never know when a wicked hunger can strike a man in the middle of the night."

She saw the long black lashes on those intense green eyes bat once, then he glanced to gauge the reaction to his thinly disguised double-entendre. *Think, silly woman, the man is expecting a reply. Something witty, droll, preferably!* Her problem: she was of two minds. Miz Goodie Two-Shoes sat, her knees clamped together, trying to ignore how her womb had contracted into a hard knot from the impact of this man on her senses. Yet, deep inside was a wild woman yearning to be set free to indulge in all the wild fantasies slipping into her mind whenever she looked at him, at those beautiful hands she wanted on her body. A small voice whispered that this man was the one to grant all those wishes.

Taking the easy way, the coward's way, she said, "Leesburg has a decent-size grocery. In the mid '60s the town had a Kroger and a Gateway—back when gas was little more than a quarter a gallon."

He arched an eyebrow. "You weren't alive back then."

His comment gave her pause. How *did* she know these things? She could clearly summon the two stores to mind, could see the Texaco station with the sign showing gasoline at 22¢ per gallon. Memories of lazy summer evenings, people out for a sunset stroll, some gathering around the Dairy Queen to exchange pleasantries. Strange, these images were in shimmering sepia, devoid of all other color. But he was right—that had been over a decade before she was born. So strange, she could see the tableaux so clearly, as if she had *lived* them.

"You know small towns—everyone's always talking about the good old days," she lied, at a loss to explain the vivid montage in her head.

"How about a trade? I'll feed you breakfast, and you show me the best places to shop. A nice way to pass a rainy morning, eh?"

Asha hated to admit it, but she liked Jago. He was sex and sin, with a dash of humor and a jigger of mystery. She couldn't recall the last time a man so intrigued her, lured her, despite her mind screaming to keep as far away from him as possible. She'd always had problems of zigging when she should be zagging, but what the hell? What was the worst that could happen—he'd be a total bastard like Justin St. Cloud, her ex-fiancé? She glanced over at the black-haired man who waited for her answer. Jago Fitzgerald was many things, all hazardous to her heart, but she sensed a deep streak of honor running through him. She realized now she had never sensed that in Justin.

"Deal, but I need to stop at the bank. The Windmill is low on change and I want to make a deposit while I'm there."

Jago frowned slightly. "I hadn't considered it, but you have to drive quite a distance to make large cash deposits."

"Not much cash these days. Everyone uses debit or

credit cards; still, sometimes I have a large deposit when Keeneland Racetrack is open—as it is now. Take a left up here and we can go down to the river and eat at The Cliff-side. They have a marvelous breakfast."

"Avoiding my questions again."

She laughed. "You didn't ask a question that time."

"Love, you alone are reason enough for some yahoo to come at you one night after closing, but add in a bank deposit—"

"Don't get your macho up. No one would dare bother me."

Jago made the turn and headed down the winding road toward the Kentucky River. The countryside was gloriously colored in brilliant oranges, yellows and reds—autumn at its peak. The gray mist of the light rain only amplified the dazzling beauty, each turn in the road showing another painter's delight. Jago didn't seem to notice. His eyes were on her as much as the road.

"This time I'll ask a question. Why would you assume no one would bother you?"

She shrugged. "Because I carry."

"A gun?" Surprise registered in his dark eyes.

She nodded. "I have a permit, and I'm a crack shot."

"So, what do you tote, Pistol-packin' Mama?" He chuckled, as if still not believing her claim.

"A Colt Python Elite, four inch barrel, blue carbon finish."

"Geez, Louise—that's a .357 Magnum, 'the Rolls Royce of handguns.' Ever had to use it, Annie Oakley?"

"Nope. Gossip spreads around this neck of the woods like wildfire. I'm a crazy foreigner with a Magnum. They leave me alone."

Shaking his head, Jago smiled. A smile that was both a warning and a promise. "Well, Asha Montgomerie, don't count on that cap pistol keeping you safe from me."

Staring at Jago Fitzgerald, *safe* wasn't a word that came to Asha's mind.

* * *

"Wow," Jago exclaimed in surprise as they pushed through the double doors of The Cliffside Restaurant. He put a hand to the small of Asha's spine, rubbing lightly as he paused to take in the long café. "It's like stepping back in time."

"The Cliffside was built in the 1930s when tourist trade and river traffic kept this place hopping. Barges ferried coal and other stuff up and down the river. There used to be several marinas for pleasure boats," Asha informed him.

Noticing the Wurlitzer to one side he said, "Hey, they have a jukebox like yours."

The comment caused Asha to chuckle. "No, not like The Windmill. No one has a Wurlitzer quite like ours."

The waitress behind the counter looked up from reading a newspaper. "Well, lookie who's come to slum. Morning, Asha. What can I do you for?" Taking a couple glasses from the rack, she filled them with ice and water and put them on a tray. The buxom redhead—with a hairdo that made her resemble a Bubble Cut Barbie come to life—looked Jago up and down. "And what can I do *you* for, handsome?"

"Don't make me get out my cattle prod, Ella," Asha kidded.

Ella Garner patted her over-teased hair and shrugged with a disappointed sigh. "I don't blame you. I'd slap a brand on his cute little tush, too. Where would you like to park that sexy rear?"

"Since Jago is new to the area—," Asha started only to be interrupted.

"*Jay-go*? Oh, be still my beating heart. I ain't never seen a Jago on the hoof before."

"—I thought we might eat on the porch, Ella," Asha finished. "Let him have a gander at that breathtaking view of the river."

"Sure thing, honey." Snatching up a couple menus, Ella led them to the side dining room, which had three walls of windows. She waited until they were seated before placing the water and menus in front of them. "Only, I think you need your eyes checked, Asha Montgomerie. What leaves one breathless is sitting across from you, silly woman."

Jago's eyes skimmed the menu, and then he looked to Asha. "Any suggestions?"

"Country ham, eggs as you like them, Ernie's buttermilk biscuits and hash browns." Asha folded the menu and passed it back. "For us both. My eggs sunny-side up, please, and a tall glass of grapefruit juice."

"Same on the eggs and juice," Jago agreed, passing his menu to Ella. "And coffee, black."

"You want grits?" Ella asked, tapping the order book with her pencil, waiting for his answer.

Jago blinked. "Grits?"

Being perverse, Asha suppressed a giggle and said, "He'll have the grits."

"I will?" Jago looked puzzled.

"Oh, you *have* to eat grits," Asha insisted.

"Okey-dokey . . . coming right up." Ella swiveled on her white waitress shoes and sashayed away.

Jago turned partway to watch the show Ella provided. Just a little ticked, Asha sighed and pursed her lips.

" 'Like Jell-O on springs,' " he quoted Jack Lemmon's line from *Some Like It Hot*.

Asha took a sip of her water, put the glass back on its coaster and then slowly pushed it around on the table for distraction. Rolling her eyes, she muttered ominously, "Strike three."

Jago gave her an easy grin and unfolded his cloth napkin from around his silverware. "Strike three? Sounds like I'm in trouble. What were my first two transgressions—just so I know why my head is on the chopping block?"

"Being a developer and a smoker." Asha unrolled her napkin and arranged her knife, fork and spoon, trying to ignore his incisive stare.

"I only smoke on the rare occasion, and being a developer is a job, not who I am. There are good developers and bad developers, don't you think?" He stretched out his legs and deliberately trapped hers between them. His dancing green eyes were playful.

Ella returned with the glasses of juice, Jago's coffee and a basket of warm blueberry muffins. "Compliments of the house, sugar," she informed with a Cheshire Cat smile.

Asha took a sip of the tart juice. "Ella, you never gave *me* complimentary muffins."

The waitress howled with laughter. "Honey, what do they teach you children over there in England?"

Asha took a hot muffin and broke it open. "Actually, I went to school in the States more than I did in Britain."

"What? Some Catholic girls' school?" Ella snorted. "You poor thing."

When Jago's stare once more followed the redhead moving away, Asha almost tossed her muffin at him. "I'd waste a perfectly good blueberry muffin."

"You're muttering to yourself and glowering at me. Should I move the knife out of your reach?" he teased.

"Might be a good idea at that, but I'll need it to butter my toast." She flashed him a wide, fake grin.

"I think you're jealous, Asha Montgomerie," he accused, clearly liking the idea.

"I think you are arrogant and irritating. Remind me never to have breakfast with you again." Asha knew she was overreacting, and she really wasn't jealous. Not of Ella. One simply did not get jealous over a vintage Barbie doll come to life. Still, the whole situation touched a raw nerve she didn't know she had.

Men looked. Men *always* looked. Tall, short, fat, thin—it didn't matter how the woman appeared or even if she were pretty—men looked. Only, following her dealings with that jerk Justin St. Cloud, the fact suddenly irritated her when it shouldn't. Her problem. Nevertheless, the past left her leery of pretty men. Women tended to go after them rather voraciously. Once she had dumped Justin, she'd made a vow never to set herself up for that heartache again.

"Men look. It—" Jago began.

Asha knew too well what he was going to say. "Doesn't mean a thing. Yeah, I've heard that before." Justin had said the same—*frequently*. Naively, she had believed him. Stupid her. She wasn't about to make the same mistake. "Word-for-word."

"She's a character—like Netta. Colorful, amusing. I don't take either of their flirting seriously."

"No one's like Netta. She has heart," she defended.

"She's flirted a lot more than Ella has, yet you didn't take umbrage with her. You just joined in the laughter." He polished off one muffin and reached for another. "Mind telling me the difference?"

Asha hadn't been piqued with Netta's come-ons to Jago, instinctively knowing her friend would respect imaginary boundaries, but she wasn't going to tell *him* that. As long as Asha had any interest in Jago, Netta might play at flirting, but it was merely teasing and nothing more; Netta flirted as she breathed. Ella was not so respectful of unspoken female territories. She bet anything that Ella would slip Jago her phone number along with the change from the bill.

Evasive, she allowed her eyes to sweep the panoramic view of The Palisades and the winding, muddy river below. The view was majestic; still, her attention was divided. Though she didn't like it, her gaze was unwillingly drawn back to the dynamic man seated opposite her in the red vinyl booth. She was saved from having to reply to his question as Ella returned with the plates full of food.

Jago suspiciously poked a spoon into the grits and eyed Asha. She stared blankly at him, then in challenge, daring him to try them, so he finally took a spoonful and put it in his mouth. He half-choked, his eyes flashing daggers, but finally forced his throat to work. Desperate, he reached for something to gulp down the mush, and she impishly pushed his coffee saucer closer.

Grabbing the cup, he took a big swallow, strangled out, "Hot," and then snatched up her grapefruit juice. Once he was done with his Trial by Ordeal, he frowned, though his eyes twinkled with humor. "You're a wicked woman, Asha Montgomerie. Remind me never to royally piss you off. Grits? They're sand!"

"You're supposed to put salt and pepper and a pat of butter on them," she said, trying to appear innocent.

He shook his head and pushed them away. "No thanks. Then it would taste like salt, pepper and buttered sand. You are *mean*, Asha. Making me eat sand is something my brother Trev would do."

"Trev?" she asked.

He nodded. "My twin brother, Trevelyn, and we have an older brother, Des."

"We are both twins! I have a twin sister, Raven." Asha was delighted with the bond of commonality. "It's not easy being a twin, is it?"

Over the breakfast he talked about having a sibling so alike, of how he understood the struggle of being outwardly like another yet so different inside, feeling the need to assert your own individuality. Her earlier peeve forgotten, Asha enjoyed learning about him. Jago was easy to talk to, flirt with. He enjoyed horseback riding—though seldom had the opportunity—loved music, old movies and sleeping in on rainy days. He took pleasure in swimming laps nearly every day, and dancing when the opportunity presented itself. The meal passed too quickly.

"I have several sisters besides my twin. My sisters Britt and BarbaraAnne—B.A., we call her—are twins, and we have twin brothers, too. We joke that twins not only run in the family, they gallop. I come from a big family, very clannish. Do you come from a large family?"

Jago pushed his plate back, sipping the last of his coffee. "Just my brothers and my mother. She's under nursing care in Ireland."

"I thought I detected the hint in your accent. You lived there?

"The accent comes from her, I should imagine. She's

Irish. We lived there when I was little, but I was too small to recall anything."

"Your father's not alive?" She watched his face cloud at her question.

Obviously, it was his turn to experience a raw nerve. He stiffened, taking a beat to rein in strong emotions, before saying in a flat tone, "My father died. I really don't recall him, though Des talks about him a lot. He's older . . . memories are more vivid for my brother."

Seeing the sparkle dim in those mesmerizing eyes, Asha reached out, and without thinking covered his hand with hers. She almost yanked it back, assuming it perhaps a little presumptuous. Instead of rebuffing her sympathy, Jago's hand quickly reversed positions, gave hers a small squeeze of thanks. Lacing fingers, they sat for some time, just holding hands, not speaking

As Asha stared into the deep green eyes, she could barely breathe, stunned by the rare moment of wordless understanding that shook the very walls of her safe little world.

Never had she felt so close to another person, not even her twin.

Chapter Six

Later that night, Asha was still trying to erect defenses against the profound connection she'd felt with Jago.

"I knew there was a reason I didn't like him," she muttered under her breath as she frowned in his direction. Ringing up a dinner ticket on the register, she was careful not to slam the drawer just to vent her peevish mood.

Netta flashed a smile while she filled glasses from the soda fountain. "I saw you drive up with Sexy Lips and unload groceries at noon. Very domestic. Convenient—him living right next door? Sigh. And me stuck in a cottage up the hill. Still, even if I were closer, I doubt it would do any good. That man keeps an eye on you at all times." She leaned close and bumped Asha's shoulder. "You feel a target on your back, sugarplum?"

A woman passed by Jago's table and paused to say something to him. Whatever the question was, he just shook his head no and grinned.

"Jerk. I forgot what a pain in the bum a pretty man can be. Women thirteen to ninety make cakes of themselves around them," Asha groused, working up a temper. "Ella slipped her phone number to him when she passed his change back for breakfast. I *knew* she would."

Netta shook her head. "Oh, there's a real shocker. I think all that Suave hairspray she uses on that helmet of hair sank into her brain long ago. Of course, she wasn't the brightest Sylvania Blue Dot bulb to start with. You know that, so why are you ticked? You think Sexy Lips will call her?"

"No," she acknowledged with a disgusted sigh. The disgust was for herself. She admitted it; she was interested in Jago Fitzgerald when her best judgment said fascination with the sexy, arrogant man was hazardous to her mental health. Already she acted like a pathetic idiot because some brainless Barbie doll had slipped him her phone number.

"Just because one pretty man was a big horse's patoot, doesn't mean they all are. It's not Sexy Lips's fault females get hot and bothered when they're around him. You know, men do the same over you. You just project that Lady Deep Freeze aura and the poor schmucks scurry off to self-flagellate for daring to look. If you ask my opinion, you'd make a good pair."

"No one asked you, Netta Know-It-All." Asha picked up a pencil and made a note to herself to call around in the morning about getting estimates on the cracked ceiling tiles—and how it's never smart to trust a pretty man. She underlined the last part three times.

"While we're on the subject of asking, find out if he has a brother like him tucked away somewhere. I'd gladly put up with the inconvenience of fighting off predatory females."

Asha stuck the paid ticket into the box by the register. "Actually, he does. Just like him. He's a twin."

Netta blinked in surprise and then grinned. "You're kidding. They cloned that gorgeous thing? Oh, there *is* a god! What's this carbon copy's name, and where can I collect him? I get off at ten."

"Trevelyn, and sorry—he's in England."

"There is a god and *She* hates me. Why is it all the best

men are in England, and I'm stuck in a greasy spoon in the middle of nowhere?"

"Don't you go calling my diner a greasy spoon," Asha teased, wagging her pencil at her waitress. "Show a little loyalty and respect here."

Netta put the full glasses on her tray, mooned, "Trevelyn," and then went back to waiting tables.

The jukebox, which had behaved all evening, suddenly switched mid-song. Asha held her breath, fearing they would be treated to an hour of "Tell Laura I Love Her." When Ray Davis of The Kinks cut loose with "You Really Got Me," she exhaled in relief.

"Still 1964," she chuckled, "but at least it's a break from the 'Tell Laura' marathon, for which my nerves are thankful."

With a big grin, Netta gave her a thumbs-up sign. "See—told you there is a god. If I ever land on *Jeopardy*, I hope one of the categories is music from the 1960s. Man, will I be able to ace that. Yeah, give me The Hollies for $500, Alex."

As Asha began to sing along with Ray, her eyes shifted casually to Jago. " 'Yeah, you really got me, so I can't sleep at night . . .' "

The front door pushed open and a handsome man with auburn hair came through, pulling Asha from her mental meanderings. Until she'd met Jago Fitzgerald, she'd never known a more gorgeous man than her brother. One might actually call him beautiful. Netta's motor would likely strip gears with Liam and Jago in the same room. It was hard on a woman's libido to see two men so utterly drop-dead gorgeous in the same vicinity.

Asha's fingernails tapped a restless tattoo on the countertop. "I could make a fortune renting them out as models for Romance book covers, then I could pay for my cracked ceiling tiles," she muttered.

"What's this about prostituting me for the sake of a ceiling? I'm insulted. I would think my bod could cover the cost of your new air conditioner, too." Liam leaned across the counter and kissed her on the cheek.

Asha's eyes slid past him to Jago, sitting in the booth halfway across the diner, noting the disconcerted look upon his face. She smiled unrepentantly. After being perturbed at breakfast, it felt good to turn the tables. Observant, Liam noted the object of her interest. He lifted his brow, a question lighting his hazel eyes.

"Jago Fitzgerald, my dinner date I take it?" Liam winked at Netta as she sashayed past. The blonde winked back.

"He's British, thirty-seven and has a twin brother." Asha reluctantly admitted, "And I rather like him."

"Any chance you might sacrifice yourself and seduce him into leaving the horse farm alone?" Liam teased.

"Welcome back, Sweet Pea. We've missed your handsome face around these parts. I was beginning to think you forgot all about us around here." Netta returned and paused to flirt with Asha's brother, slowly walking her fingers up his chest. "As for bribing—you can bribe *me* into seducing him. In fact, you can seduce me into seducing him. That'd work, too. Yeah, that's the ticket. Though I warn you, you might have to seduce me several times before it takes."

Asha chuckled. "Down, Netta, you'll overload my poor brother's hormones."

"Yeah, my hormones can't stand too much Netta razzle-dazzle first thing upon my return." Liam laughed easily. "Asha, join me for supper with Fitzgerald. I could use moral support. I'm in the unenviable position of brokering a deal for Dad when I don't want to sell. I wish you'd kept your quarter interest in the horse farm, then Mac couldn't be trying to sell Valinor out from under me."

Asha chuckled. "You silly brother, Mae didn't raise an eegit for a daughter. He'd be trying to sell The Windmill, too. Go play nice with the pretty man. If I keep you company, I'll go back to wanting to stick him with a fork."

Curious about their first meeting, Asha watched her brother walk over and extend his hand as Jago rose from his seat. The two men shook, and then both settled into the booth. They were easy on the eyes, Liam so striking with his neat auburn hair, and Jago a warrior dark. If she'd thought every female in the room buzzed in man-alert mode with only Jago sitting there, it was nothing compared to glances and drools the two men collected together.

Netta walked behind the counter, opened the glass display case and took out an Almond Joy. Unwrapping it, she popped half in her mouth, her cheek resembling a chipmunk's as she spoke. "What? They say when you're in love your body produces a chemical similar to chocolate. Well, I ain't getting any loving. I need chocolate if you want me to work."

Asha smiled. "I consider your chocolate thieving part of your salary."

Netta's blue eyes studied her before asking, "When did Liam get back from England? I thought that since he was gone so long he might've decided to stay over there permanently."

"This afternoon. He's like me—we have Kentucky in our soul, our mother's thumbprint on our lives. He only went across the pond to try and talk our father out of selling the horse farm."

"Netta, sugar, how about a refill on coffee—or are you expecting me to wait on myself?" Dwight Kennedy called from a booth by the windows.

Netta grumbled, "The unwashed masses summon." She picked up the coffee carafe, then thought better and turned back. "Make you a deal. Fix me up with Liam, and I'll keep my mitts off Jago."

Asha sniggered. The threat was toothless. When Asha ignored Netta, the waitress batted her vivid blue eyes. "Pretty please, with a cherry on top? I'll scrub your toilet for a month."

"Sorry, I don't play social arranger for my brother." She laughed at Netta's grumpy face.

"We could double-date," The blonde pressed.

Dwight yelled again, "Netta! Coffee!"

"All right, already, I'm coming. Some people just got *no* manners," she almost shouted playfully. The whole restaurant heard, and roared with laughter.

Watching Netta work the room, Asha smiled. Strange, there was nearly ten years difference in their ages, but you'd never know from their friendship. As Netta made her return pass, Asha suggested, "Come back in fifteen and we'll plot."

The woman's face brightened. "Sure thing, boss!"

Asha glanced back at Liam and Jago. Under different circumstances the two men could have probably been friends. The farm now stood between them. Valinor satisfied Liam the way The Windmill did her. Liam loved raising horses, and was good at it; though not making a fortune, the farm never ran in the red. She feared Mac had allowed his never-ending bitterness over the divorce from their mother to push him into considering the sale of Valinor without taking Liam's wishes into account.

Both men were smiling, talking easily, obviously comfortable with each other. Evidently something was said about her, for Liam turned and very pointedly looked as she wiped down the counter. A blush rose to Asha's cheeks as both sets of eyes fixed upon her, but Asha only saw the man with sable hair. Unable to look away from Jago, all around her shifted focus, blurring.

Asha swallowed hard, fighting back panic. This special bond summoned by Jago Fitzgerald scared the bloody hell out of her.

The spell broke as Monty Faulkner swaggered through the door. Asha gritted her teeth. Something was decidedly queer about Faulkner, and not as in Queer Eye for the Straight Guy, but *off*. He rarely came in the restaurant, and he never did anything out of line, but Asha hated the way he leered at her.

The man's eyes were a strange flat gold, reminding her of a crocodile she'd once seen on a school field trip to the Cincinnati Zoo. She'd gone into the reptile house along with the other children. Snakes gave her the willies, and lizards weren't much better; eschewing those exhibits, she walked to the corner and looked down. Oddly, she'd found herself staring at a glass floor with a crocodile under her. A large one. She'd watched it, assuming it to be stuffed, a harmless display. The eyes were a weird yellow-gold, lifeless like marbles. As she observed the thing, repulsed yet hypnotized, the blasted croc jumped up and snapped at her. She was terrified, seeing that yawning jaw coming at her; only when the croc bumped into the glass did she breathe again, remembering there was fortunately a barrier between them. As soon as the blasted creature understood that, too, the thing went back to lying there, alive, yet there was no life force to the reptile. It existed and killed. That was the long and short meaning to its life.

Asha recalled that crocodile when she looked at Montague Faulkner—only there was no glass wall between them.

In his twenties and thirties he'd likely been beautiful, a golden angel that would've outshone Liam or Jago. His hair was California blond, the shade few ever kept into adulthood, the mass of curls at odds with a face ravaged from time and drink. Not having a magic portrait tucked up in his attic like Dorian Gray, the ugliness of his soul was etched on his dissipated countenance.

Without waiting for Rhonda to seat him, he shoved into the large C-shaped booth at the front of the diner. Asha opened her mouth to caution him, but a breeze brushed against her cheek. She glanced around, puzzled. The door to the kitchen and the one to the front were closed. The heater overhead blew warm air; this had a distinct chill. Feeling little guilt, she shrugged and kept her mouth shut.

Netta strolled over, placing an empty tray on the stack at the end of the counter. She flashed a fake smile and through her teeth said, "Jerk alert." Going to the fountain, she drew a Big Red and then grabbed a Snickers bar. "I'm taking my break. Let Rhonda earn her keep." With that, she retreated into Asha's darkened office.

"How about some service?" Faulkner growled.

Rhonda tended to ignore people that dared seat themselves. With a perfect arched eyebrow, she glanced at Asha and frowned in distaste. Asha gave her a faint nod. With an exaggerated sigh, Rhonda went to take his order.

Asha glanced at Jago. He caught her staring and winked. When she pretended to ignore him, he leaned over to the jukebox's wallette and flipped through the selector. Pulling change from his pocket, he dropped a quarter in the coin slot and pushed the red buttons. The room filled with the slow sexy sound of the Shirelles' "Baby It's You." "*It's not the way you smile that touched my heart . . .*"

Asha's heart slowed to a deep thud that seemed to match the beat of the golden oldie. She was barely able to ring up the next check and set up the charge card. So caught in Jago's net, she jumped when Faulkner tossed his water glass across the room.

"What the *hell* is this?" he roared.

Asha started toward the table; however, Liam beat her there. "You got a problem, *Mont-a-gue?*" Placing both hands on the table, her brother leaned forward and glared.

Faulkner's face turned a motley red. "Someone put salt in the damn ice water!"

"Liam." Asha touched his elbow softly. After a second, her brother stepped back with a faint nod, recognizing she was the owner of the restaurant, not him, and thus it was her right to handle the problem. "Mr. Faulkner, is there some trouble?"

"Salt! Someone spiked the ice water with salt!"

"I saw Rhonda draw the water. She didn't put anything in it. No one but you has touched it since," Asha informed him in an even tone.

"You telling me that *I* put the salt in the water?" he snarled. He started to rise from his seat, hesitating as his eyes flicked to Liam standing behind her, and then to Jago, who materialized at her elbow. Sam stuck his head out the swinging door, a heavy metal spatula in his hand. Asha sighed. Men and their time-honored code of protecting their women.

"I didn't put salt in my own damn water," Monty insisted.

Asha spread her hands in the air. "I didn't accuse you of that, but since you broke the glass I cannot check it now. I'll bring you another."

"There better not be salt in it," he threatened.

Asha calmly got a glass of ice water and set it before him.

In a flashback to that bloody crocodile, the disturbing man moved before she could blink. Deceptively fast for a man whose debauchery had taken its toll upon his body, his hand caught her wrist in a vise grip. "You won't always have those young bucks standing behind you, missy. Remember that."

Asha met his eyes lacking any spark of humanity, only that air of a predator that killed because that was how he was created. "You don't scare me, Mr. Faulkner. I carry a Colt Python. You ever come near me, I'll start with your knees and shoot my way up without hesitation." For emphasis she smiled, formed her right finger and thumb into a gun and shot him.

"Let go of the lady—*now*," Jago growled from behind her.

A surly look crossed Faulkner's eyes, but Asha saw he was backing down. Bullies always did when they couldn't shove people around. They were only strong when they had someone weaker at their mercy. The man swallowed hard.

Faulkner bluffed it by rising in the booth. "Or you'll what, *Fancy Pants*?"

Suddenly, the jukebox turned on and Ray Peterson's voice sang out, "*Laura and Tommy were lovers . . . He wanted to give her everything . . .*"

Faulkner turned a ghastly shade of gray and released Asha's wrist. He looked at her strangely, and then his head jerked to Jago, the alarm growing to one of terror. "No. It can't be."

"*Tell Laura not to cry . . . My love for her will never die . . .*"

"This is some sick joke." Faulkner pushed himself from the booth, shoving Asha aside. Jago caught her, then moved to stand before her.

Faulkner shoved past them and rushed to the door. He yanked on it, but found it oddly stuck. As he rattled the knob, he kept staring as if the jukebox were a metal monster from outer space come to munch humans. In desperation, he kicked at the door as the song built to a crescendo and ended. Immediately, the player launched into a new song, "Last Kiss" by J. Frank Wilson and the Cavaliers.

A swirl of wind ruffled the tickets by the register, causing Faulkner to jump. Like a cornered rat, he glanced around, searching for another exit. There was one through the formal dining room, but he'd have to get past Asha and Jago in the aisle between the booths. Another was through the office, but Liam and Netta were at the end of the counter blocking him. He started toward the kitchen, only to have Sam's face pop up on the other side of the circular pane of glass, again brandishing a spatula. Faulkner spun and backtracked to the front door. As he reached it, the straw dispenser started shooting a flurry of paper-covered straws at him. The jukebox played on.

"*Never forget the sound that night . . . The cryin' tires, the bustin' glass. The painful scream that I heard last . . .*"

Faulkner wailed, yanked the door open and ran into the night.

Jago looked at Asha and lifted his brows. "Impressive. Would someone like to tell me what the bloody hell just happened?"

Chapter Seven

"What the *bloody hell* was that?" Jago repeated for anyone willing to answer. No one did. Ruddy cowards. The instant the words were out of his mouth, Asha and Netta scurried off, muttering they had closing chores to start. Jago had a hard time believing what he'd seen. Something really strange—look for-Rod-Serling-time strange—had just occurred, yet no one wanted to speak about it. Obviously, they were going to pretend it hadn't happened, and hoped he'd do the same.

"You're going to ignore my question, too?" Jago's eyes targeted Liam.

Asha's brother strolled around the counter and fetched two bottles of beer from the cooler. Perching on a stool, he handed one to Jago. "What's to tell? The man's a vulgar creep. An aging town bully. I wouldn't put it past the jerk to sneak up behind you and stick a knife in your back. While old man Faulkner was still alive, Monty got away with a lot—and I mean a *lot*. In the manner of all serial killers, he started small by shooting animals, pets, and then later, car windows of passing vehicles. No matter what he did, daddy dearest bought him out of trouble, right down to Montague committing rape when he was barely fifteen, with no charges ever being lodged—so it's told. He's been gone for a long time; most people assumed he'd moved away. Then he showed up again about three years ago, just after Dr. Faulkner died. Residents of Leesburg cross to the other side of the street when they see him coming."

Jago wasn't diverted. "That's *not* what I asked and you know it."

Pretending not to hear, Liam kept his eyes on Netta and Asha preparing to close up for the night. "I get the impression, Fitzgerald, you want to court my sister."

"*Court?* A quaint way to put it." His turn to play cagey, Jago tilted his beer and looked at the label. "If this is a dry county, how is it The Windmill can serve beer?"

"Oooo, nice duck. I'm impressed." Liam grinned, lifting his ale in salute. "The old icehouse on the edge of The Windmill's property originally straddled two counties. Some mapmaker goofed. When boundaries were drawn, there was this very narrow strip, a No Man's Land that each county claimed. They battled over it in the courts for decades. Outside of any incorporated lines, there were no laws to rule what happened here. With the two counties fighting over which one The Windmill actually sat in, and each wanting the taxes, our mother Mae put her foot down, said the only way she'd support either side was if they grandfathered The Windmill and let it continue to serve beer."

"Thank goodness for grandfather clauses." Jago rotated on his stool to observe Asha and Netta filling salt-and-pepper shakers on the tables. "And thank heaven for little girls."

Sam came from the kitchen, wiped steam from the dishwasher off his face with his apron, and then helped himself to a Budweiser. "Amen to that," he said. With an exhausted exhale, he joined Liam and Jago on the stools. The three sat and watched the ladies. "Two mighty fine women."

"Represents the breed." Liam sighed his admiration.

Jago glanced at Montgomerie, unused to men 'prettier' than he was. Asha's brother was as handsome as Asha was beautiful, though not in a plastic way like many models tend to be. Both Montgomeries were earthy, vital, sensual creatures.

Over the years, Julian Starkadder—Desmond's right hand man—had compiled extensive files on all the Montgomeries in preparation for his brother's plans. Jago knew that Liam was only a few months older than he. Had they attended the same school, Liam and he would've been in the same classroom—maybe even good friends, judging by his instant liking of the man.

"Represents the breed? Hmm . . . never heard the expression before. I'd say it applies though." Jago fixated on Asha's mobile rear, as she stretched across the tables to gather sugar, salt-and-pepper containers. The curves in those tight, white jeans made his hands itch. He took a draw on his beer; the icy cold Coors did little to stem the rising heat in his body.

"It's a horse breeders' term. You hear it a lot on the farms around here. That one special horse above all others, when their confirmation is so perfect, that the contours just make you want to run your hands over their sleek body, ache to get them between your thighs." Liam sighed, his eyes seeking Netta.

"A horse, hmm?" Jago consider the metaphor. "When I watched Asha last night, I thought of my Harley. I own a '67 Electra Glide. The bike's design, the sound when you start it—nothing can compare to it. It's riding thunder."

"A horse? A motorcycle? You young-uns." Sam scoffed. "When I look at a good woman I think of boats. I was in Florida for my vacation last year. Some guy had one of them high-priced, cigarette boats they race, tied up at a dock. This baby was neon blue and black—a Tiger XP, the owner said it was. He was nice enough to take me for a ride. Opened those engines wide. Wow. Talk about riding thunder."

Derek Whitaker, busboy at The Windmill, pushed through

the swinging door from the kitchen and went behind the counter, untying the folded apron around his hips. "Don't tell Asha, but I'm stealing a beer."

"We're mum. We men have to stick together," Liam replied unconcerned.

"You think of a good horse, Liam," Derek said, clearly having overheard. "Our new Brit here thinks of a Harley. Sam—a cigarette boat. You're all wrong. A good woman is like a Shelby—quality throughout and damn few of them about. You slide into that tight driver seat, shove the key in the ignition . . . now *there* is riding the thunder."

Liam rotated halfway on his stool. "What's that, Derek, wishful wet dreams talking? I hear Winnie MacPhee has been shooting you down for the last month."

"Forget Winnie, she's crazy." The tall, strawberry blond man offered his hand to Jago. "I'm Derek Whittaker, assistant cook and busboy. You're Jago Fitzgerald, mystery man. Not much happens in this wide spot in the road that isn't common knowledge in an hour." He sat and took a swig of his beer. "Now my Shelby—that'll make a grown man get down on his knees and cry. It's *clean*, man. Runs like a scared deer. Sad sorry shame I have to sell it."

Jago stared at Derek, incredulous. "Sell a Shelby? That might be considered grounds for an insanity claim."

The young man shrugged. "I want to be a vet. Asha pulled some strings and got me into Auburn University. Not an easy trick, even with good grades. It's the only veterinarian school in about a five state area. I'll have to travel back and forth between Kentucky and Alabama frequently, to make sure mom is doing okay on the farm and such. It's a ten-hour drive each way—the Shelby deserves better treatment. I figured it'd bring enough money to get a dependable car for me and have some cash left over to help out my mom. The problem is no one around here can afford it. I have it up on eBay with a buyer's reserve of $35,000. So far, no bid has come close. This car is mint, cherry. Black interior, black exterior, a little red pin-stripe on the fenders . . ."

Liam chuckled. "Yeah, you so much as put a hand on the door and he has to wash and wax it."

Jago took out his box of Swisher Sweets. "Okay if I smoke?" All the men nodded, so he lit up and passed the package around, each of them taking one. "What year?"

"Same as your bike—'67."

"I haven't seen it in the lot." Jago glanced through the plate-glass windows. "I'd have noticed a Shelby."

"Leave it in the lot to get dinged or for Monty to gouge its length with a key? Bite your tongue. I drive mom's truck to work." Derek shook his head.

"Have breakfast with me in the morn. Bring the car and let me take it for a test run," Jago suggested, exhaling the smoke. "If it's as cherry as you say—"

Liam butted in, "It is. A sweetheart. I'd buy it in a New York minute, only I'm saving up to purchase a horse farm—before *someone* else can." His scowl at Jago was done in play.

Eyes bright with hope, Derek asked, "You're interested—seriously?"

"Your car lives up to what you say, you have a deal." Jago leaned back against the bar and folded his arms over his chest. "Though I prefer round numbers. $40,000 okay?"

Derek nearly choked on his beer. "You're kidding."

"No, I rarely kid about bikes, cars or women." Jago knew what it was like to have a working mother, struggling to get by. Though the two looked nothing alike, Derek suddenly made Jago think of his brother, Desmond. He recalled how his older sibling had worked long and hard to make a better life for Trev and him, to see they wanted for nothing.

He and Derek would both be getting a good deal. He figured the young man could use a helping hand—and he *wanted* that Shelby.

Just as he wanted Asha.

Derek laughed. "In that case I won't rat to Asha and Netta you guys were comparing them to horses, bikes, and boats."

Chapter Eight

A rainy Friday night, and not yet eleven o'clock, saw Asha restless, edgy. She didn't want to go home and watch the telly, but there was damn little else to do around this neck of the woods. Everyone had eaten, or she'd suggest they could all go to her bungalow, put on some DVDs and she'd fix them a late meal. Ordinarily the staff went up the hill to the drive-in on Friday and Saturday nights after work, kicked back, relaxed and enjoyed a few laughs. With the rain pouring down that was a no-go.

" 'Night, Asha, Netta," Derek called, going out the door after Sam.

" 'Night, Derek." Asha cut the overhead lights on the booths, still running options through her mind.

As Netta pushed the condiments cart toward the kitchen, Liam jumped to his feet to open the door for her. Asha watched as their eyes locked for an instant, desire crackling in the air. For some time, she'd suspected that Netta had a serious crush on her brother. Tonight, Asha had noticed how Liam's hazel eyes tracked Netta with a banked fire. Searching her memory, she failed to recall ever seeing that expression on his face when he'd looked at other women. Being a Meddling Montgomerie, Asha itched to play matchmaker.

Also, she didn't want the evening over, longing to be near Jago, drawn like the proverbial moth to a flame. The man hit her senses hard. Still, she remained leery of being alone with him—afraid of the wild woman lurking just under her skin, waiting to break free. Having Netta and Liam with them would provide a convenient buffer.

Liam rose, collected the empty beer bottles and dumped them in the trash. "Asha, you have a bungalow empty?"

"Always for you, brother dear." Asha saw Netta's head snap up, the blue eyes fixed on Liam, hope banked in the crystalline depths. It dawned on Asha why her brother wanted to stay at the motel. "You're concerned about that creep Faulkner."

Liam shrugged. "He's a bully. That sort never comes at you straightforward. However, he gets liquored up—one of his favorite pastimes—he might try to jump you in the dark. Too much the coward, he won't dare bother Jago or me, but he would come after a woman. I want you on your toes, lass."

"I'm always careful, Liam. He doesn't scare me." Asha shifted her glance, seeing her brothers concern reflected in Jago's stare. Fighting a sigh, she realized she could stare into those penetrating eyes all night. That bloody connection again. Unable to stand her vulnerability, she went to stack ashtrays.

"While I have your attention,"—Jago snatched back the one he was using and flicked his cigarillo into it—"how do I get access to the swimming pool? Laps before bed would make me sleep better. It's still early and I'm restless."

Restless is the key word tonight, Asha thought. "I don't have a lifeguard. I use college kids from the University of Kentucky during the summer; I haven't been able to hire a replacement."

"I don't need a lifeguard, Asha. I promise not to run

around the pool or start water fights." He crossed [illegible]
and held up his right hand. "I'd just like the exerci[illegible]
denly taking her wrist, he examined the marks [illegible] by
Faulkner, his thumb brushing gently over the bruises already forming. His touch sent Asha's heart slamming against her ribs.

Liam championed Jago's request. "Come on, Sis, it's glassed-in and heated. You use it. Netta uses it. I use it."

"You would aid and abet your enemy? He's here trying to buy your horse farm," Asha pointed out. "Besides, neither Netta nor you will sue me."

Jago reached across the counter for a pen and paper, quickly scribbled something and pushed it toward her.

"What's this?" Asha blinked at him.

He arched an eyebrow and exchanged longsuffering glances of male understanding with Liam.

Grumbling "T.M.," she picked up the paper and read it aloud. " 'I shan't sue Asha Montgomerie if I drown in her swimming pool.' Cute."

Netta took off her apron and wriggled her shoulders clearly to ease the stiffness. "It makes me feel positively ancient to go home on a Friday night and curl up with a hot water bottle. We should kick up our heels and live a little. Of course, around here that's hard to accomplish. The drive-in is the only action for miles."

"A drive-in in the rain sounds like a good idea," Liam teased with a wicked smile.

Asha suddenly envisioned the hushed interior of a car, Jago in the driver's seat, the windshield wipers slapping while the movie played unnoticed. The intoxicating scent of his citrus and bergamot cologne would mix with the heat of pure Jago Fitzgerald, wrap around her and drive her mad with wanting.

Maybe she'd be better off going to bed and reading a good funny romance or a sinister vampire tale. Dawn Thompson's *The Ravening* waited on the nightstand. If she were near Jago and those dark green eyes for too long, she might do something foolish. Maybe do it twice. Three times.

"We could call it an early night—" Asha started, only everyone practically screamed at her.

"*No!*"

They couldn't have timed it more perfectly had they rehearsed it. Asha smirked, seeing their faces, all innocent grins.

Though Netta had flashed a dazzling smile, pleading was in her blue eyes. "We could . . . go for a swim," she suggested hopefully, "and save the drive-in for tomorrow night."

Liam nodded. "A swim sounds good. The drive-in can hold."

Asha almost licked her finger and drew an imaginary hash mark in the air. Score one for the sassy blonde. Not only had she maneuvered Liam into a swim, she'd lassoed and was ready to brand him for Saturday.

Asha studied his countenance. Clearly, Liam wanted her to play the vanilla filling between the Oreo cookies of Netta and himself. Asha also was beginning to suspect he wasn't above tossing little sister under Jago's nose, hoping to influence the man over the purchase of the horse farm.

Another time she'd have been ticked at her brother seeking to use her in such an underhanded fashion. Since it involved Jago Fitzgerald, it didn't have quite the sting.

Yeah, baby, use me!

Asha watched Jago cut through the water with the grace of a Selkie. He turned under the surface, pushed off the wall and shot a third of the way down the pool before his next stroke. His legs were long, strong, his sculpted arms sliced forward rhythmically, showing he was an expert swimmer who could keep up that tempo endlessly. Pure poetry in motion. The man had the most beautiful shoulders she'd ever seen. A fool, she could stand here all night and watch, with hardly a thought in her head—except those of wanting.

Netta came up and hung an arm over Asha's shoulder. "Hmm, see something you crave, girlfriend?" she asked, grinning.

Both women cringed as Liam suddenly did a cannonball off the diving board, the splash from the pool spraying them. He surfaced, kicked off the wall and paced Jago, mirroring the man stroke-for-stroke.

"My brother will bust a gut before he admits he can't keep up." Asha sniggered.

Netta cocked a questioning eyebrow. "What makes you think he can't? I'd say they're rather evenly matched."

"Jago says he swims nearly every day. While Liam is active, he doesn't do any exercise regularly. That gives Jago the edge. Two-to-one that Liam quits first." Asha shrugged.

"Done!" Netta did a pass with her hand, pointing to the chaise lounges. "Let's plop our fannies down and watch the show. Better than television, and less fattening than chocolate."

"I thought there wasn't anything you liked more than chocolate." Asha spread a towel and then stretched her legs out on a chaise.

"Sugarplum, if I had your brother near for 365 days a year, I'd give up chocolate in any form." She studied Asha intently. "Do you have a problem with that?"

"You giving up chocolate?" Asha laughed, shifting her eyes to the swimmers, and enjoying the show.

"Would it create a sticky situation if I were to see Liam?" Netta's expression was serious.

"You mean you cannot see him?" Teasing, she waved a hand before Netta's eyes. "Maybe you're suffering an overdose of chocolate."

"Get stuffed, Asha. I'm serious. You and I are nearly ten years apart in age, but our friendship isn't something I'd risk lightly."

"I get along with you like a sister," Asha said. "As far as Liam, you're adults—you don't need my approval."

"I want it, though." Netta glanced at Liam, who lagged a

meter behind Jago now. "I'm a couple years older than he is. I'll be forty come January."

"That means anything? You don't look it. If I hadn't taken your job application, I'd guess you were about my age. As for my idiot brother, you have my blessings. You'd be good for him. Sometimes he's too wrapped up in the horse farm. I worry about him should this sale go through. Also, he's lonely, I think."

Liam surfaced under the diving board, held on to the drain with his left hand, and snorted water from his nose. Jago did another lap, then surfaced to take hold with his right. Their words were low, but then their laughter rang out, filling the glasshouse.

"I won the bet." Asha wiggled her toes.

"I'm telling you, if you don't latch on to Jago Fitzgerald and hogtie him, you've got rocks for brains, sugarplum. There aren't many with such elegance, raw sexual power, grace and smarts, and he's got them in spades."

"Jago scares me, reminds me of a beautiful black wolf. He hangs back, watching, singling me out of the herd. It spooks me."

"Yeah, I thought that when he showed up. I *told* you—he was waiting for you."

"Why me?" Asha mused, slightly unsettled by the idea. Her little voice warned she needed to consider that further, but then her eyes met his across the pool, locking, and all thoughts fled her besotted brain.

"When you have the Big Bad Wolf cutting you from the pack, you learn to smile and play Little Red Riding Hood. 'My what a big tongue you have—all the better to . . .'" Netta's sexy laughter taunted Asha. Rising, the blonde untied her robe. "Remember, wolves mate for life. Now, that drop dead gorgeous brother of yours reminds me of a Siberian tiger. That loose-gaited stalk belies all that muscle. Excuse me while I go bungle in the jungle."

Netta strolled the length of the pool, long-legged and

barely covered in her baby-blue striped bikini. Her saunter was natural, with no jiggling, as if she'd learnt to walk with a book on her head like a runway model. Both men couldn't take their eyes off the sexy blonde. It wouldn't have surprised Asha if the water at that end of the pool rose ten degrees. Netta stepped up on the diving board, then jack-knifed perfectly into the water.

Jago turned back to Asha and lifted his brows, challenge in his dark eyes. Quite odd, she read his mind so clearly, that almost tangible link between them rising again. His unspoken question could not have been plainer—*Can you top that?*

Asha was suddenly riddled with near crippling self-consciousness. When she'd changed in the bungalow, instead of donning her royal blue suit that she usually wore, the super sexy one she'd purchased years ago for a honeymoon trip to the Bahamas snagged her eye. The wedding had been cancelled two days after she'd bought it, when she'd caught her fiancé giving the stiff one to his blonde-bimbo secretary. The swimsuit had stayed forlornly at the back of her drawer for over five years, never worn, the original price tag still attached.

A black-gold maillot weave, the one-piece suit covered more of Asha's body than Netta's bikini—at least the front did. A deep scoop neck plunged low on her breasts and had French-cut legs, very flattering. The back was what tended to be not all there. The straps met on the shoulders and merged into an inch-wide strip that followed the line of her spine down to the thong bottom.

At least she'd been smart enough to put it on and give her reflection a hard inspection in the full-length mirror before coming to the pool. She'd lost seven pounds since she bought it, which only accented her 34D chest. Asha had never felt comfortable in a bikini, though surprisingly, she felt at ease, confident in this bit of nothing. Or had. Now she wished she'd played coward and gone with the more sedate suit that covered her arse!

Once more Jago demonstrated their fey connection. Turning his back to the pool wall, he stretched out his beautiful arms along the drain in a signal that he wasn't moving until she took off her black robe. This ability to read him unnerved her.

What would it feel like to make love to a man so attuned to you that his thoughts brushed your mind? The near telepathy would see her arousal stronger, as she would know what he felt, experienced, doubling their passion since he'd feed off her reactions, too.

Ignoring the hard fist to her womb, she slowly rose to her feet, meeting his dare. She untied the belt around her terry robe, and let it slide off her shoulders to pool around her feet. His smug smile vanished, and one of Jago's arms dropped off the edge of the drain.

"Hope he didn't skin it." She chuckled. Shoulders squared, she sauntered the few paces to the side stairs where she entered the pool's shallow end, aware that Jago's eyes tracked her every move.

As she used the steps to enter into the tantalizingly warm water, Asha glanced down at the silken liquid gently lapping at her legs. Strangely lightheaded, a spinning sense of déjà vu overwhelmed her. She blinked.

Everything shifted.

The pool was no longer enclosed in the glasshouse, but open to the air. A soft spring breeze stirred the circle of red, blue, green and orange Japanese lanterns . . .

Laura listened to Gene Pitney crooning the poignant "Town Without Pity," the record spinning on a player set up underneath the wrought-iron staircase that went straight to the roof of The Windmill's clubhouse. She half-heartedly took in the paper lanterns that ran along the rim of the sundeck, illuminating couples slow dancing in the deep shadows. Young men wore tuxedo jackets, while girls in full-skirted formals had their hair up in angel curls.

"Junior prom for Leesburg High," she muttered.

Her sigh was dejected. Small wonder. The previous week had seen a flurry of activity in the small town. Excited for weeks, the girls had picked out formals and had their shoes dyed to match their gowns. Fearing not being able to get in for the all-important day, they had set up appointments well ahead of time to have their hair done at Juanita's Wash & Curl.

Laura failed to share the excitement of this night. Oh, her gown was beautiful—a pale yellow, a shade most girls couldn't wear without looking sallow. On her, it was perfect. Like her classmates, she'd also had her shoes dyed the same delicate shade of her formal.

"Just going through the motion," she confessed to the soft night.

Drawing the line, she'd worn only one petticoat and not starched so it stood out like an ironing board. She had fixed her own hair, eschewing Juanita's beehive or angel curls specials, and wore it up, but in a simpler style, with a hint of the Victorian era. She felt pretty. Even so, she wished she was anywhere but here.

Because Tommy wasn't her date.

"Jerk." She choked back tears.

If Tommy had escorted her, the night would've been magical. She'd nearly made herself sick for weeks before working up the courage to ask him. He'd been home, up all night cramming for finals, and looked deliciously sleepy when he answered the front door. Ooooh, she had just wanted to step against him and kiss that sexy mouth good morning. Instead, she'd made silly chitchat until she finally stammered out the words and asked him if he would take her. He'd smiled, listened to her request, and then laughed. He'd laughed!

"No way am I escorting you to the Junior Prom, Laura," he'd said, "so just get it out of your pretty head. No college man in his right mind would be caught dead at a party for a bunch of juniors."

Her joy at him calling her pretty had soured as he'd shattered her dream of going with him. After that she'd wanted to stay home, but her mother wouldn't hear of it, and when Erica Valmont put her foot down, there was no changing her mind. With mild distaste, Laura had accepted a date with nerdy Junior Donner—their mothers' doing. Junior didn't have a date either. It was hard to be the only ones staying home. With their class so small—only thirty-three—if you failed to attend you may as well hang a billboard around your neck announcing, 'I'm a loser and can't get a date.' Thus, she'd come in the beautiful formal, feeling as pretty as a faery princess. A princess who lacked her prince.

The night was almost hot, odd for May. The gentle breeze brushed against her bare arms with a gossamer touch, pushing her to feel restless. The pool whispered a tempting lure.

"For a double-dog-dare, I'd unhook my garters, bunch this damn petticoat up and go wading." And she meant it.

There was a lull in the tunes as the hired disc jockey, Rusty Rogers, from WAKY loaded 45s onto the spindle changer. Lesley Gore's clear voice sang out that it was her party and she'd cry if she wanted to, cry if she wanted to, cry if she wanted to—causing Laura to glance up. She saw the group of college kids coming up the concrete stairs winding up the hillside to The Windmill's clubhouse. Tommy was halfway back in the group of seven couples. Her heart dropped, and then started a slow thud as their eyes met.

He was so handsome! He was wearing a white shawl tuxedo and wore it like a man, instead of like the juniors playing grown-up. Most of the guys still wore their hair in a pompadour in the front and combed into a ducktail in the back, a stubborn holdover from the late '50s, showing styles were slow to die here. Brylcreem still made a tidy profit in Backwater Kentucky! But not Tommy. His hair was short, kept that way because the thick black curls were too wavy to do much else. The look suited him. He was elegance and male grace . . . and with another girl.

"Damn him! Oh, how I'd love to kick him in the seat of his pants!"

Catching her eyes on him, he smiled. Tears threatened, but he wouldn't be able to see them from that distance. She reeled from the pain.

"The bastard couldn't take little old Laura to her Junior Prom because a college senior couldn't take a junior in high school, eh? Yet, he dares turn up with a date, he and his snotty college friends crashing the party. Ooooh." She spun away, unable to look at him. Putting a hand to her stomach, she feared she might puke.

The night had been crappy enough without having to face the one person in the whole world—the only person—she'd wanted to escort her.

In her girlish dreams, Laura envisioned Tommy, handsome in his tux, them dancing slowly in some dark corner. Tommy stealing a first kiss. It'd been painful enough to have him laugh at her after she finally sucked up the courage to ask him to take her. His crashing the party with a girlfriend was about as cruel as he could get.

In the background, Lesley Gore wailed obscenely about her boyfriend coming to her party with another girl, acid to Laura's wounds.

Heading off trouble, the chaperones confronted the group. The junior class had paid for the party, so Laura hoped they'd send them packing. If Tommy were closer, she'd likely dump the punch bowl over the jerk's head.

After words were exchanged, the group from the University of Kentucky was permitted to go up on the sundeck and dance—as long as they behaved. "Fat chance of them behaving." UK kids wanted nothing to do with a teen dance where there wasn't liquor. That left trouble. The chaperones were shortsighted to think otherwise. Laura noted a few guys already staggered while navigating the narrow staircase. "I bet my pale yellow shoes they've been drinking."

The last one to the stairs was Tommy the Rat—with his date, Joy Dinwiddie. He paused with his hand on the rail and smiled at Laura. Joy pushed at his back, nudging him to go on up. His smile faded as he felt the blast of Laura's icy fury, and a question lit his dark green eyes.

Tommy stared at her with an unreadable expression. Flashing Laura a dirty look, Joy pushed at him again. He shrugged the blonde off and started toward Laura. Unable to face him, she turned away. He caught up with her in a couple strides. Grabbing her bare upper arm, he pulled her around. His incisive stare lanced her heart.

"Laura, what's wrong?"

"Bastard. Are you that cruel and insensitive?" Her long lashes batted away the tears.

He seemed puzzled. "Cruel? What do you mean?"

"God, you're thick!" she growled. "Did your IQ suddenly drop? Or is this punishment for me daring to hang around, hoping someday . . . ?"

Laura couldn't go on. What a silly fool she'd been. It stopped here and now. Tommy Grant was bane to her. She tried to jerk away from him.

Tommy tugged her back to face him again. Before she knew what she did, she slapped him. Hard. She read the shock on his face. Part of her was stunned, too. Part wanted to do it again.

"What the hell was that for?" He blinked, still not believing that his adoring acolyte dared raise a hand to him or stare with such loathing.

"You have to ask? Well, Mr. Suddenly-Stupid, I begged you to bring me to this dance. But no. Something about no college man in his right mind would be caught dead at a party for a bunch of juniors. Now, what do I see? Seven BMOCs here. You arrogant, think-you're-so-damn-hot college men are here to cause trouble and make fun of us. Well, jump in your cars. You aren't wanted here." She tried to shove away from him, but he held her by the upper arms. "Leave me alone. In fact—just leave."

One of the chaperones—Mr. Taylor—came over. "Laura, is everything all right? Is there a problem here?"

Tommy held up his hands, backing off. With a strange expression of regret, he spun on his heel and headed to the stairs, taking them two at a time. Laura glanced up to the sunroof, still seething with anger. Tommy stood, staring down at her, his hands on the white railing. Even from this distance, she saw his uncertainty. Unable to bear staring at the man she both loved to the depths of her soul and now hated with a warrior's passion, she rushed inside the clubhouse and into the ladies' changing room. She wanted to bawl like a baby, but wouldn't give him that satisfaction.

A box of Kleenex was on the shelf before the long mirror. She beelined to it. Pulling out three, she carefully dabbed at the tears to keep her mascara from running. Hearing chatter headed into the women's lounge, she rushed toward the changing rooms; she couldn't face anyone now.

She scooted into the last stall and closed the louvered door as the voices drew near. Sitting on the bench, she leaned her head against the wall, trying to find some peace. Maybe they wouldn't linger.

"Well, I feel sorry for her," the soft voice of Melody Hayden said.

Another laughed—Patti-Sue Moran. "I don't. She's such a spaz. For the past two years she's dogged Tommy Grant. Like he'd ever want her."

"She's cute," Melody defended.

"I'm cute, too," Patti-Sue sneered.

A third voice, Maddy Paddington added, "She's got a set of knockers. Guys stand to attention when she goes by."

"They're too big. More than a handful is too much." Patti moved to stand before the mirror to apply lipstick; through the louvered slats, Laura spied her preening.

"I heard it was more than a mouthful. Either way, she's got 'em." Maddy snorted.

Patti leaned forward and pressed her lips together to set her lipstick. "It won't do her any good. Joy Dinwiddie's putting out. She'll get knocked up to land Tommy. Watch. It's sad to see poor Laura follow him like some lovesick puppy.

Tommy's always complaining to my brother how you open the door and she falls into his home."

Melody pushed the other girls toward the door. "Come on, the guys have waited long enough."

Laura hadn't realized she was crying until a tear hit the back of her hand. Forcing herself to her feet, she walked to the mirror and frowned at her coon eyes. Getting soap from the sink dispenser, she carefully washed the black from under her lower lashes and repaired her face.

The door swung open and Melody rushed back in. She jerked upright, seeing Laura before the mirror. "Ooooops . . . you heard."

Laura summoned her strength and turned to face Melody. "It's always good to know what people really think about you. I prefer honesty to two-faced pretenses."

Melody looked ashen. "Patti is such a snot sometimes. She's jealous of you. We all are. You're so pretty. You just never tried to fit in."

"I'd want to fit in with a bunch of vicious backstabbers?" Laura started to push past her, only Melody caught her arm. "Let go," she snapped.

"Look, I'm sorry," Melody apologized.

"Thanks, but no thanks."

Laura shoved by Melody and out the door. She went straight up the stairs to the roof to look for Junior, where she'd last seen him, hoping he'd take her home; her dad worked second shift at the Corning plant in Danville, and her mom didn't have a car to come get her. It was nearly ten miles or she'd walk all the way home. In despair, she glanced down at her pale satin shoes not made for walking on pavement.

As she reached the roof, her eyes alit on Tommy sitting on a chaise along with the other college kids. Joy sat right behind him. Laura seemed unable to move as Tommy and she locked eyes. He stared at her—trying to judge her mood, she guessed.

Whatever he felt, it didn't matter. She merely wanted to

find Junior and get the hell out of here, but first, she had to stop staring at Tommy.

Joy leaned against his arm, deliberately brushing her breasts against him. Laura felt like vomiting. She couldn't stop the picture of Tommy and Joy having sex from flooding her mind. The image would keep her from sleep tonight; of that she was sure.

Tommy smiled, as if hoping to draw one from Laura. Damn him! She wanted to dump an ice bucket in his lap. Flashing him a Medusa-on-the-rag glare, she went in search of Junior.

She asked several people. No one had any idea where her date had disappeared. Despite everyone staring, Laura didn't care. She just wanted to leave.

Melody was suddenly at her elbow. "Laura, what's wrong?"

She almost recoiled from the other girl's touch, except she was desperate. "I came with Junior. I want him to take me home. I don't feel well. I think I'm going to be sick."

"Junior went off with Jess and Carl a bit ago. Carl's brother is a bootlegger. Bet they're off drinking. You don't want Junior to drive you home if he's liquored up," Melody warned.

"Well, he has to take me home sooner or later." Laura was nearing panic. She didn't know how much longer she'd be able to hold it in.

Melody grasped her hand. "Take a deep breath, Laura. Don't give these idiots a show. Let's you and me go dangle our feet in the pool. When my dad comes to pick me up, he can drive you home. We don't want you out with Junior. That jerk can't handle liquor. Why did you come with him?"

"His mother and my mother . . ."

"Enough said." Melody rolled her eyes. "How I ended up with Davey Dean. Mothers and their well-meaning intentions are a pain in the tush."

"What's up?" John Carlyle inquired from behind Melody and Laura.

Melody's eyes flicked to John and then guardedly to Laura. "Laura's looking for Junior. She wants to go home. I told her she's welcome to come with me when my dad picks me up."

John reached out and roughly took Laura's arm. "That's okay, I'll take her."

Laura leaned back. The bourbon fumes mixed with the cinnamon breath spray he used to mask the alcohol made her stomach roll. John was with Tommy's group. And very drunk.

"Thanks . . . I'm going with Melody." Laura tried to pull away, but his grip tightened.

"Don't be like that, sugar. Let go of that Goody Two-Shoes image and live a little." John leered. "Come on, baby, I'll take you."

Suddenly, Tommy was there. "Let go, John. She's just a kid."

Laura wanted the roof to open up and her to fall through; maybe she'd break her neck and none of this would matter.

John chuckled. "Kids don't have tits like that."

The music fell silent so everyone heard his vulgar comment.

"Take your hand off Laura—now, John, and apologize to her." Tommy's voice was steel. He moved between them, like some medieval knight ready to do battle for a damsel.

"Tommy, what's she doing now?" Joy whined at his elbow.

Tommy picked up Joy's arm and pulled her toward John. "Dance with John, while I take Laura home."

Laura yanked away. "Melody is giving me a ride. You stay, Tommy, and play with your little friends. Come on, Melody."

"Right behind you, hon." Melody flashed Tommy a killing glare.

"Laura . . ." Tommy turned to follow her, only to have Joy latch on to his arm.

Laura didn't slow. Her steps carried her down the stairs, and to the shallow end of the pool. She finally stopped and gasped for breath.

"Laura, stay here. I'll call my dad to come and get us. This crowd's getting ugly. There's going to be trouble. The chaperones should've never let those college kids stay." Melody patted her arm. "I'll be right back."

Laura kicked off her satin shoes and sat down on the concrete edge, little caring if the rough surface ruined her gown. Tomorrow she'd burn it. Neither did she worry that she wore stockings. The water felt like liquid silk. Surprised, as she'd had no idea the pool was heated, she closed her eyes, wishing she could swim. It would be so lovely to swim until she was exhausted; then her mind wouldn't be filled with images of this horrible night.

Gathering her skirt, she stepped down on the half-moon steps, into water swishing over her knees. It was so soothing.

Suddenly, someone took hold of her arm and pulled her back. She blinked to see Tommy leaning toward her. "Come on, Laura, I'm taking you home." He tugged her in his direction . . .

"Asha? Asha?"

It took Asha a minute to adjust. Once more, the pool was covered over like a greenhouse and it was October, not a May night over four decades ago. Jago held her arm and hauled her from the pool. Netta and Liam were behind him, their expressions etched with the same look of worry. Jago led her to a chaise, then pushed her to sit.

"Are you all right?" Netta padded over and sat on the lounge next to her and gave her a hug.

"I'm fine." She grasped for any excuse to ease their concern. "Just a little lightheaded. I haven't drunk enough Pepsi today. My sugar's down. If someone will get me a cola?"

"I'll fetch it." Netta jumped up and hurried to the clubhouse.

Liam and Jago exchanged glances, clearly dubious. Asha glared at them, defiant. That was the only explanation she was going to offer.

How could she tell them she'd just slipped into another person's life?

Chapter Nine

Jago broke the surface of the water and then grabbed the edge of the lime green air mattress Asha lazily floated upon. The lowly male in him was mesmerized by that sexy display of glorious curves, as if she were served up on a bed of lettuce—an open-face sandwich for him to devour. And boy, did he hunger to do just that! Overriding the primitive pounding in his blood was concern about Asha zoning out on them earlier.

"Are you all right?" he queried, playfully trickling a handful of water down that barely covered spine and derrière.

Asha shivered, then laughed. "You mean have I relapsed into *zombieitis* in the five minutes since you last asked?"

"I guess I'm being a pain?" He chuckled.

"No, you're rather sweet. Thanks. Really, I'm fine." She reached out and stroked his cheek with her thumb. Her smile vanished; the look in her cat eyes turned into one of a soul-deep ache as they traced over his face. Instead of dropping her hand, she traced his jawline, then her index finger outlined his lower lip.

Mercy. Jago's body twanged, the sound of a taut bow being plucked. Sexual, yes, hitting his groin with the force of receiving a kick; then the vibration moved up his chest and lodged dead center. In his heart. Oh boy, he was in trouble. Her expression of such wonder demanded a kiss, but he knew it was a trap. The instant he kissed her, he wouldn't want to stop. While sex on an air mattress definitely had possibilities, not with an audience and especially not when one over-protective brother would be one of the watchers.

He settled for gently taking her wrist, his thumb brushing the now livid bruises left by that jerk Faulkner. Anger boiled in him that the creep had dared touch her. Leaning forward, he pressed a light kiss to each purple mark. Asha's eyes dilated; those long, black lashes batted surprise at the gesture. Another punch to his gut.

He treaded water, slowly towing the raft toward the shallow end of the pool, out of splash range of Liam and Netta, who were still diving off the board. Mesmerized by Asha's lovely face, he worried about what had happened to her when she entered the pool. *Not enough Pepsi* just didn't cover what he'd witnessed. Other than appearing pale, she seemed to have recovered. Even so, Jago couldn't erase the scene from his mind: She had entered the swimming pool and then froze like a statue.

As he'd watched her, a minute of puzzlement passed before the realization hit him that something was wrong. Okay, he'd been drooling—a horny idiot, no blood in his brain, that had gone *south* the minute she'd thrown off her black robe and revealed that killer body in all its glory. It'd taken a minute for logic to override his libido. Could anyone blame him? Nothing could've prepared him for Asha in the barely-there suit. The metallic fabric shimmered, woven so it appeared dark gold one instant, then nearly black the next. It hugged her breasts and hips as though spray-painted on, the iridescent flicker of material emphasizing her to-die-for body. The impact stunned him, his whole system going into sensory meltdown. He'd remained where he was, waiting for Asha to come to him, afraid if he moved even one inch, he'd go after her, lay her on the poolside and take her, right then and there.

Never had his gut twisted in such an agony of animalistic wanting. His arm had slipped off the drain, skinning his elbow as he absorbed the psychic punch of seeing her. He'd have bet a chunk of change Miss Asha Montgomerie would come out in a prim and proper suit, not something that made Netta look like she wore a Mother Hubbard. Finally it registered in his hormone-riddled brain that Asha had frozen in mid-movement as she entered the pool. Blood drained from him; he raced to reach her, Liam behind him. His heartbeat was rapid, erratic. Not from swimming. From dread. He told himself there was nothing wrong with her, yet he couldn't quell his panic. He'd reacted the same way when that creep had dared touch her in the diner, only this was tenfold.

Though there wasn't anything in Julian's report on Asha having it, epilepsy was his first thought. Terror gripped him as he feared she'd slip into a *grand mal* and would slam her head against the steps before he could reach her. Instead of a seizure, she merely stood, unmoving, cold to the touch. Her heartbeat, though a little slow, was strong, steady. He looked into those tawny eyes, dilated, unfocused. Downright spooky.

Then they'd fixed on his hand, where he had hold of her arm, and blinked several times. Gradually, color flooded her waxen skin. Releasing a breath he didn't know he held until then, warm relief had flooded through him.

He didn't like to think Asha had lied to him, but the way she evaded his questions afterward caused him to feel certain there was more to it than a lack of sugar. But for the life of him, he couldn't deduce what.

Like the bizarre incident in the restaurant earlier, biding his time wasn't easy when he wanted to demand answers.

Desmond and Trev were often bulls in a china shop when they wanted something done. Jago preferred to hang back, study a matter from all angles, and then ultimately decide the best course of action. At this moment, he felt the pounding of his rash Mershan blood. He wanted to grab Asha and insist she tell him what she was hiding, shake the answers out of her. Even more compelling was the urge just to kiss her senseless.

With a groan of agony, he surveyed the tiny strip of metallic fabric that followed the line of her graceful spine down to the thong and then her firm round buttocks. How was a man to stay sane, let alone carry on an intelligent conversation?

"You're sure you're fine?" he asked again.

Her eyes roved over his face in a ghostly caress. He felt it as if it were a physical touch. His body jerked, painfully.

"Want me to do a handstand to prove it?" She stuck out her tongue at him playfully.

"Oh, brother." He rolled his eyes, envisioning her doing handstands in that bathing suit. "In that case . . ."

Before she anticipated his actions, he'd flipped the mattress sideways, just for the thrill of catching her. His right arm was under her thighs and his left across her back; Asha felt nude in his embrace. The idea slammed into his body with a wall of fire. It wouldn't surprise him if the water in the pool around him started to boil.

"Someone shoot me—please," he muttered with a laugh.

Her gaze fixed on his chest, then slowly traveled up his neck, his jaw, mouth and finally met his stare. He'd never felt a woman's eyes move over him the way Asha's did: lasers burning into his skin. His heart pounded against his ribs to the point of bruising. Just remembering to breathe was an effort.

As with most things in his life, he usually was willing to hang back and study a woman from all angles. Asha made him want to forget his staid nature, pushed him to do something rash such as grab her by the hair and drag her off to his lair—*hmm*, bungalow—and make mad passionate love to her. It was unsettling, these desires, these needs that

Asha provoked in him. That lush small mouth opened slightly, as if she could almost taste his kiss. He noticed her breathing was as erratic as his. It caused her breasts to rise and fall in slight jerks. Closing his eyes, he fought for control. Opening his lids, he looked into the fathomless eyes he could drown in.

"You do know where we're headed, don't you, Asha?"

She stared at him with a doe-in-the-headlights expression, shook her head yes, then no. He had the feeling she was barely aware of what she did. So was he.

It was that simple: One door closed in his mind and another opened. Staring into those amber eyes with a dark grey circle around the iris, Jago accepted Fate. He'd looked into the eyes of many women, yet somehow as he gazed into Asha's he couldn't recall any of them.

Life suddenly became very complicated.

He doubted she was anywhere near ready to trust him enough to let him close. He scared her. While part of him rose to that power, reveled in her female skittishness because it bespoke how strongly their chemistry worked on an animalistic level, it meant he'd have to bide his time, earn her trust. Not an easy prospect when the craving to claim her burned in him, to brand her as his, a need as elemental, as vital as drawing his next breath.

Romance was complex enough, but when you tossed in the fact he was here flying a false flag as part of Desmond's schemes, any sort of a relationship would be built on extremely treacherous ground. How could he say *trust me* when Asha didn't even know his real name? She knew he was connected to Trident Ventures' attempt to buy the horse farm. Clearly she was devoted to her brother, and there was little doubt Liam Montgomerie wanted to hold on to that farm at all costs. Once she understood the full scope of Mershan International's plans, Jago had a feeling the fur would fly.

Tamping down on the flickers of rising dread, he sighed and put her on her feet. Double damn. If he were Trev he'd go after her, no holds barred, and allow the chips to fall where they may. This wanting of Asha went bone deep. Not just the physical craving, it was everything beyond that: He wanted her *in his life*.

His chest had a strange pressure. Accepting how his world had changed in just two days would take a bit of time. Even so, he wouldn't run from the enormity of what was happening between them. This was the one area where he let his Mershan blood rule: When he saw something he really desired, he didn't hesitate. His Harley back in England, the deal he'd made with Derek for the Shelby—both were impulsive purchases. He'd never regretted the motorcycle and figured he wouldn't be sorry for buying the car. He'd *had* to have them, so he didn't hesitate. That same drive to claim Asha burned in his gut. He wanted to stick her in the Shelby, drive non-stop to Las Vegas and marry her. He couldn't. He might look like Trev, but on the inside, that path wouldn't suit his conscience simply because it wouldn't be fair to her.

Asha laughed musically. "You keep asking if I feel all right, only I think I should ask if *you* feel okay. You have the strangest expression on your face."

Looking for a release of his frustrated mating drive, he stalked her, backing her up to the end of the pool. "I'm *not* all right. What did you expect? You'd waltz in here in that *take-me* swimsuit and I'd not go into hormone overload? Here's the plan, Asha—"

"Oh, you have a plan, do you? Smart man." Eyes dancing, she laughed.

He growled as her back hit the edge of the pool. Planting a hand on the wall on either side of her, he leaned to Asha, invading her space. Letting her feel the heat off his body. "One time offer—you and that itsy-bitsy, backless suit get out of this pool, wrap that robe around you, and get the hell to your bungalow before I count down from one hundred, or I'm coming after you—and if I get my hands on you, nothing will stop me from taking you. Do you understand, Asha?"

He leaned closer. He could almost taste her mouth, the hint of Pepsi on her breath, and it was nearly enough to let loose the primal lust rippling under his skin. Asha nodded. Still, she foolishly played with fire. He figured coming at her like a Category 5 hurricane would send her running. Rather surprisingly, he could see her mind struggling. One part of her wanted to run and not look back; the other was tempted to dance with the devil. The thought skittered through her mind to do something wild and wicked. He could read her that plainly.

"Don't consider it, my Scottish lass. I mean every word I say. Run, or there won't be any sleep for either of us tonight." He smiled a predator's threat, then began counting. "One hundred, ninety-nine, ninety-eight . . ."

He lifted her by the waist and plopped her cute little tush on the pool edge. Her cautious side finally kicked in. She blinked, slowly rising to her feet, water dripping from her body. He kept counting. Grabbing her robe, she clutched it to her chest. Her brown eyes softened, intense longing swirling within. Blasted woman wouldn't let him be chivalrous!

"Damn it, Asha—seventy-nine, seventy-eight . . ." With an easy push, he levered up on his arms, dragging his body out of the pool. Water sluiced off him. "Seventy-three—I get my hands on you, there's *no* turning back." He made a swipe at her as if to grab her, then laughed as she squeaked and finally ran.

Watching that firm derrière moving away, Jago contemplated if he might've just done the most stupid thing in his whole life. *Stupid*, but honorable.

"Being honorable sucks." He sighed in frustration. "Jago Luxovius Mershan, you're one lucky sonofabitch—or cursed. Right now, I'm leaning heavily toward cursed."

Chapter Ten

Sitting on the rock retaining wall that ran around the bungalows, Jago smoked a Swisher SweetHe should be pleased. Not once all night had he gone to the refrigerator and stood aimlessly searching for something he craved.

The last piece of the puzzle had finally clicked into place: What he craved was Asha.

He'd gone to bed, slept a couple of hours, then awoken to his body on fire with need. Strange, they'd only known each other two days, but now his whole life seemed empty, shallow without her nearness. His yearning for her was a fever in his blood that no laps in the pool or cold showers could assuage.

Oh, he'd done the right thing in sending her running from him. Asha was affected by him, his sexuality, but deep down she wasn't ready to take that step of letting him in—in her bed, in her life, in her heart. She wasn't the type to sleep around. Her emotions would have to be fully engaged before she'd open the drawbridge and permit him into her inner world.

A soft breeze swirled around him, oppressively hot for

this time of year. It whispered *All Hallows Eve*, despite the holiday being nearly three weeks away. Fallen leaves scurried along, carried on the wind . . . restless ghosts bound for nowhere.

He glanced toward the restaurant, imagining a jack o' lantern on the porch, carved and aglow, wondering how Asha celebrated the old pagan fire festival. Strangely, faint notes of music floated on the night wind, the rattle of the leaves in the trees almost masking them. He cocked his head, trying to hear the direction from which the sounds came. If Asha were awake and as keyed up as he, she was asking for trouble; he could only play the knight in shining armor so long.

But the music came from the restaurant, not Asha's cottage. Tossing the half-finished cigarillo to the walkway, he ground it out under his boot, and then headed to see who would be playing music in a locked restaurant at this time of the morning.

There was no way to see into the old overseer's house from the back, so he walked around to the front to the diner. The blinds were closed along the row of windows except for one looking in behind the register where a night-light lent an orange glow. It was enough to see inside.

A man and a woman were over by the jukebox, slow-dancing. Gene Pitney crooned how true love never runs smooth while the pair seemed lost in the music. Jago glanced around the parking lot to see if a car sat off to the side. Nothing. So, the lovebirds had walked here? Maybe they were staying at the motel. He didn't want to be Mr. Buttinski, but he didn't think Asha would care for anyone just wandering in and using the restaurant for their own private party.

Jago strode to the front door and tried the handle, found it locked. Frowning, he rapped his knuckles on the glass, trying to draw their attention. No response. The couple kept dancing as if they hadn't heard. He tapped harder.

"Well, you both can't be hard of hearing," he muttered, and started around the far side of the restaurant.

He entered the motel, intent on finding the night manager. The man—who oddly reminded him of an aging Obi-Wan Kenobi—was at his post, sound asleep. Jago dinged on the little bell twice, but the manager snored along undisturbed.

Sighing, Jago headed back outside and toward the bungalows. "Great! Here I am trying to be honorable and stay away from Asha, allow her time, and what does Fate do? Gives me a Kentucky Ginger Rogers and Fred Astaire, and an aging Jedi on the lam, who wouldn't awaken if the bloody building was on fire. Worse, I'm starting to talk to myself."

Something brushed his legs. Glancing down, he discovered the fattest cat he'd ever seen, pure black and with gleaming orange eyes. The tagalong beast nearly caused him to trip several times on the path to the cottages.

He knocked on the sliding glass door of Asha's cottage. "If she doesn't answer my knock, Cat, I'll think Rod Serling is lurking about. 'Submitted for your consideration . . . a man trapped in the nowhere burg of rural Kentucky. He's about to discover that being seen, but not heard, has dire drawbacks—dum dum dum—in The Twilight Zone.' "

The light flipped on and Asha came to the door, pulling the curtain back partway. Dressed in a blue silk robe, her long auburn hair was neatly braided and over one shoulder. Her huge eyes stared at him with such longing, yet with a flicker of female skittishness. He wanted to kiss her senseless. For hours.

"Come on, Asha, open up. Trust me." Jago smiled when she unlatched the door and slid it open. "Despite wanting to kiss you 'til the cows come home, I'm here for another purpose. There's someone inside your restaurant."

"Someone?" Asha echoed blankly.

"The doors are locked, but the jukebox's blaring. I don't think they're trying to rob the place . . ."

Without a word, Asha turned and walked back into the darkened bungalow, leaving him and the cat standing there. Jago glanced down at the feline. Its amber eyes looked up at him, then to the wide-open door. The beast almost shrugged as if saying, *She left the door open—it's an invitation,* then went inside.

Jago shifted on his feet, then muttered, "Well, hell . . . the cat's smarter than I am," and entered Asha's domain.

Though in shadow, he could tell the bungalow's floor plan was a mirror of his own. His space had a motel ambience, while Asha had obviously made this small apartment into a home. He wondered at that, just as Desmond likely wondered about Asha's sister BarbaraAnne, why these Montgomerie women eschewed the fancy elegance of Colford Hall in southern England, with its fifty bedrooms, staff of servants, and near royal splendor in favor of a smaller more middle-class lifestyle. Such behavior was puzzling to say the least. The women could live in the lap of luxury, never raise a finger to cook or clean, and yet, from Julian Starkadder's reports, B.A. seemed to love her small island life on Falgannon, and Asha had deliberately set out a year ago to bring The Windmill under her total control.

He moved through the shadows, toward where she had disappeared. Light came from the room, and since the door was open, he used the cat's rule of thumb—viewed it as an invitation—and followed her. The black beast rematerialized, rubbing against his leg as he stared at Asha. She was halfway into a pair of jeans, the gown bunching up on her thighs, then waist, as she shimmied into the tight denim.

He swallowed hard as she pulled the gown off. Her back was beautiful, finely arched with strong, square shoulders. He'd like nothing more than to go down on his knees and trace that graceful spine with his tongue. Instead, he leaned against the doorframe and simply drank in her perfection. The fat cat twined around his ankles, but he was barely aware.

She pulled on a teal sweater, then tugged her long hair. Only then did she turn and see him standing there. Barefoot, she walked to the door, expecting him to move. Jago remained where he was, deliberately blocking her way, pheromones bouncing between them to where he could hardly think straight. She looked up at him, her expression unreadable.

"You're playing with fire," he warned.

Instead of looking scared of him, those haunting eyes traced the lines of his face. "Am I?"

"Damn straight. One of these days I'll stop behaving like a gentleman and show you."

The corner of her small, full mouth quirked up. "Maybe one of these days I'll *let* you."

He glared at her feet. "*Shoes?*"

She made a grumpy face and slid on a pair of old ballet slippers, then snatched up her keys off the nightstand.

As they moved around the side of the restaurant, music floated into the night: Peter & Gordon—crooning about a world without love. "Your jukebox is stacked deep with music from the 1960s. You have a passion for that era?"

"Ah . . . hmm . . . it's an . . . acquired taste, you might say." Asha looked down at the cat, who was trailing along with them. "Your familiar?"

"I figured he was *your* cat."

"Never saw him before." She paused at the restaurant door and rattled the handle. It was locked. "Hardly looks a stray, being that fat."

Tail twitching, the cat gave her a stare that said he resented the remark, that he was just pleasingly plump, thank you.

Jago peeked over her shoulder and saw the shadowy figures, still there dancing. "I knocked on the door; they ignored me."

Asha fiddled with her key ring until she found the right key. The lock turned easily, and then the glass door swung inward.

Jago nearly plowed into her back when she stopped just inside. His stare went right to where the couple had been.

Nothing. The iridescent silver jukebox with the red lights still played, but now it was Chad & Jeremy wailing about yesterday being gone.

"Yesterday isn't the only thing gone," he grumbled, stumped where the couple had vanished. "Well, they didn't slip out through the kitchen. I tried it before."

Asha went through the swinging door to double check. "Yep, locked tight," she confirmed upon her return.

"Could they've gotten out through the main part of the house where it connects to the motel?"

"They'd have to go past Delbert." Asha shrugged in doubt. "Of course, if he is napping, Sherman could march the Union army through the lobby on the way to Georgia and not wake him. Poor dear is quite hard of hearing."

She went past the jukebox, up the steps and into the main part of the house, the glass atrium opening into the rear of the motel lobby; Jago and the cat followed on her heels.

Delbert looked up as she entered. "Hey, Asha, what you doing up? Something wrong with our counterfeiter's bungalow?"

"Counterfeiter?" Jago echoed, eyeing Asha.

She had the grace to blush. "All those hundred dollar bills you toss about."

"Mae always thought she'd be a writer. Good imagination our Asha has." Delbert chuckled. "Just sometimes a bit too fanciful."

Asha stuck out her tongue at him. "Did anyone come through this entrance?"

"Well, you did—"

"Anyone *else*, Delbert?"

"Nope, been quiet all night."

"Except for the jukebox playing?" Jago pressed.

Delbert eyed the younger man guardedly. "Uh . . . yeah. Tends to do that from time to time." Seeing the black cat rubbing against Asha's legs, he clearly seized upon the kitty as a change of subject. "That cat belongs to our counterfi—

to Mr. Fitzgerald? You have to pay a deposit when you have a pet. What's his name?"

"No idea," Jago replied, but the beast rushed back to him, purring loudly.

Delbert frowned, confused. "You don't know your cat's name?"

"I don't have one." Jago tried to step back, but the cat wound around his legs.

Asha sniggered. "Seems he's not on the same page as you. 'Night, Delbert."

" 'Night, Asha, Jago—Kitty."

Asha sped off, back into the restaurant, so Jago hurried to catch up. He waited until the door to the lobby was closed before insisting, "I *did* see a man and a woman in here dancing. So where did they go?"

She didn't reply, just shrugged.

He caught her arm, pulling her around. "I didn't imagine them, Asha."

"I never said you did. And I don't have an explanation. At least . . ." She hesitated.

"At least what?"

"At least one you're willing to hear," she finished lamely.

The jukebox suddenly switched to another Pitney tune, a haunting ballad. "*Something's gotten hold of my heart, keeping my soul and my senses apart . . .*"

All questions about the intruders vanished as Jago was caught in the power of the moment. The reddish glow from the Wurlitzer lent a decorative feel to the dim restaurant. But it little mattered; he couldn't see anything but Asha. She drew him, mesmerized him, made the world new again. There was some strange bond, a connection between them. Something ancient, primitive.

He sensed she was aware of it and as puzzled by it as he. His besotted mind searched for words to define his feelings. Love? *Oh, it was love.* He was falling hard, and at a speed that was utterly terrifying. This fey link made him feel as if he'd known her all his life, all that had come before was merely a waiting game, passing the days until they met.

"Auld souls," he whispered, reaching out to run the side of his thumb back and forth across that faint cleft in her chin, as he'd envisioned doing when he first stared at her two days ago.

Asha's eyes locked with his. So many things were there: surprise, awe, intrigue . . . a glitter of a tear. *Damn,* Jago thought. He'd never considered a half-formed tear could bring him to his knees.

"Auld . . . souls?" she echoed, as if she wanted to know more yet in the same breath was terrified of his answer.

He nodded and took her wrist, pulling her into an embrace, slow-dancing to the music. "You feel it, too. As if we've known each other before. Always."

The Pitney song ended and was replaced by the soft voice of Dionne Warwick crooning. "*. . . could you be the dream that I once knew . . .* ?"

Jago lifted a brow. "See, even the damn jukebox knows."

Asha nervously licked her lips, trying to smile. "That Wurlitzer has a mind of its own. I actually got fed up with it, sold it once. Had an offer of $35,000 for it and its wallettes. When they came to uninstall it, they ran into . . . hmm . . . trouble. It damn near electrocuted them every time they tried to take it out."

He chuckled. "Why didn't you just cut the power?"

"We did. It kept coming back on. So it stays here . . . playing all these tunes from the '60s, along with a handful of others it deems worthy enough." Determination was behind her words as she added, "Where it belongs."

He chose to ignore the challenge in her eyes, daring him to say he would buy The Windmill. "When you dance with the devil, lass, there's hell to pay."

"I hadn't kenned I danced with Satan himself."

"Live 'n' learn, lass, live 'n' learn."

Jago loved how they fit: Her height perfect as if she were crafted just for him. He wouldn't have to bend far to cap-ture that small, full mouth. He stopped dancing, just rocked with her as he sang along with Dionne, then lowered his head to hers.

Knowing it was madness, he brushed his mouth against hers. She tasted sweet, with a tart hint of lemon. She tasted exotic, she tasted . . . familiar.

He should never have kissed her, not even this light brushing of lips. The fathomless hunger that had prowled within him for the last ten months sprang to life. He needed her more than air, needed to brand her as his to claim her in the most primitive way, as a man claimed his mate.

His hands slid up and down her back, urging her against him. She melted, pliant, molding those lush curves against his hard planes. That blew his mind. He inched back, trying to find something solid to lean against, finally coming against the front of the Wurlitzer with a jolt that jarred the song to end abruptly.

He spread his legs and pressed Asha closer, a sigh rolling through his thoughts, a whisper of *I'm coming home.*

"*I AM THE GOD OF HELLFIRE, AND I BRING YOU . . . FIRE! I'LL TAKE YOU TO BURN . . .*"

Startled, Jago leapt up off his feet, knocking them both off balance. The cat squalled as Asha stepped on its long tail, sending the creature scurrying under the table of the nearest booth. Out of danger, the beast watched as the humans went down in a tangle of arms and legs. Asha tossed her head back, laughing; tears came to her eyes and she had trouble catching her breath.

Jago leaned on one elbow. His other hand on his heart, he rubbed his chest. "Jeez Louise! What the hell is that?"

"The Crazy World of Arthur Brown's 'Fire.' Asha named the '60s song.

The jukebox screamed, "YOU'RE GONNA BURN!"

"Well, I was on my way to doing just that"—he glared at the machine—"before you scared me out of ten years of my life, you possessed pile of junk!"

Chapter Eleven

Asha glanced out the restaurant window, watching the steady rain. It had stopped just after she returned to the bungalow from swimming last night, but this morning came down as if settling in for the rest of the day. She looked forward to rainy days, relished the smells, the sounds, the lazy pace. In Scotland they called it *the soft*, and it made her want to go walking aimlessly for hours. It soothed her soul. Renewed her. She was aware most Kentuckians didn't share her delight. When she gave in to the urge and strolled through the pouring rain, locals observed her with a jaundiced eye. "Crazy foreigner," they muttered and shook their heads.

Typical for a rainy day, the customers stayed away from The Windmill, as though they were made of sugar and would melt should raindrops hit them. The restaurant was virtually dead, which pleased Asha. She enjoyed leisurely days in the diner. They had a special feel.

Even the jukebox had been quiet.

Winnie MacPhee sat in the corner booth with two dozen

scratch-off lottery tickets, working her penny furiously. At least, that was her excuse for still being here. She kept glancing out the plate-glass windows, same as Asha. Asha looked for Jago. Winnie looked for Derek.

An hour earlier, Winnie's yellow Beetle convertible had zoomed up, and she'd sashayed her tight little buns into the restaurant, claiming to be starving for one of Sam's biscuit-and-sausage gravy breakfasts. The meal had been unhurriedly eaten and the dirty dishes removed, though to Winnie's disappointment it wasn't Derek but Mike clearing them away. Tuesday through Friday Derek worked afternoons and nights; on weekends he pulled a double shift, doing mornings as well, augmenting his savings for veterinary school. Winnie was aware of this routine. Except this morning, Derek had sent word through Delbert that he would be late. So, Winnie sat, one eye on the parking lot, scratching lotto tickets.

Asha admitted she was in a grumpy mood. She'd anticipated having breakfast with Jago, only his bungalow was empty, his car gone when she'd gotten up. Hoping he would still show and they could share a morning meal, she'd skipped eating. Now, her tum was rumbling due to the smell of Sam's cooking. He was preparing crawfish etouffee and grumpy about being forced to use crabmeat.

"Crawfish or crabmeat, it smells delicious." Asha inhaled and sighed.

The door pushed open and Netta came in, grumbled something unintelligible that might've been a "good morning," then grabbed a cup of coffee and a Mars bar, clearly hiding behind her dark Wayfarer sunglasses. When Asha tilted her head, silently asking how it went with Liam after she'd left, Netta's brows lifted.

"Don't ask." She shook the candy bar in warning. "Don't even think about it."

Asha had just finished writing out all the paychecks, as Netta plopped down on the stool beside her. With her perfectly manicured nails, she thumbed through the checks until she found her own. Seeing the amount, she scooted the sunglasses down to the end of her nose to look over them.

"I gave you a raise," Asha explained.

"Much appreciated, boss. However, if Rhonda sees this she'll pitch a hissy fit," she warned, holding the check in the air.

Asha shrugged. "Let her. You work harder than she does. In the year since I hired you, money has gone up steadily around here. One of the best things I ever did. You keep people coming back with your chatter. Everyone adores you. As for Rhonda, I'm fed up with her calling in sick or coming in an hour late several times a week. Business is growing, so I am considering taking on a couple part-time waitresses. While I'm making changes, I thought you'd make a better hostess. You interested?"

Netta stalled by sipping her coffee and pretending to glance at the morning newspaper. Finally she gave Asha a half-hearted, "Could be."

Sam pushed through the kitchen door with a load of glasses for under the counter. "Morning, Netta. You want some breakfast?"

She ripped open the Mars bar wrapper with her teeth, took a chomp and waved the candy. "Thanks, already got it."

"Girl, that ain't no fit breakfast. Shame on you." Sam chuckled, shaking his head.

Once he'd ambled back to the kitchen, Netta leaned on the counter with her elbow. "So, why did you go hot-footing it away from Sexy Lips last night? It looked like you two were getting quite chummy in the shallow end of the pool. Then, pow—you were off running like you're practicing for the Boston Marathon."

Asha closed the ledger-style checkbook with a loud snap. "Don't ask me about Jago, and I won't ask about Liam."

"Well, hell, that's no fun." Netta huffed, then turned and

greeted the old man shuffling down the aisle. "Morning, Delbert."

"Morning, pretty lady." Delbert sat at the end of the counter, leaned back and called to Sam through the open space in the wall. "Two eggs over-easy, bacon, a side of hash browns and tomato juice."

"Comin' up." Sam nodded and gave him a wave. "Glad *someone* knows what a fit breakfast is around this place."

"Good Lord, what the hell is that?" Netta laughed.

They all turned. The cat from last night precariously walked along the narrow ledge of the windows, peering inside. Aware of their attention, he jumped down and ran to the door; standing up on his hind legs, he pawed at the glass.

Asha chuckled. "A wet cat is a funny sight, but one doing a Goodyear Blimp imitation is beyond words."

Picking up the plate Sam placed on the warmer, Delbert asked, "Why doesn't your counterfeiter let his kitty inside? He should take better care of his pet. Cats don't like to be out in the rain."

"Counterfeiter?" Netta pushed her shades to the top of her head. "Did I miss something exciting?"

"Just our Asha being overimaginative—again." Delbert poured himself a cup of coffee. "She raised a question whether Fitzgerald is a counterfeiter because of all the hundred-dollar bills he tosses around."

Netta walked over, and tapped on the glass window with a long red nail, getting the cat to bat at her finger. "He's Jago's cat? Cool."

"Not exactly," Asha said. "I think the cat's declaring adoption. Anyone ever see him lurking about The Windmill before?"

Delbert stabbed his egg yolks with his fork. "He's not a stray—not unless he goes around eating small dogs. From the looks of him, he hasn't missed a meal in a blue moon."

"We'll have to name him," Netta suggested brightly. "How about Flexie—you know like the old cartoon?"

"I think you mean Felix." Delbert paused, toast halfway to his mouth. "Maybe Fitzgerald wants to name him, it being his pet after all. The cat must be waiting for him to come back."

Asha tried to sound casual, but nearly cringed when the words came out sounding too eager. "Jago went somewhere?"

Delbert nodded, leaving both Asha and Netta in suspense. After a couple slurps of his coffee, he informed them, "He went off first thing this morning with Derek."

Asha noticed Winnie's head snapped up at the mention of Derek's name. Delbert returned his attention to his breakfast, leaving all three women hanging. Unwilling to give him the satisfaction, Asha went to the fountain and fixed herself a lemonade. She took a drink, waiting until Delbert finally decided he'd milked the pregnant pause for all it was worth.

"Figured you'd know about it, Asha, seeing as you were with him all night," he said, deadpan, gray eyes watching her for a reaction to his prod.

Netta made a big *O* with her mouth and lifted her eyebrows. "Glad one of us had a good night."

"Delbert's yanking your chain. I went to bed, then Jago came rapping at the door before dawn saying someone was in the restaurant." Asha shook a finger at the night manager. "You're being naughty, Obi-Wan."

"Didn't find anyone, did you?" Delbert inquired, in a manner that convinced Asha that he hadn't expected them to find anyone.

"No, we didn't."

Netta nodded. "Ahhhh."

"Ah," Asha agreed.

The jukebox spluttered to life for the first time all morning, the lights glowing. Asha held her breath, waiting to see what the deranged thing would play. "You better be good after last night's performance or you will be playing, 'They're coming to take me away—ha ha, hee hee'."

* * *

Asha couldn't stand the kitty crying in the rain any longer; she let him onto the glassed-in porch off the end of the restaurant. From there, he could see into the lunchroom and have a nice dry place to clean his fur. It was either that or play dodge-the-kitty each time someone went in or out of the restaurant. She bundled him in a towel and gave him a good rubdown, then left him on the glider swing. She warned, "Sorry, Puss. No kitties allowed in the diner." Before dashing off to her 11:00 a.m. appointment at Juanita's Wash and Curl, Netta went and patted him.

The Windmill was still dead. No lunch rush. *No Jago.*

After the jukebox had gone into spinning "Purple People Eater" endlessly, Asha had unplugged it and now had on her portable CD player. She glanced over at the silent Wurlitzer and stuck out her tongue. "Nanabooboo—and not a single one of them from the 1960s."

She turned up the music and set about decorating the restaurant for Halloween. She loved this time of year. Kentucky's landscape was stunningly gorgeous painted with brilliant reds, oranges and yellows, especially along The Palisades of the Kentucky River between Lock 7 and Lock 8. She was going to bedeck the diner first and then the pool clubhouse, where she planned to toss a big Halloween bash, costumes not optional. The drive-in would run movies from dusk to dawn—B horror flicks from the early '60s, back in the heyday of Vincent Price and Christopher Lee. Nearly vibrating with the anticipation, she dragged the big box of decorations from The Oriental Trading Company out of the office. She sorted out the black garland with little metallic ghosts and started hanging it behind the counter.

Sam poked his head out of the kitchen. Seeing she was occupied on the ladder, he tiptoed past with a plate, heading toward the glassed-in porch.

"Taking a lunch break, Sam?" she called, hiding her laughter.

"Damn, woman, you scared me." His teeth flashed in a big grin. "I thought the cat that ain't got a name might be hungry. I fixed him some leftover chicken."

"He doesn't look as if he's missed many meals," she pointed out.

"Don't mean he ain't hungry. I don't like anything to go hungry."

Asha was rocking her hips to "The Phoenix and The Ashes" by Brolum—a Trad Scottish group—when she heard a low-throttle rumble. A black car slowly pulled into the lot and parked in front of the restaurant. Still on the stepladder, she bent down to see it was Derek's Shelby. Oddly, he pushed out of the passenger side: Derek *never* let anyone drive his baby. He had a hemorrhage if anyone so much as got a fingerprint on the bloody car. Just asking if you could drive it sent him into an apoplexy. She noticed Winnie watched, too, curious. Jago climbed out of the driver's seat.

As the men came through the front door, Asha went back to hanging the metallic garland, pretending she couldn't care less that Jago had finally returned; she wouldn't give him the satisfaction of knowing she'd anticipated spending the morning with him. Glancing toward Winnie, she noticed the girl had shifted into the same cold-shoulder routine, an instinctive universal mode of handling men that most of the poor things had never learned to offset.

"This should prove interesting." She chuckled softly.

All buddy-buddy, Derek and Jago sat on stools at the counter. Derek thumped his fist on it. "Service! What sort of greasy spoon, jip joint is this? I want service!"

Asha continued hanging the garland. "Sorry, management reserves the right to refuse service."

Trading smirks of silent communication, they waited until she finished. Derek casually glanced over his shoulder at Winnie in the back booth.

Figuring she'd made them wait long enough, Asha climbed down and went to stand before them. "What will you gents have?"

"Coffee and two of anything that goes with breakfast," Jago ordered, not bothering to look at the menu.

Derek said, "OJ, scrambled eggs, sausage, and half a dozen of Sam's buttermilk biscuits."

"Hmm . . . maybe you should've gone to see Ella at The Cliffside. I hear she passes out blueberry muffins—to men. I'll see if Sam's still serving breakfast. Since we are preparing for the lunch rush now, it might be too late." Asha wrote up two tickets, went to the window and attached them to the wheel, then spun them around. Sam was cleaning the grill, his back to her, so she dinged the bell to get his attention.

"You gonna ding that stupid bell one too many times, girl, and I'm going to toss it out the door. I ain't deaf like Delbert. Just holler. Whatcha want?" the cook asked.

"I was checking if you are still serving breakfast, but I see you've cleaned the grill for the lunch crowd, so I guess not." She smiled playfully.

"You gone loopy, girl? *What* lunch crowd?" Yanking down the tickets, Sam scanned the orders. "Morning, Jago," he called through the opening. "Ignore Asha. She's been listening to "Purple People Eater" too long. I'll have breakfast up in about ten minutes."

She poured juice and coffee for both men. Only then did she make full eye contact with Jago. His suppressed smile said he was aware he received the cold shoulder. When she continued with her silence, he crooked a brow and nodded to the Wurlitzer.

" 'Something wrong with the deranged jukebox?'—he asks hopefully," Jago queried.

"I gave it the morning off."

He laughed aloud, an infectious sound. "Wonder why."

Sam poked his head through the open space. "Hey, Jago, I fed your cat chicken for lunch. Hope that's okay with you."

"My cat?" A question lit Jago's eyes.

Asha pointed to the glass porch, where the black kitty stood waving his paw. "I'll just add the chicken on your tab."

"Oh, I get it. He belongs to The Windmill and is trained to go around mooching, then you add his meals on the tab. Neat way to pad the bill."

Asha chuckled. "Sorry, you're not getting out of it so easy. You're the one who came dragging him in. He's your cat, Charlie Brown."

"What would I do with a cat? I have apartments in New York and London," he replied.

She shrugged, hoping to sound casual. "Maybe you should consider settling down somewhere. A cat needs a good home." Asha tried to meet his stare, but those green garnet eyes bore into hers, seeing all. She knew, though she'd tried to make the suggestion sound playful, that it had come across as an expression of her hunger.

Idiot! She mentally kicked herself. A man like Jago Fitzgerald wasn't interested in a home, kids and kitty cats. He was sex and sin. Oh, he would be open to a passionate affair with all the trimmings, and despite her vow never to trust a pretty man again she wanted all those hot, sleepless nights, lost to the glory of their bodies. But that's all it ever would be. *Take him as he is, what he offered and be thrilled with that much*, she told herself.

Then why did she see *everything* in his eyes? Tomorrows. Children, fat cats and SUVs. Jago would fit so well with her house on the river. Feeling ridiculous for painting such images in her mind with a man she barely knew, she almost fled when he offered her a grin.

"Yeah, maybe I should consider settling down," he said. "Any ideas where me and the cat might find a good place to plant roots?"

She swallowed hard, struggling for a reply. Daring to hope opened one to all sorts of pain; she knew that only too well.

Sam saved her by announcing, "Breakfasts are up."

Jago motioned to Derek. "Why don't we move to the table, then we can finish our business?"

"Sure thing." The redheaded man nodded, and climbed off the stool to collect the meals.

Asha echoed, "Business?"

Derek grinned. "Yeah, Jago is buying the Shelby. We took it for a test drive this morning to prove that it lives up to my praise."

She wasn't sure why the deal bothered her, but it did. Like a slap in the face, it was a chilly reminder of why Jago was really here. All her dreams of what might be vanished as the trepidation settled in her stomach. "You're buying his Shelby?"

Jago nodded, his eyebrow arched, saying he sensed her shift in mood. "Yes, I just have to write a check."

"Warming up? You're chafing at the bit to buy the horse farm, so you wile away your time keeping the skills sharp with Derek?" That would teach her to fantasize about a stranger. It just proved she didn't want to have the babies of a bloody developer!

"Whoa, lass! Off on a tangent again before you have all the facts." His tone was chiding, though he gave her a half-smile.

"Ease up, Asha. He bought the car at the price I asked and then some. You know what that money means to me. He's my faery godfather." Derek glanced uneasily to Jago and then back at Asha. "You should kiss the man instead of taking a bite out of his ass."

Jago's eyes danced. "Oh, she's welcome to take a bite of my arse anytime she fancies—or kiss me. I'm game for either."

Asha knew she had overreacted, but had a hard time shifting into reverse gracefully. She stuck her tongue out at him. "Bah, humbug."

He picked up the Halloween witch doll from the counter and wiggled it in front of her face. "Wrong holiday, lass."

Feigning disinterest in the two men as they ate, Asha went back to hanging decorations. The dishes were soon shoved aside, Jago took out his checkbook and Derek pulled a piece of paper from his pocket that looked like a title to a car. With a grin, he pushed it across the table.

At the other end of the diner, Winnie suddenly slid from her booth. Two spots of red stained her pale cheeks as the young woman stood, hesitating for a breath. Stinging from six weeks of Winnie shooting him down every time he asked her out, Derek had ignored Winnie since coming in, clearly not in the mood for more of her games. When he continued to pay her no heed, she marched to the counter, tossed a handful of bills and the used lottery tickets on the top, then slammed out of the restaurant. Her yellow Beetle squealed tires leaving the lot.

"Beau Derek?" Jago's voice rang through the diner. "I just bought a car from Beau Derek Whittaker?"

The Jukebox suddenly groaned to life, causing Asha to glare at it. The monstrosity had been unplugged! She'd done it herself, but chords of "Hey Little Cobra" by the Rip Cords now blared forth. "*Hey, Little Cobra . . . You're gonna shut 'em down . . .*"

Asha tossed the crepe paper pumpkin down to the counter. "That's it. Where's my pistol? I'm going to show you, you deranged metal monster, how *I* shut 'em down."

Asha had forgotten. Fed up with its antics, she put her hand on the Wurlitzer, intending to yank the plug from the wall socket—again. Only, the instant she touched the shiny metal, she received a shock that knocked her back about three feet and onto her arse. She didn't black out, but it was damn close. She couldn't move. Similar to how a person must feel like after being hit with a Taser, she just lay there numb and stared up at the people gathering over her, concern etching their faces.

Rule number one around The Windmill: never touch La Jukebox in a threatening manner. She groaned.

Jago was the first to reach her. Poor man was a ghastly shade of gray, all the blood having drained from his face. Sam, Derek and even Delbert hovered at his shoulders. They were speaking, yet their words were distant. She wanted to assure them she was fine, but all she could manage was to breathe.

She tried to lift her right hand to cup Jago's beautiful face. Damn him. Damn *her*. She'd vowed never to get involved with a pretty man again, and yet here she was falling in love with him. Falling in love? How could she believe that, when she barely knew him? Here only three days and still she could not imagine life in her contained little world without him. The overwhelming sense of futility nearly made her cry. She was happy here at The Windmill. This was where she belonged. A man as sophisticated, as high-powered as Jago Fitzgerald would never settle for living in the middle of Nowhereville, putting up with her collection of oddball people who, some might say, life had tossed away. The Windmill was a haven for lost souls.

Jago Fitzgerald was not a lost soul. But *she* would be when he left her.

The tears came. Not heavy, just one in each eye. Frustrated, she couldn't even move her hand to wipe them away before he saw them.

"Don't stand there. Someone call a doctor!" Jago demanded.

Netta came through the front door, returning from having her hair done, dropped her purse and rushed over. "What the hell happened?"

Sam gave her a furtive look. "Damn jukebox. She was going—"

Netta frowned and leaned closer. "Unplug it. Sugarplum, don't you know to sneak up on that thing yet? Frontal attacks only get you knocked on your ass. Quick, someone give me a quarter." She held out her hand and Derek placed one in her palm.

Stepping over to the jukebox, she inserted the coin and pushed H-13. Instantly, the Wurlitzer came to life and began playing "Tell Laura I Love Her." Netta smiled at the thing and patted it gingerly. "There, you metal demon. Your world is right again."

Jago stared at them all, clearly not believing. "Have the whole bunch of you gone nuts? She needs a doctor, *not* a spin doctor."

"Chill, Sexy Lips. I've been zapped by that psycho box before. Stuns you for a few minutes, then everything comes back to normal. Give her a minute and she'll be right as rain," Netta assured him.

Asha noticed other people standing behind Netta. Focusing, she saw a young man and woman. Strangers, they must've come in just after she was shocked. Then it hit her. They weren't strangers after all. She'd seen them both before.

Last night.

She lifted her hand as the twenty-something man stepped nearer. A handsome lad with emerald eyes and short black hair, she could well understand how Laura deeply loved him. "Tommy," she whispered.

Delbert's head snapped back, then he glanced to where Asha looked. A myriad of emotions flooded the man's dear face: surprise, hope, disappointment, wonder . . . regret. All were so clear in those faded green-gray eyes. The emotions coalesced into a desperate hunger as he swung his eyes back to Asha. "You see him?"

As feeling returned to her body, Asha gave a faint nod and struggled to sit. She blinked, then tried to clear her vision to look at the two people behind the others, but she felt dizzy.

"Her, too?" Delbert pressed, shaking. "You see her?"

Asha nodded weakly.

Jago's head swiveled between them, as though trying to

figure out what the hell they were talking about. She used his strong arm to sit up. She liked the solid feel of Jago Fitzgerald—a man you could lean upon. A man she foolishly wanted in her life, despite that it could only see her hurt.

"I . . . am . . . fine," she said slowly, hoping to comfort him. "Help me stand, please. Wow, cheap buzz." She tried to laugh it off, hating people fussing over her.

Jago didn't look so ashen, but he was still pale. That brought a fleeting smile to her lips, registering his extreme reaction meant he cared. Even if just in passing.

It was Delbert who now worried her. He backed up several steps and then dropped down to sit on the end of a booth bench. Netta noticed, too. She went to him, leaning down to look at his eyes carefully.

"Are you all right, Delbert?" she fretted, patting his hand.

His head gave a bob. "Please don't worry, pretty lady. Just a wee bit of excitement. You young ones need to recall I am . . ." He rolled his eyes as if thinking. "Well, let's say older than dirt. Where does the time go? Everything doesn't seem that long ago, but it's nearly half my lifetime. So much sadness. So much waste."

Asha moved past Jago to her aging friend, more concerned about him than she was for herself. She'd taken a shock, but was quickly returning to normal. She was less certain about Delbert Seacrest. When she reached to touch his arm, wanting to take his pulse, he caught her hand, squeezing firmly. That eased her concern some. His grip was strong.

He gave her a fleeting grin, clearly afraid to believe. "You . . . saw?"

Asha nodded. "Yes, I saw them."

Jago put his hands on his hips. "Saw who?" When no one answered, he threw up his hands. "Every time something totally bizarre—I mean *Outer Limits* time—happens around here, everyone ignores me. There was no one there. I think you and Delbert both need to see a doctor and that so-called jukebox needs an electrician."

Liam came in, shaking the rain off his windbreaker. "Hi ho, everyone. Another dull day around The Windmill, eh?"

Chapter Twelve

With a smile, Asha eyed the e-mail from B.A. It illustrated her sister's quirky Scottish humor. It read: *Help! Falgannon has been invaded! Ravishment looming*!

Asha hit delete. She'd give her big blonde Amazon of a sister a ring tomorrow night—provided phone service to the isle in the Hebrides was working; it wasn't that unusual for the island to lose telephone and internet service for a week at a stretch. B.A. had just launched a new Web site called Isle of Love, advertising for brides because there was a shortage of marriageable females on Falgannon, thus the invasion part of the message didn't raise an eyebrow. Since most women sighed over a man in a kilt, Asha figured her sister would in short order find mates for the island's 213 bachelors.

Pacing restlessly to the office door, Asha looked out into the dining room. After things had calmed down from the earlier excitement, everything went back to normal for the quirky place. Later, they'd all dined on Sam's prime rib, baked potato, and garden salad special. Now, Jago sat in the far, family-size booth with Derek, Mike, Sam, Delbert and Liam, playing poker. A rainy Saturday night like so many others. Yet so different. Only here a few days, Jago fit seamlessly into their lives. She could tell the men liked him.

She liked him. Maybe too much.

She studied Jago interacting with the eclectic men in her life. Judging them. They likely missed it, but she saw how he lost to them on purpose. He was patient, astute, and little got past his incisive mind. Her crew was out of their league in dealing with him. Bloody hell, *she* was out of her league with him.

Jago looked up, his green eyes locking with hers. Their power, their force took her breath away. All around her faded to a blur. She trembled as his mind crawled under her skin, brushed against hers. There wasn't any way she could hide from him. No shield. No protection: the power of their attraction wrapped around them, bonded them into a moment when the whole world held its breath.

Damn! She'd come into the shadowy office trying to get away from him, what he provoked her to feel. Hadn't she learned the hard way never to trust a pretty man? "Then why are you standing here falling for the jerk?" she whispered.

"Because women are fools." Netta came to stand by the door. "No use hiding in there, sugarplum. You can tell yourself to be smart, to remember this or that. Bottom line, we lack even an ounce of self-preservation and will still stick our finger in the socket knowing . . ."

Asha prompted, "Knowing?"

"We dream for something we can never have." Netta sighed sadly. Asha followed her friend's vivid blue eyes to Liam.

"Hell, Netta, we could form our own Maudlin & Misery Society." Asha marched over to the desk, opened the bottom drawer and pulled out a bottle of 12-year-old The Macallan Scotch. "I've been saving this for a rainy night. This qualifies. There's nothing more disgusting—"

The stupid Wurlitzer took that moment once more to

come to life. Asha gritted her teeth as Gene Pitney blasted out how it hurts to be in love.

Holding the bottle in her hand, she waved it and pointed with her finger. "Someone needs to murder that creepy thing."

Netta laughed and snatched the bottle. "Brandishing this accomplishes nothing." She tugged the stopper from the neck, paused and said, "Here's to beautiful men and foolish women who adore them." Then, Netta took a big slug. She wiggled her eyebrows. "Ooooh, that's good Scotch."

Asha claimed the bottle and inhaled a swig. "Whisky without the E, mind you. I'm a full-blooded Scots lass. I dunna need a friggin' E in me whisky. The Macallan is the only malt distillery to use sherry wood exclusively. Its nose shows hints of sherry, lemons, pears and honey. 'A bewitching mouth feel'—whatever the hell that means."

"It means it's a damn fine whisky." Netta sniggered and took the bottle back. "Here's to the late, great Gene Pitney. God bless you, Gene. You sure belted one soulful tune."

"*Brits* appreciated Pitney." Asha snagged The Macallan and motioned to the couch. When the fat cat pussyfooted into the office and jumped up on the sofa, she asked. "How did *you* get in here? I put you on the sun porch."

Netta flopped down, her feet bouncing in the air. "Maybe whommmmever plugged in the jukebox again let him in."

"Well, then *they* can wait on customers. I'm off the clock." Kicking off her shoes, Asha started to propose a toast, then paused trying to think of someone worthy of a salute. With a smile, she said, "Here's to Leanne Burroughs. One damn fine Scottish Romance writer."

"Oooh, here's to men in kilts who speak in lilts!" Netta threw back her head and laughed. "I is a poet and don't know it."

"A Highlander doesn't have a lilt. He speaks with a burr."

"Ahhh . . . even better. Does Liam own a kilt?" Her eyes flew wide. "Is it true what they say a Highlander wears under his kilt?"

"Or doesn't wear, you mean?" Asha goaded, "You'll have to ask my brother about that."

"Ask, hell—I want a demonstration."

From the doorway, Rhonda cleared her throat. "I hate to interrupt this little party . . ."—meaning just the opposite—"but I need to speak to you, Asha." She glared at Netta as if she were something found on the bottom of her shoe, then tacked on, "alone."

Asha had felt this coming for weeks. There was a certain devotion from the people employed at The Windmill. The workers were 'family' and Rhonda never developed that sense of belonging. To her, it was a job going nowhere. While Asha was an easy employer, encouraging people to be individuals and secretly delighting in their quirkiness, Rhonda took advantage of Asha's gentle indulgence as an employer.

"I'm sure whatever you have to say can be said before Netta. Not many secrets are kept around The Windmill." Asha pulled her friend back down on the couch as Netta started to rise. "Sit. We're having a nice time."

Flashing the blonde a disgusted look, Rhonda pulled out her paycheck and flourished it. "What's this about?"

Asha blinked and shook her head. "Whoa, hold that still if you want me to look at it. I presume you're referring to the thirty hours pay instead of forty."

"Yes, I am." Rhonda put a hand on her hip.

"Well, you worked thirty hours. I paid you thirty hours."

"I can't live on that."

Asha nodded in understanding. "Most people can't. That's why they work forty hours and get paid for forty hours. You were late twice and missed a day. And before you say you were ill, I spotted you having lunch at Turfland Mall with George Wilson."

"I can get a job hostessing at the Howard Johnson's in Lexington," Rhonda threatened.

Asha smiled. "Then I suggest you do so. See how long you last working *there* thirty hours a week and calling in sick all the time."

Spinning on her heels, Rhonda stormed from the office, then out the front door. Netta gave a little wave. "Bye, Rhonda."

With a shrug, Asha eyed the cat crawling into her lap. "Dismissing Rhonda from mind . . . I know why I don't trust Jago, but why do you think you can't have Liam? Personally, I think he's haveable."

"I wish." The two words reflected Netta's doubt.

Asha eyed her. "Sorry, fess-up time. Why are you putting Liam beyond reach? Inquiring minds want to know."

"Oh, you think a couple slugs of Scotch and I'll reveal all? I'm cheap, but not *that* cheap."

"Yep. A side property of The Macallan—it's a truth serum in disguise." Asha shoved the bottle at her. "Come on, confession's good for the soul. Why is a sexy blue-eyed blonde going home alone every night?"

"Like you, sister woman, I was burned. He wasn't drop-dead beautiful like Jago or Liam, just a sweet boy. He wore those horned-rim glasses, was so studious, and determined to be a lawyer. I suggested we live together to cut expenses. He wouldn't hear of it, insisted we get married. *Insisted*." She sighed sadly. "It didn't take much convincing. I would've jumped through hoops for him. I pulled two shifts to make ends meet while he went to school full-time. We had this dingy little apartment over on Rose Street in Lexington on the edge of the University. But we were happy."

This was the first time Netta had talked about her past, other than a vague reference here or there, so Asha was curious. "What happened?"

"Rich grandparents. His mother had run away when she

was young, after she'd gotten pregnant. More likely they kicked her out when they learned about it. After her death, some private detectives finally tracked him down. They invited us to visit them—in their big fancy house on the hill. They wanted to forget the past and were delighted to have found their grandson after all these years. However, they were less than thrilled with me. I didn't know Armani from Wang. I laughed too loud, my hair was too bleached. I was too—" she waved her hands in the air—"everything. Common. They always got that same expression that Rhonda had on her face, like I was something they stepped in. Oh, they were subtle, careful to hide it from Jon. To make a long story short, in the end he preferred their money, and they preferred he have a wife more suited to their rich world."

"Ah . . ." Understanding dawned within Asha. "I don't trust pretty men because I was burned by one and you—"

"Don't trust rich men. They don't mind slumming about with trailer trash like me, but they aren't the type to stick around." She winked, saying Asha arrived at the crux of the problem.

"What's that you said when you gave me advice?—not all pretty men are alike. Maybe you should give Liam a bit more credit. He chooses to live here not England. And you, Netta Reynolds, are anything but common."

On the Wurlitzer Gene Pitney wailed, "*—true love is worth all the pain, the heartache and tears . . .*"

Netta shuddered. "We're going to have to seriously do something about that jukebox. It's sinister."

"Guess we can put the help wanted sign in the window Monday morn." Asha took the bottle back. "So, is that maybe a yes on the hostess job? I'm suddenly in urgent need of one."

Jago had noticed Asha watching him from the shadows of the office, her eyes full of longing. Much to his vexation, that look of reservation was there as well. Asha simply didn't trust easily. Fortunately, he was a patient man. *Yeah, keep telling yourself that*, his mind mocked. Only it wasn't easy. He couldn't think of anything but her. When he noticed how her bronze tresses shimmered under the recessed lighting, his brain conjured images of his hands fisted in those long strands. Or the way her eyes flashed fire when she was fearful he'd cheat Derek—it made him want to see them flash with another sort of flame—passion. And when she rocked her hips to the music, his besotted mind blanked his vision, leaving him seeing her over him moving in the same pagan rhythm. The past days were nothing but a montage of Asha. At night, alone in his bed, it played over and over in his head.

Never having loved anyone outside of his mother and brothers, Jago wasn't entirely sure this was love. The words seemed too pale for what burned through him. Obsession. Compulsion. Fascination. Hell, he couldn't think of another word to fit, so he guessed it must be love. The instant Jago looked into Asha's amber-brown eyes he'd been lost.

He'd feel peculiar, befuddled by the enormity, if he hadn't noticed the same sort of expression on the face of Asha's brother. Possibly, there was something in the air. They say April in Paris is for lovers. He'd match October in Kentucky.

"The hairs on the back of my neck always stood up when my sisters were out of sight and it suddenly got quiet," Liam commented, tossing in two dimes to the poker ante.

Jago pitched in two to match, and raised him three. "Only you don't feel very brotherly toward Netta, eh?"

"Not the least." Liam hesitated, glanced to the door, then threw down his cards with a frown. "Damn, I fold. I can't concentrate on bloody cards with Netta on my brain. Let's see what they're up to."

"Excuse us, gents." Jago folded his hand and slid from the booth behind Liam. "It's been a pleasure. Maybe we can do it again—soon?"

As he passed the jukebox, he glared. The thing was playing a hit by The Troggs, the singer crooning how he wanted to spend his life ". . . *with a girl like you.*"

"*Now* you play love songs, you menacing monster," he grumbled.

He nearly bumped into Liam, who had stopped short. Nudging with his elbow, Liam pointed for Jago to look. The two women were sprawled on the sofa, laughing hysterically, a half-empty bottle of Scotch on the floor at their bare feet. The fat cat, draped over Asha's lap, lifted his head and meowed a hello.

Jago leaned against the doorframe drinking in Asha. Her mass of auburn hair spilled over her shoulders; she looked deliciously rumpled. Hell, he was jealous of that damn feline. He'd like to go over there and curl up on her lap.

"You're drunk." Liam laughed.

"Me, too," Asha chirped with a big smile.

Netta took a deep breath. "Not me. I'm just pleasantly mellow. We've been toasting Gene Pitney, men in kilts, *various unnamed males*—to protect the guilty—and trying to figure out what costumes we'll wear for the Halloween bash."

"Earthshaking events all, but I thought we had a date for the drive-in." Liam sat on the arm of the sofa, grinning.

The blonde turned her head, rolling her big blue eyes up at him. "Sure do, hon. You can slum with me anytime."

Liam's eyebrows arched. "Slum? Where the hell did that come from?"

"Ignore her, she's drunk." Asha flopped forward to pick up the bottle, dislodging the cat. Jago's hand closed over hers and removed her fingers from around the glass.

"I think you've both had enough for one evening." He held The Macallan out of her reach as she followed it up, snatching at it.

"Hey, I'm toasting my new hostess—Netta."

"Congratulations," Liam said behind her. "A fine choice."

Jago held the bottle to the side, his long arm keeping it

away from Asha's grasp. She finally stilled as she realized in reaching for the bottle, she was flush against his chest. Her eyes narrowed on him in that mix of female skittishness and a plea of *I'm yours for the taking*, which hit like a blow to his solar plexus. Breathing was impossible.

This self-imposed abstinence was going to short circuit his brain, and would push him into doing something very foolish before he considered all he faced in falling for this woman. Well, if he was going to suffer, then so could she! He lowered his head slightly, to where the scent of Asha filled his senses. She wore a light perfume with a touch of lemon and jasmine, which did little to cover the scent of the female underneath; silly woman had no idea how it made him want to toss back his head and howl like a wolf in rut. He let her feel his warmth, let her drink in his male pheromones, then watched as her pupils dilated with a hunger that matched his. Saw the power of surrender unfurled within her eyes.

Leaning close so that his mouth was against her hair, he said lowly, "Auld souls whisper ever so softly when they're near."

"And what do they whisper?" Asha almost swayed, and he thought it from the sexual buzz between them, not the whisky. The corner of his mouth crooked up.

"They whisper that little girls who go around without shoes get their tootsies stomped on by fat cats."

Glancing down, Asha finally noticed the black puss standing on her bare feet and rubbing against her calf. She smiled crookedly.

"Jago's coming out to the farm in the morning," Liam announced, reminding them both that they weren't alone. "He wants a tour of Valinor."

Asha stepped back. Worse, Jago saw her withdrawing from him mentally as well.

"So he can get a better idea of the price tag?" she asked pointedly.

"Sheath your dagger, little sister. I invited him. He likes horses, and I'm always willing to show off my stock." Liam chuckled, turning to face Jago. "A warning, my friend. Our grandmother Maeve was of old Pict blood and lived on Falgannon Isle in the Hebrides. The women of the Picts carried these strangely curved daggers. After a battle with the Vikings, they'd go around with that arched knife and castrate prisoners. Maeve had copies of an original cast, and presented them to each of her granddaughters when they turned twenty-one. My sisters are warrior women. Tread carefully around them."

Jago bent down and patted the cat, who was trying to climb up his leg. "Warning heeded. Thanks. Asha has a tendency to lose her cool when someone mentions me buying things. I guess that explains why prickles creep up my spine when she eyes sharp objects."

"I thought you ladies might like to join us. I could fix breakfast," Liam suggested.

Netta smiled brightly. "Sexy as hell and can cook. You'd make someone a great wife."

"Is that an offer?" Liam asked, challenge clear in his words.

"*Laura and Tommy were lovers; he wanted to give her everything* . . ." the jukebox began in the other room.

Everyone groaned.

Liam pulled Netta to her feet. "Shoes on, ladies. We're out of here. Colin is showing a Vincent Price-Roger Corman film festival. If we hurry, we'll be in time for *The Haunted Palace* and *Masque of the Red Death*."

Jago frowned. "Aren't those films from the '60s?"

Liam shrugged. "Ask Asha. She'll know. She's the film buff in the family."

"1963 and '64, respectively," Asha said, sliding on her shoes. "Why?"

"It just seems everything is from the '60s around here," Jago commented, following her from the office.

Asha waved at Delbert. "Close up for me, please. I'm off on a hot date with our counterfeiter."

"Hot date? Counterfeiter?" Liam echoed, opening the front door for Netta.

"Hey, what about your cat, Jago?" Delbert called. "You want me to put him in your bungalow?"

"Stick him wherever you want. He's not my cat."

Chapter Thirteen

The chubby black cat was stretched out on the Jeep's dashboard, pretending to sleep. The only sign the thing was alive was an occasional snap of the long tail, generally when the speaker, hanging from the passenger window, grew too loud. *The Haunted Palace* reached the point where Vincent Price ties up Debra Paget as a sacrifice to the monster from the pit and then the growling creature comes for her. In true horror flick fashion, she screams—and screams! The feline opened one eye, glared at the speaker and then at Jago, with the telepathy of *do something*.

Asha finished the last of her food and washed it down with the icy Pepsi. Not that she'd been hungry, but after she mentioned the concession stand served a mean chili dog, Jago had insisted on having a couple. She gathered he was a bit of a junk food junkie. When he returned, he'd had one for her. Smart man. One whiff of the tantalizing aroma and she was thankful he'd gotten an extra—she might've pulled her gun on him and hijacked one.

The cat lifted his head and sniffed the air again.

"Don't even think about it. You move, Fat Boy, and you're

going to fall off the dash," Jago addressed the feline before he stuffed the remainder of his second hot dog into his sexy mouth.

"I'm not sure he's comfortable there," Asha commented. "The dash isn't really wide enough for him."

"The silly creature put himself up there. He can get down, climb into the back seat and stretch out, if he wants—after I finish eating. You were right—they are super chili dogs. I fear I could become addicted. Guess the good concession food is one of the reasons you're packed even on a rainy night."

"The drive-in fills a lot of bills. Parents and grandparents come to catch the magic of memories. Young people are finding it's a neat place to hang out. It's a super value. If you go into Lexington and see a movie at a cinema, it's over eighteen dollars for a guy and a gal—just for the tickets. Then they soak you at the concession stand. Wisely, we keep prices reasonable. It's one price for a carload. So two couples can double date and have plenty of treats for less than half the price of a cinema. Plus, you're getting three movies instead of one. You don't have to get dressed up. No need for a babysitter; the whole family can come. They can talk all they want without someone shushing them. A whole evening of entertainment instead of two expensive hours. It's the best bargain going. Most of the younger people haven't seen many of the old movies we show so they get a kick out of them."

"Not to mention you can steam up the windows and ignore the movie, if you wish." He laughed lowly.

"Hmm, there is that." Thoughts of steaming up the windows with Jago suddenly saw her body temperature spike.

"How's the setup? You still use films?" Jago seemed truly interested.

"No, we're high-tech—DVD projection. I deal with a firm that packages the movies, and they have a large selection. They send us the intermission and movie lead-ins you used to see at the drive-ins in the '60s—you know the one with the hot dog doing tricks? They even include old Woody the Woodpecker cartoons. The old way, you had to buy films outright or rent them. Shipping and handling was murder. This is so simple now. We plan ahead what we want, place our order and they are shipped in little packages, licenses all handled for us."

"No worrying about the film breaking, eh?"

"Nope, the whole thing's very efficient. In fact, they're currently producing portable screens and offer them to places that have seasonal parking lots, such as fairgrounds, churches and lodges, big open spaces that aren't used all the time. Halloween weekend we'll close and won't reopen until March. Of course, they use your own car's FM Radio to broadcast the soundtracks instead of the pole speakers we still maintain. We did a survey if people wanted the better FM sound or the full drive-in experience. It was nearly unanimous that everyone loved the old-time speakers."

Jago's eyes skimmed the grassy lot. Built on a hillside, the rows were terraced so that each line of cars was higher than the one in front of it. An efficient layout, it took up less acreage than a flat lot and had good viewing from any slot. "You have what—room for four-hundred cars?"

"Near that. We generally average a hundred-fifty on a good night. The capacity with the DVD and satellite projection is around four hundred for a single projector, so I think drive-ins may come back slowly—at least in this limited fashion."

"At ten bucks a car . . . plus refreshments, three nights a week, thirty-eight weeks a year. Not a bad chunk of change. I can see the portable drive-in idea catching on with those sorts of figures. I might be interested in investing venture capital for this. I'll have to look into it."

Jago gathered up the trash and stuck it in the thin paper box, then leaned between the seats to place it on the backseat floor. Before she realized what he was doing, he shifted, nearly leaning against her. For a second he stared into her eyes, his breath fanning over her face. It was the first time she'd ever ranked the smell of chili dogs as sexy. Just as she figured he was going to kiss her—and she was going to let him—he reached past her and released the lever, reclining her seat back.

Raising up, those dark eyes flashed. "I missed something."

Asha could only lie there craving chili dog kisses and inhaling his potent male scent as he loomed over her. So close. Too close. Not close enough. "What?" she croaked.

"This." He lowered his head to kiss the corner of her mouth, his tongue lashing out to swipe her lips. "Mmm . . . chili sauce. Tastes better on you than on the hot dog. Of course, I might need a little more comparison."

His lips brushed hers. Soft, savoring, the contact sent a deep shiver scurrying over Asha's skin. Oh, how she wanted that kiss! The scent of Jago and his cologne was a lethal combination weaving around her, intoxicating as a $5,000 bottle of The Macallan. His high male heat radiated from him, sinking into her, snaking under her skin with a consuming need.

He pulled back, his eyes studying her. She stared up into his beautiful face, knowing this was true love. Fire rockets, Mardi Gras, dark and dangerous nights of hot sex, the scare-you-down-to your tippy-toes, forever kind of need that makes you so vulnerable. *Makes you want to do the wild thing right here in the front seat at a drive-in,* she chuckled to herself.

Jago Fitzgerald terrified her. He was a throwback, a dark-age warrior who could claim, conquer. Despite that terrifying prospect, she could no more pull back from sticking her finger in the socket than command herself not to breathe.

"You're not going to warn me and start counting are you? Because I'm not walking home in the rain." Her words were nearly a whisper.

He grinned. "Between the steering wheel and the gearshift, I think you're reasonably safe."

"Sort of the male version of a chastity belt?" Asha laughed. "Men have been getting around those obstacles for decades."

"We lads relish the challenge. Kiss me, wench—you've been dying to for days."

"Me?" she squeaked.

That was all she got out before his warm lips closed over hers again.

He was right—chili sauce tasted better on him than on the hot dog. She just didn't kiss Jago; she experienced him—his flavor, the warm scent of his body, the feel of his hard muscles. She moved her hands up his spine, chafing at the obstruction of his soft sweater, craving to feel them on his flesh.

Sexy Lips was a good kisser. Oh, was he good! As her arms slid around his neck, he nibbled, licked and sucked with a warlock's magic, sending waves of pleasure down to the tips of her toes. That sensation rushed right back upward, hitting her womb with a punch. Her breasts tightened and her brain . . . well, her brain was suddenly focused on the stupid gearshift obscenely in the way. Maybe if they could switch seats, then she could turn to straddle him. At times like these a woman wished she could twitch her nose like Elizabeth Montgomery on *Bewitched* and have gearshifts and clothing vanish in a poof.

Insistent knocking pounded on the glass. "Hey, Asha! Come on, roll the window down."

They glanced up at the face, nose nearly pressed against the glass, peering in the passenger's side window. Jago's eyebrows lifted and he gave her a quirky smile.

"Um, Asha, not sure—either John Waters or Steve Buscemi is rapping on the glass. Neither prospect is comforting."

Asha laughed and pressed the window button on the door to roll it down.

"Should you do that?" Jago teased. "Maybe he's that guy in the hockey mask. Remember how when a guy and gal make out in those slasher flicks, some fruit loop—who looks *just like him*—goes berserk and hacks them up."

"I heard that," the ferret-faced man snapped, but his nasally tone was playful. "Just remember, buster, to sleep with one eye open from now on. Sorry, me and my machete interrupted the great make-out scene here, but I wanted to give you the list of the movies I got for Halloween weekend, Asha. Sorry, I couldn't track down the license for *The Maze*. I really wanted to see that frog guy. He sounds cool. But they were able to get all the others for us. A super lineup, even if I do say so myself."

"That's fabulous, Colin. Thank you. It should be great fun for everyone," Asha complimented.

"Hey, a Hammer Halloween. Chris Lee and Peter Cushing ride again." The thin man leaned in halfway through the window, and stuck his hand out to shake. "Hi, Jago. I'm Colin Hughes. Call me Oo-It. Everyone else does."

Jago's eyes shifted to Asha in amusement, then back to Colin, as they shook hands. "Nice to meet you, Colin."

"You can call me—"

"Oo-it," Jago finished.

"Yeah, everyone—"

"Else does." Once again, Jago finished Colin's sentence.

"Yeah. Sorry I haven't been down to the restaurant to say a welcome, but I was busy tracking down these movies for Halloween. We're having a big bash. You still going to be here?"

"Yeah, I plan on it."

Colin spied the cat sprawled on the dash and his eyes lit up. "Wow, what a great cat! Hadn't heard you had a cat, Jago," he said, scratching the beast's chin.

"I think it's more like he has me." Jago chuckled.

Colin asked, "What's his name?"

"I'm not sure." Jago shrugged. "He hasn't deigned to tell us yet."

"You should name your cat. Cat's gotta have a name." Colin stopped scratching the purring feline and smiled sheepishly. "Well, I'll let you get back to the 'hot and heavy.' Night Asha. Nice to meet you, Jago."

"Nice to meet you, Colin."

"Thanks again, Colin." Asha waved. "I appreciate all the effort to get the movies."

"Sure, anytime." He stuffed his hands into his pocket and shrugged. "You know I'd do anything for you, Asha."

Jago watched the strange man pull up the hood of his

sweatshirt and trot off into the rain, back toward the concession stand. He raised his brows. "Oo-it?"

Asha chuckled. "Colin stuttered from childhood. Not bad, mostly when he became excited. When something put him into a dither, he'd go 'Oo Oo Oo-it' over and over again before he calmed down enough to get anything else out. He's been Oo-it since he was six. Mostly he's outgrown the stutter, but the nickname stayed."

"He doesn't mind?"

"It's done in love and he knows it. He's sweet. He's the first one there to shovel your drive after it snows or to cut your lawn. He runs the drive-in and maintains the grounds around all the businesses. Quite handy with anything electrical. My guess is he's a borderline genius, but few ever paid attention. We're lucky to have him."

"Hmm. Where were we?" Jago started to lean toward her, but the black cat jumped off the dash and in between them. He bounced on his hind legs, then butted Jago's chin with his forehead, and not gently either. Asha heard the crack. Jago dodged as the purring cat kept trying to *bonk* him again. "Oww, you bloody feline."

"He loves you." Asha sniggered.

Taking hold of the pest, he held the cat still, and glared into its eyes. Then Jago turned his head slightly and said, "I'd rather *you* love me."

Caught off guard, Asha's heart dropped as she stared at him. There was just enough light from the dash to show he'd uttered the words in seriousness. She wanted to summon a jest, but she couldn't think of anything, other than *I'd rather you love me, too.*

Things were moving too fast for her to reveal that. You just didn't fall in love so quickly. Could you? She feared the answer. Did she dare trust this man—a man so self-assured, a pretty man used to big-city lights? Could he fall for someone who was happy here in this quirky little spot so far from the beaten path? Foolishly, she'd let down those cocooning walls, permit him into her safe little world with no reservations, blindly surrender to the passion shimmering between them. *Love him*. But for how long? How long would Jago Fitzgerald be content to stay in her Nowhereville?

She jerked when a blaring car horn shattered the spell. It kept on in a long stream as if stuck. With a sigh, Asha looked to row H, slot thirteen. Sure enough, there were taillights of a truck that had just pulled into the empty space regulars had long ago learned not to choose. Soon everyone was honking horns in protest.

A shadowy figure played across the screen as Oo-it held up his raised middle finger in front of the projector in added protest.

Jago laughed. "Is this some sort of drive-in ritual? An insiders' joke?"

Asha couldn't answer. She stared through the rain at the red taillights of the black truck, suddenly feeling so far away.

When Tommy pulled into row H, slot thirteen, Laura groaned in disappointment.

First, it was pouring rain. That alone had caused her to fear he might cry off coming to the drive-in. Now, the eighth row? There were seventeen rows at the drive-in, and all couples seriously dating made a beeline for the last one. You had to reverse a car into that line as it butted up against the ten-foot high yew hedge that surrounded the lot—ideal for young lovers. The locals jokingly had dubbed it "Rubber Row," since the bright light of day revealed spent condoms everywhere. Tossed out car windows, they'd caught on the evergreens and hung there like bizarre Christmas decorations. When you glanced back to that string of cars, it was an oddity to see one without fogged windows. She so hoped Tommy would pull his car into the last row! She wanted to steam up the windows with him.

In the long, empty hours of the night, her body ached for Tommy. She was a virgin, but she knew what her body wanted. She'd slid her hands over her breasts imagining they were Tommy's. Not enough. It only made the ache worse. In her mind she'd hoped tonight was THE night.

Now, row H, slot thirteen. An unlucky number. Often she felt unlucky, born under a bad sign. But maybe that was changing. She was making progress: Tommy finally had asked her out!

After the fiasco of her prom night, she'd dreaded he might never speak to her again. Frankly, she wasn't sure she wanted to speak to him, either. Then, after a miserable month of them ignoring each other, he'd started showing up wherever she was. When the girls had gone to see Vincent Price's The Tingler *at the theatre, Tommy had suddenly taken the seat next to her. At the Dairy Queen, she'd been eating a banana split and talking with Reanne Masters. Tommy came up, sat down and ate half her sundae, as if it was the most natural thing to do. When her mouth dropped open in shock, he fed her spoonfuls of the soft ice cream.*

It unnerved her a bit, to be honest. For two years she'd worked hard to 'casually' be where Tommy was, hoping to garner his attention. Suddenly, this past month, he'd turned the tables and dogged her steps. She'd washed the car last Sunday; he had come over and helped. When a bunch of the kids went down to the Kentucky River for a picnic at the sandbar before Lock 8, Tommy had been in the group. He'd swum with her: later, after dark, sat beside her and roasted marshmallows by the bonfire. Then, in the moonlight, he'd walked her up to the Lock Keeper's bell tower. He said out of the blue, "I guess I'm going to have to ask you for a real date."

She'd gotten a little huffy. "Don't do me any favors, Tommy Grant." She'd whipped around to go back to the others by the fireside, only Tommy caught her arm and pulled her close. He leaned her back against the tower's frame and kissed her until her toes curled. Her first kiss.

When he finally broke away, he said, "We both know where this is all heading, but let's take it slow, easy. First step—how about going to the drive-in next Friday night?"

Now, she sat in Tommy's car at The Windmill, hardly able to believe this wasn't another of her hungry dreams. She looked at Tommy as he shut off the car, reached for a speaker and hung it on the glass, rolling it half way up. She sighed at those beautiful hands—hands she'd envisioned upon her body. Oh, when she stared into those green eyes, slow and easy never came to mind.

She knew they preached good girls don't. Well, she was Tommy's girl now. She wanted to be his wife, his lover. Good was the last thing on her mind.

All these beautiful fantasies constantly filled her, where Tommy was hers and she belonged to him, body and soul. Only, in those sparkling dreams, she was never the one making the moves. Tommy was older. She'd always imagined he'd know precisely what to do and not need a push.

As Woody Woodpecker ha-ha-ha-HA-ha-ed his way across the screen to the soft lull of the windshield wipers, Laura wondered how Tommy would react if she pounced on him.

"You're quiet tonight, Laura," he commented. "A penny for your thoughts."

"A penny? I think they're worth a quarter."

He smiled slowly, shifted in the seat to slide his hand into his left pocket. He pulled out a coin, took her hand and put the quarter into her palm, then leisurely closed her fingers around it. It was hot—hot from his body heat.

"There's your quarter. Now what's on that pretty mind?"

She sighed. Sometimes men were so thick! Very deliberately, she dropped the quarter down the front of her top, lodged it between her breasts. She'd worn a deep V-neck sweater, hoping to give Tommy a few ideas. Guess she'd have to hit him over the head. "If you want the quarter back you have to go and get it."

Tommy stared at her, not blinking, as if she'd lost her mind. She wondered if she'd suddenly begun speaking a foreign language.

Then he moved—so damn fast it scared her.

He shifted, one hand on her neck, the other on her waist,

pulling her against his chest and kissing her. Not sweet, closed mouth kisses, either; these were dark and hungry, his mouth open on hers, molding her, shaping her, turning, his tongue thrusting into her mouth. Hell, her first kiss had been just the week before at the bell tower. This was French kissing! For an instant she wasn't sure she liked it.

The girls were forever gossiping and sniggering about French kissing; she'd always wondered what it was like. It seemed so wicked, so racy. She'd imagined Tommy kissing her like that, but this wasn't anything like her daydreams. It was . . . more. So much more. Suddenly, she liked his tongue dueling with hers.

Tommy devoured her with a hunger she didn't know could exist. Oh, her body pulsed with urges. This was painful. Her breasts were sensitive, hard, aching for Tommy's hands on them. Her womb cramped with a desperate need, and she knew nothing but Tommy inside her would ease the feeling. Fire skittered through her blood.

Tommy broke their kiss, resting his forehead against hers. "Damn it, Laura, I said we needed to take this slow."

She smiled, hearing the breathless hitch to his words. "Slow? I forget the definition of the word."

"Do you know how long I've wanted to kiss you like that?" Tommy ran his left hand up and down her ribcage.

"No, how long?"

"Too damn long." He moaned and closed his mouth over hers again, taking her to heaven. Then Tommy scooted sideways to gain a better position, his elbow hitting the steering wheel, causing the horn to beep . . .

Tommy cursed, "Damn . . ."

"Damn it, do you hear me, Asha?"

A pounding ache spreading through her brain, Asha blinked. Jago had the dome light on and was speaking to her in worried tones. The cat jumped around her, then stuck his wet nose against her cheek before Jago pushed him gently aside.

"It's okay. She's coming around." He laughed derisively and then shook his head. "You've got me so upset I'm talking to the stupid cat."

The cat whipped his head around as if he resented being called stupid.

"Asha—damn it, do you have epilepsy? I know some people don't have full seizures, they sort of phase out sometimes. If that's the case, I'd like to know so I can be prepared how I should handle these spells."

"Sorry . . . just a little woozy." Her head ached and her stomach suddenly was queasy. Maybe that part was the damn chili dog. "I phased out?"

"Yeah, just like you did at the pool."

"I do not have epilepsy."

"Don't lie to me, Asha."

"I'm not. Really."

"Then I think you need to go see a doctor and have a physical," he suggested.

No, it was *more* than a suggestion. Like all men used to authority, he just commanded and expected to be obeyed. Still, she smiled, knowing it came from concern. Reaching up, she stroked his cheek.

There was a growing pain in her head, but she knew there was nothing really wrong with her—at least, nothing a doctor could fix. Being Scottish, she accepted what she was experiencing. Somehow, she was picking up images from Laura Valmont's life; however, if she told Jago that, he'd really push her to see a doctor—not an internist, but a shrink! She couldn't begin to understand what was happening to her or why. Right now, to try and reason it for herself, let alone present a case strong enough to convince Jago, was more than her poor brain was capable of doing.

"I'm sorry, but could we go back to the motel?" she asked.

Jago nodded, already raising his seat back. He leaned

over and fastened the seat belt around her, then started the car. His eyes were full of worry.

Asha almost laughed. If he was apprehensive now, it would be nothing compared to when she told him she was channeling 1964.

Chapter Fourteen

Jago stepped from the shower—his *cold* shower—and vigorously toweled off. Picking up the pair of navy sweatpants folded on the commode, he tugged them on, trying his best to ignore the throb already returning to his groin. Yes, restlessness was back, a ravenous beast growling to be sated. This time, he didn't bother going to the refrigerator to see what there was to eat; he knew precisely what he wanted and it wasn't food—though he really wouldn't mind another chili dog. He wanted Asha. And nothing but she could assuage the hot flames of hunger crawling under his skin.

The fat feline rubbed against his legs, clearly steering Jago's steps toward the kitchen. "Guess one of us wants grub, eh? Sorry, I didn't buy cat food in Leesburg— since I don't have a cat." He looked down at the shiny black beast with glowing orange eyes; the creature seemed to smile at him. Did cats smile? He shrugged. This one did.

"Colin— Oo-it—is right. You need a name, but damned if I know what to call you. I never had a pet before. You'll have to be patient with me, Puss."

While growing up, his brothers and he'd never owned a dog or cat. They'd been too poor and always moving about. Later, he'd been busy working. The bachelor's life, a lot of it spent traveling, didn't lend itself to having an animal needing you there to care for it.

He didn't dismiss what his mother had gone through to keep the family together—what Des had gone through—but he'd spent too many damn years living with the same old heartache. He was just so tired of it all, wanted Des' plans done, so he could finally move on. The bloody past consumed too much of the present, their future. Gritting his teeth, he pushed back all the memories of his mother; her pain and suffering, her constant living in fear; how the tragic death of their father and the fallout afterwards had molded the Mershan brothers into fiercely determined men.

"Men missing so much in our lives." He exhaled, bending over to snatch a can of spring water tuna from the lower kitchen cabinet. Opening it, he dumped the tuna onto a saucer for the silly feline. "Here. Chow down, pal."

With the cat happily stuffing his face, Jago considered how to kill the next few minutes. When he'd brought Asha back to the motel, she'd quickly made excuses of wanting to be up early, and ducked into her bungalow.

"Not even a goodnight kiss, Puss. The wench doesn't trust herself. The woman wants me; she just has this strongly developed flight-or-fight response going. Fine. I let her escape. Run, but you cannot hide, Asha. I only granted you a brief reprieve."

He'd accepted her brush-off on the surface, come back to his new home-away-from-home to shower and change into something comfortable, before implementing his plan to invade her cozy little bungalow for the night. He was merely waiting now, giving her time enough to go to bed and get drowsy; he had a feeling she'd be easier to handle in that state. Pacing, he ran through different approaches to use on her, trying to tumble to the right one.

He could tell Asha wanted to distance herself after the drive-in—for several reasons, he assumed. One, things had been getting pretty intense between them before Colin knocked on the car window. The other matter troubling her: these damn blackouts. They disturbed him, too. Something was wrong. The second attack had been slightly less frightening than the one at the pool the night before. Nevertheless, she'd scared the bloody hell out of him phasing out like that. Her skin grew clammy and she lacked any response to touch or voice. Her beautiful eyes turned to doll eyes. He couldn't recall his heart ever beating with that sort of fear—at least not since he'd been a small kid and his mother was in one of her black moods. That had been a child's alarm. This was a man terrified, powerless to aid the woman who was coming to mean so much to him.

"Men don't deal well with helplessness, Puss. Makes us cranky. Give us something to pound with a hammer, slice in two with a sword or screw down with a Phillips and we're in our element."

The cat looked up from his Charlie the Tuna meal and yawned. When Jago didn't have anything else to say, he went back to scarfing down the fish.

"Great. I'm boring the mouse mangler. Well, I can't take any more waiting and talking to you like a blethering eegit, so I am off to play guardian. Enjoy yourself, Cat-With-No-Name. Feel free to make use of the bed."

He turned off the lights, except the nightlight in the kitchen, and then let himself out. As he was pulling the sliding patio door shut, Fat-fat-the-Kitty-Cat came barreling out, determined not to be left behind—so determined that he nearly knocked Jago's legs out from under him. Shaking his head, Jago locked the door and walked the few steps down the stone walkway to Asha's cabin.

As he knocked on the door, he was buffeted by the winds. They whipped the trees, sending more leaves to fall, and warning that another storm was headed their way. The cat leaned against his legs for shelter. When there was no answer, Jago rapped again, a little more insistently. This time the light flicked on in the living room, and he could see the shadow of Asha coming to the door. Glaring at him with a sleepy frown, she pulled the edge of the drapes back.

She wore a thin silk wrapper, of an iridescent shade like pearl. A very sensual gown. Unbelted, it gaped open to reveal matching silk boxer shorts and a plain white, muscle T-shirt underneath. He about swallowed his tongue. With the thin cotton clinging to her breasts, the dark circles of her areolas visible through the semi-sheer material—the sleepwear was an odd combination of pure sex and a touch of innocence that was a punch to his gut. He tried desperately to remember why he'd come.

"Let me in," he said, not quite a command, but close enough. Her eyes traveled to his bare chest, then down to the cat he was wearing as an anklet. "Okay, let *us* in."

That brought a reluctant smile to her mouth. She clicked the lock and opened the door, but only a few inches. The cat rammed his chubby body through the crack, squeezing his way into her cozy little cottage. Fine, if the pussycat could do it, so could he. Placing a hand on the door, Jago pushed it open, making her step back.

"What . . . do you think you're doing?" Asha bent down to pick up the cat, clearly intent on evicting him. Jago figured he wasn't far behind, unless he did some quick convincing. She groaned as she hefted the feline into her arms. "Ugh. No cat is this heavy. You must be a nose guard for the Chicago Bears in the off season."

"We've come to keep you company—that's what we are doing."

Asha shoved the cat against his chest, hard. "Take your—"

"Pussy?" he supplied with an impish grin. He just kept his hands on his hips, staring at her as she pushed the cat at him again.

She pursed that kissable mouth. "When in America . . . They use that word *differently* here."

"Oh?" He gave her his most innocent expression. "Do tell. How do they use it?"

"Eegit, take your cat and leave. You're not getting in my bed by flashing that sexy chest." Asha tried to appear grumpy, but didn't quite succeed. She sounded breathless.

"My chest is sexy? Guess it matches my sexy lips, eh?" He moved forward, stalking her as she backed up, until the kitchen bar hit her backside. Placing a hand on either side of the counter, he trapped her. He leaned near, letting her feel the high heat of his skin. She clutched the rotund cat to her chest like a shield. "Want to see what else on me is sexy, Asha?"

He moved closer to where she could only inhale his male pheromones. He tilted his head to the side of her face, nuzzled the hair against her ear. If she was getting as much of a buzz off him as he did her, he'd better stop pushing her buttons and ease down a notch on the sexual play. "This night is going to be hard enough—no pun intended there—so I better back up before you jump my bones and I can't fight you off."

"You arrogant . . . Ooooh . . . *me* jump *your* bones?" Asha fussed.

"See, Puss? The cat doesn't have her tongue, after all." Jago chuckled, then lightly kissed her cheek. "Relax, Angel May, I didn't come over here to offer myself up for your depraved sexual abuse."

"You didn't?" She blinked, confused. Disappointed?

He chuckled at that expression. She looked so deliciously rumpled that he wanted nothing but to take her to bed and make love to her—all night. Though it might put a crimp on his libido—tonight was about making her trust him. He wanted hot sex with Asha. Hey, he was male and she intrigued him, lured him, taunted him more than any woman he had ever known. Only, he wanted more than one night with Asha Montgomerie.

As matters stood, the whole situation was pretty complicated. His falling in love with Asha hadn't been part of

Desmond's plan. He needed to gain her trust or things between them could spiral out of control, maybe destroy them both.

"You, me and What's His Name are going to bed—to sleep. Just sleep, Asha." He reached out and cupped her cheek. "Your spacing out scares me, lass."

"Oh . . . that." She wouldn't meet his eyes, but instead looked down at the cat she was holding. "Nothing to fash about."

"Okay, I won't. Nevertheless, you had an occurrence last night. Another tonight. I'm *not* leaving you alone. End of discussion."

Ridiculously, she shoved the cat at his chest again. "What makes you think you can come in here and dictate anything to me—"

His hands took her upper arms and yanked her to him. The poor puss was squished between them, but Jago didn't let that stop him. He kissed Asha, took her mouth with every ounce of ravenous need she provoked within him. Not gentle, he channeled all the fear she'd caused with the two blackouts into passion, let loose the hunger that had him prowling to the refrigerator several times a night for months. The pounding drive to mate promised this was the one, the only woman for him. Fortunately, the cat was still between them and squirming. That last shard of reason stopped him from lifting her atop the counter and taking her right there.

The cat squealed, bringing back sanity. Every muscle tensed within Jago as he reined in his out-of-control emotions. His mind swam, dizzy from wanting her, as he brushed his lips once more over hers. Asha nearly caused him to come undone as she opened her mouth, giving him access to her warmth. Leaning down, he scooped her and the cat into his arms and then carried them to the bed.

Setting her down, he pondered where the bloody hell all this chivalrous nature came from. "Tonight, I just want to be near you—make sure you are all right."

The cat stomped happily across the duvet, long claws puncturing the material. The silly beast was smiling again.

"I'm glad one of us has something to smile about," Jago muttered.

Jago wasn't getting much sleep.

Just as his body stopped going off like an Asha Geiger Counter and he'd start to doze, she'd shift in her sleep, bump some sexy body part up against him and it'd cause his groin to stir to life with an insistent ache. This time she rolled when he was on his side, shoving that cute little tush up against his loins. To make matters worse, as he was trying to keep from gritting his teeth until they cracked, the blasted cat stalked up his body and decided to perch on his hip. As long as Jago kept his eyes open, the bloody feline stared at him, smiling. Giving up, he pulled the sheet over his head and pretended to sleep.

After several minutes, the animal shifted and lay down, still on his hip and thigh. While he knew the thing didn't weigh fifty pounds, it sure felt like it. The longer they both remained in that position the heavier he became.

He considered dumping the pest, but he'd have to move to do that and he rather liked lying spooned against Asha. It would be snug, cuddling like this on snowy winter nights. The vision was easy to conjure with the wind still blowing outside. Some sort of shrubbery was at the back of the bungalows; the breeze forced the small limbs to scratch at the bedroom window. In his mind snow howled, piling up deep, stranding Asha with him—and the cat—for days. Maybe at Christmastime.

He smiled at the dream. Nearly echoing his mood, the cat noisily purred. Absently, Jago reached out his hand and patted the pussycat's head, oddly finding comfort in ruffling the animal's fur. Maybe having a kitty was a good thing.

A discordant note filtered through his dreams, causing him to awaken. He listened, trying to pinpoint what had pulled him away from something beside chestnuts roasting before an open fire. There was nothing. Nothing but the scratching of the bushes against the glass. Not a sound he heard normally, still the winds had been going on for several hours. Why did the scraping bother him now?

Almost holding his breath, he lay there listening. The refrigerator in the kitchen kicked off, so the silence was stronger. Nothing but the non-rhythmic scraping of the bushes. *Scratch . . . scratch . . . scratch*. Feeling as if he was listening for something that wasn't there, he sighed and started to relax again. He smiled in the darkness. Maybe if he was lucky, sexy Asha would wake up horny and want to have her wicked way with his body.

The dissonant noise came again. And it wasn't just his mind conjuring the sounds; the kitty heard. He'd stopped purring and his head turned toward the window, ears alert. What finally convinced Jago something was not right: the cat's ears laid back and he growled lowly, similar to a dog.

Carefully pushing the cat off his leg, Jago slid from under the sheet and out of the bed. Trying not to disturb the sleeping Asha, he moved in silent steps to the window. His instinct was to yank the shutters wide and confront whatever dared intrude upon his domain. Instead, being his usual careful self, he tried to peek through the cracks of one panel. The scraping stopped. It left him holding his breath and waiting for the noise to come again. He stood frozen for a minute, then decided to beard the devil and snapped open the louvers.

The gray light of dawn greeted him. His eyes strained, trying to see in either direction to the edges of the building. Nothing. The European snowball bushes provided a splash of autumnal color, but blocked him from seeing if there were footprints on the ground.

His head snapped around as he heard a faint tapping near the front door, almost like a bird pecking. " 'Only this, and nothing more,' " Jago muttered to the cat, who still lay on the end of the bed, also looking in that direction.

Quickly crossing the bedroom, Jago headed through the living room. Asha's purse on the counter caught his eye, and he recalled that she carried a gun. Opening the handbag, he found the revolver, the weight feeling as if it was made for his hand. Quickly checking to see it was loaded, he walked straight to the patio doors and silently unlocked them. With a jerk he pulled them open.

Again, there was just the wind lowly whistling through the trees. Jago glanced in both directions, but spotted nothing out of place. No footprints on the walkway, but since the wind had dried off the dew that wasn't atypical. Barefoot, he stepped out into the damp morning. Going to the corner of the bungalow, he looked toward the rear of the cottages. He paused, listening. No odd sounds. A beat-up truck puttering along the road in front of the restaurant was the only manmade sound.

Walking toward the other end of the cottage, near his own, he tried to put a finger on the vague feeling gnawing at him. Before, when he'd heard the noises, he almost sensed something *off*, a danger lurking close. Now there was a void. Nothing.

He glanced down to see the cat curving around his leg. "Maybe just my imagination," he said to the feline, and he might have accepted it as truth but for the cat's attitude. The puss was calm, curious and just tagging along. No laid-back ears, no growling. "Oh well, the riddle remains unsolved. Come on, race you back to bed. There still might be a chance Asha will wake up and want to abuse my cute little bod."

As he placed his hand on the door to her bungalow, he heard the phone ringing in his cabin. He looked back and frowned, wanting to ignore it. There would only be three people calling him—Des, Trev or Julian. Des wanted regular check-ins, progress reports. Trev would want to gloat, which Jago could do without. But there was also his mother to consider. Always in frail health, she seemed to be slipping away from them both mentally and physically.

Though Des refused to admit there wasn't anything his money couldn't fix, Jago feared she was slowly losing her battle with cancer. Sighing resignation, he headed back to answer the call.

Snatching the phone off the table, he barked into it, "This better be good. It's not yet six a.m. here."

Not wanting to leave Asha alone in her bungalow, and yet thinking it best she didn't hear any of the call, he moved to the front door, where he could watch Asha's cabin. He was still uneasy about the earlier noises.

"My, you're chipper this morn. Sorry, did I wake you? It's time for elevenses over here."

Trevelyn sounded too damn smug. He was lucky he was several thousand miles away or Jago might be tempted to make his twin look a little less like him. Sometimes it was damn irritating to share the same face with one so totally opposite in temperament.

"I suppose there's some purpose to this call other than to piss me off?"

"Grouch. Isn't it enough to want to know how my twin is doing in Hicktown?" Trev chuckled, only it grated on Jago's nerves.

"Don't call them that." He didn't snap, but his tone sounded short. He was irritated, defensive and really didn't feel like putting up with his twin's arrogance.

"Oooh, touchy. Tell me little brother"—Trev referring to the fact that he'd been born first, by a whole twenty-one minutes—"are you falling under the spell of Asha Montgomerie?"

"You know, I'd really like to punch your face right now, Trev," he said, but it lacked real force, just typical brothers fussing.

His twin laughed. "It's been a while since we had a donnybrook. I'll give you a rain check, how's that?"

"You're on. And for your information—I'm not under the spell of Asha."

"That's good to know. The Montgomerie sisters descend

from the *Cait Sidhe*—so I am told by Raven—a race of witchwomen from the Picts. Looking into her eyes, I can believe it. They light a fire under a man's skin, set flames to licking at his brain. I was concerned you were not strong enough to withstand their witchy magic."

"No spells, no magic," he stated flatly. "I'm in love with her, and if all these Machiavellian plans don't ruin my chances, I want to marry her."

"You're daft, man!" Trev's disbelief was clear, his tone derisive. "You don't even *know* her. What? How long? Four days? You been pulling at some jug of Kentucky moonshine, Bubba?"

"No moonshine. It doesn't change anything."

"She must be one hot lay—"

"Again, be thankful you're on that side of the Atlantic, Trev, or I'd mop the floor with your pretty face. Of course, it won't be so pretty after I finish rearranging it, but then you'll appear handsome—all scarred like a warrior true."

"Bloody hell. You haven't gone to bed with her yet, have you—"

"Goodbye, you SOB." Jago punched the end-call button, breaking the connection. When the phone started ringing in his hand again, he stabbed the ringer-off button, and then looked at the cat. "Just be happy you don't have a twin brother. They're the bane of life."

As he started back to Asha's cabin, he glanced up the hill toward the drive-in. He noticed that on the far end of the last row, you could see down onto the bungalows from there. The black truck—at least he thought it was the same one that had gone up the road a few minutes ago—was parked there, motor off. Jago stared at the vehicle for several minutes, then went back to his cabin to slip on shoes and a sweater. He tucked Asha's gun into his belt, intent on going up the hillside, checking out who owned the truck, and what he was doing in the drive-in at this hour.

When he came out, the truck was gone, no sign of where it had vanished.

Chapter Fifteen

Jago's head hit the pillow, a sigh and a smile on his lips. He had driven demons away from the door—with the aid of his trusty sidekick . . . *What's His Name*—vanquished an irritating brother with his rapier repartee, and now both the conquering heroes were ready for a well-earned nap.

Rain now lashed at the window, but it was a soothing sound, nothing like the noise that had come before. Sleepy, Jago rolled over and pulled Asha back against him, the action natural, as if he'd done it a thousand times. The heat in his body instantly escalated; his poor aching groin complained. Still, he did his best to ignore that hard cramp of lust, reminding himself, after the last ten months of feeling little more than apathy, it was oddly enjoyable to experience this voracious need.

Asha rolled in his arms until she was facing him. The minx was awake. Uh oh, visions of gasoline and lit matches came to mind. She wiggled her toes, performed a small, drowsy stretch and then rubbed her ankle against his. She asked groggily, "Where did you and your shadow sneak off to?"

"We went chasing monsters away from the door."

"Ah, knights in shining armor are so sexy." She gave a low, throaty chuckle that nearly made him come undone.

"This is nice." He hooked his leg over hers and used it to nudge her closer. "Rainy, lazy morn. Just us cuddling."

The cat waddled up his thigh and rumbled a deep purr, causing them both to chuckle. He butted against the back of Jago's arm. If he were human, he'd be saying, *What about me*?

"Just . . . *nice*?" She ran the tip of her index finger over the edge of his upper lip, then his lower. Her glowing eyes studied his face, hungrily taking in every detail of his reactions to her.

"Okay . . . very nice."

Stroking her thumb over his eyebrow, she said, "You know, the cat will need a rabies shot and all the childhood kitty disease shots and boosters so you won't have to worry about him getting sick."

The feline's head jerked up at the mention of shots and he glared at Asha.

Jago laughed. "I don't think he's keen on the idea of someone poking him with a needle. Can't say I blame him. I don't like needles either. Big bad Trev nearly faints at the sight of them. It's so funny." He kissed the tip of her nose. "Only, why am I expected to foot the expensive bill of his continued existence? He seems to have done very well before showing up here to adopt me."

Annoyed, Asha started to shove away from him, but he held her firm. She struggled in his arms. "Oh, yeah, I can see where a cat would crimp the style of Mr. Jetsetter—"

"Whoa, Asha, I was teasing. The ridiculous beast is growing on me." He glanced at the cat, who was settling down to take a nap on his hip. "Literally. I'm playfully protesting—adjusting—to something new, unfamiliar to me. We can find a vet Monday and haul his sorry arse there, and I'll happily pay the bill. Things are moving a little fast—for us both—but we know something rare, something special is happening between us. I'm sure each of us has been burned in relationships before. It would be nice if we came programmed to go straight to the person who was the perfect mate for us. But then, maybe Fate tosses us some jerks along the way to make certain we appreciate how extraordinary it is when the real thing walks into our lives. I could tell you where I think this is heading, but then I doubt you're ready to believe me. So, why don't we just relax, listen to the rain and enjoy being together. Or . . . I could tell you that when you walked through the door of The Windmill, it was like you materialized from the sun's blinding shafts, an image branded into my memory, so that when I'm old and gray I'll recall that instant and how it moved me . . . *changed* me."

Feeling his life distill to this single moment in time, Jago reached out and took her braid. With slow movements, he undid the stretchy band around the ends, then unwound the three sections of auburn tresses. In the dimness of the bedroom her hair appeared almost brown. He couldn't see the golden threads woven through the mane, but he could feel the silken softness as he pushed his fingers into the heavy mass. He arranged the long length over her shoulder, draped it so it fanned out. His mouth crooked at one corner as he noticed how the strands fell across the outer curve of her breast, almost clinging to it.

"Smart hair . . . lucky hair." He lightly traced the roundness of her full breast with the tip of his index finger.

She half closed her eyes; her breathing shifted, shallow, faster. "I . . . I cannot think . . . when you are doing that, Jago."

"Me neither." He closed the path of his finger to where he was circling just around the rim of her nipple. "Thinking is highly overrated anyway."

"Hmm . . . I agree." She shifted, pushing on his shoulder until he was flat on his back and she was on her knees, straddling his hips. She said with a wicked grin, "Before this goes any further, I think I should warn you that I'm multi-orgasmic." She leaned forward and impishly lapped at his nipple with her hot little tongue. His breath drew in on a hiss and he had to fight to keep his body from bowing off the bed.

"Ah, you are? Clever lass . . . ah . . . you are. Impressive. Delightful. Am I lucky or what?" He chuckled, thinking how happy Asha made him.

That caused him pause. He'd been content before—pleased, thrilled, entertained. He'd enjoyed various aspects of his life, such as when he saved Mershan International a bundle in a takeover. But had he ever really been happy? Just happy?

She ran her hands up his chest and then over his shoulders. "Well, actually, that's not quite the truth. I think I *would* be multiorgasmic if I had a man worthy enough."

"Even better. Certainly sounds like something that would make me 'rise' to the occasion. So you *think* you could be this 'sexual marathon maven' if someone were to hold *up* his end of the bargain?" He gave a faint up thrust of his pelvis to punctuate his question.

She flexed her hips so that the V of her crotch settled perfectly over the ridge of his erection taut against his belly. "Ah, think? I'm rather positive I could be."

"I think you would be, too. Multiorgasmic is my new favorite word."

His hands on her waist, he splayed them, then worked them up her ribcage, holding her tight. He jerked her to him, his mouth opening on hers, hot, demanding a response, demanding her surrender. Covering her lips with his, Jago coaxed, wooed, teased, challenged, until she opened and allowed his tongue the entrance he solicited. He sighed, having found what he'd been seeking his whole adult life.

The weight of her breasts rested on the tops of his hands, tempting him to enjoy their fullness. He loved the feel of the cotton T-shirt, how the material stretched out over them. His deft fingers moved upward, squeezing her breasts. She liked that. Oh, did she like that! Only, she wanted more. He rubbed his thumbs over her nipples, felt them hardening as the knot of desire tightened within them both.

Rearing up, he captured one tight budded breast with his mouth and drew on it through the thin cotton, sucking hard. She cried out as the spasm of a climax ricocheted through her, shocking her, catching her off guard. Clearly, she'd never expected the orgasm to hit before he was even inside her body. Neither had he.

"One," she gasped, then laughed.

"Oh, that's a tossed gauntlet if ever I heard one." His mouth moved to her other breast, pleasuring it with teeth and tongue, sucking rhythmically until he made her shatter yet again. This time she was anticipating it, tried to resist but couldn't, then finally succumbed to the force. He smiled at the play of expressions on her face revealing all.

"Ah . . . ah. . . . oooh," she panted.

Jago grinned unrepentantly. "Two."

Scooting back so that he was half sitting up, he kissed her luscious mouth—gently now, just for the sheer delight in kissing, as if he could do it for hours. Then he grew cognizant of the soft cotton pressing against his bare chest, the spots damp from his mouth, and the friction was suddenly unbearable. He wanted to be flesh to flesh with Asha and nothing else would do.

Evidently, the same thought filled her, for she pulled back to let her hand dance over his feverish skin, snaking it between their bodies. Her tongue tip peeked through those well-kissed lips as she placed her palm along the blatant bulge in his sweatpants. Then she was pushing them down, her fingers curling around his rigid, pulsing length. He was hard, very hard, and heavy in her grasp, pure male power, a visible manifestation of how deeply he wanted her. Her thumb rubbed back and forth over the ridges in his flesh, making his body buck with each gentle, curious stroke; then she brushed her thumb pad up and over the tip, almost savoring his softness.

"Enough of that. I can only stand so much torture before our little experiment is blown . . . umm, so to speak."

He shoved her onto her back and pulled her silken boxers slowly over her hips. Rotating so that he was over her lower body, he sifted the fingers of his right hand through the soft curls to find that cute little button, one of her control points that could push her into a shallow climax. He circled slowly with his thumb, then he leaned forward and closed his lips about the tiny knot, grazing it with the sharp edge of his teeth. Heat of longing burned between her legs, nearly scalding him. Her hips started to move, but he pinned one thigh with his chest, the opposite with his elbow, until she had to lie there and take the sweet torture. She reached down and fisted her hand in his thick hair; the fingers at first tugging back, then holding him there. Her low moan skittered along his skin, killing any idea of holding back.

Being a smart ass, he couldn't resist. "Three."

He rose up on one knee, positioning himself against her hot slick opening and then entered her in one sharp thrust. She nearly keened in release as her body both protested his invasion and yielded up her surrender. Her strong internal muscles closed about his erection, squeezing its length.

"Four," he groaned.

Teeth gritted, he was determined not to give in to his own release until she was thoroughly satisfied that she was multiorgasmic. However, there was nothing to say *he* had to do all the work. Still inside her, he gently rolled until she was sitting on top of him again. Her hoarse cries told him she still rode the edge of her last climax, so he flexed strong against her inner walls, the tip of his cock finding and butting up against that little walnut-shaped nerve, the key to her achieving a deep orgasm. Two strokes and she came apart. Loudly.

"Five, Asha."

He nipped the side of her neck, then sucked hard. He'd mark her: that idea made him almost growl ferally. Marking his mate with his brand of possession pleased him. A very primitive urge. Very empowering. Off in the distance, Jago heard the slow roll of thunder. It made him smile, wondering if he really heard the rumble or if it was just the magic of Asha.

"Do you hear the thunder?" he asked.

"Hmmm?" Too caught up in the splendor of their passion, that was all she could reply.

"Let's see how long it takes to reach fifteen." Grinning like an idiot—a very happy idiot, he said, "We're riding the thunder, lass."

With a low groan, she put her arms around his neck and held on.

Still tired from the lack of sleep—and a rather vigorous morning of healthy, demanding, 'multiorgasmic' exercise—Jago stifled a yawn. Arching a brow, he watched the black Jaguar slowly roll down the driveway of the horse farm and park next to Liam's red Viper and the farm's pickup truck. What's His Name curled around his boot and rumbled loudly as Asha and Netta climbed from the Jag.

Asha wore a navy, scoop-neck sweater, the sleeves pushed up to her elbows, her ever-present heavy Celtic cuff bracelet on her right wrist. Her long auburn hair had, once again, been tamed into a proper braid that hung over her left shoulder and down to her waist. She was so bloody beautiful she robbed him of breath. Her head turned in his direction, obviously assessing him as he did her, though she was hiding behind a pair of dark sunglasses.

"It's wary-time again, Puss. She let down that drawbridge

this morning in the pale gray light. Now her fight-or-flight response is kicking back in, making her scared—especially after I did a cut and run with barely a good-bye kiss. You and I might be in the doghouse . . . so to speak." The cat meowed up at him. "Now, do I give her space and let her repair that invisible wall between us, or do I immediately push her buttons and remind her how she moaned when I was inside her?"

There were no two ways about it: Asha was obviously ticked at him. After teaching her just what a 'climax virtuoso' she was, he'd dashed off with barely an explanation of where he was going. In the heady heat of lust, he'd forgotten that he'd made an appointment to buy another Harley from one of Derek's friends. The man, a long-haul truck driver, was going away for two weeks immediately after church was out in Leesburg. A half hour late, Jago had to fly to catch the trucker before he left. Now, he could tell the quick kiss and the "be back later" he'd tossed over his shoulder hadn't gone over well with her at all.

Tail twitching, the fat feline watched Asha as if giving deep thought to the problem. He looked up to Jago, *meerrrrrrred* and then offered one of his silly smiles.

"Yeah, that's what I thought. Look out, Asha, this knight errant is on a mission," Jago said lowly. Bending down, he scooped up the feline and half draped him on his shoulder before heading to greet the women.

As he approached he could see Netta's face was scrubbed free of make-up; her hair wasn't styled, but pushed back in a ponytail. That fresh-face look made her appear twenty-something instead of her age. She glanced around tentatively, clearly ill at ease and trying to hide it. Once again, Jago sensed a vulnerable young girl lurking under that veneer of brass and sass, one who obviously had been hurt deeply. He wondered if she knew this rarely seen side of her slipped through now and again. He doubted it, figuring she would ruthlessly quash it if she were aware.

He'd been raised with two brothers, but in an odd way Des, Trev and he had been the caretakers of their mother. She suffered from what they now called bipolar disorder, and at times the mood swings were near crippling. For small children who didn't understand what was happening to their mother, the ordeal had been frightening to watch. In a role reversal, her sons were the protectors; they had watched over her, soothed her when the dark malaise gripped her soul and demons of fear came knocking.

Maybe that accounted for the emotions that rose within Jago as he smiled at Netta. He'd never had a sister, but he suddenly experienced a spike of brotherly protection toward this unusual woman. Netta's vulnerability touched the same chords of protectiveness within him.

Asha stuck her hands in her back pockets and approached. Her hesitation was apparent, as she pushed the Foster Grants down to the end of her nose. "I like your fur muffler." She reached out and patted the cat. "He still needs a name, though."

"He hasn't told me what it is yet. In India they believe a cat has three names—the name you give him, the one he answers to and his real name. I'm waiting until he cuts to the chase and gives me number three." He leaned over and kissed her, soundly. "I'd say that's a good morning kiss, but I've already had one of those. And it was *good*. On a scale of one to ten . . . hmm . . . I would say—fifteen?"

He watched her blush crimson, her amber eyes widening at his taunt before she shoved her sunglasses back in place.

"Glad *some* of us were kissed good morning." Netta flashed Liam a glare that said *eat dirt and die*, the strength not lessened by the old-fashioned Wayfarer sunglasses hiding her eyes.

"I have a headache," Asha announced. "I hope you have some aspirins, brother mine. I'm out. Someone—just before he ran off with no explanation of where he was going—stole my last two."

"In the medicine chest, top shelf. Help yourself." Liam replied with an easy grin.

Netta shrugged and started walking after Asha. "I guess I'd better keep her company."

Jago leaned his arms on the fence rail, watching the retreating women. The cat climbed off his shoulder and entertained himself by walking along the fence top, nearly falling twice. "Not having any sisters—"

"Lucky man. I have seven. I must've gotten your share." Liam tapped Jago's arm. "How about I bum one of your cheap-arse cigars. They're growing on me."

Jago withdrew the package from his pocket and held it out. After Asha's brother had taken one, he removed another for himself, then flicked his lighter for them both. "I was wondering, what it is about women having to go to the bathroom together? Is there some unwritten law which poor males aren't told?"

"If there is, they must cross their hearts, spit on the floor and take an oath never to reveal the deep dark secret." Liam exhaled a stream of smoke, as he watched the stallion prancing in the pasture. "Being a gentleman, I'll pretend to ignore that you shagged my sister last night, and instead ask what you think of my horse?"

Jago stared at the chestnut thoroughbred, recalling Liam had used the term *represents the breed*. The stallion fit that. Never had he seen a more beautiful horse. Something inside him craved to possess this animal the same way his heart craved to possess Asha.

"You're wrong about last night." He waited a heartbeat before clarifying, "It was this morning. As to your horse—I want him," Jago declared, hungrily observing the animal prancing about the paddock.

The corner of Liam's mouth tugged up in a half-smile. "For a man who lists his residence as London, England, you seem rather intent on acquiring a lot of big ticket items that need a home and care here. Sort of like a man setting down roots. Derek's Shelby, Dale Winston's Harley this morning . . ." What's His Name came waddling along the fence, getting the hang of balancing his *fattitude*. Liam chuckled. "A cat. My sister."

Jago laughed. "I didn't acquire the cat . . . he acquired me. And your sister is not up for discussion. Stop changing the subject. I want the horse, Montgomerie."

"Seems you're the one changing the topic, and no discussion needed. If you hurt her, I'll beat the ever-loving shite out of you," Asha's brother chuckled.

"She has the power to hurt me—maybe more." Jago's response was both truthful and evasive.

"Fair enough." Liam stared at him in assessment. After a moment he seemed satisfied and returned the topic to the horse. "I'm not sure Thor's Thunder is for sale. He's special."

"Name your price. I won't quibble." Jago set his jaw, resolute in wanting to own the animal.

Liam smiled. "I haven't decided he's for sale. I'm thinking of him being the foundation of a new breeding line for the farm—"

"Provided you have a farm. If Trident buys it then I can get the horse anyway," Jago teased.

"*If* Trident buys it. I'm still determined to hold on to Valinor. I've a few aces left up my sleeve. Also, even if your firm gets the horse farm, Thor's Thunder won't be a part of it. He's mine. I bought him with my own money. He doesn't go with Valinor. Besides, if I put him on the market, his price tag would be pretty steep."

"I can believe it. And he'd be worth every penny. Again, name your price. Whatever it is, I'll meet it," Jago said determinedly. "Consider—if you sell him for his pretty price tag—that would be a nice drop in the bucket to fight Trident."

"You do play hardball, don't you?" Liam arched a brow. "For a man just passing through you are collecting a lot of 'toys.' Now you want my horse."

Jago placed both of his arms on the upper rail of the fence and settled his chin on his hands, watching the stud. His glance flicked to Asha and Netta coming out the front door of the house. "A man is only passing through when he doesn't know where he's headed."

"And do you know where you're headed?" Liam pressed.

Jago hesitated. He'd only known Asha for a few days, and he never acted rashly. He was the cautious Mershan, the quiet twin, the one who was content to watch his two nearly overpowering brothers—men who thought they could remake the world according to their wishes. It was sitting hard on his conscience that their plans would cause a backlash on Asha, Liam and their siblings. At times, the pain of the past overwhelmed Jago, so he could only imagine how deeply it had scarred Des who'd suffered most, and understood what drove him. He loved his brother. Yet, none of that would stop him from claiming Asha.

"I know where I've been. I'm not happy there," Jago admitted with resolve, with sadness. "And only a fool doesn't see what is before his face."

Asha came up and patted What's His Name, and then glanced to the horse. "Isn't the stallion gorgeous?"

"He is indeed. That's why I'm buying him."

Surprise lit her face. "His sire is one from the line of hunters bred on Falgannon Isle by the Mackenzie twins. I hadn't realized Liam was selling him. Thor's Thunder is his pride and joy."

"*My* pride and joy now." Jago flashed a devilish smile. "I'm buying him."

Asha glanced to her brother. "I didn't know you were putting him on the market." It was more of a question than a statement.

Liam shrugged, and gave her a secretive smirk. "I haven't said I would."

Jago's smile spread wider. "You will."

Asha took off in a jog, calling over her shoulder, "Wait 'til you see *my* baby. He's all mine. And you can't buy him."

Jago watched that cute little derrière bounce in her snug jeans as she trotted to the barn to fetch her horse. He grinned and petted the cat. "I won't have to," he said under his breath. "He'll be mine, too, when I marry you."

CHAPTER SIXTEEN

Asha glanced over at Jago by the edge of the barn's hayloft. The tall, double doors were wide open, permitting him to stare out at the gentle, late-afternoon rain. His elbow was propped against the doorframe, as his eyes skimmed over the rolling scenery of the countryside. One of the most beautiful times of the year for the state, vivid autumnal hues kissed the panoramic view of Valinor's perfection, breathtaking in the falling mist. When the sun punched holes through the clouds, a rainbow magically arched over the barn. Kentucky certainly was putting on an awe-inspiring show for Jago Fitzgerald.

Even so, Asha wasn't sure he truly appreciated Nature's display. He was in a pensive mood. Often given to brooding herself, she permitted others the same space to be contemplative. Poor man, a lot of changes were happening in his world all at once. Likely it was as scary to him as it was to her that they'd started a relationship, despite barely knowing each other. He now had a Shelby, a second classic Electra Glide—she didn't want to know how much he'd paid for that toy—and now he was determinedly trying to buy her brother's horse. She smiled at What's His Name chasing imaginary mousies in the loose straw across the loft's floor—at least she hoped they were imaginary! And Jago had a cat—though he was still protesting the point of who owned whom. These were weighty responsibilities for a man a bachelor too long.

An odd memory came to mind about her grandmother, Maeve, telling her to get a man young and raise him the way she wanted. *After twenty-five they're too set in their ways and not worth the trouble*, she had assured her granddaughters. Of course, Maeve came from another era, when people married and had families in their early twenties. Had life ever really been that simple, or were there just less options to confuse things back then?

She had a feeling Jago was worth the trouble.

"I generally spend Mondays and Tuesdays at the river house," she told him, trying to sound casual.

Not waiting to see his reaction, she picked up the pitchfork and stabbed the sharp prongs into a bale of clover hay. Pushing it to the opening in the floor, she dropped the feed through the trap door. Being nosy, the cat poked his head over the opening and peered at where the hay bale landed.

"Watch it, bud. You lean over much more and you'll lose your balance. You're not the most graceful of putty tats," she fussed at the feline.

That finally drew Jago's attention back inside. He took a couple of steps, leaned over and snatched the cat by the tail, then kicked the trap door shut. "I'm not in the mood to find out if kitties really do land on their feet when they're dropped. My luck, you'd be the exception to the rule and I'd have a puss with four casts on his legs expecting me to tote him around." He turned to Asha. "So, do I get an invite to the house on the river?"

"Despite Indian summer temperatures, it's a little cool to go swimming. I enjoy a brisk swim, but most people don't. However, I thought we could—if you were of a mind—take the boat out for a ride, maybe have a picnic on the sandbar near the lock. The view of The Palisades is breathtaking from the water."

"I'd be open to a dunk in the river—especially if I had something to warm me up for all the trouble. Think we can arrange a little heat afterward? Do we need to pack, or can we just jump on the Harley and head out?"

"You merely want to take your Harley for a ride. Sigh, used and cast aside. And here I thought you might be a lad who'd enjoy a 'roll in the hay'—literally," Asha said with a theatrical waggle of her eyebrows.

"A 'roll in the hay' would top the list of my *101 Things To Do On A Rainy Sunday Afternoon with Asha*. Riding my vintage Harley would be second. A close second, mind." Jago's eyes flashed playfully. "Only, I figured rolling around in the hay wasn't a smart option. If brother dearest pops up here and finds me 'teaching you to count', he might get a little irate. Brothers are known to be rather Neanderthal where baby sisters are concerned."

"Hmm . . . how do you know Netta isn't teaching him *one . . . two . . . three* . . . right now? Maybe they are already in the hot tub. Could be why we haven't heard a peep from them in the hour since we've come back from horseback riding."

His face brightened as he grinned wolfishly. "Hot tub? Your irritating brother—who won't sell me his horse—has a hot tub?"

"Liam isn't annoying. I rather think you two are evenly matched in being stubborn."

"As I said—irritating."

"You just like to buy things. You bought the Harley this morning. You don't need to purchase the horse today."

"I want the horse," he persisted.

"You are bloody unrelenting when you want something."

"Yeah, I am. Very persistent." He kept coming, in his stalker mode again. A predator on the prowl.

Jago caused her blood to buzz with a mix of anticipation and terror—terror she'd be hurt because there was no shielding her emotions from this fascinating man, this beautiful man who half-killed himself this morning teaching her the magic of 'counting to fifteen.' *Crash and burn* was the mantra of her Doubting Thomas side these days. Even so, there'd be no walking away from him.

"Come on. The rain has stopped. The sun's peeking out. I want to ride my bike."

"Oh, gor. I've never ridden one of these things before," Asha said nervously. She accepted the black leather jacket Jago handed her. "Thanks, it's beautiful. What did you do . . . mug his wife for it?"

"I bought the jackets and helmets, too. His old lady is expecting in February and wants all traces of the motorcycle gone. She was afraid that if the jackets were there, it would tempt him to buy another bike down the road. It's a little big for you, but will do for now," he said, adjusting the snaps at her waist.

Taking a helmet from the handlebars, he pushed it on her head. Being slightly claustrophobic, she instantly hated the thing. Still, she gritted her teeth and tried to grow accustomed to the necessity, knowing the protection was vital. Even so, some part of her couldn't exorcize her mind's eye of the foolish image of riding the Harley with her hair blowing in the wind.

Taking her hand, Jago led her to the bike. He instructed. "Remember, right is wrong. Get on the bike from the left side. Put your hands on my shoulders and then mount it."

"Like climbing on a horse."

"Yep." He swung his leg over. "Just like it."

"Or like a man wearing an earring," she kidded.

Jago laughed softly. "You made me think of a friend—actually, my brother's right-hand man. He wears an earring."

"Oh? In his *right* ear?" She slid her leg over the leather seat and then lightly bit his left earlobe.

"No, his left. And if Julian came anywhere near you, I

might have to beat him to a pulp." She thought he growled, but he started the bike, warming the engine up, so she wasn't sure.

That deep throttle thunder was unlike any sound she'd ever heard. There was a majestic power to the noise, akin to a lion's roar in the jungle, proclaiming he was king. Jago smiled. "Feel the rumble between your legs. It's riding thunder."

Asha settled on the seat and put her feet where he told her. Then he pulled her arm about his waist, so that she was pressed flush against his back. She tried to control the riot of sensations thrumming through her body. The low-throated vibration of the bike, being plastered against a very hot male, proved there was something very sexual, very intimate about riding the Harley with Jago.

He set the bike to wheeling down the drive, scaring the horses in the pastures on either side. As he pulled onto the main road he slowed, but then he throttled the bike and it roared, flying off down the highway. Asha gave up trying to look at the scenery, just turned her head and laid it against Jago's back. The landscape, buildings and trees all went by in a blur; she closed her eyes and relished the rushing sensation and the warmth of Jago's body. The whole experience was peculiar, in that she gave over everything to him, accepted him to protect and care for her. Trusted him completely.

The ride was relaxing and yet deeply profound in ways that she had trouble expressing. She felt strange, glorious, alive. She quickly learned to lean when Jago did, working with him, them becoming a part, an extension of the bike. Riding the Harley with Jago was very much like having sex. No wonder men loved these machines!

The word caused her pause. Love. She was in love with this man. It was too damn soon. She knew so little about him. Still, that didn't matter. She had opened her heart to him as she had never opened it before. That terrified her more than flying down the highway at 60 mph with the wind ripping at her.

Jago was right. They were riding the thunder.

Jago loved the feel of the Harley. Pure ecstasy. He opened the throttle and let it rip, then glanced down at the tach, seeing there was still power left to call upon. If it were just him on the monster, he'd run the bike full out, but since this was Asha's first time, he took pity on her and kept within the speed limits.

As he leaned into a curve, he noticed a reflection in the rearview mirror. Since the trees heavily lined both sides of the road, with leaves still half-clinging, the afternoon shadows were long and in heavy contrast. At first he thought it was just a trick of light. But the distraction kept catching his eye.

Finally, on the last curve, he noticed what kept pulling his attention: a black truck. It hung back, nearly out of range of his mirror. Generally, he wouldn't even pay it mind. Only, the memory of the truck being parked up at the drive-in when it was closed came to mind.

Prickles rippled up his spine.

Tommy, what's he doing?

Asha's grip on Jago's waist tightened as the voice filled her brain. *Not now*, she prayed.

Before, when she'd been assailed with the memories of Laura Valmont at the pool and the drive-in, she had totally zoned out. At the pool Jago had been there; he would've caught her if she'd fallen. In the car, she had faced no physical danger, but here, losing consciousness, and slipping into a past that happened over four decades ago, could be costly. She might fall from the bike, or cause Jago to lose control. The prospect was scary. She gritted her teeth and tried to fight the images.

Oh, please not now. Her mind tore in two. Part of her was

on the back of the motorcycle with Jago. Another part was channeling images from Laura and the 1960s.

Tommy, I'm scared.

Asha was scared, too. She faintly shook her head as if she could dispel the overpowering recollections of Laura, but the insular feel of the helmet made it harder to fight the flashes. The narrow, winding road Jago had taken seemed familiar, though she'd never been on it before. However, Laura Valmont had, in a fire-engine red Ford Mustang.

Pulling back from the past sucking at her, she grew aware Jago had picked up speed. The sense of everything zooming by in a blur was dizzying. Her arms tightened about him and held on for dear life. *Please, stop! Oh, bloody hell, please stop*! She wasn't sure if the thoughts were hers or Laura's.

She tried not to squeeze Jago too tightly, yet it was hard to judge. Instead of bringing the motorcycle to a halt, he gunned the engine. The bike almost jerked on the back wheel. She gasped as the Harley roared down the road. They were nearing the cliffs. Have mercy, Jago surely wouldn't take the old abandoned road? Glancing up, Asha caught sight of the reflection in the review mirror; she then risked turning her head to see. A dark truck bore down on them, keeping pace with the motorcycle's flat-out speed. As the pickup gained on them, Jago again goosed the Harley, nearly causing the back wheel to spin on the wet pavement. The monster leapt forward, keeping them out of harm's way.

Asha held her breath as the truck inched closer and closer. Her heart racing like the motorcycle engine, the sound of the tires on the wet pavement, the roar of the Harley—all blended into part of the nightmare from the past. She swallowed her own panic. It doubled, as she tasted the terror of Laura Valmont.

A scream ripped through her brain as she struggled for the last vestiges of reality. She could not lose consciousness at this high velocity. She would die. Jago would die.

We're together. We'll always be together. Just like the song, our love will never die.

Never die. Never die. Never die.

Just as Asha opened her mouth to let her scream meld with Laura's, Jago cut the bike to the left and shot down a narrow side road, barreling down the dilapidated lane. The truck roared on past. Jago skillfully spun the bike in a 180-degree turn, so that he sat, legs braced, facing the mouth of the small road. He waited, gunning the Harley, clearly fearful the idiot driver might come back.

Shocked by the experience, and still being drawn into the past, Asha climbed off the bike, barely aware of what she was doing. Some part of her mind recognized Jago's concern; even so she couldn't stop as her steps carried her toward a strange, deserted building at the back of the nearby lot. It called to her. Without knowing why, she had to go to it—was compelled to go to it. Strange, the thing being out here in the middle of nowhere . . . similar in fashion to The Windmill.

The damp weeds of the field were up to her thighs. Most were dead, except for the creeping honeysuckle and wild rose briar on either side of a faint path, some patches nearly over her head. Several long canes reached out, almost snatching at her; she dodged as her steps carried her on. Broom sage, Queen Anne's lace—all dead, long dead, and not just from this past summer, but the summer before that and likely several summers long ago. Judging by the looks of the derelict land, it hadn't been cleared this decade, possibly a decade or more before that. Who knew the last time it was used?

The building wasn't cared for, only half-heartedly secured against vandals. As if no one ever came here; no one cared if they did. So weathered, the wood of the plank siding was a colorless grey. Plywood had been nailed across the front of the place, covering the windows and doorway. Someone had spray-painted a peace sign and the words

Hell no! We won't go! in red on one warping board. The Vietnam era? The paint was fading away.

Asha paused at the bottom of the steps, contemplating if the porch was safe, but then decided to go around to the back instead.

Behind her, she heard Jago calling, but his words were carried away on the waves of memories fighting to surface within her. As she circled around the side, she heard a flapping noise. Her steps slowed as she neared.

The sound came from an odd addition to the building. Originally, she'd judged, the structure was a simple L-shaped house. Possibly someone had lived here once. At some later date, the extension—what looked like a small pavilion—had been grafted onto the back. There were no walls to this part of the structure, just sheets of unpainted plywood covering the two open sides. One wooden panel had been pulled half down, hanging diagonally by a single nail. Behind the boards was a heavy circus tent-quality canvas, gray from age and ripped in a couple places. The wind caused the end to flutter, the metal grommets of the rings knocking against the wooden post.

Asha hesitated for a moment, uncertain if she wanted to pull back the sailcloth and see what lay beyond. Just as she worked up enough nerve, Jago touched her arm. Her mind snapped back.

"Asha, are you all right?" He reached out and brushed the back of his hand to her cheek. She offered Jago a fleeting smile, trying to reassure him, only her attention remained divided. The clanking of the metal grommets against the poplar wood post was a siren's song, calling her.

In a sad voice, she told him, "It seems so small now."

"What's small?"

She heard his words—ignored them. Moving forward, she grasped the canvas and lifted it back. In a flash, everything about her surroundings shifted, changed—as they had by the pool. Instead of the dingy, forlorn pavilion, the white canvases were rolled up to the roof and tied back, leaving everything open to the night air. Colored Christmas lights were tacked along the poplar wood rail that ran along the outer edge of the small skating rink. Eydie Gorme's "Blame It On The Bossa Nova" played over the speakers hung on the walls. The skaters could rock to the music while going around and around. Laura loved the dizzying sensation, loved the spinning colorful lights, similar to the feeling of being on a merry-go-round.

No, no, the bossa nova.

Then she saw him, standing by the post, watching her. *Tommy.* So handsome. And she loved him more than she loved life.

"Asha, damn it." Jago jerked her around by the arm to face him. "What the hell is wrong with you? And don't bother telling me you need a Pepsi."

With a faint shudder, Asha's mind returned to the present. She glanced about the dingy building. No Christmas lights. The hardwood floor was ruined by the decades of the lack of care and intruding rain. No music. No skaters. No Tommy and Laura. However, Tommy Grant and Laura Valmont had once stood here on a hot summer night over four decades ago. For some strange reason she was being shown their young lives, their special passionate love.

Though all about her was now back to normal, an oppressive air of sorrow lingered; it pushed against her mind to where a tear came to her eye. She wasn't sure why seeing a beautiful memory like the one she had just experienced should leave her so profoundly shaken. The couple's love was so clear, so beautiful. Laura and Tommy were extraordinary people. Though these flashbacks left her rattled, she felt Laura was giving her a gift. That gift should bring joy, happiness. Instead, she was overcome with a poignant, heartbreaking sadness.

Silent tears streaming down her face, she smiled at Jago, trying desperately to hang on. Just hang on. "I wish I had known them."

Poor man, he stared at her, totally confused, fearful. "Who?"

"You're now sorry you went to bed with me, eh, Jago? You're scared I'm crazy as a loon." She reached up and touched his beautiful face, cupped his cheek. "I'm not sure I can explain, since I don't really understand myself." Dropping her hand, she walked in a small circle. "This used to be a skate rink. They came here on summer nights. Played music. Mostly the girls skated. The guys just watched them in their tight pedal pushers. They decorated with strands of Christmas lights, made it festive. Others would park their cars out here, and would sit on the hoods observing, too. The nights would flicker, alive with lightning bugs, turning everything magical. It was a gentle time. A happy time."

As she talked the images grew so strong, the music filtered around her. " 'I wonder what went wrong, with our love, a love that was so strong,' "—she sang the lyrics to the tune she could hear.

"Del Shannon's 'Runaway,' " Jago identified.

Asha's head whipped back to him, almost hopeful. "You hear it?"

If he could hear it, too, maybe she wasn't going insane. She gave him credit. He listened for a minute, but then shook his head no.

"You're hearing Del Shannon?" he asked solemnly.

She chuckled, trying to make light of the bizarre situation. "Actually, no. You'll think I'm totally nuts. I'm now hearing 'Alley Oop.' "

" 'Alley Oop'?" Jago huffed a small laugh, but concern filled his dark green eyes. "Sorry, I missed that one."

"I'm sure it's on the jukebox at The Windmill. I'll play it for you when we get back." She smiled, fighting the tears. Her tone sobered. "I'm not crazy, Jago."

"You just go around hearing 'Alley Oop'?" He shoved his hands in his back pockets and looked at her, guarded. "I read once about a guy, his tooth was turning his mouth into a radio. Somehow, he was receiving music through his filling. Maybe you need to have your fillings checked."

She shrugged. Walking to the rail, she put her hands on it and gazed out at the abandoned property. "It might account for the music. Only it doesn't cover Tommy and Laura."

"Tommy and Laura?" he echoed, his disbelief rising. "The lovers from that song on the demented Wurlitzer?"

"Yeah, 'Tell Laura I Love Her' by Ray Peterson. It was very popular in the early '60s."

"Maybe you're fixing on that song—for some reason?"

"Tommy Grant and Laura Valmont. They used to come here. They were very much in love."

"Used to? Were?" he challenged.

A flock of birds were suddenly flushed from the stand of trees, the crows' caws filling the late afternoon sky. Jago took her elbow. "Come on, we can figure out Tommy and Laura later. We need to get out of here. Now. The sun is already starting to go down and I don't want to be out on the bike after dark. Do you know anyone with a black pickup truck? A Ford. Not a new one."

"Around here? Half the farmers, most likely. There are some trucks that are from 1940s still in use."

"I think we were being followed."

"That nut in the truck?"

"Yeah. This morning I noticed a black truck in the drive-in, parked in that corner where it could look down on the bungalows." Jago encouraged Asha to sit in front of him this time, clearly not trusting her to safely hang on behind him.

"I wouldn't worry about that. Colin drives an old Ford truck. It's black. That was likely him cleaning up the trash left from the night before."

"Any reason to think Colin might mean you harm?" he asked as he handed her the helmet.

She shook her head. "Sorry, you're barking up the wrong

tree there, Jago. Colin would never hurt me. There isn't anything he wouldn't do for me."

He shrugged, unwilling to let go of his doubts. "Colin is in love with you. Maybe he resents you letting me into your life."

He gunned the engine and set the Harley wheeling down the road.

Chapter Seventeen

"I'd say I want to buy this house, but I think you might hit me," Jago teased, as he poured The Macallan Scotch into two old-fashioned glasses and then added a dash of water and a couple cubes of ice.

Asha merely smiled as she diced carrots, a cucumber and fresh mushrooms for the salad. Her eyes filled with pride as they followed him around the living room. He couldn't contain his covetous gaze; he savored the rugged beauty of the honeyed oak and red cedar plank-covered floors, ceilings and walls, the high, exposed beams overhead. The whole front of the three-story, A-frame was mostly glass, with no curtains to obscure the breathtaking view from the lodge at the top of the hill. It opened onto a huge deck, which jutted out slightly over the hillside.

What's His Name zoomed about the house, his tail vibrating like Jeep in the old Popeye cartoons. Upon arrival, he'd first rushed to the kitchen—as though making sure the house came with the necessities—then he'd dashed here and there, checking everything. Poor thing nearly wore out his fat self.

Once his inspection was complete, he started to spray the fireplace to mark it as his. Asha had tossed a throw pillow at him, screaming, "Don't you dare!" and warned him they had made an appointment at the vet's on Friday. She grumbled something about turning him into a eunuch if he sprayed the first thing in the house. He must've believed her for he behaved after that. He quickly established his favorite spot on a window seat near the river stone fireplace. Just a minute ago, he'd run over, hopped up on the recessed window and focused on a squirrel, sitting and chattering on the deck rail in the twilight. The cat turned his head and gave Jago one of his funny smiles, the orange eyes clearly saying, *Yeah, this will do*.

Jago scratched the kitty's broad head. "Yeah, this will do nicely, Puss," he murmured lowly.

"Stop whispering to that mangy cat," Asha teased.

The cat whipped his head around and glared at Asha, clearly saying, *Who's mangy*?

"You two can conspire all you want—I'm *not* selling this house. My house. Mac left it sitting, neglected for years. I've spent a lot of time getting it into this shape." She shrugged. "I guess it has memories for him—about my mum—ones that he'd rather dismiss. Only, I find peace here. When I cut the deal to trade him my shares in the farm for his part of The Windmill, I made him toss in the house to balance the exchange."

"Why do you stay at The Windmill motel when you have this absolutely marvelous castle atop the hill to live in?" This was biting at Jago, had been from the start, how the Montgomerie sisters were often at odds with their upbringings, seeking quiet, less flamboyant lifestyles than that of the ancient English manor, Colford Hall.

Asha shrugged, going to the refrigerator and removing cheese. "This is a *home*. I love coming here, working on it, bringing it back to life. Only, it needs more than just me." She concentrated on running the block of aged cheddar back and forth across the hand grater, clearly avoiding his stare. He could see she didn't want to say, *It needs a family*.

"I love this house, lass. I can't imagine one more perfectly designed. It's elegance and style, and yet comfortable, welcoming—you feel like you could put your feet up on the coffee table without breaking some unwritten law. It conjures images of hot summer nights grilling outside, fireflies flickering in the woods, or spending a Sunday curled up by the fireplace with a good book as snowflakes fly by the window. Here the world seems so far away, like we're the only ones for miles around." The sound of a car in the drive broke Jago's fantasy. He leaned to see out the back door. "Well, almost. Your brother's Viper."

"Liam—the worm." Asha wiped her hands on the apron about her waist, then untied it.

"And Netta," he added.

"Maybe they came for supper," she said hopefully.

"With suitcases? Yeah, right." Jago arched his eyebrow and then lifted his glass in salute. "Fe fi fo fudder . . . I smell the blood of a nosy big brother."

Tossing the apron on the island counter, Asha flipped on the porch light for them. "I'm not sure fudder and brother really rhyme. This is *my* home. While he's welcome for supper, I didn't invite him for a co-ed slumber party."

Liam opened the door of the screened in porch for Netta. Juggling a sack and his leather duffle, he permitted her to come on through to the kitchen. Asha pulled open the inside door and gave them a grin. Netta rolled her eyes and lifted her shoulders in a faint shrug, letting Asha know this wasn't her idea.

"For you." Netta chuckled and handed her a bouquet of cut mums.

"Thanks . . . I think." Asha gave Liam a big fake smile, her eyes flashing daggers. "What a surprise. It's been so long since we've seen you, Brother Dearest. What—an hour and a half at least?"

"I missed the scintillating conversation and delightful company," Liam said, nonplused. He dropped his duffle and held up a sack with his other hand. "We brought steaks and a strawberry pie."

"Which you stole from *my* diner." Asha crossed her arms and glared at him.

Undeterred by her cool welcome, Liam leaned over and kissed her cheek. "I knew you wouldn't mind. Hey, I cooked and fed you brunch. Payback time."

"I'd be delighted. Go fire up the grill; we can get the steaks going. I wouldn't want you out past your bedtime." She took a vase from under the sink, ran it half-full of water and then plopped the flowers in, not bothering to arrange them.

Liam turned and accepted the Scotch Jago handed him. "Dream on. I'm not driving back on that narrow cliff road in the dark." Raising the glass, he offered a big grin. "Especially when I have been drinking. Fancy meeting *you* here, Fitzgerald."

"Jago, don't abet his fibs by feeding him The Macallan. He doesn't deserve it." Asha growled. As the cat waddled over and sniffed Liam's leg, she smirked. "Sic him, Putty Tat. Him you can spray all you want."

"Haven't you named that animal yet?" her brother inquired.

"Liam, why are you here?" Asha asked, picking up the chopping knife.

Liam ignored the question. "You will learn, Jago, the men in my family strictly abide by three rules concerning my sisters. A matter of sheer survival, actually. First rule—never let any of them behind the wheel of a car when they're pissed. Second—keep them away from sharp objects." He took Asha's hand and removed the knife from her grip. "And third and foremost—protect your *breall*. Of course, being males perhaps we should've made that rule number one."

"Breall? Which is?"

"*Breall*—Gaelic for that which a man most treasures."

Jago laughed. "All rules duly noted and filed away for future reference." Accepting the long grill lighter from Asha, he repeated her question, "So, Liam, why are you here? Brother's protective mode stuck in engage?"

"And here I thought you wanted me to seduce him to leaving the horse farm alone," Asha taunted when Liam again failed to answer.

Jago picked up the cat and started outside. "This night could get very interesting. Puss."

"Or stay very, very dull." Netta fixed Liam with her blue eyes.

Jago wasn't sure if that was a comment or a threat.

Despite still being mildly irked at Liam for pulling his big brother watchdog routine, Jago was in a mellow mood after the delicious steak and salad. He thoroughly enjoyed being at the river house, and had enjoyed the fun time outside grilling with Liam and What's His Name. Most especially, he loved the sweet promise of many more like it.

His frame of mind soured after they had finished dessert and were getting ready to go to bed.

"Jago and I can bunk together in the master bedroom. That way, Netta and you each have a room." Liam announced, as if that decided the matter.

Jago couldn't help it; his eyebrows lifted at the suggestion. Obviously, brother dearest was a chess player, with plans on capturing Queen Netta, while protecting Queen Asha. *Over my dead body*, Jago swore to himself. "While I like you, Montgomerie, you're not whom I had in mind to cuddle with tonight."

Liam shrugged. "Beggars cannot be choosers."

"I was invited. That puts you in the beggars category, eh?"

Asha made a sour face at her brother. "This is my home. I'd appreciate you letting me decide where guests sleep."

Liam tossed up his hands. "Fine. You decide."

"Thank you," she replied, getting clean sheets from the linen closet. "Netta and I shall sleep together in the loft, and you two get the rooms on the landing."

Liam looked disgruntled. "The beds in those rooms aren't full-size, just old-fashioned three-quarter beds. The loft one is king-size."

Asha grinned impishly. "Yeah, I know." She shoved the sheets to his chest, and then pinched his cheek. "'Night, 'night, William Francis."

"Francis?" Jago almost snorted. "As in The Talking Mule?"

"Up yours Jayyyyyyy-go. *No one* is named Jago." Liam sneered good-naturedly and pushed the sheets back to Asha. "Seriously, the king-size bed would give us males more room. Three-quarter beds were *not* designed for men's bodies."

Jago said, "I'm almost afraid to ask what a three-quarter bed is?"

"Instruments of torture. Two inches shorter in length than a regular bed and about five inches narrower. Mickey Rooney would never complain, but I have to scrunch up or my feet hang over. I'll have a pinched nerve in the morning," he warned his sister.

"You should've thought of that before you invited yourself to a sleepover." Asha shoved the sheets at him again and then walked off, leaving the two men standing in the hall of the landing, staring at each other.

Liam glanced at his sister going up the stairs, and then down at the sheets and pillowcases he held. "Well, bugger."

"Not working out as you assumed, Mr. Chess Master?" Jago's snigger slipped out when he saw Liam's flummoxed expression.

Liam exhaled his disgust. "Enjoy wiggling your toes all night, Jayyyyygo."

"Sure, *Francis*." The cat shot past Jago's legs, heading straight for the bed. "Yeah, well, *I* won't be the one sleeping alone tonight."

"This has to be the longest night of my life," Jago grumbled to the fat feline a little while later. He paused from his pacing back and forth like a caged panther in the landing bedroom. His skin on fire, there was no sleeping. When he'd lay down, he'd half drifted, images of his morning with Asha flooding his mind, haunting, tormenting him. Opening a jalousie window to let in the cool air, he leaned on the frame, permitting the night's dampness to flow over his bare chest. He'd love to go jump in the river, let the water bring down the temperature within his body, however they'd arrived at the river house too late to explore the bank and discover if swimming was safe here.

Just as his muscles relaxed and his groin stopped its insistent throbbing, he heard steps on the stairs, coming down. His head snapped up, and he knew without doubt that it was Asha. He was not sure how, since he'd never before heard her steps when she was trying to be silent. Maybe it was the animalistic mating instinct she aroused in him.

"Looks like I might get lucky after all, Puss," Jago nearly purred, heading to the door. The beast yawned and stretched, then settled back down on the bed.

Asha had reached the landing and was coming down the hall as he opened the door. Wearing a black silk wrapper, she gave him a sleepy, sexy half-smile—which died as Liam's body filled the opposite doorway. He glared at her in brotherly fashion and then he nearly growled at Jago. Jago glared right back.

Asha put her hands on her hips. "Enough is enough, Francis. Go to bed."

"I will, if you will." Liam flashed a threatening grin.

Jago wanted to shove the man's teeth down his throat, especially when Asha went back upstairs.

An hour later the scene was repeated, only this time the shoe was on the other foot. Netta came downstairs, likely heading to the kitchen for something to drink since her steps lacked any stealth. Liam was waiting to waylay her. Jago made sure to time it so he got to his bedroom door just a heartbeat after Liam popped out of his. The cat was sitting on the end of the bed, watching as if things were getting interesting. Asha's brother was grinning like a slaphappy fool as his eyes took in Netta in the red robe. That grin fell off his face as he saw Jago.

"I could really grow to hate you, Jayyyyyyygo," the man snapped.

Netta laughed, gave Liam a little wave and continued on past.

Jago stretched, folded his arms and then leaned against the doorframe, showing he was staying until Netta went back upstairs. Which is what happened. Netta came back, wearing a milk moustache, which Jago was sure Liam would love to lick off. Instead, he just glowered at Jago. Once Netta was in the loft upstairs, Jago gave Liam a little wave that aped Netta's and turned back to his bed.

A pillow came flying through the hall, hitting him in the back of the head.

" 'Do wah diddy diddy dum diddy do.' " Jago laughingly sang the old Manfred Mann lyrics as he climbed into bed and scratched What's His Name's ear.

"What are you doing?" Liam asked, coming into the kitchen a couple hours before dawn.

Jago looked up. "And here I would've thought you a rather highly intelligent male. What does it look like I'm doing, *Francis?*"

Liam opened the refrigerator and shrugged. "Slicing lemons. I figured that much. I meant, what are you doing *with* the sliced lemons."

"Well, I'm not going to run them all over your sister and lick off the juice, that's for sure." Jago was in a slightly perverse mood so he pushed the 'brother button' with glee.

"Ah, you tread into dangerous territory there."

Jago flashed his teeth in a predatory grin. "I'm the one with the knife."

"Ah, you're still pissed that I invited myself for the night." Liam took out the remaining half of the strawberry pie. "So what's up with the lemons?"

"I couldn't sleep, so I'm making lemonade. I'm thirsty."

"Frankly, I need something a little stronger," Liam remarked.

"Me, too, but figured it best I keep my wits about me or I might be tempted to mop the floor with that pretty face of yours."

"Oooh, someone's grouchy."

"It's four in the morn and you're down here." Jago arched an eyebrow. "And you aren't grouchy, *Francis?*"

"True. Scotch go well with lemonade?"

"Scotch goes well with anything, but who says I will share my lemonade?

"You *are* ticked. I'll share my pie," he chuckled.

"It's not your pie. But share anyway." Jago took the sliced lemons and use the electric juicer. "Point of curiosity. You were fine yesterday morning about me sleeping with Asha. So, why the overly protective brother routine now?" Pouring the juice into a pitcher, he added sugar, water and ice. Stirring, he watched Liam, waiting for the answer.

"I had no problems—until you came back from the bike ride. Asha was pale, shaken. Giving her a royal scare on the Harley, not caring if—"

"You really want me to pound on you to relieve my frustrations, don't you?" Jago exhaled his frustration. "I didn't scare her on the bike. Two peculiar things happened. Some guy in a black truck—maybe—tried to run us off the road, and then we came across some sort of old pavilion in the middle of nowhere. She says it was used as a skating rink back in the '50s and '60s."

"Edgar Casey's old place?" Puzzled, Liam accepted a glass of lemonade and carried it and his pie to the table out on the glassed in porch. He pulled out a chair and sat down.

Jago took a chair at the end of the glass-topped table. "I have no idea what it was called. There were no signs—outside of a Vietnam protest spray-painted on the boards covering the windows. That tells me it's been boarded up since the '70s."

"Yeah, Old Edgar was a bootlegger. Not that I know

much about him, mind. A bit before my time. Delbert has talked about him once or twice. He and his wife lived in the house. He built it himself on the corner of her mother's land. Mommy dearest owned a big antebellum house on top of the hill, and when she died, Edgar and the missus moved up there. Long gone now. Burned down. After they moved up to the manor, they decided to turn the old house into a moneymaking venture. He built that old pavilion on the back side for a skating rink. He would haul in a trunkload of beer and bourbon on the weekends. Was a big thing around here. Casey's was miles outside of the city limits, so there wasn't much they could do about it. No one cared. They kept it respectable. Why would that upset Asha?"

"Not sure. Know anyone with a black pickup—good condition, but not too new? I don't know trucks well enough to know the year or model."

"Dozens. A lot of farms have them. A lot of older people still have them—original owners. Oo-it drives one. Why?"

"Colin came to mind. You think Colin might want to harm Asha?"

"Enough with these questions. Oo-it wouldn't harm a fly, let alone Asha. He might kill for her, might die for her, but he wouldn't touch a hair on her head in malice."

"I thought of Colin first thing, and asked Asha. He loves her, you know. I wondered if he might be upset about me in her life."

"Gor." Liam paused several heartbeats to half drain the glass of lemonade. "You've seen too many movies. You can rule out Oo-it."

Jago sighed. "She said the same thing, that he wouldn't harm her. Sorry to be so vague. We were on the bike and I noticed—at least I thought—someone might be following us. The afternoon sun tends to throw long shadows where the trees are heaviest. In a helmet, it was hard to spot at first. Something kept catching my eye, just out of sight of my rearview mirror. Then as I took one turn, I finally got a look. Black Ford pickup. '60s, maybe early '70s. I couldn't see it well enough. Then suddenly it roared up, bearing down on us. I was doing the speed limit, trying to take it easy on Asha since it was her first time, but I kept having to speed up. Then it seemed as if he was pushing us. It got rather dicey, so when I spotted a small lane I zoomed into that."

"Okay, I concede that a hair-raising ride from being chased by some jerk would account for Asha coming back to the farm scared."

"She wasn't the only one. I got the sense this guy was out for trouble. Of course, that was just my impression. I might be wrong." Jago shrugged. "I couldn't see anything the way the afternoon sun kept bouncing off his windshield. Then he sped on past. That's when we found the old house and rink. The damned place is so overgrown with briars you can't really see it from the road. Yet, Asha went straight to it."

"I'm not sure she ever knew about it. As I said, that was a bit before her time."

The pie he was eating suddenly turned bitter in Jago's mouth. "Yes . . . and no."

"What the hell is that supposed to mean?" Liam reached for the pitcher, pouring more lemonade.

"Asha went to the house as if she knew precisely where she was heading. For a moment, she paused at the front, but then her interest was pulled to the rear. She circled to the back and found it partially opened. Almost in a trance, she went into the rink area. Very spooky. She began telling me about the rink, how it had been decorated with Christmas lights strung around the railing. I didn't see any still up, though I did find rusty bent nails as if someone had tacked something to the old handrail. She talked about them playing music, the girls skating, the males watching . . . couples sat on the hoods of their cars taking the night air. The way she talked about it—well, it was as if she had been to the rink back then. No, that's not right. In that breath, it was as though she could see it—as though a part of her *was there*."

"She's never been there," Liam repeated. "This place closed down long before she was born. Some huge skate rink opened in Lexington and everyone went there instead. Casey died, and his wife never tried to keep the business going, so they say. Once they closed the old road, no one goes to the river that way anymore."

"I told you, I assumed it had been boarded up while the Vietnam draft was still going on. I can't figure it. But I swear to you she was seeing it, even singing songs from the era. Dell Shannon's 'Runaway' . . . and she mentioned one called 'Alley Oop.' She said she could hear the music, asked me if I could."

Liam frowned, said nothing, just pushed a glazed strawberry around with his fork.

"These blackouts—"

Liam's head snapped up. "Plural?"

Jago nodded. Scooting his chair back, he propped his ankle upon his opposite thigh. "One at the pool. Then last night at the drive-in . . . she did the same thing. She was normal one minute, then the next staring at me with doll eyes. FYI—that's why I stayed with her last night. She scared me. I didn't want to leave her alone. I was quite honorable and refrained from 'shagging' her—as you so quaintly put it. Sorry, she had other notions this morning. Has she ever experienced blackouts before?"

Liam shook his head no. "Of course, I've been gone two months, back to England, so I can't speak for that time away, but she's never had any occurrences such as these before. Did she tell you what happened at the pool and the drive-in?"

"No. Lack of Pepsi was the excuse at the pool. Second time, she ran from me. This afternoon at the rink was the first she talked about them. I watched her, Liam. She heard the music. She almost had me believing I could."

"We come from a 'fey' family and tend to accept that there are things in the world at which others might scoff,"

Liam said. "Although, this is a puzzler. I have no idea what's happening to her now. This is the first I've heard of any of this."

Jago pushed on, sharing his fears. "The kicker—she mentioned something else. A Tommy and Laura."

Liam paused, then decided he didn't want the rest of his half-eaten pie and shoved it away. "Why do those names ring a bell?"

"That damned song on the jukebox."

"Yeah, but it's not the song. There's something else, something that strikes a memory."

Jago recalled the last names that Asha had told him at the pavilion. "Tommy Grant and Laura Valmont?"

"Yeah . . . now I recall. Some sort of accident on the road where you were today. A long time ago, they were in a terrible car crash. Died."

" 'The cryin' tires, the bustin' glass, the painful scream I heard last.' " Feeling gut-punched, Jago recited the song lyrics, and was suddenly filled with a sorrow so intense that tears came to his eyes.

"That's not 'Tell Laura I Love Her.' That's—"

"Yeah, 'Last Kiss.' It plays on the jukebox a lot, too." Jago fixed Liam with a hard stare, fighting to keep at bay the overwhelming pressure to break down and cry. Not sure why. "So, you're going to tell me what it is with that damn jukebox?"

"Oh, surely you've guessed—The Windmill is haunted."

"Thank you, Rod Serling." Jago wanted to make a joke of it. How serious can you be—a *haunted* Wurlitzer? Then why did he already half-believe Liam?

Getting up, he walked to the picture window overlooking the river, staring into the coming dawn. The night-light hit the large pane so it became a ghostly mirror, reflecting his own likeness, and then Liam's behind him. Slowly lifting his hand, he placed his fingertips so they touched the reflected ones. He was a logical person, used his senses to tell him what was real and what was not. A haunted jukebox? He wanted to laugh how ridiculous the idea was. Only, sometimes you had to open your mind to things you cannot touch.

Like love.

Chapter Eighteen

Enchanted, neither day nor night, the pale light of dawn crept over the riverside, bathing the majestic Palisades in tones of sepia and gray. Asha drew deep solace from this time of day, when the world was still sleepy and nothing stirred; not even birds sang their wake up melody. A wood nymph alone in a mythical kingdom, she stood dipping her toe into the edge of the river and inhaling the earthy scents of water and land. Reaching out with her senses, she drank in the peace of this tranquil instant of half-light.

With a dreamy sigh she shed her robe, the black silk pooling about her feet on the pure white sand. She paused there and permitted the damp morning air to caress her naked form. At ease with this state, she leaned her head back and shook her long hair, setting the thick mass to swing against her hips. She closed her eyes savoring the feel—sensual, liberating. But then, she didn't need anything to awaken that side of her nature. Her traitorous body had throbbed a plaint all night long, yearning to be with Jago.

Preparing herself for the biting nip, she stepped into the

bracing waters and walked out to the middle where it was chest deep. She inhaled sharp breaths until growing accustomed to the pool. Shivering, she had a hard time holding on to the slippery bar of Ivory; it popped out of her hand and tried to float away. She playfully snatched it back, then headed toward the water coming over the top of the high cliffs. The quivers in her body grew stronger as she pushed under the brisk, stinging spray, yet she relished the invigorating flow.

It wasn't really a waterfall. The lodge sat on a small inlet, a finger that jutted out into the river, and when it rained, the runoff at the top of the cliffs spilled over to form a small cascade. After ages of this, a deep pool had been hammered out under its base. Thick ferns on each side shielded the spot from view, lending the spot a secluded feel of paradise found.

Allowing the buffeting water to rain down upon her, Asha embraced its icy slap. Her teeth chattering, she worked the white bar into thick foam, lathered her skin, and then allowed the suds to wash away as quickly as she soaped up. The coolness of the spray muted the heat in her body. Her breasts tightened painfully due to the cold, but that little compared to the ache within her, continued wanting of Jago all night.

Wanting him still.

Closing her eyes, she imagined Jago's strong hands upon her body. She envisioned him touching her, stroking her, caressing her, slicking soapsuds over her breasts . . . and lower. She sighed wistfully. Much lower. Such thoughts provided no ease, merely increased her yearning for him, churning the hunger 'til the force devoured her mind.

Exhaling frustration, she was still disappointed that plans hadn't gone as she'd hoped when she invited him to the river house. She'd pictured a relaxed, cozy meal; just the two of them—*well, three,* she chuckled, thinking of the kitty and how he had inserted his fat self into their lives. Maybe they would've built a small fire, sat before the fireplace and just talked, really seized the chance to get to know each other better. They were lovers now, yet there was so much of his life she knew nothing about. There were a thousand things she wanted to ask, so many little secrets to discover about this beautiful man with whom she was falling in love.

No, that wasn't right. She wasn't falling for Jago. It was much too late for that. Despite everything moving too bloody fast, she was in love with him. Loved him. She sucked in a breath and tried to contain the panic those words caused to surge within her. Yet, terrifying a thought as love was, she knew she couldn't hide from the fact. Men like Jago Fitzgerald didn't grow on trees. A woman would have to be batty not to risk all, hoping to come away with the gold ring. Literally. Well, she was no coward. She was a prideful woman, true. All Montgomerie women were. But Jago was special. She would do what it took to make him want to stay with her in this perfect little pocket of the world she was creating.

"First, I have to get rid of a pesky brother. He ruined the beautiful evening I planned. I'm lucky he didn't have a bloody chastity belt with him," she grumbled, the words nearly drowned by the gentle falls.

Stepping from the hard spray of the spate, prickles of awareness skittered up her spine, a throwback to the virginal maiden sensing a very male presence, intruding upon her private realm. Her head turned in the direction of the perceived threat. Stunned, she dropped the bar of soap; the white square bobbed away and was rapidly carried downstream and out into the swift river, though she neither noticed nor cared.

He must've entered the water while she was under the falls, while the noise blocked her from hearing. A pathetic, blethering idiot, her mouth hung open as she watched the naked man surface, rising like a Celtic water god. She couldn't breathe, her heart dropped and then erratically slammed against her ribs. It was ridiculous that a man could make her feel so foolish, so utterly out of control, but then love had a strange, magical way of doing that.

Placing a hand to her heart, she forced herself to breathe at an even pace, marking time as he waded toward her through the hip-deep shallows, coming onward with a focused intensity that sent goosebumps up her spine. The water was chilly, yet she scarcely noticed anymore. His heated predator's gaze held his prey mesmerized. That last ounce of the timid wood nymph, fearing the power her love gave him over her, screamed, *Flee while you can*. Her heart didn't heed the warning. She would stay right here, waiting for Jago.

Water sluiced off his muscular chest and long, beautiful arms as he reached up with both hands and pushed back the black curls on both sides of his head. Jago's body was hard and lean; he walked with that loose-gaited stalk of a big jungle cat. Coming straight to her. Straight *for* her. The water was deepest nearer the falls, hitting him at mid-chest as he moved closer.

He stopped before her, his dark eyes languidly moving the length of her naked form, barely hidden by the crystalline waters. Too arrogant by half, he prolonged the maddening tension by remaining motionless, just looking. Though confident within herself, under Jago's intense scrutiny she began to fear he wasn't pleased by her body. When they had made love in the bungalow, they'd been shrouded in half-light and shadows. Desperately, she wanted to please him. She wanted to slap him for his arrogance. She wanted to kiss him.

The corner of his mouth finally twisted into a sardonic smile as he reached out and wrapped his hands around her neck, the strong thumbs caressing the column of her throat and tilting her head back. With a hunger that was nearly terrifying, his mouth covered hers. There was no gentleness, no teasing; this was a warrior laying siege and refusing to accept anything less than complete surrender.

Sharp pangs of desire lanced through Asha's body, grinding, twisting painfully inside her, while overpowering emotions blotted out logical thought and vanquished any residual qualms. Only the primitive urge to mate remained. She would walk through fire for this man.

In the manner of an artist memorizing each detail, his eyes traced over her face. There was a quiet desperation, a raw hunger in the dark green depths, as though he held something very precious to him, something he feared he might never possess. That rattled her.

"You want moonlight and roses? Gentle kisses to your hand? Words of love? Promises? You deserve all that—and more, Asha. I can give you those things. Later. Much later. Right this minute, I want you—all of you. Here. Now."

His thumbs drew a line down her throat, the strong hands splaying over her shoulders, along her arms, finally to clasp her waist. He yanked her body against the length of his, let her feel his erection pressing insistently against her belly. Her whole body tightened in a biting voracity that clawed at her muscles, her mind, ripped through the good girl façade and let loose the wild woman craving to be set free. In echoed response to his touch, her womb contracted into a hard knot that pushed past agony. She burned in a hunger so devastating that the power humbled her. The questing fingers slid over the curve of her hips, then around her derrière, cupping and squeezing her firmness.

As if sensing how close to the edge she was, he broke the kiss and gasped, "Open your legs for me, lass."

Lost to their passion, she barely understood what he asked. Fortunately, her body responded by instinct. She shifted her legs and his hand pushed between their bodies, long fingers sifting through her dark curls, along the swollen folds hot with her fevered desire. She flinched at the intrusion, at the two fingers chilled from the water; the contrast of the high heat within her body and the iciness of his invading touch only served to heighten the sensations. They didn't stay cold for long; her liquid arousal poured on to his clever magician fingers, quickly warming them.

A breathy moan escaped her on a sigh, as a white-hot spasm pulsed through her. Jago saw she was near to climaxing, smiled at her rapid surrender. Triumphant, he brushed a kiss against her lips. "Wrap your legs around my hips," he laughed, "and hang on."

She slid her arms around his neck and let the water's buoyancy help her obey. He grabbed her hips and lifted her to position his erection against her body. His penetration came with a hard thrust, shocking her, making her spine arch until she breathed in, taking him fully inside her. That brought her breast up high. He caught the tip of her right nipple, sucking hard, in the same rhythm as he bucked within, causing the muscles of her internal walls to tighten about his searing flesh.

"Ahhhhhh . . ." Consumed by the sensations of their bodies being joined, Asha moaned low in her throat as the explosion spun through her body.

"Shall we start counting, lass?" Jago teased. Then he brought her down savagely, slamming upward within her. From that angle, his movements easily forced her to shudder with another release.

"Ah, counting?" She admitted truthfully, "Not sure . . . I . . . can."

His buttocks flexed as he used how she floated to help her move against him, with him. "This water is so cold . . . it's having an odd effect, lass. It's slowing down my climax . . . so this might take some time."

"Oh, pity that." She chuckled as she locked her ankles behind him. "Guess I'm glad I am multiorgasmic then."

"*You're* glad?" Laughter rumbled in his chest.

Despite their touching ability to laugh even within such an intense focus of emotion, Asha felt the pure animalistic need unfurl within his muscles. His hands on her hips guided her to rise and fall ever so slowly along his rigid erection, sending sensations to whip through her blood. Her brain experienced a bubbling vibration, drawing her closer to faintness. Pushed by a frenetic appetite, her hands clutched his shoulders, her nails scored his flesh; even so he refused to increase the maddening pace.

As he took her mouth with his, his gasping breath echoed hers. His ravenous desire was a power unleashed. There was no controlling it; both of them were helpless against its voracious fire that consumed them, destroyed them, remade them, born from the flames like mating phoenixes. This was raw, primeval, as elemental as a stallion claiming his mare. Despite the primordial earthiness of their emotions there flared something bright, something rare that existed both born of their passion—and beyond it. Plunging himself to the hilt, he pushed her agony and ecstasy higher and higher. . . . until the world exploded.

With some last shred of sanity, Jago dragged them to the white sand and collapsed with her. Minutes passed before either of them had any sort of reasonable functions, but finally the world came into focus and Asha stared up at his beautiful face, at the green eyes, shining with cherished emotions.

She wanted to gift him with the words in her waiting to spring free. Wanted to tell him how much she loved him, that her surrender to him was complete, body, heart and soul. Over the past days she'd suspected he was falling in love with her, yet she still worried if she deluded herself, saw what she wanted to see. Thus the words remained locked within her fragile heart, waiting, hoping for him to speak.

Instead, he reached out and pulled her to him, kissing her with such tenderness that tears arose in her eyes. Breaking the kiss, he wrapped his arms around her and held her tightly.

"Sometimes less is more." He laughed softly, referring to her reaching two climaxes and a third shared together. "I needed to be with you last night, lass. You're under my skin, in my blood. Desire is too mild a word for what you evoke, provoke, conjure within me—and it crawled under my flesh until I couldn't think. I was nothing but a caged tiger prowling my room, a beast wanting its mate." His hand cupped her cheek, his thumb stroking gently. Those piercing eyes drank in her countenance as if he beheld the most rare and treasured thing in his life.

It wasn't a declaration of love . . . but it would do. For now.

Chapter Nineteen

Just before lunchtime, Liam finally reversed the speedboat out of the boathouse and slowly pulled into the current, positioning the bow upstream. He'd just spent the better part of an hour showing off the numerous bells and whistles of his 'toy' to Jago.

The black Crownline 255CCR pleasure boat was small enough to navigate the river for skiing, yet was a dream for outings because it provided all the comforts of home: a head compartment with shower, sink and vanity; a small refrigerator and microwave; a stereo, MP3 player, DVD and satellite dish. The backbench where Netta and Asha sat could convert into a sundeck, and even had a built-in cooler.

With the smile of a proud papa, Liam ended his spiel about its fabulous wonders with, "And, no, you can't buy my boat, Jago."

They all laughed, but Asha didn't blame her brother. Jago's eyes held a covetous twinkle—the same hunger he had shown when he looked at his Shelby and the Harley.

Grinning wickedly, Jago flicked the ashes off a Swisher

Sweet and pointed out, "But the boat matches the car and bike. All three are solid black."

"Ah—fortunately, my horse isn't black." Liam lifted his eyebrows, and then spun the wheel, moving the powerful boat into the middle of the swift river.

Tossing away the half-smoked cigarillo, Jago settled into the Tri-Tech bucket seat across from him. "I don't mind. In the horse's case—*my* horse—I'll make the exception. Besides, his name is Thor's Thunder. I'm partial to riding thunder."

His eyes flashed, speaking a silent message to Asha. She rolled her eyes.

"Men and their toys," Asha grumbled under her breath, watching her brother show off the controls to Jago.

Netta gave a bored smile. "You said it, sugarplum."

Liam gunned the boat's engine, and it was just sit back and enjoy. The twenty-five-foot cuddy was a smooth ride, even when the water level was up, as it was now. The powerful engine could easily rip along at sixty mph Doing that speed in a car and in an open boat were two different things, to Asha's way of thinking. Fortunately, Liam took pity on Netta and her, and kept the pace down to around forty. Even so, the air almost pounded her.

Asha shifted on the bench, feeling as though they were flying down the waterway. Closing her eyes, she leaned her head back and reveled in the sheer beauty of the October day. Gorgeous, with near-summertime highs—a record, according to the radio—everything seemed conjured to make their outing on the river faultless. She soaked up the warmth, knowing there wouldn't be many more days like this before cold weather came.

Childhood memories of coming to the lock sifted through her mind. Of course, in comparison, everything seemed much bigger then. The cliffs were higher, the river wider and deeper, and the falls over the weir surely closer to Niagara. Strange, the perspective you have of the world when you're small.

The water was high and rather muddy after the recent rain. She noticed Liam kept a sharp eye out for any debris, which might not show, hidden just under the surface. So far, it wasn't proving to be a problem.

She had to admit that her brother was playing nice with her pretty man, even letting him drive the boat—which meant the trip to the dam was taking three times as long. Near the last bend before reaching the falls, Liam just had to show off and permit Jago to learn how to handle his baby. They'd ended up riding back downriver a good part of the twenty-mile stretch to Lock 7 along the steepest part of the Palisades.

As they sped past the cluster of warehouses near Camp Nelson, Jago swiveled around and asked, "What are all those buildings?"

Holding on to the back of his seat, Asha inclined forward, delighted to give him the historical information. She smiled when he reached out and took her right hand and twined his fingers with hers. "That's part of the old Quantico Complex—landings and warehouses for tobacco and distilleries, for back when this river was the lifeblood to central Kentucky. During the eighteen and nineteen hundreds, this was the only way to move material, people and crops. Seagram's-Canada Dry still has warehouses at the top of the new bypass, a reminder of those bygone days."

"Canada Dry?" he chuckled.

"Yeah, I always thought that funny. Distilleries have for centuries been drawn to invest in the area. Also, Kentucky tobacco was the highest grade fetching British money to pour into the Complex. Second sons from Scotland and England came here, settled and made their fortunes. The complex developed its own microcosm, homes, secondary businesses such as ferry landings, taverns, a sawmill, gristmill and even a gunpowder plant. That proved vital during the Civil War. Strange to think of how busy an area this once was, the heart of Kentucky commerce. Even into the 1950s it still had heavy barge traffic, and on weekends was riddled with pleasure-boaters and water-skiers. Of course, that was when people swam in the water with little worry about the quality. Now it's polluted; abandoned mines, malfunctioning and nonexistent septic systems, animal waste or runoff from crop chemicals are in the upper portion of the watershed. The state is working to improve the quality, and they're making inroads."

"Odd, it seems so deserted," Jago commented, turning to watch what had once been a thriving community disappear into the distance. "So all that grew up around the warehouses and businesses? It's similar to what happened—on a smaller scale—with The Windmill."

Asha gave a faint nod and settled back on the bench. His observation unsettled her deeply. He was right; there were similarities between the old Quantico Complex and her teeny community 'round The Windmill. And while her feelings for Jago made it too easy to forget what brought him to Kentucky, if somehow Trident Ventures ever got their hands on The Windmill it wouldn't linger as a relic of how days had once been; it'd be leveled and turned into a shopping mall and apartments, their quirky way of life lost forevermore.

Burying the sadness those thoughts brought, she tried to re-summon her pleasure in cruising along the picturesque river as it twisted and turned, each bend more breathtaking than the last. The watercourse remained deserted and quiet except for the full-throttle roar of the speedboat.

As the escarpment rose, she once more tilted forward to speak to Jago. Due to the higher velocity Liam was now running at, she nearly had to shout to be heard. "Up there is Boone's Cave. When the old cliff road was still in use you could glimpse it in the curve of one bend. Supposedly, Daniel Boone spent the winter there hiding from Indians. Very small, they say, about three-feet tall and continually wet, but if you crawl in far enough there is a room, which opens up and is dry. Those cables up there"—she pointed at the ones that ran from the lower Camp Nelson area to the very top of the opposite hill, up the nearly four-hundred-foot incline—"used to be for a cable car. Long time ago that took people past the cave."

"Not much to look at." Jago seemed unimpressed.

"I guess that's why the Lookout Restaurant and the cable car went out of business in the 1950s." Asha chuckled, but the small laugh died as Jago leaned close, cupped her chin and kissed her. All thoughts of playing tour guide fled her smitten brain, as she stared in his beautiful green eyes, so deep and dark, so full of mysteries. *I love this man, love this man, love this man*, her mind chanted like a mantra, but while she had opened her heart, trusting him, trusting in love again, it still terrified her what he made her feel, forced her to feel. She swallowed hard, trepidation clogging her throat. Her emotions were too strong to handle, so she smiled and sat back, giving pretense of enjoying the remainder of the ride.

They passed the rare house or farm. On a flood plane, the area remained relatively undeveloped. The closing of the locks from Versailles and Salvisa all the way through to Heidelberg had effectively broken the river into small strips, isolating them. Not as picturesque as the Cumberland area, this still had an untouched natural look. The river snaked through the high limestone cliffs, finally widening into a broad, fertile plane, bordered by tall wooded ridges all dressed in the fire of autumnal reds, oranges and yellows.

As the dam came into view, Liam throttled back. Lowering the boat to a speed that just kept it from being swept downriver, he moved closer to the falls, so that Jago and Netta got the full impact. It was a deceptive weir, the last timber-crib dam and all-stone lock to be constructed on the Kentucky River, built three feet higher than the other thirteen.

"In deep summer the level gets so low there's no water over the weir. Men often sit on it and fish. However, it's not a place to fool around. A man tried to cross it several years back, and was swept over and drowned," Asha said. While it appeared smaller than in her childhood memories, her awe and respect, maybe fear, of the dam remained stark in her mind.

"They concreted the gates closed?" Jago asked, frowning.

She nodded. "Closer up to the structure, you can see its poor condition. It was built at the end of the century and opened in the autumn of 1900. The Army Corps of Engineers still owns them, but it's clear they're not maintaining these complexes. Locks 1 through 4 are still kept up. The rest either are welded shut or, like this one, have the gates blocked with a concrete barrier."

Turning the boat, Liam maneuvered to the beach just below the waterfall. "Jago, if you'll take the wheel—just hold it steady while I tie it off."

Her brother opened the trap in the windshield and climbed the steps to reach the long bow. Uncoiling a blue nylon rope, he held the end and jumped to the white sands. He looped it securely around a limb of a tree at the edge, and then signaled Jago to cut the engine and drop anchor.

Netta looked around, unmoved, first at the massive edifice, which even from a distance showed its century-old age, and then to the murky water. "This is what we just got our brains beat to death at 60 mph for? That thing is ready to collapse! Now I have to wade in water that could be a questionable health hazard to get to the sand? I'm *so* underwhelmed. We could've stayed at the lodge and played splashy-splash in the nice clean pool under the falls."

"But the boys couldn't drive the boat if we did that," Asha pointed out with a chuckle.

Liam tightened the rope so it was stable and held out his hand. "Stop your grumbling. You don't have to wade in the possible biohazard water. You can jump into my arms and I shall catch you."

"Oooh, I get to jump your bones! This might prove interesting after all." Netta winked at Asha, then undid the buckles on her neoprene lifejacket. "This ugly yellow does nothing for my complexion. Must've been designed by a man. A woman would've had a better fashion sense."

She accepted Jago's hand to help her up the two steps to the bow. Being the perfect gentleman, he aided her across the rocking boat, and then to jump into Liam's strong arms. Netta squealed in delight as she was caught and he swung her playfully around in the air.

Jago turned and held out his hand to help Asha next.

"You guys go on and gather the wood for a fire and get it started. Since our ride took a bit longer than anticipated"—Asha glared at both men—"I'm snagging a Pepsi and then will fix the shish kebabs so we can cook them over the fire. I'm starving and want lunch. If I don't get fed immediately, I'll start gnawing on anything sticking out."

She looked comically at Jago's fingers, but he smiled and lifted his eyebrows. "Anything sticking out? Delightful possibilities there, lass."

As Asha pulled back the stairs to go down into the galley, she nearly screamed as something popped out. "Damn it, how did you get in there?"

Jago spun, still on the bow. "Who?"

"Him." She pointed as the fat cat waddled to the midship. The feline hoisted his rotund self onto the backbench and stretched out. "You really need to name him, Jago. It's hard to fuss at him when he doesn't have a name."

"Me? I'm new at this cat business." He laughed. "Silly beast. He must've crawled in there when Liam and I were carrying on the food and beer and gassing up the boat."

Asha shook her head. "Well, hie yourself off and go help gather wood. I'm sure your cat is as hungry as I am. He hasn't eaten anything in a couple hours."

Going down into the small, but luxurious cabin, Asha headed to the built-in refrigerator for a can of Pepsi. Popping the top, she took a deep drink to kill her thirst. Prickles tickling the back of her neck, she knew Jago had followed her. Even so, her heart skipped a beat when she turned and saw he blocked the doorway. He had that hungry tiger grin on his face again.

"This damn boat is a male's wet dream," he said. "You have the entertainment center, refrigerator, and head within arm's reach of the bed. You and I are going to have to gag your brother and kidnap this boat. 'Counting' on a boat could be a lot of fun," he kidded.

"Could be, but if your nameless cat sprays anything, Liam will have a hissy fit."

Jago tilted his head in playful calculation. "Hmm . . . but maybe if my cat damages his precious toy, he'll sell it to me."

"There you go. Of course, you could buy your own boat. Crownline does make more."

"Oh yeah, that's the ticket—one longer and with three times the bells and whistles." Ducking, he came down the steps. "It wouldn't be half the fun if it didn't make Liam pea green with envy."

She sniggered and lifted her soda in salute. "Want a Pepsi or a beer? One-up-manship is thirsty work."

Removing the can from her hand, he sat it in the sink. He then reached out and took her waist, pulling her against him. "What I want is *you*. I can't stop craving you."

Jago's mouth covered hers, taking it with the same raw passion that had pushed them this morning. All the desire, all the grinding sensations came roaring back one hundredfold. Pure agony. Pure rapture. And Asha couldn't get enough. Her hands clung to his back, digging her fingers into the strong muscles, tasting him, yearning for him until it was sheer madness.

The boat rocked as heavy-footed Liam landed on the deck. "Hey, Puss, didn't know you came along," they heard him say.

Jago broke the kiss, but still held her tightly to him. "Can we bolt the door and do a *one-two-three . . . cha cha cha*? It might save my sanity."

"Hey, down there. You guys coming?" Liam called.

Jago groaned, then laughter rumbled in his chest. "*This* guy sure the hell is trying."

A last kiss to his neck, Asha sighed and stepped back. Picking up the Pepsi, she took a big drink and then pressed the cold can to her forehead. "Suck it up, Sexy Lips. Let's go feed me lunch, and then we can see about drowning him in the lock."

Asha moaned, eating her third marshmallow. It was slightly charred, just the way she loved them. She didn't really have room for another, but it had been a long time since she'd had marshmallows toasted over an open flame. "I'm not sure, but I think food tastes better cooked over a fire the way our ancestors used to do it."

They'd roasted large chunks of steak in the kebobs, and eaten the delicious meat with potato salad, slaw and baked beans they'd brought. Now as the afternoon slipped away, they toasted the treats and just enjoyed the soothing sound of the falls.

Jago took the other marshmallow off his skewer. "I didn't know anyone liked theirs incinerated like I do."

"Yeppers, toasty is not nearly enough."

Liam handed one—not charred—to Netta. "Someone needs to nudge that cat and see if he's still alive."

What's His Name had romped in the sand while they fixed lunch, and then he'd eaten his share of the steak before passing out on the edge of the blanket. Jago reached over and ruffled his fur, but the silly thing didn't move. "Guess I'll have to get him a kitty life jacket if he wants to keep riding in the boat. They do make them."

"Oh, he'll love that . . . *not!*" Asha laughed, taking his hand and rising. "Come on. There's just enough time to go see the lock before we have to leave."

Netta reached for another marshmallow. "You sugarplums run along and go see the dam. I'm staying here and sticking my tootsies in the sand. I'm as close as I want to be to that scary thing."

Asha suddenly felt strange, that odd time slippage pushing in on her thoughts again. She now recalled a fragment of Laura Valmont's memory of coming to the beach with Tommy for a group cookout, how they'd shared their first kiss under the old bell tower. The image of Laura—so pretty, in bright pink pedal pushers and a white cotton blouse—seemed so vivid, and for an instant the vision of Tommy was nearly as sharp as Jago. The two images blended and separated within her mind, and she saw how much Tommy's eyes were like Jago's. His were darker, but both pairs were very green and held the same incisive intelligence.

Auld souls. Jago had said that to her in The Windmill as they slow-danced to Dionne Warwick.

Holding hands, they climbed the path up the small hill to what once had been picnic grounds near the lockmaster's house. Over to one side there was still a dilapidated table. The falls were even more deafening up here. Asha looked down on the flattened area of concrete, which ran the length of the immense structure. Once it had been solid: now it was breaking into sections, cracking badly. The mortar wasn't even gray any longer, but a dirty brown from the last two floods that had gotten up over the whole area. A notice painted on the concrete warning to stay off the complex, no trespassing, was now faded and mostly covered in silt. She pondered what the state would do, when and if the dam gave way. Lexington and the surrounding towns drew millions of gallons of water from the river. It didn't take an engineer to see that the locks really needed replacing. The past summer already saw water rationing hitting the larger towns. What if the locks weren't repaired or replaced? Would another big flood wash away the weir? Endless questions arose as she stood with Jago watching the water churn.

Jago gave her a contemplative smile as he stared at the concrete structure. "I have to admit Netta is right. It's crumbling and not very attractive." He almost had to yell to be heard over the falls. "Yet there's something unique, special about this place."

Asha nodded. "I'm glad you like it. I always have. I don't

come often, but I have pleasant childhood memories of my brothers and sisters, my parents, back before their divorce."

The falls kicked up a thick spray, the breeze picking up the moisture and swirling it about them. Droplets clung to Jago's black curls. In a brilliant shard of time, the sun crested just over the tree line of the ridge, refracting through the mist to create a rainbow to arch just behind him. She didn't need that bit of Elfin magic to know how precious Jago was to her. She was glad of the mist for it hid the tears that came to her eyes.

She bit back words yearning to be set free, to let him know how deeply he touched her heart, how quickly he'd become a part of her life, her soul. Only, she was still too unsure how he would accept the words . . . if he would accept them. Would he believe her? People said I love you too frequently, devalued its importance.

Foolishly, she'd once thought she loved Justin. Now she saw she had loved the idea of being in love. Her pride had been stung over the breakup, and ridiculously she'd permitted the incident to cause her ego and self-confidence to suffer. As she stared at the handsome man, sharing the simple pleasure of the lock, she knew beyond doubt, she'd never experienced what he brought her.

"What's that?" He pointed to the tall A-frame structure at the pinnacle of the hill behind them.

"The bell tower." She tugged on his hand leading him toward it, aware that was the spot Tommy had first kissed Laura, the recollection strong in her consciousness.

Sadly, the fifteen-foot tower was now neglected, same as all the support and maintenance areas of the whole complex. Benches had been built into either side of the open A-frame, where people could sit and wait for the lockmaster. She explained, "Anyone wanting to be locked through, landed and rang the bell, and eventually the lockmaster came and would start the locking process. People going downriver would pull in, then the water would lower and the gates opened on that level. Those coming upriver entered and had to wait while the lock filled. I can recall swimming here and having to get out while the barges were passing through, how dangerous the water was rushing from—"

Asha caught herself. She realized she'd never seen a barge locking through. *But Laura had.* Jago never said a word. Even so, she saw comprehension in his eyes. She wondered if he felt any of the past that swirled about them like the mist conjured by the falls. The air was so laden with moisture; it beat down upon them like rain, mixing with the tears that trickled down her cheeks.

He pulled her to him, kissed her mouth, her cheeks, her forehead and each eyelid in turn, in a quiet desperation that touched her soul. Then his mouth claimed hers again, this time with searing passion, and something gentler: the rare, elusive power of love—their love and Tommy and Laura's. He backed her against a rounded column of the tower and kissed her.

The beauty, the poignancy lanced her heart.

Suddenly the bell rang out, causing them to break apart. Curious, they glanced up, wondering what had set the old metal clapper to sounding. The pull-rope had long ago broken off, dry-rotted with age and exposure; someone would have to stand on the bench to reach it. Looking at the wooden planks, it was doubtful they would hold weight. The breeze was not strong enough to move the heavy bell.

Shaking his head in perplexity, Jago turned her to face the waterfall. He locked his arms about her, flexed his strong muscles and pulled her back tightly against his chest. For several minutes they just stood like that, him rubbing his cheek against the side of her head. Swaying slightly, they soaked up the contentment of being with each other, and just enjoyed the sound of the falls.

"What's on the other side?" He leaned his head, his mouth next to her ear and nodded toward the cliffs of the far bank. "Up there?" His tone was casual, but she picked up a sense of quiet purpose within the words.

"Just the cliffs. Men often get dropped there, so they can fish from the ledges. Others tie up where we did and then walk across the waterfall."

"You're kidding. What madness is that?"

"Crossing as you see it now, you'd be swept over. It'd be a miracle if you didn't die. However, during summer the water often gets so low you see the riverbed on the upper pool. I've seen it where the bottom is showing about a third of the way from this shore. When it gets like that, there's no flow over the weir. No falls. There's a service path, a lip along the front of it; you can easily cross then. Sometimes, men are foolish enough to walk that with the water running high. But with the force of that water—millions of gallons a day—you don't play with it."

"What's behind the cliffs?"

"A forest."

"And beyond the forest?"

"Farmland along Highway 27. I should imagine that's near the Buena Vista turnoff."

"Bue-nah viztah? Don't you mean bwe-nah vees-tah," he teased about the way the locals pronounced names.

She smiled. "I was here visiting mum once at the lodge, and they had tornado warnings on the radio. The announcer was new to the area, and he gave the alarm for Garrod County, with the normal French pronunciation. The DJ came on and said to tell them it was Gar-rod County, with the hard G sound, or they wouldn't know it was for them."

"Okay, so what does being near Bue-nah Vista have to do with what I asked?"

"We followed the river coming to the lock. It snakes around and around, miles to ride down, but not that far as the crow flies. That's one of the highest peaks in the area, hence the name. You can see the river in the distance from the highway, right there at the turn off. If I recall correctly, farms are there."

"Then you wouldn't have much trouble getting up there on that last knoll before the cliffs?"

"You'd have to walk through the woods." Asha turned to look over her shoulder at him. "Why? You're thinking of buying that, too?"

"Now, be nice." He shrugged. "I noticed a reflection up there. A flash. I wondered what was up there, how easily you can access it."

"A reflection?"

He nodded faintly. He stayed, holding her in the embrace, watching the river. After a couple minutes, he said, "There."

Asha had to blink the tears from her eyes to spot it—a hard glare, like off a glass or a mirror, right at the crest of the woods. Since the afternoon sun was setting behind the cliffs, she started to use her hand to block the harsh light to see better. Jago caught her hand, preventing her from lifting it.

"Don't." His quiet tone was making her uneasy.

It could be anyone—a hiker, a farmer, even someone camping. With the woods and river undeveloped, it drew people hiking or canoeing. As she followed Jago down the path to the beach to pack up and leave, she pondered why she had the feeling whoever was up there was none of those things.

Chapter Twenty

As Asha walked down the center isle between the booths of the restaurant, Melvin Johnson called to her over the Wednesday breakfast clatter.

"Hey, Asha, what the hell *is* that?" Using his fork he pointed at Sam who fed the fat cat on the glassed-in porch. "Did you get Sam a new combination garbage disposal and dishwasher?" Everyone joined Melvin in a good laugh.

"I think the thing has declared himself The Windmill's official mascot, though he's really Jago's cat," she answered, pulling a small strip of clear tape from the dispenser she carried.

"Really? Didn't know the Brit had a cat." Taking a sip of his coffee, Melvin watched her.

"A recent addition," she commented with a smile.

He stabbed the yolk on his egg and then sopped it up with his toast. "Gossip says that man's been adding a lot the past few days, buying Derek's Shelby and then Dale's Harley. Who'd he buy the cat from?"

She chuckled. "In this instance, I think the cat acquired him."

"What's with the sign?" he asked next.

"You're full of questions this morning, Melvin." Asha taped the corners of the plastic HELP WANTED sign to the front window. "I'm hiring a couple part-time waitresses so that you and the others will stop grousing at me about not getting service fast enough."

"Where's Netta? She always keeps my cup topped off." Melvin held up his half-filled mug, letting her know it was in need of attention.

"Netta is at Juanita's getting her hair done. Besides, she can't do everything around here. The lass needs some helping hands. I let Rhonda go—though I am sure she'll put it about that *she* walked out on me." Asha poured coffee for Melvin. She looked out the big windows, spotting Netta's beat-up Hyundai pull into the lot and park at the side where employees did.

"That ain't Juanita anymore," Melvin informed her. "She died about twenty-five years ago. The owner is Daisy Mason now; she just never changed the name of the beauty parlor since Juanita's is sort of a local landmark in Leesburg. She bought it from Juanita's granddaughter after her granny died. She tried for a few weeks to call it Daisy's Wash and Curl, but everyone grumbled; she changed it back to keep them happy."

Asha paused and considered Melvin. "You were around here back in the '60s? Did you know Tommy Grant or Laura Valmont?"

"Yeah, I did." He took a sip of his coffee, hesitating. "Tommy was already at UK when I went to Leesburg High. Laura was in my American History class, though I didn't know her well. She was a grade ahead of me and only moved to Leesburg a year or so before, if I recall right. My cousin, Junior, took her to the prom."

Asha thought back on the prom night she'd witnessed through Laura's eyes, recalling how Laura had hunted for Junior to take her home after she fought with Tommy. It was so strange, to already know the pieces of the past of which

Melvin spoke, see them so vividly in her mind. Laura Valmont's memories were now hers.

"She didn't socialize much, just followed Tommy around all the time." Melvin's eyes shifted uneasily to the jukebox. "They used to come here a lot, played that thing all the time and slow-danced in the aisles, like all the kids did back then. The Windmill and the old skate rink were about the only places for young people to hang out."

Asha watched the Wurlitzer, which sedately played the beautiful "Greenfields" by The Brothers Four, almost expecting it to switch in mid-song to Ray Peterson crooning about Tommy and Laura. She muttered under her breath, "Yeah, damn machine is being good *now*—Colin is running around with a screwdriver."

She shivered when the song hit the lyrics, "*We were the lovers, who strolled those greenfields.*" Turning her attention back to Melvin, she asked. "What happened to them?"

The man made a sour face, clearly uneasy with the subject. He shrugged. "Died."

Asha felt as if she'd taken a hard blow to her heart, all the sadness she'd experienced at the skating rink returning tenfold. For some reason, Laura's ghost was touching her life, showing her the past. It made her grasp the back of the booth to steady herself. "Died? How?"

"That's right—you didn't grow up around here, did you? Maybe you'd better ask those who know more about them. There's one or two around," he said cryptically.

"Melvin, I'll have Sam double the *filè* powder in your gumbo Thursday night," she threatened.

"People around here respect the dead, give them their rights. You don't speak of those who died violently. It calls them back, holds them here when they need to move on." Clearly uncomfortable, he checked his watch. "I need to get to work. I'll let you know about my brother-in-law, if he'd be interested in that job replacing the ceiling tiles. Can I get my ticket?"

Asha nodded and went to the front to check him out.

Melvin's reaction bothered her, but she didn't push. He picked up his usual peppermint from the bowl by the register and unwrapped the cellophane. Popping it into his mouth, he then scooped up his change and stuck the coins in his pants pocket. His gray eyes showed regret. He hesitated before going to the door.

"Look, it ain't a memory I use for gossip," he offered as a reason for his behavior.

She nodded, understanding more than he'd ever know. "I wasn't gossiping. I'm truly interested in what happened to them."

Melvin shot another fleeting glare at the Wurlitzer. "Yeah, guess you have cause. They were two nice people, very much in love, and died tragically. A car crash out on the old river road, along that dangerous stretch back before they put in the bypass and the new bridge. Tommy evidently crossed the centerline, trying to pass a cement truck, and too late saw a semi bearing down. He swerved, judging from the tracks on the road, but the Peterbilt smashed into the Mustang's side, killing Laura instantly. I didn't see it happen, just came up minutes later. Tommy was alive for a few moments when we reached him. The steering wheel shoved half into his chest, he was holding her hand and trying to call her name. It wasn't pretty, Asha." Tears filled his eyes. "To this day I'll never forget those poor people. They should've had a good life, had grandkids by now. I didn't know them all that well, but coming upon that wreck left deep scars in me. Taught me the value of each day, you know. Sometimes life just ain't fair."

Netta waltzed in through the front door as Melvin departed. He barely muttered a hello to her before rushing out. She lifted her brows, shrugged and came around the counter with her shopping bags.

"Melvin seemed upset. Anything happen? La Jukebox from Hell carrying on again?"

"Just some unhappy memories." Asha finished drawing a Pepsi for herself, then really took a look at Netta.

Shock was too mild of a word. Her friend had on chicly tailored black slacks, a charcoal blazer with small gold buttons and a deep blue shell blouse that made her vivid eyes seem all the more arresting. Her hair color had been toned down to a lovely shade of golden blond and the wild curls and waves were gone. In their stead was a sleek coif that ended in a small French braid, elegant and reminiscent of the beautiful actress Kim Novak. "My, aren't you stunning!"

Netta did a 360-degree spin to show off. "My first day as your new hostess. Will I do?"

"You'd do to meet the Queen, though it's a bit wasted on the bunch around here. They love you as you were. But you're beautiful either way."

Winnie MacPhee raced into the restaurant, beelined to the empty booth and leaned in on her knee. With a determined look to her eyes, she snatched down the HELP WANTED sign from the window and rushed to the counter. With a nervous grin, she pushed it toward Asha.

"Why did you go and take my sign down? I just put that up." Asha had a feeling where this was going, and she wasn't sure it was a good idea.

"It says two part-time waitresses. How about one full-time instead?" Winnie stood there grinning.

"Actually, the idea was to have two waitresses to cover the supper. Netta is my new hostess. That leaves Cathy as my only waitress through the week. I have Denise on Fridays and Saturdays."

"Yeah, but if you had one that came in and worked the lunch and dinner shift both, especially one with a lot of energy, maybe you don't need two. Anyway, I want to be one. I can start whenever you like." She waited, looking optimistic.

Asha glanced to Netta, who merely gave her a blank stare. She was clearly making no comment, though Asha had a sense Netta echoed her own trepidation.

"Up front—I have concerns because of Derek," Asha admitted. "I'm not sure it's a smart move to hire a waitress who is fighting with my busboy."

Winnie clapped her hands together. "I won't be a problem. Promise. I'll be busy waiting on customers; he'll be in the back, or clearing tables. We won't have to bump elbows too often. Look, you pay better than the café in Leesburg or the Dairy Wiz. I don't want to eat up my salary in gas driving all the way to Lexington and back each day—the traffic out of that town is a major headache during rush hour. Ah, come on, Asha. The Dish Barn is cutting back on my hours. I can't live on twenty-five hours a week. Choices are limited. Give me a chance. Please?"

Asha sighed, knowing she was a soft touch. "Two weeks. If I catch Derek and you fussing, I'll toss you out on your ear. No too-short skirts, too-low tops or perfume—customers might be allergic. I provide the smock aprons; you get five. If you want to work full-time, you can work 11:30 am to 7:30, Tuesday through Saturday, twelve dollars per hour plus tips."

"Oh, thank you! Also, may I have one of the employee cottages? I'd really like to move out of my parents' home."

Asha chuckled, knowing if she let the girl have one of the cottages there went the 'two-week trial'. Still, she understood how hard it was for the kids trying to stay in the area. Choices on where to live and jobs were not good; most were forced to go elsewhere to find both. She'd always liked Winnie, and poor lass, her mother had a tongue like an adder. It must be hard living with such an overbearing woman. When Asha came back to take over running The Windmill, she'd turned it into a sanctuary for people seeking the slower path in life.

Asha trusted her fey voice, as she had with Netta and Sam. "Okay, you can have a cottage."

Winnie hopped up and down and nearly jumped over the counter, leaning close to hug Asha. "Oh, thank you, thank you, thank you! When do I start?"

A low throttled rumble sounded, as the Shelby swung into the lot, Jago behind the wheel. Asha watched Jago stop directly in front of the door in the *No Parking* spot, and he and Derek got out. They'd gone to the courthouse to get the car title transferred, why Jago beamed like a proud daddy about to pass out cigars.

"You can start today if you like. My new hostess," she motioned to Netta, "can walk you through things and get you settled. The smocks are in the locker. Netta will show you where. Once you get your own personal locker set up, come back and fill out the application, the W-2 form, and I'll give you a key to a cabin."

"Come on, sweet thing, I'll get you squared away." Netta smiled and pushed open the kitchen door.

At the same time as Netta took Winnie into the kitchen, Jago and Derek pushed through the front door. Asha chuckled as both men looked back to the black car, their expressions easy to read. Jago grinned, possession clear in his eyes. Poor Derek had the wistful, sad look of one saying good-bye to his beloved.

Jago turned to see Asha watching him and gave her a drop-dead, sexy smile. "It's mine. All mine. Well, it's property of Trident Ventures until I get the money transferred here."

"Yeah, I guessed that's what put the grin on your face." She chuckled. "Of course, your Harley might get jealous."

Coming around the counter he opened his arms wide. He looked damn delicious in his black jeans, leather jacket and blue T-shirt, an irresistible bad boy that had stolen her heart.

"Hey, there's enough of me for both." He kissed her cheek and whispered, "Enough for you, too . . . if you say pretty please with a cherry on top."

Putting a hand on his chest, she resisted the urge of fisting her fingers in the cotton and yanking him to her for a kiss that would knock his socks off. Instead, she pushed him back a step. "Cool it, Sexy Lips. I'm gearing up for the lunch rush around here."

"In that case, fix me a glass of iced tea, and if I may, I'll borrow the phone in the office to make some calls."

She winked. "Only if you say pretty please with a cherry on top."

He shoved against her hand, invading her space in challenge. "I have interesting ideas about maraschino cherries and whipped cream."

"I have a passion for maraschino cherries," Asha confessed. Swallowing hard, she tried to think of something utterly witty and so sexy it'd make *him* swallow hard. Only, visions of Reddi-wip and sexy, sinful cherries filled her mind. Heat flooded her body as she blushed.

To hide her reaction, she turned away to fix his iced tea. Jago just laughed, knowing how he'd pushed her buttons. Fine, let him. She'd get even later.

Derek grumped, "If you two are finished playing lovebirds, can I have a beer? And don't gripe that it's too early in the day, Asha. I just sold my Shelby. I need something a lot stronger but will settle for a Coors."

Chatting happily, Netta and Winnie came from the kitchen. The girl's jovial expression died when her eyes locked with Derek's. Flashing a fearful look at Asha, she quickly followed Netta into the office. Setting the Coors on a paper coaster, Asha excused herself and followed them.

Going to the file cabinet, she took out the papers needed to employ Winnie and a set of keys to cabin #11. "Sorry, it's been locked up for a year. You'll need to air it and vacuum the inch-thick dust. You can take the papers onto the porch to fill in everything. This one is for your doctor to fill out. I'll reimburse you for the physical, but I need your physician to certify you're healthy enough to work. Other than that, I'm an easy employer. I run The Windmill like a family. That means Derek and you get along on the clock. On your own time, whatever you do is your business, but here you're happy campers. Any questions?"

Still smiling, Winnie shook her head no and held out her hand for the keys. Asha hesitated for a heartbeat, hoping her instincts were right. She loved the harmony of The Windmill, and didn't want anything to disturb that. Looking into Winnie's warm brown eyes, she had to go with her inner voice that said this girl would fit in. Oh, she didn't expect it to be all sunshine and roses. Derek's feelings would have to be soothed. Even so, she dropped the keys into Winnie's palm, comfortable with her decision.

"I'm so excited." Winnie followed Netta from the office, only to bump into Colin.

"Hey, congrats, Winnie gal. I just heard. You need help with anything at the cottage let me know. I'm a handy guy. Electrician, plumber, carpenter, painter, Jack-Of-All-Trades . . . that's me. I work cheap, too." He followed her down the long aisle to the glass porch, discussing what needed to be done for her to settle in. "My cousin in Leesburg has a furniture store. I can get you wholesale on anything you need."

Jago snatched up his glass of tea and kissed Asha on the cheek. "I'm off to borrow your office. You get lonely, come on back, lock the door, and we'll discuss your passion for maraschino cherries."

"You wish," she chirped.

He smiled, gave her a pat on the fanny. "Damn straight I do." Then he vanished into the dark-paneled room.

As the door closed, Derek stormed behind the counter. "What's Winnie doing here?"

"She's my new waitress. And I'll tell you the same thing I told her—I don't want any trouble between you two."

"Then you shouldn't have hired her. Winnie's crazy. She hounds me everywhere I go. This is the one place she's left me alone; she knows you won't put up with her nonsense," Derek argued.

"Which is precisely what I told her, and I mean it. If there is any trouble, I'll let her go." She cautioned, "There *won't* be trouble. Right?"

Colin returned and started changing out the stool that was wobbling.

"Then let her go . . . now," Derek insisted.

Pausing from unscrewing the stool's padded seat, Colin frowned. "Ah, ease up, Beau Derek Two, you're just grouchy because you sold the Shelby. Winnie's a good kid. And frankly—if you were to ask my opinion—"

Derek snapped, "I didn't."

Colin ignored him. "—I think your imagination and ego are working overtime about her hounding you. There aren't many places to go around here. I see you more than she does and I'm not stalking you. She needs the money. They cut her hours nearly in half at the Dish Barn."

"What would you know about it, Oo-it?" Derek sipped his beer and glowered.

Asha sighed. "I'm saying this once. I won't stand for bickering—from anyone. I want peace and quiet around here."

The Wurlitzer suddenly cut loose with a very noisy song from The Trashmen: "Surfin' Bird."

"A-well-a everybody's heard about the bird . . . B-b-b-bird, bird, bird, b-bird's the word."

They all stared at the jukebox with mouths open.

Asha groaned. "Damn thing! It's too early in the day for this nonsense."

"I'm getting a headache. Think I will take two aspirins and clock in." Derek dropped his empty beer bottle in the trash bin. "Dishwashing will look good after ten minutes of 'bird is the word.' "

"Colin, do you own a sledgehammer?" Asha rounded the counter to stare at her haunted jukebox.

"Hey, why don't you call up the Sci-Fi Channel and tell them about it. They could do one of the 'Ghost Hunters' shows on it." Colin leaned forward, and lifted Asha's hair away from her neck with the end of his screwdriver. "Wow, did you ever get nailed—euphemistically and literally. By what? A giant leech? Man, that's some hickey. Could be the grandfather of all hickeys. Hey, you recall that old movie *Attack of the Killer Leeches*? Actor Leo Gordon did the screenplay for it. I gotta get that one for the drive-in. It was so low rent it wasn't even a B movie. Maybe a D movie . . . ha ha ha."

"Colin, now isn't a good time." Asha tapped her foot in impatience.

"Anyway . . . these giant leeches were in this swamp of some nowhere spot in Louisiana, and they went around putting some major suction on their victims. I think Jago must be one of them leeches in disguise. If you ask me—" Colin turned around and, not watching where he was going, slammed hard into Jago, who had come from the office. He grinned sheepishly. "Oh ho, thought you were on the phone, Jago. Lovely weather we're having, eh? Found your costume for the Halloween bash yet?"

"Not yet. I was searching for a killer leech costume—they're fresh out." Jago's eyes twinkled with a suppressed smile as he reached out and pulled the unlit cigarette from Colin's mouth. "Smoking is bad for your health."

"Sheesh, some people are grouchy this morning. Hoo-hoo . . . you could just come as you are, but since the idea is to come as something totally different, a leech mask would be redun—"

"*Killer* leech," Jago teased, trying to keep his face straight.

"Yeah, well . . . hmm . . . how about coming as King Kong? That'd work. Or Oscar the Grouch." He offered a winning grin and waved his screwdriver. Then his eyes glanced down and noticed what he was doing, and worried that Jago might view it as a threatening gesture he quickly stuck the tool in his back pocket. "Not my day, I fear. Just remember you can't punch me in the face. Asha wouldn't like that. She'd think you're a bully. Then she might not let you play giant leech with her again."

Jago's chest vibrated with a suppressed chuckle. "Colin—shut up."

"You know, I get told that a lot. I don't mean to be irritating. It just sort of slips out naturally."

"Really? That surprises me." Jago swung his leg over one of the stools at the counter and asked Asha, "So, how about a lunchtime ride on the Harley with a killer leech?"

"Sorry." She smiled. "I must work, but I'll join you for lunch in a bit if you're still around."

"Plan to be. What's good on the menu?" His green eyes flashed devilishly. "Besides maraschino cherries?"

Chapter Twenty-one

Singing an old Smoky Robinson tune, Jago rounded the corner of the restaurant. "'What can make me feel this way . . . my girl . . .'" In high spirits, he executed a Motown spin on his heels and then laughed to the cat trotting alongside him. "Damn jukebox has me doing it, too, Puss. Of course, the tunes from that period were ones you could sing along with, upbeat tunes. That's why so many turn up in commercials these days. And hey, *I'm* so happy, but it's not the song. She makes me that way. I don't ever recall being this happy."

The cat glanced up and meowed, his pointed look saying, *What about me*?

"Hey, you're getting to sleep in a comfy bed with two warm bodies and eating twelve square meals a day thanks to Sam. What more do you want? Sheesh, there's no pleasing some pussycats—"

He stopped as the bungalows came into view. He'd meant to bend over, pick up the cat and drape him over his shoulder. Instead, he just petted the kitty absently, his eyes on the cabins across the small courtyard. The patio door to his was not fully closed, and was oddly open about six inches. Seeing the sliding door cracked set off alarms in his brain, similar to how he'd felt the morning he'd heard scratching at the window. A fine edge of unease began to inch up his spine—the same as when he'd spotted the reflection on the other side of the lock.

He recalled: after Liam and he had taken Asha and Netta back to the lodge, they'd driven over to the spot where you could see the river from Highway 27. Unfortunately, it had been getting dark, thus they only made a cursory inspection, little more than affixing the lay of the land in Jago's mind.

Liam and Netta stayed that night as well. "Another sleepless night," he grumbled to the cat. "No opportunity for me to practice 'counting' with Asha again. I got even, Puss. Just for spite—I rousted his arse at dawn and forced him to go tramping through the woods with me."

Too sleepy to offer much of a protest, Asha's brother had gone along on the excursion, possibly to work off his own excess hormones. Liam had seemed uncaring that someone had watched them from the cliffs. Finding a wadded up wrapper from a pack of Marlboro cigarettes on the ground near the spot where Jago had noticed the reflection had done nothing to change that apathy either. Nor was Liam perturbed by tire tracks in the muddy ground at the edge of the woods where someone had parked, hidden from view.

Liam had shrugged. "So? Someone walked through the woods, birdwatcher, hiker, camper, some guy fishing—no telling what he was doing up here. Seriously, I don't think it's anything to get concerned about."

Jago had squatted and examined the tracks closely. "Could be a truck that made the tracks."

"Again, I have to say, *so?* You drag me from my bed for a trespassing litterbug?" Then it had finally reached Liam's foggy brain. He'd slid his hands in his coat pockets. "You're thinking about the truck that harassed you on the bike ride on Sunday."

"Yeah, and the truck at the drive-in earlier."

"I told you Oo-it drives one. So do half the farmers in the area. And don't get paranoid. Some people around here see a biker and think 'goddamn Hell's Angel.' Some Bubba with a brain a couple cans short of a six-pack and another six in his belly, probably decided to give the biker a good scare. Thought it a high old time."

"But Asha was on the Harley," he argued.

Liam had rolled his eyes. "Hey, big bad biker's molls don't get respect from Billy Bob Joe."

Jago chuckled, shaking his head. He didn't think Asha would like being thought of as a moll.

Now, looking at the open door of his cabin, he couldn't dispel the odd sensation that once more crawled over his skin. "I locked it this morning before I left with Derek. I'm careful about that," he told What's His Name. When the feline rubbed against his calf and glared at the bungalow, ears flattened against his head and his tail snapping, Jago exhaled in frustration. "Okay, maid service? Maybe she forgot to close the door after she left?"

Approaching slowly, he paused to examine the lock built into the frame. There were scratches around the core that someone fumbling with a key might make. But, as he ran his fingers along the mechanism where it seated itself into the wall, he spotted what looked more like gouges, as though someone had used a lever like a crowbar—or a big screwdriver—to snap the weak lock.

"Back to Oo-it—again. First, the black truck, now the screwdriver . . ." With a sigh, he glanced back to the restaurant, thinking about Colin running around all morning with the oversized tool. "He smokes, too, Puss. I wonder if they're Marlboros?"

His mouth compressed into a frown, knowing Asha wouldn't be happy he even held the suspicion, yet there was little way to avoid it. He stared at the curtain rippling in the wind, trying to decide a course of action.

He discounted this being the carelessness of the maid; she might scratch the lock putting in the key, but she wouldn't take a lever to the thing. Colin was in the diner—working on the stool. Jago knew they advised people facing a possible breaking-and-entering situation not to go inside; call the police and let them handle it. "What police? We're in the middle of bloody nowhere." He fingered the bent lock.

Jago doubted there was a county force, so he'd likely have to call the state troopers. No telling where they were or how long it would take for them to arrive. He'd bet whoever had done this was long gone. To be on the safe side, he could go back and get Asha's gun, but he didn't want her in the middle of this until he learned what had happened. Walking over to the Shelby, he fished his keys from his pocket, opened the trunk and removed the tire iron from the jack.

"Not that I need it, Puss. Des saw both Trev and I were fully trained in Savate, since we had to be in some pretty dicey places around the world." He chuckled. What's His Name looked thoroughly unimpressed.

The curtain flapped softly, stirred by the breeze, as he took hold and slowly pushed it back. Just steps inside, he paused. Everything was silent, so still that he heard his heart thudding, strong and slow in his blood. His eyes flicked to his briefcase sitting on the table next to his laptop, then soundlessly he moved into the living room. He listened intently, not with his ears, but with that fey primitive sense a man tended to ignore at times. Jago found that when he failed to heed that inner voice, he later paid for it. That sixth sense detected a presence lingering in the air, though from someone long gone. A rapid inspection of the rooms confirmed that impression. No one was in the bungalow. Jago didn't spot anything missing. Even so, there were clear signs to him that someone had entered and been through his things.

A sloppy maid who didn't close the door? That was believable. It's what he *wanted* the situation to be. Except, that tingling sense said some person had come into his cottage and snooped. Why? For what purpose? His briefcase looked as if it had been left untouched. Going to it, he saw that was not the case. A lever had been put to use on the latches, too. Both had been worked loose. When he lifted the lid, the papers were not in the neat order as he'd left them.

Pulling out a chair, he sat down with a thud, dread bubbling up inside him. Slowly shifting through the folders, the worry spiked when he saw the white envelope stuck into the pocket slot. He hadn't left it there. Only too well he knew what was in it. Regardless, he opened it, compelled to scan the contents again.

The cover letter wasn't there. Jago felt like puking.

On a letterhead for Trident Ventures and addressed to Desmond, with copies to Trev and him, it had confirmed all the arrangements for Trident's hostile takeover of Montgomerie Enterprises, how the arrangements would be kept under the table until everything was in place. Once the maneuvers were complete, a press release would be issued announcing Mershan International was buying out Trident. In essence, his brother would be CEO of a company that owned Trident Ventures and Montgomerie Enterprises as subsidiaries. Desmond's vengeance would finally be complete.

He went through the case again to double check. Maybe the snooper had mistakenly placed the letter in one of the other files, which contained information on the buyout for the horse farm, the offers and counter-offers between Trident and Asha's father. Nothing that would be damning. Not like that letter would be.

Only the letter was gone. What remained was the question: Why would anyone break into his bungalow and steal that piece of paper that had little value to anyone but him?

Jago stalked back into the restaurant, his eyes sweeping the room. Colin had just finished tightening the nuts on the stool. Jago couldn't help it; his eyes fixed on the man's big-ass screwdriver and couldn't look away.

Sensing that all was not right, Colin glanced up. He rose with a slight frown. "It's called a screwdriver, Jago. You poke it into things and *screw* with it. I'd think you'd be rather familiar with the concept."

"Watch it, or I might have to show you a new place you can put that damn oversized tool—as in, where the sun doesn't shine," he warned.

"Hoo-hoo . . . someone got up on the wrong side of Asha's bed this morning." Colin grinned unrepentantly. "You don't scare me, Jago. I told you before; you can't beat on me; Asha wouldn't like that. So save the high camp. You'll come to adore me soon enough. Everyone does."

"Okay, I adore you." Surprisingly disarmed by the chatter, Jago laughed. Easing back on the temper, he went to get a beer from the cooler. "Can you use the monster tool to change a lock on the bungalow?"

"Is this a test? No one said anything about a test. I'm really good on killer leeches, Vincent Price and Boris Karloff. Did you know Karloff's real name was William Henry Platt? Remember the old Song "Monster Mash," where the guy sounded like Karloff? Karloff actually sang the song himself on television once! Now how many people know that?" The man beamed at his esoteric acumen.

"I'm sure you are a killer at Trivial Pursuit."

Colin fetched a Dr Pepper and twisted off the top. "So why do you need the lock changed?" Using the cap, he arched it into the trashcan. "He shoots! He scores!"

Observing the strange man with the irritating, yet oddly likable personality, Jago shook his head. In his role for Mershan International, it was commonplace for him to look high-powered corporate executives in the eye, wait for them to 'blink,' then walk away with whatever Desmond had wanted from the negotiations. His incisive mind, the ability to assess quickly another's strengths and weaknesses served him well, thus saw him a good judge of character. It didn't ring true Colin would break into his bungalow simply to steal a letter that had little value to him. Except . . . except he could use it to show Asha that her lover was lying to her. It was clear Colin was in love with Asha: only was it puppy love or obsession? Would the need to discredit Jago push him to follow them around, spy on them and look for damning evidence to use?

Damn it! His suspicions all followed a chain of logic, yet as he studied the oddball it was hard to reconcile Colin the Stalker with Colin the 'Basketball Superstar.' The two profiles were in such conflict; he liked Colin and that alone made him want to trust him, despite circumstances piling up.

"Someone broke into my bungalow. Bunged up the lock. It will need another. Can you do that, or will we need to call for a locksmith—provided Leesburg has one."

Asha came from the office, scowling. "Did I hear right? Your cabin was broken into?"

Colin rolled his eyes. "City boy shows up and we have a crime wave. Mwahaha. I leave the keys to my truck on the floorboard so I know where they are at all times. That's how scared *I* am about someone around here stealing anything."

Asha stalked out of the diner, obviously heading to the cabins. Jago looked at Colin and then Sam, peeking through the serving window, then followed her.

"Hey, wait for me! I'm the one with the screwdriver!" Colin called, rushing to catch up.

Asha stood frowning at Jago's door, hands on her hips, the fat cat dancing around her ankles wanting attention. A hot autumn wind whipped through the trees, sending the dry leaves to the ground, forecasting bad weather. She pulled her long hair over one shoulder and held on to the ends to keep it from flying about her face. "You're right. Someone forced the lock. When did this happen?"

Jago shrugged. "I locked it when I went off with Derek. It was this way when I came back. Of course, with that damn juke box screaming 'bird is the word,' someone could blow the place up and you might not hear."

Colin scratched his head, looked at the other bungalows. He reached into his shirt pocket and took out a pack of cigarettes and tapped one out. Marlboros. Jago groaned. Colin took Jago's scowl as censure. "Hey, Asha bitches at me already for smoking. Besides, you smoke those cheesy Swisher Sweets."

"Yeah, I do," he replied absently, wishing Colin smoked anything but Marlboros.

Taking the cigarette, the handyman stuck it into his mouth, but didn't light it. "Hey, Jago, someone have it in for you? You a drug runner or a diamond smuggler? Why would someone hit your pad and not bother any of the other cabins? I get it—Jago equals James, doesn't it? Jago Bond! They were after your super spy secrets." He sniggered.

His using the word *secrets* caused Jago to want to hit something.

"What was stolen? I'll replace it even if the insurance doesn't cover it. We've never had anything stolen from the motel before." Asha sighed, looking disappointed.

Jago's stomach muscles tightened as if he'd taken a sucker punch. He turned to glance around—or more precisely, he pretended to look about for clues so he didn't have to meet her beautiful eyes. "Nothing was taken." Lightning streaked across the sky, followed by a thunderclap nearly overhead. Scooping up the cat, he took Asha's upper arm. "We'd better get inside. Storm's going to break any minute."

"Hey, guys, I'll dash up to my house, see if I have anything to repair that lock," Colin shouted over the rising wind, then started to jog up the hill.

Jago and Asha barely made it to the glassed-in porch before the rain hit, pounding on the concrete drive and walkway at the front of the restaurant, with a soothing sound. They left the kitty on the porch—much to his grumpy meowing—and went into the diner. Asha headed to the office to take a call from a supplier, leaving Jago at the counter to finish his slightly warm beer. Jago took a seat on the stool that Colin had fixed, and watched Sam carry in a stainless steel bucket filled with crushed ice, and empty it into the built-in bin under the counter.

"Where's the usual lunch crowd?" he asked the cook.

"Won't be one. Damn storm will keep everyone away. Watch. Oh, a couple might brave the rain. You'd think people around here are made of sugar. Damn shame, I've been cookin' all morning," Sam grumbled shaking his head.

"So what's good for lunch? I'm in the mood for Tex-Mex for some reason."

"Tex-Mex? Bah! You want some good eatin', try my Cajun cookin'. I fixed my *Chicken What Du Hell* as the lunch special. It'll make your soul sing." Sam offered him a big smile as he dumped the ice shards into the bin and closed the lid.

Jago finished the Coors. "I'd noticed your accent. You're from New Orleans."

"Sure am. Katrina got me. Had my own restaurant. Nothing fancy, mind. Just good eatin'. Mama Lou's Down-Home Authentic Cajun Cooking. That damn big-ass sign was the first thing that Katrina got. Not much longer after that, the water came. The Army Corps of Engineers and the Emergency Preparedness people did this computer mock-up to study what would happen if a Category 5 hurricane ever hit New Orleans. They even aired it on the Discovery Channel the year before it happened. They did nothing. Sat on their hands and said there was no way to evacuate the city. Didn't rebuild the levees. Wouldn't stop dredging the river. So, the worst happened, exactly like that computer show warned. And the poor unsuspecting people paid. Whole town paid and is still paying. When I saw the water rolling in, I got in my truck and drove north and kept going, following the Blue Highway. Finally landed here late one night. My Aunt Bessie used to work for Asha's mama, was a cook for her. I used to come stay with her in the summers. So there I was—no home, no family, no business and too damn old for anyone to hire me. Asha did. The gal has a heart."

"Will you ever go back?"

"I love the Big Easy, but that life is over. I belong here at The Windmill now." Sam's black eyes studied Jago closely. "What about you? You got a car, a cat and a 'cycle now. Hear you're planning on getting a boat. You gonna keep our girl?"

"I sure plan on it."

"She won't live anywhere else, you know. You prepared for that? The Windmill is a haven for lost souls. It's Asha's purpose. Netta was lost. Derek was a punk headed for trouble, now he's going to be a vet. Delbert doesn't have anyone but us. Oo-it has been shunned all his life; no one ever looked close enough to see how smart that man is. I sure needed a home and job." The cook paused. "Only, our gal was lost, too. She needed roots, a reason in life. All that money and that big damn house in England never gave her that. Her mama always returned home to Kentucky; ultimately it destroyed her marriage because Mac refused to give her what she needed, what she found here. Best think on that. Asha is like her mama; why she came back here to make a go of it."

"Strangely enough, I guess I was lost, too." Jago admitted. "I never realized it until now. I need roots and a purpose in life, too. I'm happy here."

Sam huffed. "Figured that might be the case—why you started collecting your toys. What about your business trying to buy her out?"

"Sticky wicket, but I'll handle things. We'll work something else out."

"She ain't gonna be happy if you buy that horse farm out from under her brother," Sam counseled knowingly.

Jago picked up a quarter from the counter and, with a magician's practiced slight-of-hand, made it vanish. "I'll have to work a little magic to see Liam holds onto it, don't you think?"

"Sounds smart to me."

After Sam ambled back to the kitchen, Jago stared out the window, watching the rain. The old man's gentle prodding had summoned something he'd been hiding from—his lying to Asha. He needed to come clean with her. Soon.

He swallowed back the rising bile, recognizing it might mess up Desmond's plans, and by damn, he owed everything to his older brother, knew all the sacrifices Des had made, what he'd suffered. More father than brother, Des had always been there. He loved his older brother; this whole takeover of Montgomerie Enterprises would make Des a billionaire several times over—or destroy him if everything turned sour. One wrong move and their plans would come crashing down like a house of cards. His telling Asha everything might set that in motion.

Despite that fear, he couldn't continue to love her, couldn't give her the words in him, the words she wanted to hear. He had no right to offer her the future he so desperately wanted until she knew all. There was no other way. He wasn't stupid; he knew this was the necessary next step in their relationship. Only, he was so bloody scared. Scared of losing her. He'd never known true happiness. Until Asha. He didn't want to make a choice between Des and Asha. He loved them both. Damned if he betrayed Des. Damned if he lost Asha by telling her the truth. Damned if he continued lying.

Asha came from the office and fixed a lemonade. She gave him a smile that hit his heart. A coward, he swallowed back his need to come clean, and instead soaked up the radiant happiness she brought to him.

"Well, that's sorted out," she informed him. "I have a caterer from Lexington doing the Halloween party. They were giving me a headache about orange and black cupcakes."

Sam stuck his head through the serving window. "About time you got in here, girl. My *Chicken What Du Hell* is ready. Somebody needs to eat it. Set yourselves down and enjoy. Might as well, with that storm this place will stay dead."

Jago laughed, following Asha to a booth by the window. He watched as the cook brought out two plates heaped with food. "Not sure what this is, but sure smells good."

"Tastes even better. Make you forget about Tex-Mex. Enjoy." Sam grinned and shuffled back to the kitchen.

The dish turned out to be big chunks of roast chicken, noodles, tomatoes and onions, in a lemon sauce with a hint of white wine. It was delicious, as Sam promised, but Jago couldn't fully enjoy it because his guilty conscience gnawed at his mind. He cleaned his plate so didn't really have room for cheesecake. Even so, he accepted the dessert and coffee, prolonging what he knew he must do.

When he finished, he pushed his plate aside. "You mind if I smoke?"

"Go ahead. I rather like that cherry smell." Asha took another bite of cheesecake and smiled dreamily, savoring the taste.

Jago exhaled a stream of smoke away from her, and fought off panic. His hand shook as he reached to pull the ashtray closer. Stalling. "We need to talk."

Lightning suddenly struck across the road, the following thunder reverberating through the whole diner. The lights flickered and then died. There was something strangely intimate being in the empty diner in the dimness. Jago hoped it was not an omen of Asha's reaction to what he was about to tell her.

"Asha, we've only known each other a few days; somehow it seems longer. As if I've known you for years. I think it best if I tell you a few things—"

"Asha! Oh, Asha!" Colin ran into the restaurant. "Oo-oo-oo—it's so exciting!"

Feeling like he just escaped the hangman's noose, Jago laughed uneasily. "Oh? I'd have never guessed."

"Asha . . . you are . . . not . . . going . . . to believe this. This is . . . soooooo cool."

Asha smiled, getting up to refill her lemonade. "I can hardly wait to hear."

Colin beamed proudly. "I got a phone call from Stuart Hersh."

Jago pushed out of the booth and followed her to perch on a stool. "Who's Stuart Hersh? A locksmith?"

"Funny. Nope, Hersh handles the bookings for Bobby 'Boris' Pickett. I'd tried several months back to see if Pickett could come to the Halloween party and perform. I mean, would that be cool or what? He was booked solid—popular time of the year for him—so it was no go. But get this—Hersh called to see if we still wanted to hire him. There was a cancellation. He said Pickett's hosting a Halloween party in Louisville on the Friday before Halloween, and then one on Saturday and Sunday in Lexington. So, he'll be in the area. If we give him lodging from Sunday through Thursday, he could do our Halloween gig on Wednesday. We could announce it at the drive-in. We could do some posters and handbills. So, can we?"

The lights flickered on, then the jukebox slowly came to life and began playing "Monster Mash." Jago stared at the shiny Wurlitzer. "Freaky."

"See? Even the box wants Bobby." Colin nearly danced in place. "Can we, huh?"

"Sure. That will be great fun," Asha gave her consent, amusement twinkling in her amber eyes.

Jago ground out his cigarillo in the ashtray, and opened his mouth to ask Asha if they could go somewhere quiet where they could talk, but Delbert came in. The cat dashed in between the old man's legs, sending everyone scurrying to catch him. The silly beast proved quick for a pussycat that had two speeds—waddle and stop.

Jago smiled at the antics, watching Asha, adoring her, and realizing their talk would have to come soon. That damn letter was out there. He had to tell her himself before someone else did.

Chapter Twenty-two

It proved to be a perfect All Hallows Eve, warm, yet with a nip in the soft breeze. Asha couldn't have conjured a more beautiful day for The Windmill's Halloween bash. The remaining leaves of the sugar maples and oaks were still ablaze with oranges and the occasional splash of brilliant reds, setting the countryside afire with this magical time.

Inside The Windmill, a fat jack-o'-lantern sat on the end of the counter, a sappy, toothy grin carved into the face; its softly flickering candle cast a pale amber glow across the darkened diner. Even the jukebox endlessly playing "Tell Laura I Love Her" seemed part of the delightfully supernatural ambience swirling in the air.

Her hips softly swaying to the soulful ballad, Asha stood by the diner window, sipping a lemonade and absorbing the beauty of the landscape. She sensed a peace, a rightness in this day, in her world. Since there were still a lot of preparations for Halloween night, she had closed the diner after the lunch rush and now stood in the silent restaurant with the lights out, enjoying the tranquil moment.

Twisting the clear rod to open the Venetian blinds, she observed Jago washing the Shelby—with a little 'advisory help' from Colin and the cat that still didn't have a name. She figured any minute Jago would turn the hose on Colin, who kept pointing out each patch Jago missed. The instant Jago wiped down the car so it wouldn't spot, the cat jumped up on it and padded across the hood. Smiling, she watched Jago pick up the pesky feline and place him down with a pat, then rewashed the tracks. The scene was nothing out of the ordinary, yet one of those instances in time she so treasured.

Unhurried, she relished this moment of solitude; there hadn't been many of them in the past few weeks. All had shifted and changed with Jago's coming, with his quickly slipping into being a part—the focus—of her world. The speed with which he fit into her life, and then morphed into her heart still left her breathless, often scared. Despite the fear, she embraced the spellbinding madness of being in love, truly in love.

Jago used his bungalow as an office for his business concerns now as his days and nights were spent with her. He cheerfully helped out with all The Windmill's businesses, and seemed genuinely to enjoy himself. Interested in every aspect, he about drove Colin nuts with questions about the drive-in's projector system. Asha smiled, thinking how much good it did Colin's ego that Jago wanted to hear his opinions.

Some days after breakfast, Jago accompanied Liam to Valinor and learned about running the horse farm. That made her nervous. Still, Liam seemed happy with it, so she figured her devious brother had an ace or two up his sleeve. Being a 'Meddling Montgomerie,' she had to fight the urge to prod Jago and Liam both about the status of the sale; she didn't like it hanging over their heads. At such times, she simply took a deep breath and reminded herself it was Liam's business. He'd have to take care of the farm, just as she'd take care of The Windmill. Whatever the case, she didn't want the situation to intrude on her relationship with Jago.

Her brother appeared increasingly happy—at least where the farm was concerned. His romance with Netta on the other hand, oddly appeared stalled. Such a beautiful man, women were usually ready to kill simply to gain his notice; her arrogant brother wasn't used to anyone keeping him at arms' length. But that was precisely what Netta was doing. Asha suspected Netta had cold feet and was running scared. Again, she bit back the temptation to butt in and play matchmaker. She really felt Netta was good for Liam—or could be if she stopped throwing obstacles up between them. Asha knew she wouldn't appreciate Liam trying to interfere between Jago and her, so no matter how hard it was, she reined in and left Netta and Liam to work matters out between themselves.

Outside these small worries, everything was so perfect between Jago and her. The final piece to the puzzle, he completed her world. He was liked and respected by all at The Windmill. The only troubling aspect: she occasionally caught a questioning expression in her employees' eyes when they thought she wasn't looking. Concern. They clearly approved of her loving Jago, only they held reservations, were fearful she would be hurt if things suddenly soured.

She would've dismissed their anxieties completely if she hadn't caught Jago with a similar glint in his eyes. That had caused her heart to miss a beat. Several times he'd approached her saying, "We need to talk" only to have someone intrude. She assumed he wanted to discuss where they were headed in their affair. Continuing to build upon their relationship would soon require more permanent changes in their lifestyles, such as how he would handle his job with Trident Ventures. Everything was just so ideal, she hesitated to broach any aspect of his connection to Trident.

Right now, she was very much in love and wanted to savor that special magic. All else could hang.

Especially, on this night. Halloween! She was eager to see what Jago would dress up as. A smile tugged at the corner of her mouth as she contemplated his reaction to *her* costume.

With a happy sigh, she gathered her purse and locked the restaurant. " 'She did the Mash . . . the Monster Mash . . . ,' " she sang softly as she walked along the sidewalk and rounded the building. Just before she turned to go toward her bungalow, she waved to Jago and Colin still futzing with the car. Evidently tired of playing carwash, What's His Name came running after her.

"You missed a spot, Jago."

In response, Jago's hand flexed around the large sponge as he gritted his teeth. He really liked Colin, enjoyed the quirky chatter the man kept up, only right now he wished his hand was around Colin's scrawny neck and not the sponge. Dropping it into the pail with a plop, he picked up the hose and sprayed the car.

"Black cars are a pain. Show every smudge you miss." Colin pointed with his cigarette toward a slowly appearing streak. "You missed another here."

"Thank you. I don't know what I'd do without your help," Jago replied.

Colin stopped inspecting the car, looked at Jago in his cut off jeans and made a sour face, though his eyes flashed merriment. "You know, Jago, those shorts do nothing for your legs."

He knew Colin was deliberately pushing his buttons, trying to get a rise out of him. The runt was rather good at it, too. Jago re-sprayed the fender and seriously considered turning the hose on Colin. Instead, he reached over, pulled the unlit cigarette from the pest's mouth.

"Stop baiting me just to relieve your boredom." Snapping

it in two, he flicked it away, trying not to laugh. "Smoking is bad for your health—in more ways than one."

"Asha and you keep telling me that, and I keep reminding *you* that you smoke those funny little cigars. *Swisher Sweets*," he said the name in a high, mocking voice. "Frankly, they're something a guy wearing shorts would smoke. Even the name sounds—"

"Anyone ever tell you what a pain in the bum you are, Colin?"

"Bum? That's what . . . an English rear end?" He chuckled. "Sure, all the time. I'm growing on you. *Told* you. Seriously, if you'd just give in and call me Oo-it, then I wouldn't irritate you so much. Everyone expects a Colin to be well behaved. An Oo-it can say or do anything and everyone laughs."

The cell phone sitting on the car dash began to chirp. With a smile Colin opened the door and reached for it. "Phone's ringing, Jago," he informed him redundantly, squinting to study the small buttons. Once more, the urge to let Colin have it with the hose tickled within Jago.

"Thanks, I might've missed that," he chuckled.

Colin punched the button and started talking, "Oo-it's Wash-o-rama. You pay it, we spray it. What can I do you for?" A big grin spread across his face and his eyebrows lifted. "Ah, *Trevelyn* . . . yes, the hired help is here, and yes, you may speak to him. However, remember this is a business, and we frown upon personal calls, just so you—"

Jago jerked the phone out of Colin's hand, shooting him a glare. The quirky man sniggered playfully. "Trevelyn? Bet he wears shorts, too."

Jago frowned at Colin, clearly indicating he should go away and not eavesdrop, but the pest just blinked his intelligent eyes and played innocent. It was too much to resist: Jago finally pressed the lever on the hose and let loose with the spray.

"Hey, hey!" Colin danced out of range. "Just for that, I'm

going to go find your cat, kidnap him and hold him for ransom."

"Well, while you're torturing him, see if he'll reveal his name." Laughing, Jago finally put the phone to his ear. "Hello, brother dearest. I'm rather busy at the moment, so make it short, please."

"Yeah, they're getting ready to put you in a padded cell. I leave you alone for a few weeks and you get into trouble. Oo-it's Wash-o-rama? Kidnapping and torturing your cat? What cat? Even more pressing, what the bloody hell is an Oo-it?"

The voice on the other end of the phone sounded different, the Brit accent stronger now. Also, Trev's tone resonated with a tension, though being Trev the Omnipotent, he was trying to screen it. Someone else might miss these small changes, but not Jago; attuned to the man who was his mirror image, he always knew when Trevelyn was trying to hide something. Judging by his own situation, he figured that 'something' had to do with Trev being around Raven Montgomerie. Curiosity ate at him, made him ponder just how involved Trev was with Asha's twin.

"Oo-it is the nickname for a quirky but strangely endearing character who works at The Windmill. Whole place is full of them."

"Similar to Falgannon Isle. When I talk to Des, he sounds like he's hip deep in oddballs. He's also getting a hint of a Scottish burr; and you, brother dear, are acquiring a Kentucky twang," Trev teased.

"While you are growing veddy Brit. Consider yourself lucky you didn't go to Falgannon or here and escaped the local color. Your finicky temperament couldn't handle it."

"Oh, I wouldn't say I avoided eccentric people. There's a small band of Gypsies camped on the Colford property. I'd think people living in wagons in this day and time ranks up there with out of the ordinary." Trev exhaled, obviously stressed or tired. "How are things going?"

"I detect a note of concern," Jago said.

"I wish this was all done. The pretense of being Trevelyn *Sinclair* wearies me. I've been buying up Montgomerie Enterprise stock left and right all week, yet keeping it slow enough not to draw attention. We're gaining inroads. Still, I'd prefer the takeover to be a *fait accompli*. I dislike not being in contact with Des or you. I ring and ring and can't reach either of you. I keep having dreams of the sisters getting together and comparing notes—then all hell breaks loose."

"Between us, I'd prefer we just drop the plans, tell them the truth, now, before your dream becomes a reality . . . a nightmare."

"Knowing what it would do to Des? It'd not just ruin him financially, but also what it would do to *him*. This isn't about money. You know that," Trevelyn argued. But there was less conviction to his words than there had been three weeks earlier.

Jago's hand gripped the phone, fighting to keep from tossing it against the nearby tree. "There should be another way. The takeover will happen; Des has the wheels in motion and there's no stopping it. Only, we can come clean first. Lay all our cards on the table. Do the deal straight on."

"Des wants it this way. We owe him—"

Jago leaned his head back. Breathing in and exhaling slowly, he reached for a control that was rapidly slipping away from him. "Don't start. Just don't bloody start. I've heard the song and dance, chapter and verse, until I am ready to puke, Trev. This is *not* the way. It can't be the way—"

His phone chirped at the same time his brother cut him off. "My other line is ringing, Jago. Let me take it. It's Mershan International's line, so it will be Julian. Hold—"

"That's my phone saying the battery is low." Jago jumped at the excuse to break off the conversation that threatened to ruin his whole night. "I need to recharge it. I'm out for the night, so call me tomorrow. Not early. Remember the time difference."

"No! Wait—"

The line went dead. Whatever his brother wanted, it could wait.

Asha adjusted the long, black wig on her head and stepped back to study the effect in the mirror. Her sister B.A. was a beautiful blonde; her twin, Britt, was a stunning brunette. The remainder of the Montgomerie sisters took after their father and had various shades of auburn hair. To see the blue-black wig on her head, a shade similar to Jago's hair, was startling to say the least.

"Wonder what Sexy Lips will think of me as Morticia Addams?" She had been speaking to the cat, but looked around and noticed the creature had vanished.

The bungalow was small—not many places he could disappear. Checking the kitchen proved the still nameless kitty wasn't there feeding his face. Wondering where What's His Name had vanished, Asha headed to the bathroom and flipped out the lights. The patio door was closed, so he hadn't gotten out that way.

She shut the closet door, but felt a cool draft coming from across the room. As she stared in that direction, unease skittering over her skin, the louvered shutters moved apart, pushed inward by a breeze as though moved by ghostly hands. Going to them, she took hold of the knob and pulled them wide. The window was raised about six inches—enough for the cat to climb through.

"Even a fat cat," she muttered in puzzlement.

There was no screen covering the window. They were on all the bungalows, so why was hers missing? Feeling a chill creeping up her spine, she recalled Jago's cabin had been broken into. Though nothing had been taken, she didn't like that someone had violated his privacy. Now her screen was gone and the window open. She hadn't left it that way.

Maybe Jago had forgotten to close it and she hadn't noticed before. That still didn't explain the screen. Nothing had happened to any of the bungalows or the rooms since the incident of Jago's broken lock; regardless, she didn't like the feel of this.

Putting her hand on her hips, she glared at the window. She went to the kitchen and found a screwdriver and two screws. Coming back, she closed the window and locked it. Then, where the bottom pane met the top, she very carefully twisted the screws into the wood at an angle on each side, only partway, effectively stopping someone from raising it. Closing the louvers, she hooked them shut, too. She'd check on where the screen had vanished later. Right now, she had to hustle; she didn't want to be late to her party.

The Shelby was back in its usual parking space, but as she stepped outside, Asha saw the lights in Jago's cabin were off. Evidently he had already changed into his costume. She guessed the cat was with him.

Feeling as if she'd forgotten something, she decided to go around and check on Delbert, suggest he close down the lobby early and go to the party. The dear man's spirits seemed a little down for the past couple of weeks. She was worried about him. Maybe a few laughs and a dance might cheer him up, she hoped.

She entered through the atrium, but he wasn't about. She started to leave, but then her little voice nagged at her to check on him. Going down the hall off the side of the lobby, she followed it back to the rooms where Delbert lived. The door was ajar, but she hesitated before entering.

Peeking around her doorframe, she called, "Delbert?"

No response. Seeing light cast across the floor, as though a reading lamp was on in the bedroom, she slowly entered. Delbert was sitting in an overstuffed chair in the far corner. She smiled at the touches of old-fashioned décor about the room, the lace doilies on the tables and one on the back of the chair. Someone had spent hours making them. Delbert was sitting with a large album across his lap, the narrow beam of the lamp directly on it.

"Delbert?" She knocked on the doorframe, trying to draw his attention. "Hey, Delbert. I'm looking for an escort to this big Halloween bash. I thought Obi-Wan might like to do the honors."

His posture was so forlorn that her heart squeezed. He looked up at her, and she saw his cheeks were streaked with tears. Worried, Asha rushed to him, frightened something was very wrong. She reached out and gently touched his arm.

"What's a matter? Are you all right?"

He sucked in a deep breath and gave a forced smile. "I'm fine. You look different with black hair, Asha. I always had a thing for Carolyn Jones. Used to watch that silly show each week just to see her in that black dress, those eyes flashing wickedly."

Trying to lighten his mood, Asha imitated Morticia and did the Addams Family snap of the fingers. "And do I do her justice?"

"You are beautiful, girl. Inside and out. Not many people are. I'd like some pictures of you and your Jago for my album."

"Certainly. All you want."

His trembling fingers reached out and stroked the edge of a photo. "He reminds me of Tommy, you know, same curly black hair. Oh, he doesn't really look like him. But the eyes . . . sometimes I stare at them and I recognize it's Jago, but for a breathless moment I see Tommy."

Asha's heart dropped. "Tommy Grant?" *Maybe you'd better ask those who know more about them. There's one or two around.* "You knew Tommy?"

"A handsome boy. He grew into a great young man. I was so proud of him." Such sorrow filled Delbert's eyes as he looked up at her. "I don't think I ever told him . . . I can't remember . . . but I don't think I told him how proud I was to be his uncle."

"Uncle?"

"His mother was my older sister. Margaret Seacrest. Maggie, we called her. She married David Grant. Damn, so many mistakes in my life, girl. Too late to change things. My life's over. Just regrets now. Tommy's father was killed, hit head-on by a drunk driver. Maggie didn't have a way to support herself. You see, it wasn't expected of women back then. They married and stayed home to take care of the kids. That was the way of things. Women didn't have careers. Only, Maggie had a son to raise. I took over supporting them. I didn't have that much to give. Did what I could. I was a struggling lawyer, you know. Hard to build a practice in Leesburg. Times were tough. I worked long and hard, and much to my shame, often I resented that I was caring for Maggie and Tommy, instead of a wife and son of my own. Wasn't good of me. I shouldn't have done that . . . thought those things."

"Delbert, don't be too hard on yourself. We're only human. Sometimes we're less than perfect, think or say things we really don't mean. People who love us understand."

"I bought him that Mustang. They died in that car. Maybe if I hadn't bought it . . ."

Asha took his hand and clutched it tightly. "Sadly, bad things happen to good people. You buying a car had nothing to do with that."

The old man's hand trembled as he nodded. "But they were so young, Asha . . . had so much to live for. Would have gotten married in a year, had children. They . . . would've made a beautiful son. He'd be about the age of your Jago now." Delbert looked down at the picture of Laura and Tommy. "I feel them here. As if they didn't move on. My sister died by her own hand. Took pills one night. She couldn't live with losing both Dave and Tommy in car accidents. I used to come here, eat at the restaurant, or go to the drive-in. Play their song. After a spell, when people figured I should stop grieving and get on with my life, they began giving me pitying looks. '*Poor Delbert, not right in the head*.' I had a heart attack when I was in my early sixties. A bad one. Nearly died. Your mama, god bless her soul, came to the University Hospital and picked me up. Brought me back here. Not sure where I would be without her."

"She did the right thing. You belong here with us."

"It was a good day you came back after your mama died. I feared this special place would one day be swallowed up by developers."

She grinned. "Won't happen. I'm holding on to this place. And now I have Jago. He'll be my warrior. He'll fight for me, fight for The Windmill."

Delbert nodded. "Then I can die in peace."

"Like bloody hell you will." Glancing at the pictures of Tommy and Laura, Asha wanted to see them. Just not tonight. Delbert needed to get out and ease his troubled heart, be with the rest of the Windmill family. Closing the album, she took it from his hands. "Some rainy afternoon I'd love for you to show me all the pictures and tell me about Tommy and Laura. I think I have a few things to tell you as well. But this night is magic. I shan't leave unless you come. Tommy wouldn't want you here alone."

He let her take the album. "I'm old, Asha. Life passed me by."

"No, it didn't. You just live at The Windmill where time tends to stand still. You have a lot of years ahead of you. Stop wasting them with regret. We have so much to do here, and if I have my way, you'll have a godson to bounce on your knee." She shrugged. "Maybe next year?"

His grin was real. "Godson? You going to marry Jago?"

"Yeppers. Sure am. I haven't told him yet—men like to think it's all their idea." She took Delbert's arm and wrapped hers around it. "So, for now this is our little secret."

"You are a special lady, Asha Montgomerie. He's very lucky to have you."

"Actually, he is. Now let's hurry. We wouldn't want to miss Bobby 'Boris' Pickett doing The Mash."

"You think he might sing 'Purple People Eater'?"

She laughed aloud. "I'm sure if you request it he might. If not, Colin and I will do a version for you."

He chuckled. "Now that would be a sight to see."

Chapter Twenty-three

But I'm lost for words
When I hold you close
Because you take my breath . . .
Away.

The beautiful ballad "Lost for Words" by Mike Duncan was softly playing in the background, yet suddenly Jago could barely hear it. He'd just asked Colin who the artist was, and where he could buy the CD, because the song seemed to reach into him, touch his heart. Duncan's voice was haunting, compelling. Then he had looked down the terraced hillside and saw Asha coming up the winding concrete stairs, and he was truly lost for words, too. Lost to anything, for that matter. All the festive party noises, the wild costumes and the Halloween decorations faded to a dim blur as he stared at the woman he simply loved more than life.

" 'And you take my breath. Away,' " Jago sang.

He'd loved Asha from that first breathless instant when she materialized from the brilliant sunlight and walked into the restaurant. In that moment, he had accepted Fate. Now he couldn't breathe as he watched her trying to climb the stairs and not trip on the 'spider leg feet' of her costume.

His mouth quirked up as he noted the black wig she wore. It threw him. She carried off the outfit well, making a surprisingly sexy black-haired lass. But then, he had a notion she could show up baldheaded and in a burlap sack and he'd love how she looked. He leaned on the wood rail post like a sap, drinking in the vision of Morticia Addams helping Obi-Wan Kenobi up the steps.

"Hey, Asha sure is a hottie in that get-up, eh?" Colin elbowed him with a big grin and then snapped several pictures. "Oo . . . oo . . . oo . . . it. I know, I can sell you copies for a buck. Eh? Great set of knockers she's got. Want me to get some close-ups?"

"I may kill you some day." Jago's threat had no teeth, though.

Colin wasn't fazed either. "I'm growing on you. Told you, I would."

Jago chuckled and then summoned a proper glare, looking Colin up and down. "How the bloody hell did we both end up in vampire costumes?" he asked.

"Us? What about *him?*" Colin asked, swinging around and lowering the camera to snap pictures of the pudgy cat, wandering around in a Dracula cape. "Silly kitty, I think he likes the costume."

Asha entered the glasshouse, then pulled up when she saw the three of them. Steepling her hands before her mouth, she tried to contain her laughter . . . and failed. "I feel like I'm watching an old episode of 'What's My Line' on the Game Show Channel. *'Will the real Dracula please stand up?'* "

Jago grinned and raised his arms to flourish his cape. "I tried to buy a giant leech costume, but they didn't have one. I bought the next best bloodsucker."

"And What's His Name, too?" she patted the vampire kitty on the head.

"I thought about a bunny costume. They had a pink one

for kitties, just like Ralphie in *The Christmas Story*, but figured he'd think it beneath his dignity." Jago lifted a strand of her black wig, toying with it, just needing to touch her.

"I didn't know fur-covered hogs had dignity." Colin sniggered. Then suddenly his eyes grew wide. "Oo . . . oo . . . it's Bobby!"

Jago chuckled seeing the guest of honor coming around the pool with Derek—*both* in Dracula capes. "It's an epidemic!"

"There's a distinct lack of originality around this place, Asha. We need a five Drac limit on this party. Any more show up flapping a cape, I say we chuck them out on their keister." Excited, Colin rushed over to snap pictures of his idol Bobby Pickett.

"Too late!" Jago raised his glass in salute as Liam, in the Count's full regalia, escorted another Morticia Addams in through the glass door.

"Well, this is a fine how-do-you-do." Asha and her 'spider feet' wiggled over to face Netta who was equally lovely in the black wig. The two stared at each other, and then slowly circled to examine the other closely, their two sets of fake spider feet bouncing as they turned 360-degrees. Almost as if in mirror, both women raised their arms, glowered at each other and then in complete unison did the Addam's finger snap.

Everyone broke into a riot of laughter, including the two women.

Winnie came out of the clubhouse in an Elvira getup. She paused, then blinked at seeing the two Morticias and the six Draculas. "Gee, I haven't even had a drink yet," she said.

"OO . . . oo . . . it! Wow!" Colin nudged Jago in the ribs again, referring to Winnie's black dress, cut lower than the Morticias. "Bet you wish Asha came in *that* costume." He ran over and clicked at Winnie in her sexy outfit, moving in closer until he was obviously snapping chest shots.

Liam pointed out with a bemused smile, "It seems the party should've been 'Ladies in black and Vamps only theme.' Halloween Express must have sold every Drac and Morticia costume they had."

"Bite your tongue," Netta chided. "I'll have you know I made my costume from scratch."

Asha sniffed envy. "No wonder yours fits so well."

"Thanks, I sew all my clothes." Netta shrugged shyly.

Jago was impressed; the quality of her costume vastly outshone Asha's bought version. "You have a true talent, Netta. Ever thought about turning your skills into running a boutique? You could do a very exclusive, upscale store in one of the Lexington malls."

For a moment, Netta's blue eyes shone with possibilities, then she clamped down on the dream. "Costs money. But I'll keep it in mind."

"Gather round, kiddies," Colin called over the music and chatter of the guests. "Time for Bobby to do The Mash. Don't forget to get a copy of his autobiography, *Monster Mash, Half-Dead in Hollywood* or his CD. After he performs, he'll autograph them for everyone."

"What about 'The Purple People Eater'?" Delbert asked, picking up What's His Name.

Jago swirled one side of his cape around him and quipped, "Purple-people-eater? More to the point, I vant to know vhat ever happened to my Transylvania Tvist?"

Bobby Pickett joined the laughter, then shook his finger. "Hey, bud, that's *my* shtick. You and the cat butt out. I work alone."

The night passed too quickly, Asha thought. The bash was a big success, drawing a huge crowd, with Bobby Pickett proving as popular as ever. It was a crowning moment—though it was repeated several times through the night due to encore requests—when he performed "The Monster Mash." Colin stared at the man in complete adoration.

It caused her pause when on a break Pickett thanked her for having him perform at the party. "This has been a really great gig," he said. "The place hasn't changed in all these years. Just endures, like my song. You even still have that funny neon windmill marquee for the drive-in."

Asha was ladling punch into the black and orange paper cups for everyone. She stopped and considered his words. "You were here before? At The Windmill?"

"Yeah, back in 1963. When the song was still really hot—the first time around. The song went to the Top One Hundred three different times," he informed her proudly.

She forced a smile as he took the cup of punch and walked away. Glancing up the hill to the drive-in, she watched the pink and aqua neon tube lights outlining the wooden windmill, flicking back and forth so it appeared to be turning. Pickett had performed in the autumn of 1963, less than a year before Tommy and Laura had died. A circle had closed.

A shiver crawled over her. While there hadn't been any more incidents where she slipped into Laura Valmont's life, she suddenly felt rather distant, the past sucking at her. Once again, the glass walls, rendered nearly invisible by the night, started to fade, giving way to a time when the pool was unenclosed.

"Asha." A hand grasped her upper arm and gave a small shake. "Asha, damn it."

She blinked three times before she saw Jago in his Dracula costume in front of her. Trying to fake it, she smiled. "Enjoying the party, Vlad?"

"Don't try to shine me on, Asha. This time I want an explanation," he demanded.

The man was bloody insistent, so she tried to distract him by waving the promise of hot sex under his nose. "Vlad the Impaler. Hmm, think you'll be *up* to a little *impaling* in awhile?"

"Your wish is my *impale*, Morticia." She started to walk away before he could question her further, only Jago jerked her around to face him. "Imminent debauchery aside, I want answers. I'm male, so I can be led around by my"—he glanced down with a wicked grin, then raised his hand and wiggled his little finger—"uh, pinkie, but that doesn't mean I'm forgetful. As soon as the blood comes back to my brain, I'll remember I wanted answers to a certain situation."

Asha nodded, realizing despite the playful teasing he was quite serious in wanting to know about her spells. "You can have answers, Jago. Just, later. When we're alone. The party's nearly over and I want to enjoy the last few minutes."

"Okay, reprieve granted. Nevertheless, I want an explanation soon, Morticia."

"Hey, Asha," Delbert called, rocking in a glider, with the Dracula kitty sitting contently next to him. He patted the empty space on his other side. "Come sit by old Obi-Wan."

"Why, Delbert Seacrest, you're tiddled!" Asha chuckled going over to him.

He gave her a mellow grin. "May the force"—a hiccup popped out, shaking his whole body—"be . . . with you." With that, he almost fell forward.

"That's it, Jedi Master. No more punch for you. Come on, Jago. Let's help Delbert home and tuck him up."

They each took an arm to aid Delbert to his feet. As they helped the elderly man along, Jago slowed just enough to snatch up his copy of Pickett's book and two CDs—"The Monster Mash" and Mike Duncan's, on loan from Colin. "Mr. Pickett, it's been an honor. Thank you for coming," he said.

"I was delighted to do the gig. Maybe you folks will have me back next year, but as a guest. I'm finally retiring next month."

"Count on it." Jago waved the Mike Duncan CD. "Oo-It, thanks for letting me borrow it."

Colin beamed. "Hey, you finally called me Oo-it! Told you I'd grow on you."

As the cat waddled past, following them back to the bungalow, Bobby called to the kitty, "Good night, Clint."

Jago, Colin and Asha said in unison. "Clint?"

* * *

Humming the theme to *The Good, the Bad and the Ugly*, Asha snapped out the light in the hallway leading to Delbert's rooms. Sam came around the corner, still wearing his Darth Vader costume sans the mask, and gave her a smile. "You run on with Jago, and enjoy the rest of trick-or-treatin'. I'll keep an eye out on our Obi-wan."

"Thanks. 'Night, Dark Lord of Sith." She kissed his cheek. "See you in the morn."

Jago returned, toting the fat cat on his shoulder. "The office is now closed and locked tight. Almost the Witching Hour, sexy lady. Shall we go raise a little magic?" He took her hand and led her out toward the bungalows.

"I thought since the party was winding down, we could go up to the drive-in and watch the horror movies until dawn," Asha suggested as he opened the door and put Clint inside.

Instead of replying, Jago swung her around and pinned her against the wall, kissing her slowly, thoroughly, his hands rubbing up and down from her hips to her breasts. He tasted like pineapple sherbet and rum from the punch. He tasted like Jago. Her hands did a little roaming, too. She loved the hard muscles of his back, the broad shoulders, loved how their bodies fit so perfectly as she pressed against him.

He broke the kiss, panting. "Go get out of that dress—"

"Mmm, that's an idea." She nipped his chin and rubbed against his strong body like a cat.

"—and put on jeans." He nibbled on the lobe of her ear.

"Jeans?" Asha looked up into his glowing eyes, thinking she must have misheard.

"Yep. Jeans and your leather jacket. I'm taking your for a midnight ride on the Harley." He pushed her toward the bedroom. "Hustle that sweet arse, love. Vincent Price, Chris Lee and Oo-it are waiting. I'll go get the Harley. I'd help you change, but if I did that we'd never make it to the drive-in. Colin worked hard to get the films. He'd be disappointed if we didn't put in an appearance."

"You're sweet. It is important to Colin." Asha kissed his cheek. "But we don't have to stay until dawn."

"Hum, when we come back you can reward me for being sweet with a little private trick-or-treating?"

Still in the Dracula costume, Jago revved the Harley as she came out. Clint stood inside her bungalow, his nose pressed to the glass door. His tail snapped as he realized he was being left behind. In his vampire getup, he looked particularly comical—a true Kodak moment!

Asha practically danced across the patio, swung her leg over the Harley and climbed on behind him. "Where's my helmet?"

"We're just going up to the drive-in. I thought you might enjoy riding without one." He looked over his shoulder and grinned wickedly. "Sort of like having sex without a rubber."

Their eyes locked as they both thought the same thing: He hadn't used a condom with her. She wasn't on birth control pills, either. As she'd told Delbert, maybe next year he might have a godson. Of course, she had no idea how Jago felt about that.

So in tune with each other, Jago read her concerns. He brushed his lips against hers, then said, "Tomorrow, lass. We have a lot of things to talk about, important concerns. Tonight, I'm taking you for a ride up the hill. We'll watch a movie to make Colin happy. Then we can come back, get fussed at by Clint the Cat for abandoning him, and finally, I'm going to make love to you so slowly, so exquisitely, that you might even count to twenty-one. Now hang on while we go riding thunder."

Pushing his cape over to one side, Asha slid her arms around his waist. She leaned her head on his back and just let him take her where he wanted. He kept the speed down, gliding up the hill and then through the gates of the drive-in. He cut the headlight and coasted into the parking lot. Jago motored along the first row, turned and climbed up to the top and then finally back down to the concession stand. Slow and easy.

Some of the partygoers had already straggled up to the drive-in to sit on the lounges on the small porch off one wing, which had been decorated for the holiday.

Colin waved. "Hey, Drac has a Harley! Where's Clint?"

Jago balanced the bike until Asha dismounted, then set the kickstand. "Who's up for chili dogs? My treat."

"Hoo hoo, free food, I'm game. Bet I can eat more chili dogs than you, Jago. I once ate a frog on a bet for ten bucks." Rubbing his hands, Colin started after Jago. "I'm sure Netta will want one, too."

Netta waved and rolled her eyes. "No, thanks. After the frog story, I'm not in the mood for mystery meat. But I wouldn't mind a Big Red, lots of ice, and an Almond Joy."

Asha followed Colin and Jago inside, then touched his elbow. "I'm going to the little girls room to untangle my hair."

The concession stand always had a fun ambience—smells of cooking food, the sound of the movie playing outside, oddly muted, and the colorful signs and lights. As she passed along the windows she could see Peter Cushing chasing Christopher Lee. There's no place like a drive-in, she thought as she pushed into the ladies' lounge. Inside, elevator music played.

Going to the mirror, she pulled a small brush out of her fanny pack and set it on the counter. She unbraided her hair, carefully straightened the tangles and then quickly plaited it. Several women came and went, most stopping long enough to thank her for the Halloween party and for the all-night drive-in. It pleased her to know everyone really enjoyed the entertainment her small oasis provided. Looking at her reflection she saw happiness shining in her eyes.

"Glad you came back to take over the business, aren't you, old girl?" she said to her image.

As she came out of the restroom, she sidestepped the people rushing in. The current Dracula film had just ended and everyone was making a mad dash to the bathrooms and the concession stand before the next Lee-Cushing battle began. The crush made Asha feel like a fish trying to swim upstream!

She spotted Jago at the end of the line, near the cash register, and all the people became faceless blurs moving about her; she could only see him. Being female and quite territorial, she then zeroed in on two women in line behind him, all giggly and bouncy as only women 'in heat' can be. One gave her friend a gentle push, shoving her into Jago's back, trying to get his attention. Blushing, she twittered an apology as he reached for his wallet, then both women seized the opportunity to strike up a conversation with him.

"Pretty men are *such* a pain in the bum. Where's my claymore when I need it?" she muttered to herself, though strangely she didn't feel the usual surge of jealousy. She trusted Jago, was secure in how he felt about her.

Someone slammed into her shoulder, knocking her back a step. She blinked, putting out her hands almost defensively, her mind going from confusion to revulsion faster than she could form thought. Her attention shifted from Jago to the man before her, and she stared up into crocodile eyes.

Monty Faulkner stood with a faint smile upon his face, no emotions in his yellow eyes. "Oh, I apologize . . . though it was your fault," he pointed out. "You weren't looking where you were going. You should be more careful. Good way to get hurt."

"You're quite right. My fault. Please accept my apologies." Asha simply wanted away from this man—now—and tried to move past.

He had other ideas. He reached out and caught her upper arms.

Asha summoned up her Scots warrior spirit and met his odd eyes, then looked down her nose to his hands. "Please take your hands off me." Her voice was calm, something the lady of the manor would use on a serf who'd dared touch her.

"Sure, Miz Montgomerie. I just wanted to tell you how great all this stuff is that you do around here. Gives people a place to go, a way to have fun. Not since back when they had the old skating rink open has there been such a nice place to spend an evening. Super job."

She forced a smile. This man was unsettling, but she wouldn't permit him to see it. He was a bully who fed off weakness. "Thank you. I try. Now, if you'll excuse me."

For a moment she feared he wasn't going to let go, but then he released her. "Happy Halloween. Hope you get plenty of tricks-or-treats—whichever you want." Then he turned and vanished into the crowd.

Asha knew she was being silly. Every community had a black sheep, a 'Boo Radley' who creeped everyone out. That didn't mean he was really dangerous. Local gossip always blew everything out of proportion, to where truths became exaggerated legend. Hadn't Boo turned out to be the kindly protector of innocent children?

Jago came up and kissed her lightly on the mouth—a chili dog kiss—banishing Faulkner from her thoughts. "Sorry, my stomach rumbled and I had to comply." His grin faded as concern flickered in his eyes. "You're not going spacey on me again, are you?"

"Nope. Just lost in a moment of thought." She snatched up one of the hot dogs smothered with the mouthwatering chili and pushed back the paper wrapper to take a bite.

"I prefer them with onions, but I have a hot date for later." He kissed her again, his tongue finding chili at the corner of her mouth. "Like a boy scout, I'm always prepared."

"Lucky me—a man who holds his end *up*," Asha laughed.

He grinned. "You better believe it."

Asha's body rocked against Jago's as he brought the Harley to a fast stop. Instead of climbing off, she just sat there hugging his warm back. She had to admit, while the bike still scared her, she enjoyed riding with Sexy Lips. There was something rather *stimulating* about being shoved up against his back, her arms around his waist. The low rumble of the powerful engine between her legs summoned images of no-holds-barred, ride-'em-cowboy sex. The vibration from the Electra Glide moved into her muscles and then lodge in her pelvis with a quiver.

Too smart by half, Jago's chest shook from his soft laughter. "You feel it."

She nodded her head and just hugged him tighter, loving him with her whole heart. Wanting desperately to tell him how much. The need to express her feelings was overpowering, yet something warned her Jago wasn't ready to hear. This puzzled her. He was serious about her, so she didn't understand why this last barrier remained between them. Oh, he never said anything; it was just the fey connection they shared, the closeness she recognized when they'd had breakfast at The Cliffside.

He set the stand on the bike and turned so he could pull her into his arms, kissing her slowly, with the sheer pleasure of just kissing. Finally pulling back, he smiled. "Chili dog kisses are addictive. *You're* addictive. You know that, don't you?"

She smiled as he got off the Harley. "I sure hope I am."

Just inside the cottage, he paused and whispered, "Close your eyes and don't move until I say you can."

"Oooh . . . games?"

Clint the cat came to rub against her leg, meowing in complaint. She wasn't sure if it was a rant about being left alone, or that his food bowl was empty.

Music filled the darkness as Jago turned on the CD player; a catchy tune about seeing a 'UFO in the backyard' filled the small cottage. Asha liked it, thinking it rather fitting for Halloween, but Jago muttered, "Oops" and hit another button, switching it to a soft ballad about love. The tune was the same one she'd heard at the glasshouse earlier.

"Colin let me borrow his Mike Duncan CD. I'm ordering a couple copies in the morning. This guy is going places."

"Can I open my eyes now?" she asked.

"Nope." She could hear him moving closer, felt the radiant heat of his very male body, then finally the scent that was Jago filled her head. He brushed his lips over one eyelid, then the other. "Tomorrow we have a lot of words to say, a lot of things to discuss. For the rest of the night we banish words, have no need of them. From this point on—don't speak. Just experience how we communicate on an elemental level."

"I don't get to count?" She couldn't stop the smile from spreading across her lips.

His hands moved up the edge of her leather jacket and then very slowly peeled it off her shoulders, allowing it to drop to the floor. "Lass, I'm going to saturate your brain with me, with us, with sensations so devastating you won't be able to count. Just let it happen."

"I can do anything I want—I'm just not permitted to speak?"

He pulled her against his chest, lifting her slightly so he could feast on the side of her neck. "Hush, wench."

He kissed her, so lightly, so reverently, she couldn't stop tears from welling in her eyes. The kiss spoke all the words she wanted to hear, needed to hear, that told her how important she was to him, how special. The kiss spoke of a soul-deep, never-ending hunger and that only she could touch him in this unique way.

Capturing her wrists, he traced his thumbs in maddening circles on her palms, causing her nerve endings to tingle. Her mind cast back to when they'd met and he introduced himself. He'd done the same thing, marking her. Branding her. He began to rock, slow-dancing in the dark to the beautiful words. Her whole being burned with the consuming arousal. She soaked up every marvel of the magic his body worked on hers as they swayed, touching, brushing, compelled to him as if he were a magnet.

" 'But I'm lost for words . . . when I hold you close . . . because you take my breath . . . away.' " He sang the words, then he nuzzled her temple.

"You're speaking," she teased.

"Hush, wench. I'm *singing*."

Releasing her wrists, he placed his hands on her hips then circled her waist until his thumbs and forefingers released the snap on her jeans. Sliding inside, his strong fingers gave her hips a squeeze. She felt the faint ripple of surprise shudder through his muscles as he recognized his hands were touching flesh and only a little scrap of her thong.

He growled. "You wicked, wicked woman."

She looped an arm around his neck and arched to him. He leisurely pushed the jeans off her hips, down her thighs, finally leaving her to kick out of them, while he filled his hands with the globes of her derrière. She nipped his lower chin, then fussed, "You're speaking again. You said no words."

Teeth flashing in a feral smile, he jerked her against him. Taking a step, he lifted and balanced her on the edge of the counter between the living room and the kitchen, leaving her legs dangling. Her arms tightened about his neck and held on.

Taking hold of her long braid, he loosened it about her shoulders. With a smile, he fisted his hands in the heavy tresses and forced her head back, their eyes locking. Not about to let him control this beautiful passion, she locked her legs about his hips and dragged him to her, rocking against his groin. He kissed the strong column of her neck, fed on her fey essence, which she hoped would brand his soul.

His hands palmed her breast, squeezing, feeling the pebbled nipples through her thin muscle T-shirt. Her eyes adjusted to the dimness to where she saw his face clearly in the night-light from the kitchen; beautiful in his feral beauty, he was a pagan fire god come to burn her heart, her body, her soul.

She jerked in shock as he grabbed the front of her T-shirt and ripped it down the middle. He paused for a moment, just staring at her full breasts, areolas ruched against the caress of the cool air. Letting him know her arousal matched his, her chest rose and fell in short breaths lifting them, aching for his touch.

The passion flared bright, but with Mike Duncan's haunting voice flowing around them, through them this was more than just lust. This was the true beauty of their bonding. So much more. Need shuddered through her muscles. And not merely the need to have him inside her body, but to be able to speak all the words of how deeply she loved him.

He lightly dragged the back of his knuckle over that sensitized pearl at the apex of her female core, distracting her from thoughts. Asha nearly bucked off the counter in response. With a deliberateness that set her teeth on edge, he dragged her to the very rim of the counter. He pushed her panties aside; the rasp of his zipper followed. Then he was inside her, holding her rigidly. He set a rhythm so unhurried—his withdrawing, his becoming a part of her again—that she sighed in bliss, in agony.

The hot explosion rolled through her blood, slamming into her brain.

" 'Cause she takes my breath away.' " Jago gasped in near anguish, as he followed her into a release that fused their souls as one.

A tapping on the patio door came at the crack of dawn. Jago wanted to ignore it; Asha and he had barely been asleep for an hour. Nevertheless, after the scratching incident weeks before, the slightest noise outside always brought him fully awake. Sliding on his jeans, he zipped them up, then glanced at the sleeping cat and woman, his heart full of love.

He sighed. In a few hours she'd awaken, and then he'd tell her about Des, his mother and father. Strange. Had her grandfather not set into motion the events that resulted in his father killing himself, he might never have met Asha. Vagaries in the paths of life. It saddened him that everything good in his existence came with a steep price tag. Maybe he could make her see how Fate controlled their destinies, how they were *meant to be*.

Of that he was firmly convinced. There had never been a woman like Asha, never would be one capable of filling his life, his heart, the way she and her gentle love did. He so admired how she'd come back to The Windmill and worked hard to create this special family community. Not many people understood the quality of caring for others as she did.

He had a smattering of dread that no matter how carefully he explained everything, what drove his brothers, what drove him, there'd be hell to pay. Asha hadn't been forced to live with the deprivations of his childhood, watched his mother struggle to keep their family together, or how Des drove himself to rise above the poverty that had threatened them. This pampered granddaughter of Sean Montgomerie had never gone to bed hungry. He had, more times than he cared to remember. It'd be hard for Asha, born of a life of indulgence and privilege, to grasp fully what had initially compelled him to go along with Desmond's plans. Asha wouldn't take his deception well. Maybe he should take her to meet Des first, let her get to know his brother so she could comprehend how truly obsessed Des was. And why.

Maybe, maybe not. It was too late for alternatives. He *had* to tell her this morning. The lies stopped now, before he destroyed any hope of a future with her.

Glancing to the closet, he thought of the small, black jeweler's box in the pocket of his windbreaker—the engagement ring he'd ended up purchasing while in Lexington to buy the Halloween costume. He'd come out of the costumers and was getting into the Shelby when he noticed the jeweler across the street. On impulse, he'd crossed over and went into the upscale store. He wasn't sure what he wanted, or even why he'd come, but then he'd seen *the* ring: a yellow diamond, marquis-cut, a nice size at nearly three karats yet not too flashy. Asha wouldn't like anything flashy. And as he'd stared at the stone, he envisioned it on her finger, knew it was created only for her. For once, he was glad of his fey voice, pleased he'd listened to its proddings.

Of course, he could open their talk by giving Asha the ring and asking her to marry him, bind her to him before telling all. Yeah, right—the coward's way. *Will you marry me, Asha? Oh, by the way, your last name would be Mershan, not Fitzgerald.*

"She's going to kill me," he said in a whisper. Fear rising in him, he swallowed hard. No, he hadn't the right to ask Asha to be his wife until he was completely honest with her. Never in his whole life had he been a coward. He'd face the music and then crawl on his belly to kiss her feet if that's what it would take to make amends. Only, right now being a coward was damned tempting.

The rapping came again, more insistent this time. Obviously it wasn't someone poking around, but instead, trying to awaken them. The muscles of his abdomen flexed in reaction, preparing to absorb the coming psychic blow. No one would casually disturb them at this hour. Something was wrong.

With one last look at his lady, he padded across the living room to the front door. Pulling the curtain aside, he was startled to see a man in chauffeur's uniform, the cap off and tucked into the curve of his elbow. The pace of his heart increased in those seconds it took to unlocked the door.

"Mr. Mershan?" the man queried as the door slid to the side.

Jago glanced past the stranger to see a black limousine parked at the end of the small lane, parking lights on. "Yes, I'm Jago Mershan."

"Mr. Starkadder said I would recognize you by the green eyes and black hair," the chauffeur informed him, holding out an envelope. "I'm to give you this, sir."

Jago wanted to take the small square of paper about as

much as he ached to pet a king cobra. Sometimes, he wished he didn't have these fey impressions. The envelope sent blackness to coiling within him; he knew whatever words it contained were ones he didn't want to see.

Before the man began to think he was batty, he took the white envelope and broke the seal.

Come quickly. Your mother is dying.
Julian

Chapter Twenty-four

Asha jerked awake and looked around, feeling something was very wrong. Her hand reached out to the rumpled sheet where Jago had slept. It was cold. Stretching and yawning she sat up.

Reaching for her robe, she swallowed to moisten her dry mouth. "Ugh. That's dreadful! I must brush my teeth before Jago wants a good morning kiss. Poor man would pass out from my toxic waste breath." The cat mirrored her action, stretching and yawning, too. "Good morning, Clint," she chuckled. "At least we know your name now."

The bungalow was still. Too still. At the door to the bathroom she paused, suddenly torn between the pressing need to swish some industrial-strength mouthwash and to reassure herself where Jago was, that everything was all right.

Her niggling unease increased when she pulled back the curtain on the patio doors and saw Colin using a push broom to sweep leaves off the concrete courtyard before the cabins. She rolled back the door and the kitty dashed out. The cat trotted over and rubbed against Colin's leg.

"Morning, Asha." Colin gave a little wave. "Morning, Clint."

The animal usually followed Jago around, so it was odd he was with her. "Colin, have you seen Jago this morning?"

"Yeah, at dawn. I'd just closed up the drive-in and was coming down to put the money in the safe." His eyes watched her, concerned. "Figured I'd clean up the leaves while I waited for you to get up. I can go with you to deposit it. Between the Halloween bash and the drive-in, you really need to get all that money in the bank."

"Where's Jago?" Asha knew she needed to make a run to Leesburg, but had hoped Jago would go with her and they'd breakfast at The Cliffside. Then they could go for a walk along the river and have that talk he wanted.

"Gone." Colin shrugged, trying to imply nothing unusual in that.

"Gone?" Asha echoed.

"Yep. I stopped off at my house after closing the drive-in to get a couple aspirins before I took the money down to put in the safe. I looked out the window and saw this big ass limo sitting at the end of our little alley, flashers blinking. I came to check it out. Jago was speaking to this rigged-up driver in a chauffeur's uniform." He chuckled. "For a minute I wondered if this wasn't someone in costume doing a last minute trick-or-treat thing. He had on those crazy jodhpurs and all. You just don't see that around here, you know? Only, Jago went to his cabin, changed, came back out and left with him."

"Did he say anything?" Asha stuck her hands in her pockets to hide she was shaking.

Colin nodded. "He said I should take care of you and Clint until he comes back." His eyes grew sad. "Don't worry, Asha. Probably something to do with that big company he works for. High-powered outfits like that expect their management types to hop whenever there's trouble."

"Most likely." She offered him a smile she didn't feel. "Give me a half hour and then we can head to Leesburg."

"Sure thing."

She closed the door, trying not to overreact. Jago worked for a vast multinational organization. Something important had obviously arisen and his presence was needed immediately.

Figuring he'd leave her a note, she searched around. Nothing. "Jago will call," she told Clint, then went to change clothes. The words had been said more to reassure herself than the cat. They didn't work.

Especially when he didn't call that night. Or the next one.

Bleak November. The two words together were almost redundant, yet they seemed strangely created to describe this sad day. *The whole month, actually*, Jago thought. *Nearly a month without Asha*.

Wishing he were anywhere but here, he watched as they lowered the coffin containing Katlyn Fitzgerald Mershan into the grave. He'd once read there were people who attended funerals of someone they didn't know, because they drew some sick pleasure from the last rites. Well, no voyeuristic mourners lurked along the graveside today. Only Katlyn's sons stood marking her passing.

"Too bloody wet and cold," he said under his breath.

Jago sighed. The last three weeks had been a bad dream. Closing his eyes he thought back to Halloween, how the battery on his cell phone had died as Trevelyn received a ringing on another line. Julian Starkadder had been calling with news. After fighting cancer for nearly a year, Katlyn had taken a turn for the worse. The doctors were not sure how long she could last. Ever efficient, Julian had arranged for a limousine service to fetch Jago. When the tapping at the door came at first light, he'd never expected to hear the news his mother was dying.

In the half-shadows of the bedroom, packing to leave, he'd watched Asha slumbering peacefully, a smile on her beautiful face. Too much the coward, he had left her sleeping. Feeling as if his body had taken a hit from lightning, he couldn't think. Trying to form some reasonable explanation for his hasty departure was beyond him. Bloody hell, he hadn't even left her a note. He'd simply had asked Colin to take care of her when the man jogged down the hill to investigate the limo. Jago offered the excuse that a business emergency had arisen and he couldn't take time to explain, that he had a plane to catch. There were questions in Colin's gray eyes, but he merely nodded.

That seemed eons ago. Before his life had become one long nightmare of doctors coming and going, of them shaking their heads, resigned to doing little more than making his mother peaceful. Her room was private, so at first Jago and his brothers had stayed with her around the clock. In the beginning, they'd worn themselves out keeping watch. He never understood why hospitals couldn't provide succor for families at such times. Des, Trev and he had slept in hard-backed chairs until Julian had finally brought small folding cots for them to use. As the days passed, the sorrow of losing his mother grew crushing to Jago. His personal devastation was overshadowed by the fear of what her dying was doing to Desmond.

Lifting his collar against the cold hitting the back of his neck, Jago looked over to Des, watching his brother with growing unease. The rain whipped around Desmond, yet he didn't tilt his umbrella to stop the downpour from lashing against his face; oddly, he almost appeared to welcome the cold rain. Most people would assume Des was mourning. Jago wasn't fooled. The rage, frustration—perhaps even a touch of madness—were part of a ravenous beast within Des, waiting to slip the leash. God help them all if it did.

Des finally sensed Jago observing him, and looked up to meet his stare. His mother had always said Desmond's eyes were a mirror image of their father's. Trev agreed, but he was merely repeating like a parrot what he'd learnt at her knee—Jago couldn't recall their father, so he doubted Trevelyn could either. They had been babies when Michael Mershan had taken his life. The only father he had ever known stood staring at him, a wounded animal in pain. And Jago was helpless to ease his anguish.

Fearing for his brother's state of mind, he crossed to Desmond and placed a hand on his arm. "Come on, Des. It's not necessary to stay while they fill in the grave."

Desmond didn't move; sadly almost appearing rooted to the spot.

The sounds of shovels rhythmically tossing the wet dirt into the hole were the only noise the three cemetery staff made. Working quietly so as not to intrude upon the family, they finally raked the last clods of dirt onto the top and then placed the elaborate wreaths. One from each son, one from Julian.

"Des, it's over." Jago squeezed his brother's elbow in comfort.

Desmond jerked away, rage flashing in his vivid green eyes. "It's *not* over. Not 'til we take down Montgomerie Enterprises."

Disturbed by the angry response, Jago glanced to Trevelyn, hoping for his support in getting Des to leave the cemetery. Because of their bond, his twin and he often 'spoke' on a near telepathic level. Too locked up in his own grief, Trev blocked Jago's fey plea.

Fear and frustration mixing within him, Jago questioned, "You wish to go ahead with the plans?"

"You can ask that? She's barely in the ground—a woman whose life was ruined by Sean Montgomerie."

Jago braced himself, half-expecting Des to take a swing at him, knowing he'd accept the blow and not fight back. At least, not in that manner. He'd fight with words. "If Montgomerie were here, I'd strangle him with my bare hands, but taking the son-of-a-bitch's crimes out on his granddaughters isn't the way, Des. Two wrongs don't make a right."

"I'm not taking it out on the granddaughters." Desmond swallowed back a myriad of emotions—looking like a drowning man and with no way to save himself. "I'm merely claiming what Sean put up as collateral. Move the plans up. I want it done."

Placing a single red rose on top of the fresh grave, Desmond stalked off in the rain.

Alone.

" 'Oh, what a tangled web we weave.' " Jago tried to shake the sense his life was going to hell in a basket.

Trevelyn glared at him. "Shut up. Just shut up. Des doesn't need you playing conscience. For that matter, neither do I."

"Don't you?" Jago's challenge went unanswered for his twin hurried off after their brother.

"Someone shoot me—*please*!" Asha complained to the supper crowd in the diner. Everyone chuckled.

With Thanksgiving three days away, Asha was in a dither. Her to-do list kept growing, so many details to handle with the last minute preparations. At this point in the manic arrangements, she wasn't sure whatever possessed her to hold Thanksgiving at the restaurant.

As the holiday approached, she'd grown sensitive to the fact that a lot of people—especially the elderly in the area, who didn't have families to celebrate with, or the divorced or travelers—weren't looking forward to the holiday with enthusiasm. This time of year only reminded them how alone they were. Originally, she'd wanted to have a meal for The Windmill family. But as several regular customers noticed her decorating, they'd asked hopefully if The Windmill would be open for Thanksgiving day dinner. It became apparent they would face being alone. Her heart ached, thinking how Delbert, Sam and Colin would be in the same situation if not for being a part of her little world, so the Turkey Day party expanded.

Asha recalled a book her mother had given her on the clans of Scotland, just before she died. Inside Mae had written, *Some families you are born into. In this fate you have no choice. Other times, you collect special people, rare people, and make your own family*. Had Mae realized Asha was the one to come back and take over what Mae had built, to carry on, to fight for this place and its way of life, when none of her other siblings would?

The Windmill family was doing the whole turkey meal—dressing, pumpkin pie, cranberry sauce and all the trimmings. They'd open their arms and hearts to make room for anyone wanting to join them. After the first breathless *oh my, what have I done*? Asha quickly embraced the whole idea, as did everyone.

Besides enjoying the true spirit of Thanksgiving, Asha welcomed the hectic activities; her days were kept busy with ordering and decorating from morning until late at night. She went home with Clint so tired that she ached, and fell into bed to sleep. Well, sometimes she slept. She hated how often she tossed and turned half the night, wishing for Jago.

He'd finally called—at the end of the first week. She'd intended to be huffy and give him the cold shoulder, until she heard his voice. He'd sounded so tired, stressed, her mood quickly shifted to one of worry. Though she'd pressed a little, he'd only said that he had serious problems with a billion dollar deal and he wouldn't be back for a few days. Those few days turned into a few more. Then a few more. And there'd been only one call, late one night to reassure her.

"Twenty-five days to be exact, but who's counting?" Hanging a paper turkey from the archway between the restaurant and the foyer to the old house, she stopped and sat down dejectedly on the very top of the stepladder. Damn, but she missed Jago. Taking a deep breath to steady herself, she tried to pretend with each day passing she didn't become more scared she was losing him.

Sitting in the back of the limousine, Jago flexed his stomach muscles, failing to still the nervous butterflies inside him. He couldn't ever recall being more exhausted or scared. So bloody scared he wanted to puke.

He snapped open the lid on the ring case for the

dozenth time. The canary diamond twinkled as it caught and reflected the passing lights lining the interstate as the car took the turnoff. *Asha*. Her gentle spirit had sustained him these past weeks, kept him going when life pressed in upon him from every angle. Yet, while he drew strength from her love, his fear waxed as he worried over what would happen when he returned.

Time and again, he had closed his eyes and played his memories of Asha like a movie. The recollections, images of them together were a haven where he escaped when everything ground him down. There were so many happy times. Each made him ache to hold her. His worries, his grief wouldn't have been so bad if he could've held her at night. He was incomplete without her.

He snapped the case closed, his thumb rubbing over the velvet lid as he fretted. Des scared him. From their conversations, it was clear his older brother had fallen in love with BarbaraAnne Montgomerie. B.A., Des called her. On the one hand, Jago had a feeling that for once in his life Desmond had found the pot of gold at the end of the rainbow—in this instance Falgannon's rainbow. The other side feared Des was too troubled, too unable to let go of the past and might ruin his one chance at happiness. Hell, at this rate the Mershan brothers' quest for vengeance would be the single biggest mistake in their whole lives. Trevelyn was so wrapped up in Raven, but the arrogant idiot wouldn't even admit he was in love with her. At least Des admitted his feelings, even if he refused to accept his plans had to change or else.

Des was too used to getting his own way. He'd turned Mershan International into a billion dollar business, with offices worldwide. When he snapped out orders, dozens of underlings rushed to do his bidding. He hadn't counted on the Montgomerie Sisters. Foolish oversight, considering his brother had carried a picture of B.A. in his wallet for nearly fifteen years. Des was a smart man. How had he ignored the meaning of that simple act?

Jago closed his eyes and leaned his head back, so bloody exhausted, disheartened to the point it hurt to breathe. Memories flooded his brain of Desmond at thirteen, sick, nothing to eat the night before; Des dividing his supper between his brothers' plates when their mother wasn't looking. Des, getting up early to do his paper route, the bare light bulb glaring yellow in the pre-dawn hours showing Des as he suffered another spasm of coughing, so hard it nearly made him pass out. Instead of giving into the sickness, his brother had wrapped his thin muffler around his neck and slid on his hand-me-down coat. Their eyes met for a long instant. Then his brother forced a smile and said, "Go back to sleep, runt."

"Mr. Mershan, we're at The Windmill. Where do you want me to drop you?" the limo driver asked.

Home. The voice in Jago's head whispered.

"Park in the alley where you did before," he instructed.

"Yes, sir." Pulling up, he cut the engine. "Here's my card should you ever need me again. It's been a pleasure serving you."

Jago nodded. "I appreciate it. You made all this much easier."

He handed the man a hundred dollar tip, barely hearing the thanks, as he stared at the back of the restaurant and then the bungalows. The driver climbed out and helped him carry the luggage to the cottage. As he opened the door, he smiled to find Asha had pulled his Harley into the living room and Clint was sleeping on the seat.

For the first time in twenty-five days, he smiled.

"Hey, Asha!" Colin called as he rushed into the restaurant. "I just saw a limo going up the hill. I think maybe it dropped Jago off."

Asha was testing the new taps on the soda machine. The supplier had installed the Orange Crush and Grape Crush feeds to the fountain setup today. Her hand shook on the glass she was holding as she filled it with grape soft drink.

She told herself to stay calm. There was more than one limousine in Kentucky.

But then she heard the roar of the Harley and her heart did a flip. Jago was back! She tried not to give in to the excitement, the exhilaration of knowing he'd returned, but couldn't stop it. Taking a steady breath, she tried to reach down deep inside herself to find some proper indignation. How dare he go off with no explanation and two brief phone calls!

"In twenty-five *long* days," she muttered under her breath. "Okay, so I *was* counting."

"Hoo hoo . . . Jago is back." Colin rushed out the door to welcome him, followed by Delbert, Sam and Derek.

"Men. They always stick together," she informed the paper turkey on the counter.

Netta sat down on the stool, then grinned. "What's that you saying, sugarplum? Hey, your man is back. Go give him a proper welcome."

"Don't you dare hand out advice on how to handle my love life. I haven't noticed you doing so well in yours." Asha sipped her Grape Crush, determined to play hard-to-get for a few minutes. "Besides, he's the one who left. He knows where to find me."

"Don't do as I do, do as I say." Netta popped half an Almond Joy into her mouth. "One of us should be 'getting a little'—hmm . . . ah. . . . *grinning*."

One-by-one, the men came straggling in, Liam bringing up the rear since he'd just pulled up. His eyes locked with Netta's for a moment, but then he glanced to Asha. "Jago's back."

"I told her," Colin said, picking up a screwdriver to finish affixing the shelf she wanted for a potter over the jukebox. "She's doing her female deep-freeze thing."

The Harley roared again, summoning her outside. "Blasted man," she grumbled.

Netta clucked, swiveling on the stool to watch her. "You run along and enjoy Sexy Lips. I'll close up the restaurant.

Oo-it can defend me with his monster screwdriver if any male or a giant leech should make untoward advances upon my tender body—not that anyone around here would bother." She shot Liam a killing glare.

Asha wanted to drag things out and make Jago wait longer, but then she made eye contact with him through the glass door. His hair was longer, falling around his ears and neck in thick waves in bad boy fashion. Dressed in biker boots, leather pants and a new leather jacket, he was every woman's fantasy come to life. How did one resist that?

Those green eyes glowed as he watched her give in, and come out the door to him. She couldn't look away. With a warlock's power, he held her spellbound.

Jago.

She blinked as she drew closer. His face, though wearing a smug half-smile, appeared haunted. He'd lost weight, and dark shadows smudged the skin around his eyes. Had he been sick?

She stopped an arm's length away, loving him, anxious over him. "Twenty-five days and two lousy phone calls," she chided softly.

Not bothering to say a word of explanation or to beg her forgiveness, he reached into the pocket of his leather jacket and, in a magician's pass, he held out a small black box. A *ring* box. For a moment, she didn't breathe, didn't dare hope. It would be too painful if she built castles in the air only to have it contain a pair of earrings.

"Take it," was all the silly man said. He shoved the box toward her.

His eyes reflected love, yet were troubled by whatever he had been through this past month. But she saw there was a deep panic in their glimmering depths. Jago was scared. She doubted he'd ever been scared before in his whole life, so assured he was of himself and his place in the world.

She took the box with a trembling hand, almost too terrified to open it. Finally she flipped the lid back. In the dim light coming from the diner, the pale yellow stone gathered the ambient illumination and then reflected it. It was brilliant, a lovely stone, not too small, not too big. As Goldilocks might say, it was just right.

"Marry me?" Jago asked.

Tears came to her eyes as she stared first at the stone, then at the man she loved more than her life. "Yes."

It was that bloody simple.

Chapter Twenty-Five

Tommy, I'm scared. What are they doing?

Heart pounding, Asha struggled to wake up. She was Asha Montgomerie, yet somehow she was also there with Laura Valmont—and Laura was with her, in her. Since Christmas Eve, the visions of the past that had remained quiet through the days when Jago was away were suddenly back. She wasn't sure what had triggered them; vaguely, she wondered if it might have had something to do with her engagement ring, though she remained unsure quite why.

One of those silly things, she'd taken the ring off to wash dishes and forgot where she'd left it. She had panicked, fearing she'd lost it. Assuring her it was insured, Jago found where she'd placed it on a saucer. He had taken her hand, slid it onto the soapy fingers and then kissed her cheek. Silly man didn't understand it wasn't the monetary value. No ring would be like this one.

"I considered giving it to you for Christmas," he'd informed her. "Thought it might be the perfect time."

She leaned up on her tippy-toes and brushed her lips against his. "You chose the perfect time. Absolutely perfect."

Even as she spoke the words, she felt something pulling at her and had to fight against being sucked into 1964, into Laura's life. She wondered if Tommy had given an engagement ring to Laura at Christmas, or maybe planned to but never had the chance. The sadness of the possibility haunted her.

After that incident, the images began to invade her sleep, where she couldn't resist them.

The wind whipped at her hair—at Laura's hair—through the open window of the bright red Mustang. Tommy sped up when the jolt hit, rocking the whole car. Up ahead the cement truck was slowing down, making a left turn. Again a hard jolt came. Tommy spun the wheel, trying to avoid crashing into the rear of the huge truck.

Horns blaring, metal smashing, pain searing through her body, Laura screaming . . .

Asha jerked up in the bed, her scream melding with Laura's as Mike Duncan's song played insider her head.

If I only had the time
If I could find just another line
If I held you one more day . . .

So strongly did she hear it that for a moment she wondered if it wasn't actually playing. But no. Just tricks of her subconscious. Sweat covered her body and her heart slammed painfully against her ribcage. She placed a hand to her chest, willing the vibrations in her blood to slow. Every nerve ached.

Glancing out the huge bedroom window at the falling snow, she sought reassurance of where she was, who she was. She smiled faintly upon seeing the winter wonderland. A total whiteout, the weathermen were calling it. After several steadying breaths, she recalled it was the day after New Year's, and that she was snowbound at the river house. Snowbound alone with Jago? Now there was heaven!

Why couldn't they have had this snow for Christmas Eve? It would have made an absolutely perfect background for the beautiful time. She'd loved shopping in Lexington with Jago. One of the few times of the year she enjoyed going into the traffic-riddled city. There was something so special about the Yuletide decorations, the hum and bustle as they shopped for gifts for family and friends. There had been a two-story carrousel at Turfland Mall, and Jago had taken her to ride the painted ponies. He gave her special gifts, some small like the pair of garnet earrings in the shape of hearts, some silly like the Frederick's of Hollywood female elf costume—though she figured that was his gift as much as for her. The lovely vivid blue pashmina shawl. His eyes had twinkled as he asked her to model it for him—wearing nothing but the shawl. But those were stolen moments. There had been a big dinner party at The Windmill with everyone trading gifts. Half the people in the area ended up coming by to drink a cup of Delbert-spiked eggnog and wish a Merry Ho Ho.

A happy time. A busy time. Thus, she welcomed the tranquility of finally being alone with Jago—and Clint.

The only discordant note to the holidays had been a call from her brother, Cian. His cell phone battery had been running low, allowing him just enough time to wish a Merry Christmas and say he was sorry neither Liam nor she were coming home to England for the holidays. She started to explain her home was here in Kentucky now, but his phone went into its warning beeps, so he cut her off, informing her that he was sending proxies for Liam and her to sign. He feared there'd be a hostile takeover of Montgomerie Enterprises after the first of the year; if that came to pass he wanted to be in position to vote Liam's shares and hers.

Jago raised up in the bed, pushing the cat draped across his lap to the side. He touched her shoulder. "Shhhh . . . you're safe, Asha. I'd never let anything hurt you."

She melted into his arms, relishing the beautiful contours of his chest, the security she experienced in his strong embrace. Warming her very soul, she absorbed that high heat he generated. His heart beating in a calm rhythm reassured her that she was indeed protected. If only he could keep her dreams at bay.

"Sometimes I get scared," she admitted.

He leaned back, cradling her. "We all get scared now and then."

She had her cheek pressed to his chest, relishing the steady thudding of his heart, but suddenly it jumped, the beating erratic. Tilting her head so she could see his beautiful face, she asked, curious, "You get scared?"

He nodded. His right hand absently massaged the back of her neck. "The idea of losing you scares me spitless." He smiled for reassurance, only she saw the measure of his fear reflected in the dark eyes.

"Silly man, you're stuck with me and Clint." She brushed a soft kiss to his lips.

"What scares you, Asha? You haven't slept well this last week."

"Ghosts."

A muscle in his jaw twitched. "Tommy and Laura."

She nodded. "We keep meaning to have our talk, but everyone interrupts—or we can't control ourselves and jump each other's bones."

Asha had noticed a quiet desperation to Jago's lovemaking since his return, as if he used their passion to bond her to him. It even crossed her mind that he was trying to get her pregnant. Generally, men shied away from that step in a new relationship. Jago was not most men. She sensed he would make a good daddy, would enjoy raising a child. His gentleness with Clint demonstrated his caring, especially when the silly beast had done something that would cause other people to lose their tempers. Such as, when the cat barfed a hairball into his shoe and Jago didn't know until it was too late, or the time Clint jumped on his leather motorcycle jacket and started to claw: Jago had only talked to the cat in soft tones and had explained these were not good things for kitty to do. His tender patience would make him a super father. So easily she could envision him wearing one of those baby harnesses. Only, this was more than him wanting a baby with her; she had a strange feeling he sought to use a child to fuse her to him, to reassure himself in some manner of his hold on her.

"There's something to be said for bone-jumping," he joked, then kissed the tip of her nose. She yawned, then smiled and she draped herself over his chest.

"True. I don't have to exercise anymore."

"See, therapeutic sex is good for your health."

Being devilish, Asha traced a circle around his areola with the pad of her index finger and watched it tighten. Once she had his attention, she prodded, "You're doing it again—avoiding talking about Tommy and Laura . . . just as you avoid discussing your time away."

"*I'm* doing it?" He accused, "You're the one playing with my titty. You're setting fire licking at my poor male brain, then you want logical conversation? All the blood travels south on an urgent mission. If you want to talk about ghosts, stop that."

"Okay, I'll stop. I'd rather discuss why you came back looking so haunted. But ghosts are a start."

He exhaled a deep sigh. "Okay, tell me about Tommy and Laura. What? Do you think we are the reincarnation of these lovers from the 1960s?" His tone was faintly patronizing.

"No, actually, I don't have that sense. There *is* a connection. They loved The Windmill. It's theirs, too. I'm fighting to save it. You're a threat to it. I think . . . maybe they want me to know how special it is, that it's worth fighting for."

"You already believe that. You don't need two nonpaying guests to remind you." He scooted up in the bed. "And I am no threat to The Windmill, Asha. Surely you know that."

She reached for her robe and slipped it on, thinking he would keep his male brain on the chat if there were fewer 'distractions.' Clint gave a huge yawn, grumpy that his people were stirring at dawn instead of snuggling back down to sleep. She patted his head and he curled up, glaring at them with one eye.

"Yes, I do know. I think you understand what I'm doing there. Only you aren't Trident Ventures," she qualified. "They want the horse farm, and they've made it clear by pressuring my father that they wanted The Windmill, too. I know how big business works. What they want, they get, by fair means or foul."

He picked up her hand and toyed with her engagement ring. "Don't fret about Trident. They shall leave you alone."

"You have that much pull with them, Jago?"

He'd meant to reassure her. For some reason it had the opposite effect. She shifted on the bed so she could face him, wanting to watch his countenance. He crossed his arms over his chest—a defensive position, whether he was aware of the action or not.

"I will . . . in a few weeks," he answered. No further details were forthcoming.

She wasn't content with that reply; it felt an evasion. "Was this part of what took you away?"

"Part."

The one word answer set her teeth on edge.

Grrrrrrrr. More evasions! The man was beginning to tick her off. She wasn't Miz Nosybucket, hadn't pressed him on matters about his month away, assuming he'd tell her when he was ready. Men had a tendency to talk in their own time. Prod them for facts or explanations and they clammed up on you. She had six brothers to attest the only way to handle a man was to out-wait him. Even so, she didn't like how he was closing himself off from her by tossing out these half-hearted, vague responses. She'd noticed Jago's sentences grew shorter as she pressed, and wondered if he was aware how telling such actions where. He was used to dealing with the high-powered world of big business, the hired gun for Trident Ventures, which meant he was used to guising his reactions. Perhaps he couldn't use those tricks with her. She smiled.

"What part?" she pushed.

He reached for his jeans and tugged them on, evidently sussing she'd zeroed in on the chink in his armor. Going to the window, he looked out at the snow flying. His stance demonstrated he was marshaling his defenses. Also, he appeared to be working up to the one thing men seemed to have the hardest time facing—actually opening up and communicating.

Getting out of bed, Asha went over and wrapped her arms around his waist from behind. In the pre-dawn light the whole river valley was pure white, with only the dark ribbon of the river winding below. It was stunning, but she'd rather look at Jago. She hugged him tightly, loving him with all her heart.

"Jago . . . I love you."

She'd waited for him to tell her that first. Yeah, she knew he loved her, but women were silly, sentimental beings who craved to hear those three little words. She was no different. It doesn't matter a man showed in a hundred ways how much he cared; women were whiny brats and *had* to hear those words. Well, she was tired of waiting.

His breathing stilled; his strong back muscles tensed. He didn't move, and she suddenly worried if she had made a mistake. But he'd asked her to marry him. A dozen times a day he demonstrated his love. Why should hearing those simple words cause such a strong reaction, almost a denial? It scared her, and being a female who needed reassurance, she panicked.

His head dropped forward as if he experienced a crushing sadness. Unsettled by what was going on within him, she tried to laugh, to make a joke out of the situation, though tears rose, threatening to clog her throat. "Hey, I'm a silly female. Just ignore me. I merely assumed that when you gave me an engagement ring you loved me. But hey, no worries. Clint and I will adjust—"

He swung around, catching her off guard. One hand clamped hard around the back of her neck, the other her waist. Yanking her to him, he took her mouth savagely with his, kissing her with a passion that seemed fueled by desperation as much as desire. "Damn it, woman, I love you. You have no idea how much I love you. I don't know what I would do if you left me. I think I would die inside."

He pushed her back against the wall; his trembling hand came up, his fingers stroking her cheek as though he were a sculptor memorizing the contours of her face, as if he stared at the most precious thing in his world. The power of his emotions washed through her, humbled her, shamed her for her childish reaction, for her craving to hear the simple words when he gave her so much more. Words didn't begin to measure up to the strength of his need for her reflected in his dark green eyes.

"You have no idea how you complete me, make my life right, see me happy. You lack all concept of what my life was like growing up. How empty I have been all these years . . . waiting for you to come with your healing love." He leaned his forehead against her, as if seeking to keep the sexual tension from taking over and spiraling out of control.

"You haven't spoken of your past to me, outside of mentioning your brothers and your mother and father. I figure you'd tell me those things when you are ready. You and I are what's important, the life we are building here, now, the future. We will have a lot of wintry nights ahead or slow summer evenings when we can talk about memories, what made us who we are. The past is not important at this stage, Jago. Sometimes people let the past rule them too much."

"The past *is* important . . . to some. Obligations, duties, loyalty, love—all are in the mix. And yes, some allow it to rule their lives. It's frightening how the sins of the fathers are visited upon the children and even grandchildren, swept up by past events that happened without our playing any role. Yet, we are unable to break free before it's too late."

"It's never too late. You simply have to remember what's most important and fight for what you want."

"I hope you mean that. I hope—"

The phone rang, breaking the moment. She smiled. "Told you. Every time we talk, someone visits, calls or we get horny."

"Horny is more fun. I do love you, Asha." The back of his hand stroked her cheek. "Never doubt that."

"Never doubt my love either."

"I don't. I doubt myself. *That* is what I doubt." Jago growled as the phone kept ringing, saying the person on the other end clearly wasn't going to leave them in peace.

"It's a new year. The rest of the world is back to work. They don't know we're snowbound and enjoying it."

"I don't care who the devil it is, I'm telling them to go to blue blazes." He crossed the room to the phone and jerked it up. "Hello. Oh, Des. Sorry, I've been concerned, too. A lot of things happening here, as I am sure it is there."

Of course, Jago didn't tell his older brother to get stuffed. Asha could tell by how drawn his face became that he was worried about Desmond. His speaking in hushed tones reinforced that impression. Giving him space, she prodded Clint's belly. "Feed the kitty?" she enticed.

The silly cat nearly twisted himself into a pretzel, flopping around like a fish out of water, trying to get to his feet. In the kitchen, Asha opened a small can of Fancy Feast for the yodeling pussycat. With him happily feeding his face, she set about to make a tea tray so Jago and she could sit by the fire, watch it snow and enjoy a lazy morning. Maybe she would unplug the phone and stuff Jago's cell phone in the laundry hamper to ensure their peace.

As she filled the kettle, her eyes took in the rising sun, its rosy light turning the wintry landscape to pinks and purples. So beautiful, the scenery was perfect for a postcard or photograph.

A movement at a distance attracted her eyes. She couldn't focus upon whatever was up there. Squinting to see, she nearly overfilled the teakettle. Turning off the tap, she set the pot on the electric burner and turned it on. Coming back to the sink, she looked again at the far hill. The hillside was thick with pines and shrouded with heavy snow, the long shadows of dawn cast distorting shapes. Nothing. Just the falling snow. She wasn't sure what she expected to spot.

"Must be my imagination, Clint. I don't see anything. Maybe it was a deer. Even a wildcat. There still are a few long The Palisades. He'd make you look small in comparison, which with your girth isn't an easy thing to do. No one would be out tromping around in this snowstorm, so it was some forest creature." She frowned. "I don't think we have bears anymore. I hope not."

Sipping her tea, Asha went to check the stack of mail on the entry table. Typical bills and junk mail, she quickly sorted through what was important and then dumped the spam into the trashcan. When she looked back at the small tabletop she frowned. The large brown envelope with the signed proxies for Cian was missing. She'd placed it there a couple days ago thinking to mail it the next time they went out.

"Oh bother. I guess I scooped it up with the junk mail, Clint. Cian will kill me." She squatted and pulled out the stack of magazines, flyers and advertisements. The cat padded over and 'helped' her inspect everything. There were two brown envelopes—one from Publishers Central Bureau telling her she'd likely won ten million dollars. Scratching Clint's head, she laughed. "Joy and celebration . . . The Windmill's petty cash will be happy."

Pursing her mouth, she frowned when she failed to find the errant item. Fearful it might've slipped inside a magazines or the mailers, she carefully went through them, fluttering pages of the catalogues or unfolding the newspaper-style Bargain Mart. Nothing.

"Well bugger," she grumped.

"What are you two doing rummaging through the garbage?" Jago had come into the kitchen barefooted, so she hadn't heard him until he spoke.

Asha jumped from fright. "Jeez Louise. You scared me out of a year of my life, sneaking up on me like that."

He leaned down and kissed the top of her head. "Sorry, I wasn't sneaking. You and Clint were too absorbed in playing with the trash."

With a disgusted sigh of not having found the envelope, she dumped the mess back into the rubbish. Asha glared at the table and then around the room, considering if she'd set it somewhere else and merely thought she'd put it there. "I was searching for the envelope for Cian. Have you seen it? I was sure it was on the entry table."

He reached down and lifted her by her waist, slowly pulling her up his body. His braced stance was one of pure male dominance, a man wanting his mate. It humbled her. It *empowered* her. When she was finally standing, his mouth took hers for a long, slow, deep kiss that set her scalp to tingling and her body to ache in a pagan throb. Her breast grew so sensitive, craving his touch. The crowning need made it hard for her even to think.

When he broke the kiss, she nearly panted out, "The envelope? Did you see it?"

The corners of his mouth curved upward into a satyric smile. "Sounds like I didn't kiss you good enough, lass."

"Kiss me all you want—after I find that damn envelope. It's important."

His eyes glowed hungrily as he parted her silk robe to expose her breasts. Gently, he cupped them, brushing his thumbs back and forth across the stiffening peaks. Lust set free, her body burned, the core of her desire instantly tightening into a hard knot. His sensual touch was delicious, but not nearly enough. Then his clever hands moved down her waist, over the curves of her derrière, and then in a quick surprise, jerked her up and plopped her on the rickety entry table.

Jago's laughter rumbled in his chest. "Let's see if this poor table was meant for hot sex."

His fingers slid up her thighs until both hands met and he could gently massage the outside of her slick fold. He leaned close, nibbling his way up to her ear. Pausing he whispered. "The envelope? I mailed it when we went to the store for supplies."

"What . . . envelope?" she gasped, pushing the sweat pants off his firm buttocks.

He shoved into her body with one solid thrust. "Yeah, what envelope."

Chapter Twenty-six

The Windmill's Halloween and Thanksgiving bashes had been such huge successes, she decided to toss a St. Valentine's Day party at the clubhouse. It seemed the perfect occasion to break the bleak winter blues. It would be so beautiful, romantically decorated and geared to celebrate love. She thought it a shame Bobby Pickett didn't do love songs. She asked Colin to find out about Ray Peterson, to see if he was still around singing "Tell Laura I Love Her." Somehow it seemed fitting. Colin's eyes were so miserable when he told her the world had lost Peterson a couple of years before. She found it sad the man had never known how much his song had meant to Tommy Grant and Laura Valmont.

Asha had decreed that everyone was to come dressed in red, pink, black or white or they weren't getting through the door. To her delight, The Oriental Trading Company had super decorations for the restaurant and the glasshouse: wonderful spinner hearts, beautiful rosebuds under glass for the buffet tables, red heart garlands with the hearts trimmed in white lace, and a gorgeous arched banner that would serve for the entrance. She even considered putting a tent over the pool itself and buying little boats to float, creating a 'tunnel of love' just like they used to have in the old Coney Island decades ago. Colin muttered something about insurance and how a woman in love shouldn't be in charge of Valentine decorations, then flatly refused to help conjure her vision into reality. Jago, the traitor, backed him up, saying it would block the view within the pool house. Men! Such spoil sports. Despite their lack of enthusiasm, she was delighted with the way the whole concept for the party was taking shape. She had all the planters repotted with white and red miniature roses. With two weeks to go, they were starting to bloom and would be gorgeous.

Of course, she planned a private party afterward with Jago. A little red silk number from Victoria's Secret and the delivery of the hot tub for the river house were just the prescription to gift Jago with the news he was going to be a daddy. Her cute little test had showed a plus; she'd followed up with a doctor's appointment to confirm it. Thus far, no morning sickness. Placing a hand to her belly, she hoped that would hold at least until she broke the news to the papa-to-be.

She was still nervous about Jago's reaction. Deep in her heart she felt he would be thrilled. Even so, it was an odd time of mood swings between giddy-euphoria one minute and melancholy the next. That she still experienced dreams, visions of Laura Valmont didn't help matters. She had this strange suspicion Laura was trying to tell her something she was failing to understand.

She glanced up from fixing the accordion-tissue heart centerpiece as Jago and Liam pushed through the diner door. Business was slow, typical for a Wednesday. She'd taken advantage to finish decorating the restaurant. She smiled at the two drop-dead sexy men—good friends now. Only, something about their manner set off alarms. Studying them, she saw her brother gave off the impression of being relieved, though pale. Jago just appeared calm. His expression shifted to apprehension as his mesmerizing eyes met hers.

Jago came around the counter, took out a Coors for himself and one for Liam, passing the beer to her brother. As he did, he leaned over to give her a peck on the cheek. "I'd get you a beer, but I recall something about you not liking the taste—and a worry about salt being in it. I never learned why you don't like salt, though."

Liam took a swig and sniggered. "Blame that on our grandmother Maeve. She was born on Falgannon Isle and came from a long line of witches. She used to teach all my sisters these witchy tricks of the trade. One was, you should never accept salt from a warlock—that you empowered his control over your will."

"A warlock, eh?" Jago grinned. "One with sexy lips, too."

Liam's pale green eyes glanced from Jago to her. "Congrats are in order, Little Sister. We finalized the last of the details on the horse farm today."

The smile fell off her face, and Asha resisted the impulse to place a hand on her belly. "Really? I wasn't aware the deal was moving forward again, but then, I guess it's none of my business, eh? So . . . what? Is Trident going to put in a shopping mall, apartments and offices? Just what we need to ruin everything around here. What are you going to do with the stock? Do they still have glue factories?"

Both men rolled their eyes and glanced at each other in longsuffering male telepathy. She wanted to kick them both! Yes, she was overreacting; only she'd begun to believe Jago truly understood her fey spot in the world, this sanctuary where ghosts danced to a jukebox that had a mind of its own, how special a place was that had a Cajun cook, Clint the Cat, Oo-it and an aging Jedi Master. Had she deceived herself? Had she seen what she wanted to believe?

Taking a slow, deep breath, she attempted to control the wild swings of emotions within her, thoroughly aware the baby she carried triggered chemical imbalances. She also reminded herself that flying off the handle wouldn't be good for the small being growing inside her. Very carefully, trying to ignore both men, she took a glass and filled it with grape soda.

"Chill, Little Sister. Your Jago hasn't hurt Valinor, thus is no threat to your little domain."

"Oh, yeah. With Dad and you selling out, it's only a matter of time before they put in some super shopping complex, which will bring zoning laws and send my taxes through the roof! You know this place won't meet most zoning standards. It'll cost me a fortune to bring it up to code. I won't be able to pay the taxes when they are suddenly ten times, twenty times higher." She sipped the drink, holding tight to keep from tossing it into their faces.

"Jago did well by me, Asha," Liam assured quietly.

She met his pale eyes. "You sold out. The farm will be gone. How is that 'doing well' by you?"

Jago put down the bottle of beer and took her arms, turning her. "You're upset, love. The farm stays. I've fixed things because I didn't want it coming between us."

"Stays?" She was ready to burst into tears—so unlike her. Generally, if she was angry she wanted to take out her dirk and start carving her initials into someone. Never had she wanted to give in to a full-blown crying jag. *Hormones running amok,* she kept repeating in her mind.

"Yeah, Jago set up everything. Trident will underwrite Valinor financially, while I retain one-third of it and will be manager. Jago will co-manage with me. Every three years, I'll be able to buy five percent of the farm back. If I decided to leave the farm at any point, they'll give me a 'golden parachute' that will end up doubling my original share in the farm, plus some other perks. This gives me the money to expand everything—buy new stock, running the farm as I want, and not on my shoestring budget. Basically Jago and I are now partners, with Trident's silent backing." Liam held up his hands, palms upward. "You might want to kiss the man instead of being a harpy. Jago handed me my dream on a golden platter."

She shrugged and tried to joke, "Oh well . . . in that case, please disregard the hysterical rant from the loopy sister."

Jago gently pulled her into his arms, his hands rubbing up and down her back. "You okay? You seem keyed up."

"Just that time of the month," she lied. "You know the symptoms—anxiety, panic, poor judgment, depression, irritability, hostility, aggressive behavior. I think I have a few—er, all—of those."

He chuckled. "Isn't it nice that we men are such paragons of patience? Why don't you close up early? You've been knocking yourself out decorating for the party."

"Sounds nice. An early evening *would* be good." Going to the office, she leaned in to speak to Netta, making out orders for next week's food. "Hey, best hostess in the world, would you close up for me? I'm beat."

Netta unwrapped an Almond Joy. "Sure thing, sugarplum. Have Sexy Lips give you some TLC. Get some *sleep* for a change. You look tired."

"Thanks." She wished everyone goodnight, then let Jago lead her out into the February evening.

Clint came padding up, rubbing against Jago's leg. "What's he doing out?"

"Don't ask me. He was in the bungalow sleeping when I came to work. Maybe Mary let him out when she was cleaning." Asha hugged her shawl about her shoulders, while Jago fished out the keys from his pocket. "Tomorrow is February second—St. Brid's Day. By the old pagan calender, that was the first day of spring."

A cool breeze swirled around them, carrying flakes of snow with it, causing Jago to laugh as he inserted the key. "Anyone defining the first day of February as spring hasn't lived in Kentucky." He paused, caught in the breathless instant, his hand reaching up to cup her face. His thumb wiped away a stray snowflake that hit her cheek. He tilted forward and brushed a butterfly kiss softly to her lips. She started to lean into him, but instead of deepening it he stepped back.

"We need to talk." They both smiled and chuckled, sharing the same thought. "Yeah, I know we keep saying that, then twelve dozen things pop up to interrupt. No more. We *have* to talk, Asha. It's important."

"I apologized about how I reacted over the horse farm deal—" she started.

"It's not that. This is about us . . . though family is mixed in there. Yours. Mine. We need to turn off the—" The phone began ringing in his cabin. "Grrr. You and Clint get out of the cold. I don't want either of you sick. I'll be a few minutes. I have a call in to Trident to confirm the deal is settled. I might need to justify what I did. After that, all phones are off the hook so we can talk. Deal?"

She nodded, watching him dash to his bungalow. Letting Clint in first, she flipped on the lights. The cottage was chilled, so she crossed to the small fireplace and lit a match to the already laid kindling. The newspaper caught instantly, and soon the heady scent of applewood filled the air. Heading to the kitchen to feed the cat, she noticed a piece of paper taped to the refrigerator.

"If Jago's sticking a grocery list up on *my* steel fridge, his arse is mine, Clint." She dumped dry food into the bowl, then walked over to yank it down.

It wasn't a grocery list, but a typed letter on expensive vellum with the Trident Venture letterhead—had a cute little pitchfork-shaped logo. Her eyes skimmed over it, trying to take in details of what the long letter actually meant. The details didn't matter. There was only one important factor—why the letter had been left for her.

The letter was addressed to Jago Mershan.

Chapter Twenty-seven

Having trouble breathing, Asha gulped air to fight the rising nausea. She rushed to Jago's bungalow to confront him, but spotted him heading toward the front of the diner. Clint spied him, too, and was instantly on his heels. Jago was whistling to flag down Liam, as he was reversing the red Viper out of the parking lot. Finally her brother noticed Jago, flicked his lights and waited for him to jog up. She assumed the urgent parlay had something to do with the telephone call Jago had just taken from Trident.

So angry, she nearly marched over and showed them both the letter—let Jago deal with Liam as well as her. Instead, she noticed Jago had left his cabin door half-open in his dash to run down Liam. She headed there.

Inside, she looked around. His cell phone was on the table beside the open briefcase. It was only a few steps to reach the kitchen, a few more until she put her hand on the leather attaché. It seemed miles. She had no idea what she was looking for. Surely the expensive case contained other pieces of information about Trident addressed to Desmond, Trevelyn and Jago Mershan.

There were tabbed folders crammed full. Blueprints, reams of reports and spreadsheets. Her heart stilled—pictures of her with her twin sister Raven, taken last May at her grandfather's funeral. Dozens of them. There were others, too. Even a photograph of her with Justin, back before she'd broken their engagement. The manila folder seemed too heavy to hold; the glossy images slid out of her hand and all over the kitchen floor.

Then she spotted the most damning piece of Jago's betrayal—the signed proxies. She recalled hunting for them just after New Year's and Jago saying he'd mailed them. Her brother Cian needed those proxies to block the takeover bid. She could only stand there and stare. Her whole life laid there on the wooden tiles.

Coming through the door, Jago appeared frustrated. That concern was nothing compared to what flooded his eyes when he saw her there, holding the paper with the Trident Venture letterhead. He first noted her furious expression, then his eyes fell on the trident logo and the bastard knew. He knew! Finally, he saw she stood in the midst the pile of 8×10 photos, the proxies at her feet. He paled, blood draining from him.

Oh, she wanted to kick him in the seat of his pants, and this time, it wasn't a spike in the hormones. Ridiculously, he made a leap for the letter, but she backed up out of reach. When he recognized his action was nothing short of ludicrous, he stopped and closed his eyes. The corners of his mouth flexed into a grimace.

Unable to stand the sense of her whole world being nothing but a tissue of lies, she turned to leave. It was just too much. She *had* to get away, calm down until she could form a coherent thought. Stepping over Clint who rubbed around her ankles, she headed toward the door only to have Jago block her path.

Asha stared up into his beautiful face, the face she so loved; she just wanted to cry. Instead she hurled the insult, "Bastard."

"I want to—" he started to say, but she slapped him. Hard. Shocked, he reeled not from the physical blow, but the mental anguish he saw in her eyes. Seizing the chance, she pushed past him and headed back to her cottage. "Asha, wait," he called.

Jago caught up with her as she pushed open the sliding door. Damn him. She just wanted to get away for a spell. She needed to calm down, if not for herself, then for the child she carried. Despite, he wasn't going to let her do the sensible thing. When she saw it would turn into a pushing match over the door, she retreated to the fire, seeking its warmth. Needing its warmth.

They stared at each other. Lovers. Strangers. Deceiver and deceived. How could the world be turned topsy-turvy in a single heartbeat by a piece of paper?

"Mershan. Not Fitzgerald. When were you going to tell me? 'Hold it, preacher, the name's wrong on the marriage license.' Is *that* the perfect time?"

"Hold the melodrama. This will be rough enough without lacing everything with sarcasm," he suggested quietly.

Asha silently counted to ten. "Don't you *dare* tell me what to do, Jago *Mershan*. You don't have that right."

"Too bad. I'm taking it. You're white as a sheet. Please sit down—" He reached for her, but she jerked away. For several heartbeats he watched her, then finally nodded. "I was going to tell you tonight. That's what I wanted to talk about."

"Oh, please. Jerk. You asked me to marry you, and the whole bloody time you were lying."

"I wasn't. I just didn't tell you everything. My name is Jago Luxovius Fitzgerald Mershan—"

The cat padded over, curious at Asha's raised voice. "Sic 'im, Clint. Of course, be careful—you might get foot-in-mouth disease."

"Asha—

"Don't 'Asha' me, you . . . you . . . worm! How could you ask me to be your wife when you were lying?" She vibrated with umbrage.

"Because I love you so much that I'd do *anything*—"

She snatched up a throw pillow and slugged him with it. "Anything! *Anything?* Try telling the truth!"

Every time he opened his mouth, she let him have it again. He took the blows without defending himself. After a dozen, he caught the pillow and took it away.

"I started to tell you several times—"

"Oooh . . . liar! You stole the proxies!"

Jago nodded, appearing shaken, tired. "Yes, I did. Expediency . . . for us all. I just wanted everything *done*, Asha. Des will win. He always does. There won't be any stopping him. Without the proxies, Cian couldn't fight him. It would be bloody done. Over with. Finally. We could all get on with our lives. Once he takes over Montgomerie Enterprises, then I can force him to make things right for your family, as I did with the horse farm. You talked to Liam. You know I did right by him. I did try several times to explain to you, but life kept intruding. Truth? I *let* it intrude. For the first time in my whole ruddy life I was happy."

Jago spoke with such conviction, depression, that it slowed her spiraling temper. His statement shook her, simply because she believed him. He stared at her with true misery. Silly man wasn't just guilty. He was in pain, a pain so crippling that it reached into her, nearly made her forget her anger. Nearly.

"This last year, every night I'd get up, restless, couldn't sleep. I'd go to the refrigerator, open it and stand looking inside. I wasn't hungry, yet I repeated this over and over. I didn't need food. I needed love. I needed you. That first night after we met, all the nocturnal wandering stopped." He walked to the patio door and stood, watching the falling snow. "Until you, I never understood I wasn't happy. When I found you, I found my other half—what was missing."

"Then why risk it all—for what? Your brothers and you are playing some high stakes game with my family's holdings? I gather from this,"—she held up the letter—"that your brothers are behind a hostile takeover of anything with the name Montgomerie attached. My father and brother are capable of defending against a bunch of modern day pirates. What I do care about, my life here—"

"I know that. Sometimes forces push us against our will. Yes, I should've told you, only for once in my bloody life I played the coward. I reached out and held on to you like a lifeline. I was lost, no meaning to my existence. Don't you see? I'm another of your lost souls finding heaven at The Windmill. When you're that low and salvation comes along, and when you comprehend if you lose it there won't be anything left worth living for, you tend to get scared. Bloody scared. Each time I intended to tell you some interruption popped up and, like a condemned man, I welcomed the excuses." He braced his hand high on the doorframe, and leaned against it. The hypnotic eyes watched her reflection in the mirrored glass. "Yeah, I was a coward, but I haven't changed. You love me. Not my name."

"Oh!" she gasped, feeling more than panic rise in her throat.

He rushed to her. "What's wrong?"

Asha shoved him away. "Get back, unless you want me to barf all over you."

Not waiting to see what he'd do, she dashed into the bathroom and slammed the door, locking it. She barely got the commode lid up before her stomach let go. Boy, did it let go! Weak from retching, she slumped against the hamper. Clint materialized and crawled into her lap to comfort her. He sniffed her sour breath and wrinkled his nose.

"You ought to try it from my side." She jumped when Jago hammered on the door.

"Asha, are you all right?" He pounded again.

She glared at the locked door. "Go away. I really don't want to see you right now, Mr. Mershan." Her body was sending signals it was just getting wound up. "Stand back, round two is coming, Clint."

Jago yelled, cajoled and begged, though she did her best to tune him out. After tossing the rest of her cookies, all she wanted was a cool rag and to wash the horrid taste from her mouth, not to deal with a man named Mershan.

"Asha, open the damn door. Now."

"Go to hell. I want to die," she moaned, and rolled onto her side. Clint and she both flinched at the loud crash, as the door slammed against the wall. "Mr. Macho just kicked in the door, Clint. Oh, how thrilling."

Jago saw her on the floor, panicked and rushed to her. He tried to get her to sit up, but damn it, she didn't *want* to sit. The cat was hopping all over the place, though she wasn't sure if he was playing a game or trying to defend her. She didn't care. Rather, she wished both of them would leave her alone with her misery.

"Go away and let me die," she moaned.

Terrified, Jago pushed her hair back from her face. "Have you taken something, Asha?"

"I'd belt you for asking that, but I'm too tired. It's a sour stomach. Finding the man you love has been lying to you for months will do that."

"Are you going to puke more?" he asked softly.

She wanted to curl up into a ball and ignore him and the cat. "I just want to sleep . . . as soon as I rinse my mouth."

With his aid, she stood and hobbled to the sink. She washed her mouth out with water and then did a quick swish with Listermint. Tenderly, Jago helped her undress and into a comfortable nightgown; sliding under the cool sheets felt like paradise. He rushed about, doing chores for several minutes, though she closed her eyelids and ignored him. Or pretended to.

"Here, drink this."

She opened her eyes and looked up at him. He'd changed out of his clothes and just wore sweatpants. Holding out a cup, he offered a concerned smile.

"What's this?"

"Warm lemonade and honey. It cuts the aftertaste and soothes the throat."

She took the drink and sipped, surprised by how good it was. "Thank you."

"I didn't mean to make you sick."

Asha concentrated on the warm drink and tried not to take notice of his kindness. "I don't want to talk about it."

"Fine. Then you will listen to me talk. Like how dirt poor I grew up."

That caught her off guard. "Poor?"

"Yes. So poor I doubt you could comprehend it. When I was little more than a baby my father put a gun to his head and killed himself."

The cup rattled against the saucer. She saw in his eyes that he was serious. "How horrible."

"I was too young to remember, only that incident formed my whole life—maybe nearly destroyed it, and that of my brothers." Jago sat on the edge of the bed and took the saucer from her hands. "I don't want you to say anything, but I want to tell you about his death. It happened a long time ago; however it's still driving the Mershan brothers. You think I don't have the right to ask you to hear me out after lying to you, but in a strange way I do have that right and I am claiming it. You see, the reason my father committed suicide was because he was ruined by your grandfather."

"My grandfather?"

He gave a small nod. "So, do we talk?"

She pressed her lips together to keep from crying; this time it was hormonal. She looked at him. "We talk."

And they did. Jago turned out the lights and slid into the bed and cradled her—and talked. For hours. He cried when he told how his mother had died in November, how she'd been sick most of her life and had never received the proper medical care until it was too late. How she didn't have an education to support herself and three small sons. How she'd returned to her family's farm in Ireland after Michael Mershan's death. The details of the too-risky deal.

"Sean used lands he didn't own as collateral to back

chancy ventures. Emerald mines in South America, oil in the Middle East. When one venture paid off, that windfall backed another, each bonanza bankrolling the next—an empire built with a house of cards. Everything turned to gold for Midas Montgomerie. He pulled my father into his schemes, used him to lure others into them. Only, Midas Montgomerie's luck turned. Rebels took over the mines; Arabs seized oil wells; and coalmines in Wales were closed due to bad working conditions. Dozens of investments went sour."

A wave of nausea hit Asha, leaving her certain she didn't want to hear this.

"My father, poor fool, made a lot of money through Sean's early investments. Sean convinced him to entice his friends and associates into the spiraling game. A pyramid. Everyone tossed in their life savings, borrowed to get more shares. When things crumbled, my father believed all was protected because of Sean's collateral."

Asha shivered. "Sean never owned Falgannon. Colford was held in trust for my father until he inherited. The farm in Kentucky was purchased by my father for my mother."

"Precisely what my father discovered after the house of cards collapsed. The bank lost, the investors lost, my father lost . . ." He gave her a small squeeze, pressing her tightly against his chest. "The one who lost most of all is Desmond. He's consumed with the need to set things right for our mother. He's in love with B.A. I'm hoping she will be his salvation—as you are mine."

Asha resented that he had lied. Still, she ached for him. His words reached into her.

"My father's death hit Des the hardest. Des was seven. He saw my father pull the trigger. I'm sure any psychiatrist would tell you Des should've received treatment for the trauma; the act was simply too much for a child to witness and not be scarred. It's devouring him now, Asha. Mother's death only amplified the pressure. Des became our father, the only father I've ever known. I owe him everything, Asha. I'm the man I am today because of Des."

He spoke next of how his mother returned to Ireland after Michael Mershan's death, living with her father, an alcoholic. They'd resided in antiquated conditions, suffered emotional abuse at his hands until he died in a rage one night. Shortly thereafter, barely ten-years-old, Des started shouldering the burden of protecting their mother and keeping his brothers safe.

"An American writer took pity on our situation, sponsored us to come to the States. She was a nice lady. Then she was killed in a hit-and-run accident. My mum panicked, afraid they would send us back to Ireland. She took us and ran. And kept running. Anytime someone asked too many questions, she'd pack up our meager belongings and move to another town, another state. She took jobs that barely paid minimum wage, only thing she could get. Worked herself to the bone."

As he talked, Jago cried. Asha cried with him. How could she not? His pain washed through her. All the hurt, the anguish, his mother's fear and illness—Desmond's sacrifices to make sure his brothers were safe. She also began to comprehend Jago's reticence in revealing his deception. He would've been betraying Des, whom he loved like a father. She understood it all so clearly now. Understood, but had no idea how to deal with it.

All through the night he spoke of these things. And she simply held him.

In the morning, Asha was beside herself. Jago clearly had reasons for what he did, and they were not selfish, but her emotions were too out of control to be rational. She alternated between crying jags over what he and his family had gone through and wanting to belt him.

She had to get away. There was no way she could sort out her emotions and think straight. Also, she had the urge to fly to her twin's side. Trevelyn was at Colford and involved with Raven. Dealing with Jago was hard enough for her, but when she thought of Trev deceiving her sister, Asha saw red and wanted to murder someone—preferably with the last name of Mershan.

She stood by the glass doors, watching the gray morning, and trying to calm her mood. It wasn't working. She kept telling herself that her sisters, Paganne, Katlynne and Britt, were at Colford to support Raven. LynneAnne was on Falgannon with B.A.

"Only I'm alone, no sister to lean on," she said wistfully.

She picked up the phone to call Raven, then hung up. This wasn't something you broke to your sister on a trunk call. Wiggling her fingers, trying to decide, she finally picked it up and rang Colford Hall, hoping to reach Kat or Britt. Instead, a maid answered saying all her sisters were out, getting ready for a big gala for the Historical Trust.

"Blast." Asha hung up and frowned toward the closet, knowing her suitcase was at the bottom. It was silly, but she wanted to go home. Maybe back in England she'd have a buffer so she could think. Being with Jago kept her emotions too volatile. With a few weeks away, her body would adjust to the chemical changes coming from carrying a child.

Jago came out of the bedroom, his eyes filled with concern. "I won't ask for forgiveness. I don't deserve it. But you do understand, don't you, Asha?"

She gave him a small smile, staring at him, drinking in his physical beauty. Loving him. Oh, yes, she understood. Too much.

She nodded. "Please don't worry. Things will sort themselves out."

"How about taking today off and we go to the river house? It's always so peaceful there. We can talk more," he suggested hopefully.

"Sounds like just the ticket," she lied.

"Good. Let me shower and then we can be on our way."

Jago hesitated, as if not sure she was all right. Then he gave a nod and entered the bathroom, closing the door. Shortly afterward, the shower started.

Heart breaking, she crossed the room and picked up his cell phone, wallet and key ring, then reached for her purse. She wouldn't take time to pack; she was heading straight to England and Raven.

Clint staring up at her was almost her undoing. She cupped his sweet face, looking into his orange eyes. "You be a good lad. Delbert, Oo-it and Sam will feed you." On impulse she leaned down and kissed him between the ears. "Everything will be all right, so don't you worry." She just wished she believed that.

After one last look at Clint, she closed the patio door and rushed to her car. The stupid antique Triumph TR 6 cranked and whined and belched, refusing to start. She ground the starter once, making a horrid noise and was afraid she flooded it. She glanced to the bungalow, fearful. Sure enough, the door jerked open and Jago rushed out in just his gray sweatpants.

"Come on, come on, you piece of British Leyland junk," she begged and cursed in the same breath.

Jago paused and put his hands on his hips. His black hair wet, his chest beaded with water from the shower he hadn't had time to towel off, the blasted man looked so damn sexy. She loved him more than life, but if he tried to stop her she might run him down.

The motor finally caught and she released the clutch and eased forward. He'd been content to stand and glare at her while the starter was grinding away, only now it was running, so he moved to block her. Rushing up, he put both hands on the hood and made it clear he wasn't getting out of the way. She smiled, seeing his car keys, cell phone and his wallet sitting on the seat by her pocketbook.

"Hmm . . . might as well give him something in return."

Locking the door so he couldn't yank it open, she reached into her purse for the pink napkin, then rolled down the window. Seeing her do that, he came around to the driver's side.

"Cut the motor, Asha."

"Here, Mr. Mershan." She poked her arm out the window to hand him the napkin.

He looked confused, but finally took it. As he started to open it up, her foot punched the gas and the car lurched forward, leaving him standing flatfooted. Slowing to pull onto the lane, she glanced in the rearview mirror and watched him open the napkin that contained her Early Pregnancy Test with the pretty little plus sign.

He gaped for a minute, then his head snapped up.

"Buh bye, Mr. Mershan." She laughed and floored the gas, leaving him to watch her speed away.

Chapter Twenty-Eight

Jago glanced at his watch, then checked the departure time of the plane. Bloody hell, Asha was one-step ahead of him the whole way. At first, he assumed she'd finally return to The Windmill, if for nothing but to kick him out. However, Netta came to say Asha had called, and asked her to handle the restaurant while she was away, that she was going to England for a stay. The damn plane had taken off less than an hour before he reached the airport.

Exhaling his impatience, he punched the number to Falgannon, hoping to catch Des again. He wasn't pleased with their last conversation. Des still couldn't let go of the past, and it was slowly destroying him. Instead, Asha's sister picked up the phone. He almost hung upon her. Something about B.A. Montgomerie terrified him!

"Falgannon Castle," came the voice that had a similar timbre as Asha's, but was touched with the charming hint of a Scottish burr.

"BarbaraAnne, this is Jago Mershan. I'm Desmond's—"

B.A. cut him off. "Mershan? I thought it was *Fitzgerald*. Yes, we spoke briefly before, you lying bastard."

God, he loved these Montgomerie wenches! No politeness or British stiff upper lip, they came at you, wanting to cut off vital parts of your male anatomy. Must be their Pict blood. He thought of that little knife Asha kept and shuddered.

"I see you share Asha's opinion of me. I'm calling about Des. Look, I'm at the airport awaiting connections, but I need to speak with you."

"Since you hurt my sister, I'm *so* in the mood to listen."

He wished for an old-fashioned phone booth where he could sit down; wished Asha hadn't taken his cell phone. "Asha's capable of extracting her pound of flesh. I'll make it up to her if I have to crawl on my belly and beg. Right now, this is urgent. I'm calling about Des. I spoke with him last night. It upset me. Whatever happens, please keep him on the island. I'm worried about him. He loves you."

"I know."

"That's a relief." For the first time since he saw Asha holding that letter, something had gone right. "I feared, like your precious sister, you'd pull a tizzy and try to punish Des until he comes around. My brother's erred . . . in many things. We *all* have. Right now, he's in trouble. Our mother died in November and Des hasn't adjusted. It wasn't an easy passing . . ."

Her tone was sad. "I figured that out a few days ago."

An unwelcome intrusion, he heard his plane being called.

"Damn. They're paging my flight. I can't afford to miss it, and give your sister a head start. His whole life, he put Mother, Trevelyn and me ahead of what was best for him. He needs someone to put Desmond first. Can you, BarbaraAnne? Please remember above all, he loves you deeply—and don't let him off that island."

He waited for her to answer him for a couple of seconds, but finally had to hang up, not hearing her reply.

When the door opened on the small cottage, Jago sucked in his breath. In the half-light of the February evening, he thought for a heartbeat that he stared at Asha. Then after that breathless moment, he recognized the woman as Raven, her twin. He couldn't pinpoint the differences, at first glance; he just *felt* it wasn't Asha, on a deep level. Her face was faintly thinner, her hair darker. She blinked, confused, and then he understood—she was going through a similar puzzlement, thinking for an instant that he was Trev.

"Peculiar, eh?"

Eyes wary, she nodded. "I'm not sure the world really deserves two of you. One's bad enough"

"You can berate me later. I want to see Asha. Make sure she's all right."

"Asha?" Her perplexity deepened.

"Yeah, your twin, looks a lot like you but has lighter hair and doesn't have that beauty mark on her lip that you do."

"I know my sister quite well. I just don't understand why you would think she'd be here." She looked him up and down. "I see differences between Trev and you, too."

The way her mouth quirked up in a smug half-smile, set his teeth on edge. Jago reined in the irritation. "Asha's not here?"

She shook her head. "She's in Kentucky."

"She left there, was coming home to you."

"She's not here. Her home is in Kentucky now."

He half believed her, but intuition said she'd lie without hesitation for her sister. Being a jerk, he pushed past her and entered the cozy thatched cottage. A bright orange tabby appeared and danced around his feet; bloody thing was nearly as fat as Clint. The creature chased after him as he went from room to room calling Asha's name.

Raven stood by the door, glaring haughtily at him as he returned. "Chester, leave the man alone. That's not Trev," she told the cat, which paid no attention. "I think it best you leave, Mr. Mershan."

Ignoring her, he dropped down on the oak bench in the hallway. "She's not here."

"I told you she wasn't, but I guess being a lying Mershan

you expect everyone else to lie, too. Asha is in Kentucky. She rang to say she was coming, but an hour later, she called back to say she'd changed her mind and was returning to The Windmill."

He stared at her, trying to decide if she was telling the truth. It could be a joke they'd cooked up, to send him back to Kentucky, only to find out she wasn't there and he'd have to turn around and come back to England again. A perverse punishment. Almost reading his mind, she shrugged, and crossed to a hall table where a phone sat. She picked it up and punched out a number with enough digits telling him it was overseas.

She smiled patronizingly, and then held the receiver to his ear. Asha's voice was clear across the connection.

"The Windmill. Hello? Anyone there?"

Jago took the phone from Raven's hand, punched disconnect and started to dial. He paused when he realized he wasn't sure whom to call. He looked at her. "I need Mershan's corporate helicopter and jet warmed up. That's Julian's department, but I guess he's still on Falgannon. Where is Trev?"

"Trev's right here." His brother spoke from the shadow of the doorway.

Seeing his twin he laughed for the first time since Asha had found that bloody letter. "No wonder Raven saw 'differences.' " His twin had a black eye and a bruise on his chin.

Yep, these Montgomerie women were warriors. He wondered if Trev had at least remembered rule number three in handling a Montgomerie female—to protect his b*reall*.

Asha hung up the phone. No one had spoken, but she had this strange feeling it was Jago. She was sorry she'd run from him. It wasn't her style. She was still unsure what she'd do when he returned, but outside of the fun of leaving him without his charge cards, phone and car keys, she hadn't accomplished anything other than giving herself a little space to think.

Colin was replacing worn tiles on the floor in front of the jukebox; the idiot box was playing The Yardbirds' "Heart Full of Soul." He looked up, concern in his eyes.

"You feel okay, Asha?"

She picked up a pencil to add notes to Netta's orders. Her friend was learning fast and would soon take a lot of weight off her shoulders. With the baby coming, she would be a godsend. Netta was getting another promotion this payday—to manager. And pleased how Winnie was fitting in, maybe Asha would promote the young girl to hostess and hire another waitress or two.

Dropping the pencil, she picked up the glass of green tea and lemon. "Sure, I'm fine. Why do you ask?"

Colin shrugged. "You're drinking green tea instead of Pepsi, for one. And maybe the way you answered the phone; hope in your eyes—though mixed with a flash of fire."

"I'm a little tired, restless. The winds make me edgy. They rattled the panes of the windows last night and kept me awake."

"The baby making you sick yet?" He almost ducked after asking the question.

"You know, Colin, you're too damn smart," Asha growled.

He smiled winningly. "Until you came along, no one noticed. It was 'good old Oo-it—always great for a laugh.' "

"They were laughing with you, Colin. Everyone loves you."

He replaced the cap on the putty cement. "Yeah, I know. Why I loved the nickname. But Oo-it isn't *all* of me. Sometimes, names are often roles we're forced to play. Think maybe that Jago was able to forget his troubles and just be Jago here? Hey, I'm not saying that lying to you was good, and taking the proxies put him in the doghouse, but a name is just some label we stick on people. You loved Clint a long time before we learned his name. And what the heck"—he chuckled and flashed a grin—"I'm an Oo-it. Names aren't as important as a person's actions. Did Jago tell you about the drive-in project? We're partners. He put up the money, and he and I are going into the drive-in franchise business. People will have to call me Mr. Oo-it. Or how he gave Netta money to start a dress shop in Lexington? And that he's trying to line up a deal for Sam to market his gumbo recipe?"

She blinked, shocked, maybe slightly hurt. "No, he didn't. Of course, I shouldn't be surprised he forgot to mention these things. He didn't even tell me his *real* name."

"He was playing faery godfather, and leaving it up to us to tell you. Netta's dragging her heels, scared—I'm not sure she'll do it. I was waiting for my first franchise sale. Sam held off seeing if the deal happened or not. We wanted something real to tell you, not just hopes. The main thing, Jago cared enough to see *us*. Whatever his name, he's a hell of a man, Asha. Don't lose him over a silly name."

Chapter Twenty-nine

At dark the next day, a gale force gust of wind hit the side of the small diner, sending the huge plate glass windows rattling. It set Asha's teeth on edge. These sorts of windstorms hit Kentucky in November and again in March. The only time she didn't like the state's changeable and moody weather. The day had been rather warm, but now a rapidly moving cold front had blown in, dropping temperatures and sending 35 mph winds to gusts of 55 and higher. The old farmers in the area called it a nor'easter. The wind reminded a person they were human, and they and their feeble shelters could be blown down by a force unseen. Mother Nature humbled one.

When the lights flickered and threatened to go out, Asha paused from thumbing through the Crownline Boats catalogue and frowned. She loathed the winds when they howled like this, always dreading when the electricity went out, due to limbs breaking off and taking down the power lines.

"Maybe I should look at a generator catalogue instead of cabin cruisers," she grumbled to herself.

Last night had been bad enough without Jago. The winds picked up before dawn. It made her glad Colin had finished putting in new storm windows on the bungalows; that cut down on the noise some. Weather aside, she'd been restless all night: tossing and turning, endless glances to the phone, waiting for Jago *Mershan* to call. She wondered where he was, what he was doing. Missed him.

"The man just doesn't understand proper groveling protocol," she groused.

The lights flickered again. Both Colin and she glared up at them, as though it was possible to stop them from winking out by will alone. Putting down the putty knife, Colin closed the can of cement. With a worried sigh, he pushed it and the water bucket out of the pathway to the kitchen door.

"You know, Asha, talking to yourself could be a sign you're alone too much."

She countered, "My mum always said it was a mark of a highly intelligent child."

"You momma could've lived in England in a 'hall' that had fifty bedrooms, with servants to wait on her hand and foot. What did she do? Lived on a rundown horse farm and ran The Windmill. I loved her, but she wasn't your average person—you know?" Colin teased.

"What's that line—in *Lawrence of Arabia* about Brits loving desolate places?"

"Yeah, well, Larry was a queer bird." Colin stood up, wiping his hands on a rag. "Hey, I made a pun! Sorry, I'm not finishing this project tonight. I have a hot date, and I don't want to be late." Even in the fluctuating light, his blush was clear.

Asha smiled. "Hot date? Who's the lucky lass?"

"Winnie." He beamed.

She'd noticed Winnie taking an interest in Colin the past few months. He'd helped fix up her cabin into a wonderfully warm home. In turn, she began prodding him: first change, she'd taken him to Lexington to have his hair styled, eschewing Colin's monthly trip to Jake the Barber in Leesburg. Then she'd started helping him shop for clothes.

Gone were the ten-year-old, never-wear-out, hooded sweatshirts. Asha admitted the change was fantastic. Colin was very handsome. Winnie had found a diamond in the rough and was polishing him to a shine. Derek sneered and made comments about Winnie doing it just to make him jealous, but Asha thought the young woman had simply looked at Colin and seen all that potential waiting to be tapped. The two made a cute couple.

"Oh? And where are you taking Winnie?" she asked, smiling.

He gave a short snort of laughter. "She hates Lexington, is a small town girl at heart. Leesburg still rolls up the sidewalks at 8 p.m. That leaves few options. I wanted to do something special. I slipped Ella twenty bucks, and she's fixing up the porch room at The Cliffside. Roses, candlelight and maybe a little slow-dancing to their jukebox—which doesn't play 'Surfin' Bird.' I hope she likes it."

"She will. Run on and have a great night. I'm going to eat a piece of cheesecake and close up early. These winds depress me. No one ever comes when the weather is bad. No use staying open."

"Sam's off night. He's over at Melvin's playing poker. He won't be back 'til late. You'll be okay here?" Colin seemed on edge from the wind, too.

She rolled her eyes. "I've run this place since I came back; no one's cared before. Now Jago's not here, suddenly everyone's concerned I'm by myself? My purse is under the counter—with my gun. Run along and have a lovely time with Winnie. With this weather, you'll have The Cliffside to yourselves."

Colin nodded and slid on his navy windbreaker. Fixing his collar, he hesitated, eyes troubled.

Asha paused, her back to the swinging door to the kitchen. "I meant to tell you how handsome you are with your new duds and haircut."

Grinning, he bounced on his feet. "Yeah—I'm pretty cute, eh? 'Night, Asha."

" 'Night, Colin."

In the kitchen, she picked up a saucer for herself, then on impulse lifted another. Delbert might like a treat, too. And maybe now was a good time to look at his photo album. Going into the food locker, she used a pie cutter to divide the cheesecake, carefully lifting out each slice to leave the remaining pie in perfect condition—Sam got cranky when she just cut slices off with a knife. It was comical, the way he fussed at her. She might be the owner of The Windmill, but *he* was boss in the kitchen.

She carried the plates out and placed them on a tray. Going behind the counter, she filled a glass with pink lemonade for her, and snagged a milk carton out of the cooler for Delbert. Once again, her eyes went to the phone, half expecting Jago to call. With a sigh, she closed and locked the front door, flipped the sign to CLOSED, and then turned out the overhead lights.

The jukebox sedately played a Gene Pitney tune, as she picked up the tray. "You better be glad I love you, you metal escapee from *The Twilight Zone*. Someone else would have pulled your innards out long ago." Balancing the food tray with one hand, she reached out and gave it a pat. "Night-night. No 'Bird is the Word' or 'The Lion Sleeps Tonight,' eh? Delbert and Sam need rest."

Two steps and she booted something hard, nearly tripping. "Bloody hell, I almost kicked the bucket," she joked. She'd stubbed her toe on the metal pail Colin had used to clean putty from the tiles he was putting in. Using the side of her foot, she nudged it over to the corner out of the way.

At the porch, she allowed Clint out of his 'prison.' The puss padded inside, dancing, sure he was about to be fed again. His company was comforting; Asha enjoyed him being underfoot, and was sorry she had to keep him out of the restaurant. He'd been on the glider swing, staring off into the night as though he expected Jago to show up.

"Sorry, puss. I sent Mr. Mershan on a wild goose chase. My guess, he's still in England, trying to get connections back. Maybe in a day or two." Asha locked the outer entrance, pausing to stare out into the night, too. "Sheesh, I'm as bad as you, Clint. He's not coming. We'd best forget it. Come on, let's spend the evening with Delbert."

Another gust of wind slammed the front of the old overseer's house, shaking the whole structure. She was less worried about the restaurant. Five years ago, because of insurance regulations, the windows had been refitted with shatterproof safety glass, and the wood door reinforced with steel. You could take a sledgehammer to them—they'd crack, but likely wouldn't shatter. However, the main house caused her concern. Built in the early 1800s, the antebellum home was, for the most part, constructed solidly; ceiling joists were not of pine but heavy poplar. It creaked and groaned in protest, making Asha suck in a breath, alarmed, as the air seemed to push under the eaves and nearly lift the old roof off.

Dismissing her worries, she entered the lobby. "Delbert, Clint and I brought you pie," she called.

The television played in the inner office, but the room was empty. Delbert would surely return in a minute. She set the tray on the desk, then took pity on Clint and poured milk into a saucer for him. Purring, the kitty's pink tongue rapidly lapped up the liquid.

Asha's attention was drawn to the television as they flashed a weather bulletin telling of the high winds. "As Colin would say, 'No shit, Sherlock.' " She flinched as another blast of cold wind battered the front of the old house. "Clint, I don't care if his name *is* Mershan, I wouldn't mind if he were here. He could lie to me all he wants, tell me how this house has stood this long and will stand another hundred years."

Becoming concerned when Delbert didn't return, she decided to go check on him. At the turn in the long hallway, she noticed a dim light coming from his rooms. For some reason, prickles crept up her spine; her fey sense warned that something wasn't right. Pushing open the door, Asha saw Delbert on the floor, his album and his precious pictures spilt about him.

Her heart jumped as she rushed to him. "Oh, Delbert, no!" First thought was he'd had a stroke or a heart attack. She checked his pulse; he was breathing slowly, but his heartbeat remained steady.

First aid always said to keep a patient warm. She dashed to the bedroom and grabbed a blanket and pillow; returning, she snugged the cover around him. As she lifted his head to place it on the pillow, her fingers touched something wet and sticky.

Yanking her hand back, she stared at her fingers. Blood? Poor dear must've cracked his head when he'd fallen. Damn.

Sam was out playing poker, and Colin was with Winnie. No guests were currently staying with them. She'd need to call the state police; maybe they'd evac him with the helicopter from the University of Kentucky Medical Center. Then she'd ring Liam. She kissed Delbert's cheek and rushed to the lobby.

Scurrying around the counter, she opened the phonebook to find the number to dial. 911 didn't work outside of cities. Upset, shaking, she nearly dropped the receiver of the 1950s-style phone they still used. Then it hit her—no dialing tone. Flicking the flasher a couple times, she hoped to hear the reassuring hum. Nothing. The line was dead.

The lights flickered ominously with yet another strong gust of wind. "Oh, please, don't you go out—ohhhhhhhh."

She shook, trying to decide what was best to do. The drive-in was closed for the season; no one would be up there. She could drive up the hill—too long a distance to run—to the employee's homes, but they likely didn't have phones either since they came off the same major poles.

Then she remembered Jago's cell phone in her purse. Hopefully it was still charged. As she replaced the receiver, noise from the atrium caused her to look up. For an instant, she hoped Sam was returning early.

Montague Faulkner pushed through the glass doors between the restaurant and the house. A tremble went through her as she considered how he'd gotten in there. She had been the last person out of the restaurant. True, she hadn't locked the atrium. That meant he'd come in the motel entrance while she was in Delbert's room, and gone through to the diner. But why?

His bright blond curls were wild, obviously whipped by the wind before coming inside. He gave her a small half-smile, which never reached his eyes. "Ah, so you *are* here. I went to the restaurant but didn't see anyone there."

Her blood buzzing with rising dread, Asha summoned a false calm; she had to clamp down on the instinct to run. "Slow night. The weather always keeps down the number of customers." No fool, she wasn't about to say it kept them away entirely. Delbert needed help—fast. Despite that, Montague's appearing from the restaurant told her not to let this man know how vulnerable her situation was. "I'm taking advantage to catch up on a few things around this place. Is there something I can help you with?"

"Been meaning to talk to you for some time. You're always busy."

Not for one minute did she accept his surface behavior. The more normal he tried to make the situation, the louder her warning bells chimed.

"Any tree limbs down? I fear losing electric in winds like this. Such a pain when that happens. Damn lobby fills up with the customers bitching and moaning—like I can do something about it by twitching my nose." She stressed that someone might come at any moment, not wanting him to see she was alone, vulnerable. Her inner voice warned her not to ask Monty for help. Feeling panic, she didn't take time to reason out why, simply trusted her instincts. To cover her deep unease, she kept prattling, as if she found nothing disquieting about his presence.

"Some of these trees are hundreds-years old. Notice how there aren't many elm trees any more? Dutch Elm disease, they say."

As she blethered on, she made a show of straightening stuff on the motel front desk, mindlessly chattering as if it were natural for them to stand around gossiping about trees. Yet, at the back of her mind, she kept recalling all the hearsay, how they whispered this man had raped a child when he was in his teens. Also, something she couldn't define—a sense of Laura being with her—cautioned Monty was dangerous and here for a purpose. She wanted to maneuver him to where she could make a clear dash to the restaurant, and to her gun in her pocketbook.

"The poplars have been hit by a nasty bore beetle that gets between the bark and slowly kills the tree. A shame, since they have those beautiful yellow tulip blooms come spring. Guess that's why they call them *tulip* poplars, eh? They're huge, and with the poor things in bad shape, we keep losing power when limbs snap off."

Her prattle seemed to confuse him, but with the fine edge of panic rising within her, it was hard to keep up. Too many things were just now becoming clear. Delbert hadn't cracked his head in a fall: Monty had hit him. A falling limb hadn't knocked out phone service. Monty also had been the one to leave the letter on the refrigerator. He'd wanted her to get mad at Jago and send him away. Carefully, he'd chosen a time when Colin, Sam and Liam were not about. Only poor Delbert.

And her.

Quickly running through her options, Asha considered making a break to the office and locking herself in with Clint. Only, there was nothing to defend herself with, and the door was flimsy at best. She'd trap herself in the small, windowless room with no recourse.

Picking up the feather duster Delbert had left on the chair, she pretended to clean as she babbled on. Reaching the office door, she fluttered it over the top of the frame, muttering about grime, then quickly pulled the door shut to keep Clint in there out of the way; she needed to concentrate on getting herself out of this situation, and wasn't about to hand this creep a weapon to use against her.

Monty took a step toward her as she touched the doorknob, but eased his stance when he saw she merely pulled it closed. Those gold eyes watched her without blinking, once again causing a flashback to that damn crocodile in the Cincinnati Zoo. Only there was no glass wall between them here. Deep in the pit of her stomach, she comprehended she faced a man capable of killing—this she felt from Laura—with only her cleverness to save her. Right now, she could barely think.

Funny, she'd berated Jago for lying to her. Now, lies were all she had to save herself from evil.

"Excuse me, while I keep working. There's so much to do around this damn place. So little help. I'll be glad when Trident Ventures buys me out. I'm hoping to get big bucks from that. Then, I can get rid of this crazy place, go some place where it's warm and sunny."

His brow crinkled at her statement. "I thought you were hanging on to the businesses? Everyone said you refused that big company wanting the land."

She forced a chuckle, prayed her lies sounded believable. "Well, I *had* to convince Trident of that to get the price up! They've already tripled their offer. Now that they've purchased the horse farm, I'm expecting they'll offer four times the price. Bingo. Six months from now all this will be bulldozed down. Wanna bet they put a Wal-mart on the site?"

"Gone? But I thought you came back to run it, and were fighting to keep it." Monty put his hands on his hips and kept staring at her. The man didn't look convinced.

Asha tried to keep her breathing steady despite her thundering heart. She was a lousy liar. The whole family knew that. Only her life and maybe Delbert's depended upon her guile. Everything depended upon it. *Where's my knight in armor when I need him, riding to the rescue on his mighty steed*, she thought.

Oh, Jago, I love you. Nothing else mattered.

"Well, I hope my performance fooled Trident. Maybe you'll come around and a have drink at the Valentine's Party to celebrate with me." She casually dusted her way to the lobby door, only to have him step forward to block her. He was tall, close to 6-5". Scary. Nonchalantly, she swished the feathers all around the frame.

Using the dust as an excuse, she summoned a sneezing fit—a ruse. "Excuse me." *Achoo-achoo*. "Sorry, I'm allergic to—" *Achoo achoo* "—dust mites. Let me get a Kleenex."

With each sneeze, she rocked back farther into the office where he lacked a clear view. Taking a deep breath, she didn't hesitate. One foot landed in the middle of the chair on rollers, then she vaulted from it onto the desktop, sending the chair to slam into him as he leapt for her. With a hop, Asha planted her hip on the counter, swiveled and swung her legs over to the other side. All perfectly executed—except for the landing: she didn't 'stick it,' but came down hard on her right leg. Grimacing from the pain and the cracking sound, Asha feared she might've broken a bone in her foot or ankle, but spared no time for concern.

"Pain means you're alive," she muttered to herself.

Asha had a feeling she wouldn't be if she slowed down. Dragging herself up, she rushed through the little foyer between the motel and the restaurant, hearing Monty's thundering steps close behind. The short distance down the aisles between the booths seemed miles; she cried with each step, struggling to keep going on the bad ankle. Hot agony lanced up her leg each time she planted her foot, nearly causing her leg to buckle.

Frantic, she swung around the counter and grabbed her purse. Relief flooded through her when her fingers closed around the cold metal of the gun. Holding it in both hands, she raised it and pointed the Colt straight at his chest and pulled the trigger. And kept pulling it.

Horror washed through her whole being as nothing happened but *click . . . click . . . click*.

Monty flashed a smug smile, then reached into the pocket of his jacket. "Works better with these." Holding his hand up, he allowed the bullets to clatter onto the counter between them. Too late, she recalled him coming from the diner before. Now, she knew why. She watched them bounce and scatter across the oak top, ached to snatch at them. But that's what he taunted her to do, as it'd bring her within his reach.

"Told you that you wouldn't always have Fancy Pants at your back. Since he came, he's never left you alone much, glommed onto you, didn't he? I had to wait. I knew my time would come. I figured if you got a hold of that letter you'd send his British ass packing."

The jukebox suddenly clicked as it changed records, and began playing "Tom Dooley." Monty looked toward the Wurlitzer, just behind him and to his right.

"*Hang down your head . . . poor boy you're bound to die . . .*"

He flinched; his head whipped around as his eyes narrowed on her. "You do that, don't you? I heard about the women in your family—witches. You called *him* here to destroy me. I looked into his eyes. Knew them. Tommy's eyes. After that, I read up on your family on the Internet at the library. Burned a few of them during the Burning Times, they did. Some historian wrote a book about them, said they were the real thing. I also did research on how they killed witches—by hayfork and billhook."

Asha recoiled. Old pocket lore claimed pinning a witch to the ground with a pitchfork discharged her power, and then you purified her soul by carving a sign of a cross into her chest with the ugly curved blade used in handling hay bales. By the dim light of the jukebox, Monty's coppery eyes seemed to glow with an unearthly zeal. Terror roiled in the pit of her belly, paralyzing her, as within those yellow eyes she read the message that this was precisely what he intended to do to her. In her mind, she could almost see it happening. The near-clairvoyant vision kept her frozen, unable to move or think.

"Tommy, what's he doing?" Laura's voice rang clear from the shadows.

At first Asha panicked, thinking she was slipping back into the past. Oh, mercy not now! Please not now, not when she needed all her focus to survive.

Monty's head jerked around, staring into the inky darkness toward the motel. *He heard her.* Two forms materialized from the shadows—a man and a woman. The same instant the jukebox went totally nuts, hitting a groove in the record and sticking.

"*Poor boy, you're bound to die . . . poor boy, you're bound to die . . . poor boy, you're bound to die . . . poor boy, you're bound to die . . .*"

Asha dove for the bullets. Monty beat her. His arm slapped out and swiped them off the counter.

A brilliant white light shown from the road, as a car turned into the parking lot, the halogen headlights flooding the glass panes, almost blinding her. Not wasting a breath, she jerked up the soda feed off the fountain and sprayed Monty in the face as he sprang at her. And kept spraying.

The high beams came closer, and the whine of a car engine downshifting was clear over the blasting jukebox. She wanted to look, but didn't dare take her eyes off Monty. With her free hand she snatched up drinking glasses stacked on the counter and tossed them at him. Most hit, bounced or shattered, but they only kept him at bay. Then she thought of the cooler behind her. As she backed up, the sprayer jerked in her hand; it wouldn't reach any farther. Swinging out wildly, Monty caught the plastic hose stretched taught, yanked it, and almost pulled her off balance on her weak ankle. She released it fast, causing him to fall back a few steps until he could right himself. Opening the cooler's glass door, she hid behind it, using it as a shield. Once more there was glass between her and those crocodile eyes. She now launched unopened Coors beer bottles at him; their weight hit with a solid impact.

There was a pounding at the glass door, then Jago's voice called out, sending hot relief flooding through her. "Sometimes, the white knight does come in time," she whispered the reassurance to herself. "even if his armor is a little tarnished."

Still, Jago was locked out. The safety glass of the windows and steel reinforced door would permit him to see what was happening, but would hold him on that side. That wouldn't stop Jago. He'd come. Somehow, he'd come. He kicked at the lock twice, the door bouncing from the force. But it held.

She was fast running out of bottles to toss. Time to stop hiding behind the glass cooler and come out swinging. Getting a good grip on one beer with her right hand, and snatching up two more, she came out swinging hard. Monty lunged forward, but she caught him on the side of the head with the first one. The second hit his chin, shattered, and drove him back.

She shifted the third beer for her best grip, caught him full in the face. Because of the angle, she likely broke his nose. Blood streamed down his mouth and chin. Reaching the serving cart, she shoved with all her weight, catching him in the middle of his stomach, and shoving him toward the jukebox. With the shattered glass and soda all over the floor, he struggled not to lose footing.

"*I AM THE GOD OF HELLFIRE, AND I BID YOU TO BURN!*" The Wurlitzer roared out the start of Arthur Brown's song, scaring Monty, just as it had frightened Jago the night they'd danced in the diner. Monty jumped. His foot came down inside the pail that Colin had left from working on the tiles. He clomped awkwardly, trying to shake it off. It was the opening she needed. Once more she used the cart as a battering ram, slamming into him again.

Monty went down, landing against the jukebox, his palm flattened on the metal side, trying to break his fall. He fused there. As it had knocked Asha on her arse, shocking her, she saw it now fed Monty electricity much in the manner of a man in an electric chair. Monty's face swelled, his eyes bulged, yet he couldn't let go. The jukebox arched, sizzled and popped; smells of phosphorous and copper filled the air. The horrid scene went on and on.

Her leg giving out, Asha collapsed into a heap at the edge of the bar, crying, unable to watch any longer. Suddenly, arms encircled, pulling her away. Instinct arose and she struggled against them, but then Jago was kissing her face and telling her it was all right. She was safe.

Jago.

She cried harder. So much pain and worry, all the fear—adrenaline was pumping through her and she couldn't come down.

Monty howled as electricity pumped through his body destroying it. Then suddenly there was a loud explosion from within the Wurlitzer and it went silent. For an instant, Monty stood, frozen. Then fell face forward onto the floor. Dead.

Jago scooped her up in his strong arms, and carried her out of the nightmare scene.

Chapter Thirty

Near dawn, Asha sat crosswise in the bathtub—one leg propped up on the edge to keep the cast out of the water. Soaking in soothing lavender bubble bath, she reached to find some sense of normalcy.

The state police had come and gone, taking Monty's body away. Before that, the ambulance had carried Delbert, who was conscious by then, to the Chandler Hospital in Lexington. The young doctor attending assured Asha that her friend would recover completely, that they would keep him for observations. Seeing her bad limp, he'd suggested she ride with them and have her foot x-rayed. Asha hadn't wanted to let go of Jago. If she did, she'd feared she would start shaking and might never stop.

Jago had driven her to the emergency room, held her hand while they x-rayed her foot, and then as they put it in a cast. Liam, Netta, Sam and Colin were in the waiting room when they came out. Once Sam made sure she was fine, he said he'd stay with Delbert. Colin drove Jago's Jeep back to The Windmill, while Jago sat in the back holding her all the way home.

So much had happened in such a short span of hours.

The warmth of the lavender in the bath filled her mind, its calming influence making her drowsy. She closed her eyelids, but just for a moment . . .

"Tommy, I'm scared. What are they doing?"

Laura saw Tommy glance in the rearview mirror, knew he recognized Ewen hung out the passenger window, Wolf whistling and thumping on the door panel of Monty's truck.

In slow motion—yet all happening too damn fast—Monty revved the truck's engine to smash into the car again. Hard. The cement truck up ahead started to slow to make a left turn onto Richmond Pike. Laura watched, barely able to breathe as the road became winding, dangerous. The cliffs were coming up. Tommy dare not let this madness drag on there, or Monty would likely force them off one of the sharp S-turns.

The truck ahead started to slow, the brake lights only working on one side. There'd be no stopping. Tommy hit the gas, hoping to swing around the truck before it turned. As he did, Monty slammed into the car, jarring them forward. Too late, they saw the Peterbilt, barreling down on them from the other direction. The driver never had a chance to hit the brakes. Tommy attempted to swerve back, but Monty crashed into the Mustang again, pushing them forward into its path.

Crying tires, busting glass, grinding metal . . . her painful scream, as she knew everything was being stolen from her.

In movies, they show how your life passes before your eyes at the instant of your death.They lied. It wasn't the years of her short life that ran through her mind. It was Tommy.

Always Tommy. That she wouldn't marry him come next year. No Christmases, no long walks along the sandbar at Lock 8. No more kisses under the bell tower. She would never hold their beautiful black-haired son. It was all images of the life that never would be.

She tried to speak. Oh, Tommy. To kiss you one last time. To tell you how much I love you. Always will love you . . . always love you. . . .

* * *

Tommy stood there looking back as cars and trucks stopped along the roadside. The driver of the Peterbilt was on his knees in the middle of the highway crying. Poor man, it wasn't his fault. It was Monty's. He'd stolen everything from them.

Heartbreaking, yet somehow it all seemed now . . . distant.

She touched Tommy's shoulder, then laughed. Taking his hand, she tugged on it. "Tommy, this way."

"Laura, wait. I love you." He yanked her into his arms, squeezing her tightly. Tears filled his eyes and streamed down his cheeks. "Oh, Laura . . ."

She kissed him. "Shhhh! We must hurry before someone gets our booth at The Windmill. I want a Cherry Coke and then to slow dance to our song."

"But Laura . . ." He hesitated, looking back at the wreck, confused.

She reached up and gently pulled his face around toward hers. "It doesn't matter, Tommy. Nothing matters but that we're together. We'll always be together. Just like the song, Tommy, our love will never die. Come . . ."

They walked down the road, enjoying the peace. Yes, peace. It felt as if they had made this trek a thousand times . . . ten thousand. This time was somehow different.

She smiled when the restaurant, with the funny windmill outlined in neon on the roof, came into view. The music reached her ears making her smile. Ray Peterson crooned, "Tell Laura not to cry, my love for her will never die . . ."

It was odd, but The Windmill was empty when they entered. The diner never seemed to change, but offered a soothing feel of coming home. Coming home. Tommy seemed to understand. He wordlessly pulled her into his strong arms, and they began slow-dancing.

"Hey, sleepyhead. Wake up. I need to get you out of the tub before you turn into a prune," Jago touched her shoulder, bringing her awake, then started putting down a gazillion towels on the tiled floor in preparation of helping her out of the tub.

"Sorry, I must've dozed off. Lavender will do that to me." She gave him a lazy smile. "I meant to ask how did you get back to Kentucky so fast?"

"The power of Mershan International. My brother owns a Sikorsky that can almost outfly a jet, and then for good measure, he owns a jet, too."

She yawned. "I'd say I'm impressed, but I'm too lazy. You better get me out of this tub or I might drown. I'm too tired to stay above the water."

Without hesitation, Jago reached into the foot-high bubbles and scooped her out. He held her easily, so close she could see the small variation in the beautiful green eyes so full of love. Her naked body, slick with Mr. Bubble and held against his bare chest, caused her libido to roar to life, despite being too damn tired to do anything about it. Still . . .

"Kiss me, Jago, remind me I'm alive."

He kissed her, the smooth warm lips lending her their heat. Gently at first. Then deeper, more demanding, as he felt her hunger, fed off it. He finally broke the kiss and buried his face against her neck, softly crying. His tears trickled down her shoulder.

After a few moments, he carried her into the shadowy bedroom, Clint dancing on the bed as he placed her down. Turning down the light on the nightstand, Jago sat on the edge of the bed. His hands shook as he carefully tucked the blanket about her, finally shooing Clint away when he kept butting his head against her arm. The cat was upset too and wanting reassurance. She lifted her hand and managed to give him a weak pat.

Asha looked into Jago's beautiful face. "You lied to me."

"Oh, shut up." He laughed, then tears started falling again. "I don't understand why a madman would want to kill you—*kill you*, Asha."

Thinking back on the dreams, she answered, "I do, I think—as much as anyone can understand a diseased mind. He killed Laura and Tommy. They had so much to live for, their love was so special, and yet he robbed them of all of it. He was behind them when they crashed. Cruelly, deliberately, he shoved them into the path of the oncoming truck. He was jealous of what they shared. If he couldn't have it, then he'd destroy it. Like all bullies, he enjoyed crushing things of beauty." She reached up and traced the outline of his sensual mouth. "They were there."

"Who? Where?" he asked confused.

"In the diner. Laura and Tommy saved me. At one point, just before you arrived, they materialized in the shadows and distracted him, gave me time. Then they killed him—executed him."

"Ghosts, haunted jukeboxes . . . you know something, Asha, my brothers would tell you I'm a rather logical man. Yet, here at The Windmill I find all things possible." He squeezed her hand. "Only Faulkner was electrocuted by the Wurlitzer. A freak accident. It knocked you on your arse the other day—"

"The point being, it knocked me *back*. It took and held onto him."

"He was standing with one foot in water—"

"I pushed that bucket out of the way. I kicked it earlier coming out of the kitchen. Yet it was right there again for Monty to step in."

"Asha, please can we forget about this for now. It's too fresh. You have no idea how . . . *helpless* . . . I felt pounding on the glass door and couldn't reach you. Bloody safety glass! I cracked the one window, but it wouldn't shatter. I was forced to run around to get in through the damn motel entrance. Those seconds were the longest of my life." He tried to smile. "Besides, I was supposed to rescue you. You handled it yourself, my brave warrior woman. I just picked up the pieces. I should've been there for you."

"You were, when I needed you most. I couldn't have done one more thing." She stroked his hand. "Have you checked on Delbert?"

"Sam said he's resting well. Due to his age they'll keep him another night, just to be on the safe side." Jago gave a faint chuckle. "Colin said we should drive a stake through Monty's heart . . . just to make sure. I still don't get it, Asha. Why attack you? If he killed Tommy and Laura over forty years ago, why now?"

"He'd been away for a long time; most around Leesburg assumed he had moved. He only came back after his father died and he inherited the old estate. Mostly, he kept to himself, didn't come to The Windmill often. Then that night you were there and he saw you. He kept saying you had Tommy's eyes. Even Delbert saw the likeness."

Jago exhaled in frustration. "The police said they're now looking into other unsolved crimes in the area for the past three years, wondering if he's done anything else since his return. The one detective handling the case told me that Monty was institutionalized for over ten years—his father's doing—some fancy country club-type sanitarium in Ohio. He was released when the money ran out after old man Faulkner died. I guess Monty played things pretty close to his chest since, fearing they might put him back in custody."

"He'd only come into The Windmill a few times since I came back to take over the businesses. The night he complained about salt in his water—that was the trigger. He saw your eyes—so like Tommy's. Your coming here, the music playing reminded him of the accident, it all set everything off. After that, he'd fixed it in his mind I was a witch, that I had called you to The Windmill to seek vengeance for Tommy and Laura's death. He heard the place was going to be sold, then everyone in the county gossiped about me fighting to save it. I think if The Windmill had been sold, bulldozed for a shopping mall, then all the ghosts from his past would finally be laid to rest. He evidently started stalking us after the incident at the diner. Broke into your cabin to snoop. Stole the letter. He removed the screen from my window on Halloween, hoping to get in that way to leave the letter, but I returned to the cabin and interrupted him."

Jago added more details. "They believe he stole Colin's key ring to get into your bungalow to leave the letter. Colin thought he misplaced it, hunted all day for it, but then it turned up in the floorboard of his truck a few hours later. Everyone knows Colin leaves his truck keys there; he thought he'd put the other key ring there accidentally. My guess Monty had a copy made, then returned them hoping it wouldn't be noticed."

"My Wurlitzer is dead?" she asked.

He nodded sadly. "Sorry. It's silent. Enough about enchanted music boxes and evil villains. We need to talk about this." He opened the drawer on the nightstand and pulled out her EPT test. "We're going to have a baby?"

"No, *we* are not. *I'm* going to have one."

"No, *we*."

"Humph."

"Humph all you want, but my baby needs a name."

"Your baby? I thought it was our baby. Besides, names seem to have little or changeable value. Maybe we should let it grow up and then it can tell us its name like Clint did."

"Silly woman, I love you." His hand reached out and stroked her cheek.

"Actually, if I have a son we could call him Fitzgerald Mershan." She sighed sleepily and slid down in the bed.

"Him? A little boy?" He grinned. "I could buy him a little leather jacket and teach him to ride the Harley. How about Colin Samuel Delbert Wurlitzer Mershan."

"Wurlitzer?" She chuckled.

"I was stuck with Luxovius because my father was a history nut. At least, that's what mum told me." He reached out and stroked her chin. "Forgive me, Asha?"

"In time," she teased him, but then added, "but your brother Trevelyn is dead meat for hurting my sister."

"Scoot over, lass. I need to hold you. I won't be able to sleep, but I want you in my arms, to know you're safe."

She moved over and snuggled against him, feeling secure once more. Clint walked up her leg and then settled half on her, half on Jago.

Closing her eyes, she drifted. So tired. She feared sleep, thinking she might relive the nightmare of Monty again.

Instead, she drifted in fog.

In her dream, she walked to The Windmill. As she approached, the sounds of "Tell Laura I Love Her" floated through the strange sepia twilight that touched all. Everything glowed, almost as though kissed with faery dust.

She opened the door and paused.

Tommy and Laura sat in the big corner booth—their booth—sharing a milkshake. Laura and Tommy looked up and smiled.

"Can I look now?" Asha was antsy to know what was happening. Jago had blindfolded her and carried her out of the bungalow.

In the three weeks since Monty's attack, Jago had been busy spending money left and right to put The Windmill back into order. He'd made her rest and keep off her broken foot, while he handled all arrangements. Bothersome man, he wouldn't even let her see what they were doing to *her* restaurant. When the bills came in she nearly fainted at the costs. Jago said not to worry, Des was footing the bill as a wedding present. She grinned and said in that case Sam needed a new grill, she wanted her office expanded and the parking lot really needed paving.

Jago set her on her feet and removed the cloth from around her eyes. Delbert, Colin, Sam, Derek, Winnie, Netta and Liam, and many of the regulars were in the booths, waiting inside the restaurant.

She smiled in delight. Everything was new, but it was the same. They hadn't changed anything, just repaired, and replaced aging parts of her diner to where it now appeared as it must have back in 1964. Her eyes sadly went to where the Wurlitzer had sat. From the shape under the gray cloth she knew it had to be a new jukebox.

She swallowed the tears. It wouldn't be the same.

Jago nudged Colin who moved to yank the cloth off, "TA DA!"

"But . . . that's our Wurlitzer." She nearly cried, touching the nameplate that said The Windmill.

Jago draped an arm around her shoulder. "Colin, our resident genius, repaired it."

"Yeah, had a good talking to the silly box. Same machine, just a little upgrading. It now plays MP3s. I think it likes the idea of being loaded with nearly ten thousand songs." He reached over and punched some buttons; it lit up and began to play.

"Everyone's heard about the bird . . . bird, bird, bird. . . ."

Colin glared at it. "I didn't play that song."

"Back to normal, eh?" Asha laughed, and rose up on tiptoes to kiss Jago's cheek. "Thank you. I love it. But I'm not naming my kid Wurlitzer."

"You better. Or you might be listening to nothing but 'Surfin' Bird' for weeks and I don't think either of us could stand that."

"As long as I'm listening to it with you, Jago Luxovius *Fitzgerald* Mershan, I won't mind—too much."

He kissed the tip of her nose. "You're never going to let me hear the end of it, are you?"

Asha glanced to her 'family,' then down the long aisle of the booths to the shadows in the far corner, where the foyer met the house. There she saw ghostly shapes. All, once again, right with their world. Her little world.

She smiled. "Nope. Never."

"Come on. I *told* you I heard it."

Jago tugged on her hand, pulling her toward the closed-up restaurant. Looking bored, Clint waddled along behind them. As they neared the front, they paused to peek into the small window that looked in behind the register. A night-light lent an orange glow, enough to see inside. The jukebox played, its colorful lights almost appearing festive in the darkness.

A man and a woman were over by the jukebox, slow-dancing as Gene Pitney crooned how true love never runs smooth, while the pair seemed lost in the music.

"I thought ghosts moved on after closure," Jago commented.

"Finally bringing out the truth about Monty was done to protect us. They weren't *haunting* The Windmill, Jago, they choose to be here, where they are happy."

"Your sanctuary for lost souls," he chuckled.

"Not lost . . . my haven for *found* souls. Come on." She took his hand, pulling him toward the front door.

Jago hesitated. "They'll just vanish if we go in, like they did before."

She smiled. "Not this time. Come."

Asha slid the key into the doorlock and then pushed it open, not bothering to flip on the overhead lights. The music stopped, but this time the couple didn't vanish. Instead the Wurlitzer clicked, still sounding like it was changing records even though it now played MP3s. She smiled as Mike Duncan's voice filled the diner.

If I only had the time,
If I could find just another line,
If I held you one more day,
Would I find just the things to say.

Smiling she stepped into Jago's arms and began slow-dancing to *their* song. Her head on Jago's shoulder, she sighed contentment, then she peeked over to see Tommy and Laura kissing.

Special thanks to Mike Duncan for permission to use his song as part of my books and for promotional purposes.

Lost for Words
(from Lord for Words CD)

If I only had the time,
If I could find just another line,
If I held you one more day,
Would I find just the things to say.

Chorus:
But I'm lost for words.
When I hold you close.
Because you take my breath
Away.

And if I only had a way,
You would know the things I pray.
And just because I know you're mine
I could kiss you one more time.

Chorus:

Bridge:
Because you hold me up
And you give me love.
And you take my breath.
Away.

If you could only read my mind,
I could tell you one more time,
That I miss you every day.
And all the things you used to say.

KATHLEEN BACUS

CALAMITY JAYNE HEADS WEST

Tressa Jayne Turner, Grandville Iowa's own little "Calamity," is headed for the Grand Canyon State—and a wedding! It's her goofy granny gettin' hitched, and Tressa's sunny little siesta is about to have more strings attached than a dream catcher. Her cousin's keeping secrets, the roguish Ranger Rick is sending signals—more of the smokin' than smoke variety—and it seems Tressa's not the only person with an attachment to "Kookamunga," the butt-ugly fertility figurine she picked up at a roadside stand as a wedding gift. This wacky wedding's about to become an amazing race cum Da Vinci Code–intrigue. It'll be a vision quest to make Thelma and Louise's southwestern spree seem like amateur night at the OK Corral. May the best spirit guide win.

ISBN 10: 0-505-52733-2
ISBN 13: 978-0-505-52733-2

CURVEBALL

KATE ANGELL

The bad boys of baseball, they are the top power hitters of the Richmond Rogues, and the team's best hope for a shot at the World Series. But when all three have to be benched for brawling, it's the beginning of a whole new ball game, and the opposing team could win something more than a trophy—these ladies are after their hearts.

At the top of the ninth, with the bases loaded, each man realizes that happiness is just within reach, even when love throws a...*Curveball*.

ISBN 10: 0-505-52707-3
ISBN 13: 978-0-505-52707-3
